D1546422

JANE AUSTEN IN A SOCIAL CONTEXT

By the same author

JANE AUSTEN: STRUCTURE AND SOCIAL VISION

JANE AUSTEN IN A SOCIAL CONTEXT

Edited by
David Monaghan

Barnes & Noble Books
Totowa, New Jersey

First published 1981 by
THE MACMILLAN PRESS LTD
Companies and representatives
throughout the world

First published in the USA 1981 by
BARNES & NOBLE BOOKS
81 Adams Drive
Totowa, New Jersey, 07512

British Library Cataloguing in Publication Data

Jane Austen in a social context
  1. Austen, Jane – Criticism and interpretation
  I. Monaghan, David
  823'.7   PR4037

MACMILLAN ISBN 0-333-27189-0

BARNES & NOBLE ISBN 0-389-20007-7

Printed in Hong Kong

Contents

Acknowledgements		vii
Note on Page References		ix
Notes on the Contributors		xi
1	Introduction: Jane Austen as a Social Novelist *David Monaghan*	1
2	Jane Austen and Romantic Imprisonment *Nina Auerbach*	9
3	The Influence of Place: Jane Austen and the Novel of Social Consciousness *Ann Banfield*	28
4	Disregarded Designs: Jane Austen's Sense of the Volume *Marilyn Butler*	49
5	Sex and Social Life in Jane Austen's Novels *Jan S. Fergus*	66
6	'Real Solemn History' and Social History *Christopher Kent*	86
7	Jane Austen and the Position of Women *David Monaghan*	105
8	Jane Austen and the Problem of Leisure *Jane Nardin*	122
9	*Mansfield Park*: The Revolt of the 'Feminine' Woman *Leroy W. Smith*	143
10	Muted Discord: Generational Conflict in Jane Austen *Patricia Meyer Spacks*	159
11	In Between—Anne Elliot Marries a Sailor and Charlotte Heywood Goes to the Seaside *Tony Tanner*	180
Index		195

Acknowledgements

I am indebted to the Jane Austen Society for permission to use the papers by Tony Tanner and Marilyn Butler, which are based on addresses given to the Annual General Meeting of the Jane Austen Society at Chawton in 1976 and 1978 respectively.

I am also grateful to the Social Sciences and Humanities Research Council (formerly the Canada Council) for grants in 1974 and 1979 which assisted me in the preparation of 'Jane Austen and the Position of Women'.

Finally, thanks are due to Alan R. Young of Acadia University, Wolfville, Nova Scotia, who gave me the original idea for this collection.

D.M.

Note on Page References

Page references inserted in the text are to:

> *The Novels of Jane Austen*, ed. R. W. Chapman, 5 vols, third edition (London: Oxford University Press, 1973).
> *The Works of Jane Austen*, ed. R. W. Chapman, Vol. VI: *Minor Works* (London: Oxford University Press, 1954).
> *Jane Austen's Letters to Her Sister Cassandra and Others*, ed. R. W. Chapman, second edition (London: Oxford University Press, 1952).

All page references in parentheses to the letters will be preceded by the short title *Letters*. Only when needed for the sake of clarity will the titles of the individual novels be given.

Notes on the Contributors

Nina Auerbach, Associate Professor at the University of Pennsylvania, is the author of *Communities of Women: An Idea in Fiction* (Cambridge, Mass.: Harvard University Press, 1978). She has also written numerous articles and reviews dealing with Jane Austen and other nineteenth-century novelists.

Ann Banfield teaches at the University of California, Berkeley, where she is an Assistant Professor, and has published articles on narrative style and on Jane Austen.

Marilyn Butler is a Fellow and Tutor at St Hugh's College, Oxford. Previously she worked for the BBC as a talks producer. She is the author of *Maria Edgeworth: A Literary Biography* (Oxford: Clarendon Press, 1972), *Jane Austen and the War of Ideas* (Oxford: Clarendon Press, 1975), and *Peacock Displayed: A Satirist in His Context* (London: Routledge & Kegan Paul, 1979).

Jan S. Fergus, Assistant Professor at Lehigh University, has taught also at Brooklyn College, CUNY, and is currently writing a book on Jane Austen and the didactic tradition.

Christopher Kent is an Associate Professor of History at the University of Saskatchewan and is editor of the *Canadian Journal of History*. His publications include *Brains and Numbers: Comtism, Elitism and Democracy in Victorian England* (Toronto: University of Toronto Press, 1978), and he is currently working on a study of the relationship between the novel and history.

David Monaghan, Associate Professor at Mount Saint Vincent University, Halifax, Nova Scotia, is the author of *Jane Austen: Structure and Social Vision* (London: Macmillan, 1980), and of a number of articles on Jane Austen and other English, American and Canadian novelists.

Jane Nardin teaches at the University of Wisconsin-Milwaukee and is an Assistant Professor. Her publications include *Those Elegant Decorums: The Concept of Propriety in Jane Austen's Novels* (Albany: State University of New York Press, 1973) and articles on English novelists. At present she is working on the figure of the aristocrat in the English novel.

Leroy W. Smith is a Professor at the College of William and Mary in Virginia. He has previously published articles on a number of English novelists and is now preparing a critical study of Jane Austen, tentatively entitled *Jane Austen: The 'Drama of Woman'*.

Patricia Meyer Spacks, Professor of English at Yale University, previously taught at Wellesley College. She is the author of a number of books including *The Female Imagination* (New York: Knopf, 1975) and *Imagining a Self* (Cambridge, Mass.: Harvard University Press, 1976). She is currently writing an extended study of English views of adolescence from the eighteenth to the twentieth century.

Tony Tanner, Fellow of King's College, Cambridge, has edited the Penguin editions of *Sense and Sensibility* and *Mansfield Park* and is the author of two books on American literature, *The Reign of Wonder* (Cambridge: Cambridge University Press, 1965) and *City of Words* (London: Jonathan Cape, 1971).

1 Introduction: Jane Austen as a Social Novelist

David Monaghan

The subject matter of this book probably requires some justification for at least two groups of readers. Followers of the New Critical School might well wonder if an approach that starts with the writer's social context can have anything of relevance to say about the aesthetic questions that are at the centre of the study of literature. Others, who might not be hostile to the social approach *per se*, will question whether it can be helpful with respect to Jane Austen, a writer whose greatness, it has been argued, owes nothing to her experience of the major events of her day—the French and Industrial Revolutions and the Napoleonic Wars—but rather derives from her ability to create timeless fantasies.

Any misgivings readers might have about the critical possibilities of the social approach to literature would in fact be based on a rather outmoded understanding of the kind of relationship that can exist between literature and society. Certainly the Marxist critics of the 1930s tended to suggest that literature is important merely as a passive reflection of social reality and to judge greatness according to the 'correctness' of the ideology expressed rather than by any aesthetic standards. Today, though, social criticism is informed by a much more sophisticated sense of the nature of the literary work. What critics like Lucien Goldmann, Raymond Williams, Terry Eagleton and Scott Sanders[1] are attempting to evolve is no less than a synthesis of the thirties Left-wing Criticism and New Criticism.[2] Their basic premise is that a writer's social context merits consideration because there is a relationship between literary form and the structure of the social environment in which it is developed.[3] Hence, aesthetic value is not divorced from social value; on the contrary, it coincides with it.[4] Terry Eagleton even goes so far as to claim that social criticism is adequate to deal with all aspects of literature.[5] For him, the way in which a work of literature relates to the ideological world it inhabits depends not only on theme, but on style, rhythm, image, quality and form.[6] Thus, he concludes that the social in literature is not mere surface. Rather it is the matrix, and the aim of historical criticism is not simply to add specialist footnotes to the literary work but, like any authentic criticism, to possess it more deeply.[7]

The other misgiving which readers might have—that even if the social approach is illuminating for some writers, it can have no relevance to Jane Austen—is based on a persistent but quite false reading of the significance of her subject matter. It is true, of course, that Jane Austen rarely mentions the 'great' events of her day. It is not true, however, as Christopher Kent in this collection and a number of other critics before him have demonstrated, that they have no impact on her fictional world.[8] On the contrary, they are at the centre of her consciousness. Readers from the middle of the nineteenth century onwards have failed to recognise this because they have not understood how Jane Austen's contemporaries would have 'read' her novels. Far from seeing her depictions of the social life of people in country villages as escapist, they would have acknowledged them as providing an adequate vehicle for the discussion of most things of importance to their society. To understand why we must consider for a moment the conservative ideology which provided Jane Austen and her contemporaries with a common body of assumptions. According to the conservative view of things God created society with such a degree of precision that each unit, whether it be the primary one of the individual or one of the smallest social groupings of the family and the village, is a microcosm of the whole. For the eighteenth-century conservative it would therefore have appeared unnecessary to employ the large-scale methods of the historian or the sociologist in order to arrive at an understanding of the major forces at work in society. All that was required was to examine the conduct of the individual in the context of his family and immediate community. To write of '3 or 4 Families in a Country Village' (*Letters*, 401) was then the very way to write about the condition of England.

Furthermore, what Jane Austen chose to show these families doing would have been considered illuminating in her own age. Being a very formal society, eighteenth-century England placed tremendous emphasis on the moral implications of the individual's polite performance, as is indicated by Edmund Burke's assertion that 'Manners are of more importance than laws. . . . According to their quality, they aid morals, they supply them, or they totally destroy them.'[9] Therefore, Jane Austen's decision to deal with the minutiae of her characters' social lives—for what matters in her world is whether Mr Elton will dance with Harriet Smith, or whether Catherine Morland has any right to excuse herself from an engagement with the Tilneys in order to visit Blaize Castle with the Thorpes—rather than to follow Sir Thomas Bertram into the House of Commons or Captain Wentworth to sea would not have seemed to her contemporaries to reflect any intention of escaping social reality. On the contrary, they would have recognised that she was directly encountering the kind of moral questions that had to be answered if a society based on a code of duty and obligation to others was to flourish.

Since Jane Austen's literary technique is so firmly based in contemporary ideology and since, therefore, with the passage of time, it has become liable to misinterpretation, far from being irrelevant the social approach would seem likely to enhance our understanding of her work considerably. The more accurately the critic can reconstruct Jane Austen's world, the more clearly he is likely to see the macrocosmic significance of the tiny events that she describes, and the closer he can draw to a final understanding of the import and shape of her work. This final understanding, however, is unlikely to come as a result of a single and isolated synthesising effort. One of the blind spots, I believe, of the theoreticians to whom I referred earlier, is that in fixing their gaze on the final goal of social criticism—to possess fully the work of literature—they have tended to collapse the process by which this goal is usually achieved. Many fragments must be put together before a writer's universe can be completely reconstructed. Some—and in the case of Jane Austen, Alistair Duckworth's study of the thematic and formal implications of her use of estate metaphors would be an example[10]—will, of course, be large and offer at least the beginnings of a synthesis. Others, however, will be tiny, many no bigger than what Eagleton refers to disparagingly as 'specialist footnotes'. Yet all have a contribution to make.

It was the conviction that the full complexity of Jane Austen's social vision would be revealed as a result of a cumulative process rather than by a single all-encompassing effort that persuaded me of the value of a collection of essays such as this one. The contributions do indeed vary greatly in the degree of ambition with which they engage in the business of literary archeology. My own chapter, for example, is concerned mainly with placing Jane Austen in relation to contemporary thinking about the role and capabilities of women and it deals only secondarily, as in its discussion of the symbolism of household management, with how this affects our sense of the aesthetics of her novels. Much of it, then, is what might be termed pre-criticism, in that its intention is to clear some ground for the subsequent building of critical edifices (my own book-length study of formal social occasions in Jane Austen's novels would not, for example, have been possible without the clarification provided by this research,[11] and it is to be hoped that it will provide surer footing for feminist criticism than has sometimes been obtained in the past[12]). Other contributors, Jan Fergus for example, engage in the pre-critical process but then immediately employ their findings to offer fresh insights into the themes of some of Jane Austen's novels. A few are still more ambitious and concern themselves with final questions of theme and form. Nina Auerbach's chapter, for example, places Jane Austen in a Romantic context only that it might return immediately to the structure of her novels which she sees as being organised around the Romantic motif of the double prison. Similarly, Marilyn Butler turns to contemporary publishing practices as a means of providing us with a fresh way of looking at the shape of Jane Austen's novels, and Ann Banfield demonstrates the connection between a changing social reality and the evolution of literary techniques.

However, the point is not simply to judge these chapters as discrete pieces of criticism, but rather, to consider what, as a totality, they add to our understanding of Jane Austen. To begin this process we must briefly review the state of Jane Austen criticism immediately prior to the creation of *Jane Austen in a Social Context*.[13] A few years ago two works appeared that were so solid and so thoroughly documented that we were left with the sense that, if they did not have the whole truth to offer about Jane Austen, then at least they filled in the main outlines of that truth. These were, of course, Alistair Duckworth's *The Improvement of the Estate* and Marilyn Butler's *Jane Austen and the War of Ideas*. Their impact was all the greater in that they are united in dismissing the suggestion, first made by D. W. Harding and repeated over the years by a number of critics,[14] that Jane Austen's novels are socially subversive. For Duckworth, whose Jane Austen is a Burkeian conservative, and Butler, who places her firmly in the anti-Jacobin camp, Jane

Austen is totally committed to her society and its values.

Given the firmness with which these two critics would appear to have squashed the subversive view of Jane Austen, one of the most remarkable features of the essays in *Jane Austen in a Social Context* is how many of them see her as being at odds with her society. Nina Auerbach argues that Jane Austen's novels work around a tension between the security of a restricted world and its unrelenting imprisonment; Leroy Smith interprets *Mansfield Park* as a critique of patriarchalism; Ann Banfield suggests that because of her sympathy for the disadvantaged, Jane Austen's social ideal leads to a union of lovers where, at the end, there is some violation of social differences, some contamination of place; Jane Nardin traces a gradual rejection on Jane Austen's part of the aristocratic ideal of leisure; and Spacks, Monaghan and Fergus show her to be in radical disagreement with contemporary attitudes about generational relationships, women and sexual relationships respectively. Does this mean, then, that for all the weight of evidence they bring to bear, Duckworth and Butler are wrong about Jane Austen's commitment to conservative ideology? Or are these essays yet another example of the kind of perverse argumentation that enables Marvin Mudrick and others to twist Jane Austen out of shape? Or, is there any way in which the affirmative and subversive schools of thought can be reconciled?

It is this third possibility which I would like to pursue, and in order to do so will consider the chapters that give this collection a subversive tendency under two headings: the apparently subversive and the actually subversive. Into the first category can be placed the work of Spacks, Monaghan and Fergus, which does not, if looked at closely, in fact so much offer a challenge to the Duckworth/Butler thesis as it lends it support. Each, it is true, shows Jane Austen to be in disagreement with large bodies of contemporary opinion about some very basic social questions. However, they also show that it is the contemporary opinion rather than Jane Austen which deviates from conservative ideology. The conduct books and didactic novels to which Jane Austen objects so strenuously take an essentially abstract approach to human behaviour and presume to lay down *a priori* rules intended to guide the individual through any social situation he might encounter. This is precisely the habit of mind that Burke found so objectionable in the French revolutionaries. Abstract reason, he—and Jane Austen—would argue, is simply insufficient to deal with the complexities of human experience. Instead, the individual, drawing on all his reserves of Prudence (a concept involving an amalgam of morality, reason, empirical data, instinct, prejudice, feeling and a knowledge of present circumstances) must seek actively for the appropriate response to the unique demands of any specific social situation. In Burke's words, 'personal qualities should support situations'.[15]

However, if these chapters have the effect of tightening the links between Jane Austen and conservatism, the others undoubtedly seek to loosen them. They do not succeed, however, in destroying the case made out by Duckworth and Butler—it is, I am convinced, essentially indestructible—but they do demonstrate some of its limitations. Duckworth and Butler provide us with a fine sense of Jane Austen's ideological base, but they do not explore all aspects of her response to that ideology. Conservative ideology, appealing though Jane Austen undoubtedly found it, is limited in the way that all ideology inevitably is, in that, being the means by which a social group tries to justify itself, it tends to be intolerant of ambiguity and to gloss over inconsistency. What Jane Austen, as a great writer, is able to develop out of this ideology is a genuine world view, that is, a total vision of man, society and nature. The kind of relationship which Jane Austen establishes with conservative ideology is consistent with Eagleton's suggestion that 'literature is held within ideology, but also manages to distance itself from it, to the point where it permits us to "feel" and "perceive" the ideology from which it springs'.[16] The subversive element which goes into the kind of questioning which is necessary if ideology is to be transformed into world view is admirably revealed by some of the chapters gathered together in this book. Where they are limited is not in being wrong about Jane Austen (which is not to say that readers will not question some of their judgements) but in their tendency to suggest that what they are revealing is the truth about Jane Austen rather than what is more accurately a kind of subtext to the essentially conservative truth. Nina Auerbach, whose reading is perhaps the most subversive in that it unearths layers of meaning that run so counter to Jane Austen's basic social commitment that they must be something close to products of her unconscious, recognises the partial nature of the picture she presents and acknowledges the need for a synthesis of affirmative and subversive readings. Leroy Smith, however, in arguing that Jane Austen opposes patriarchy does not give sufficient consideration to the possibility that she may simply be exploring abuses to which the *status quo* is subject rather than mounting a full-scale attack on it.

Certainly, it seems to me that the world which Fanny, who always acts in accordance with traditional Mansfield values, creates at the end of the novel is essentially a reassertion of things as they must have been before Sir Thomas lost sight of his proper social role. The novel's final tendency is therefore not towards the future and change but towards the past and stability.

Taken as a whole, then, these chapters do advance the state of our knowledge about Jane Austen. Relating them to earlier social criticism makes it clear that both the affirmative and subversive readings of Jane Austen are insufficient in themselves. Affirmation of her society may be the main thrust of Jane Austen's fiction but it is in her willingness to be critical of that society that she transcends mere ideology. The final synthesis towards which Jane Austen criticism is aiming, therefore, will come out of a recognition of the diverse elements that make up her social vision, and out of the uncovering of a structure large enough to accommodate an affirmative text with a subversive subtext.

NOTES

1. Lucien Goldmann, *Towards a Sociology of the Novel* (London: Tavistock Publications, 1975); Raymond Williams, *Marxism and Literature* (Oxford: Oxford University Press, 1977); Terry Eagleton, *Marxism and Literary Criticism* (London: Methuen, 1976) and *Myths of Power: A Marxist Study of the Brontës* (London: Macmillan, 1975); Scott Sanders, 'Towards a Social Theory of Literature', *Telos*, 18 (1973–4), 107–21.
2. See Sanders' discussion of Goldmann, p. 119.
3. Goldmann, p. 6.
4. Sanders, p. 119.
5. Eagleton, *Myths of Power*, p. 2.
6. Eagleton, *Marxism and Literary Criticism*, p. 6.
7. Eagleton, *Myths of Power*, pp. 2, 13.
8. See for example, Marilyn Butler, *Jane Austen and the War of Ideas* (Oxford: Clarendon Press, 1975); Donald Greene, 'The Myth of Limitation', in *Jane Austen Today* (Athens, Georgia: University of Georgia Press, 1975), pp. 142–75, and Raymond Williams, *The English Novel: From Dickens to Lawrence* (London: Chatto & Windus, 1970), pp. 18–24.
9. 'First Letter on a Regicide Peace', *The Works of Edmund Burke* (London: George Bell, 1906) Vol. v, p. 208.
10. Alistair M. Duckworth, *The Improvement of the Estate: A Study of Jane Austen's Novels* (Baltimore, Md.: The Johns Hopkins Press, 1971).
11. David Monaghan, *Jane Austen: Structure and Social Vision* (London: Macmillan, 1980).
12. For a review of feminist criticism of Jane Austen, see David Monaghan, 'Jane

Austen and the Feminist Critics', *A Room of One's Own*, 4 (Spring 1979), 34–9.

13. For a more detailed account of the history of Jane Austen social criticism up to 1976, see David Monaghan, 'Jane Austen and the Social Critics: Recent Trends', *English Studies in Canada*, 2 (1976), 280–7.

14. The most famous of these is Marvin Mudrick, *Jane Austen: Irony as Defense and Discovery* (Princeton, NJ: Princeton University Press, 1952). For a more recent example, see Murray Krieger, 'Postscript: The Naïve Classic and the Merely Comic: *Pride and Prejudice*', *The Classic Vision: The Retreat from Extremity in Modern Literature* (Baltimore, Md.: The Johns Hopkins Press, 1971), pp. 221–42. Duckworth, pp. 5–10, offers an excellent summary of the development of the 'subversive' school of criticism.

15. 'A Letter to William Elliot, Esq.', *Works*, Vol. v, p. 77.

16. Eagleton, *Marxism and Literary Criticism*, p. 18.

2 Jane Austen and Romantic Imprisonment

Nina Auerbach

> Was not the world a vast prison, and women born slaves?
> Mary Wollstonecraft, *Maria*[1]

> 'You are a much fitter inmate for your present abode than your last, and from hence there is no danger of your escaping.'
> 'And where, then, am I?'
> '*You are in the prison of the Inquisition.*'
> Charles Maturin, *Melmoth the Wanderer*[2]

Like many women, Jane Austen has won praise for her limitations. The Victorian critic George Henry Lewes held her up for emulation because of the vast worlds she omitted: 'First and foremost let Jane Austen be named, the greatest artist that has ever written, using the term to signify the most perfect mastery over the means to her end. There are heights and depths in human nature Miss Austen has never scaled nor fathomed, there are worlds of passionate existence into which she has never set foot; but although this is obvious to every reader, it is equally obvious that she has risked no failures by attempting to delineate that which she had not seen. Her circle may be restricted, but it is complete.'[3] Over a hundred years later, we find Stuart M. Tave praising her in similarly double-edged terms for the many things she does not do. His introductory chapter, 'Limitations and Definitions', implies that the two are equivalent in her world: 'She does not fight for escape but makes the best use of the conditions, and if that's not the whole of art at least that is where it begins and where it ends.'[4]

In this view, which still prevails among many readers, Jane Austen is the artist of contentedly clipped wings. Critics such as

Lewes and Tave tend to display her as an exemplum in a cautionary tale directed at their readers, particularly their female readers, sternly recalling life's borders. As a novelist she becomes a plotter of modes of confinement for elastic imaginations like those of Catherine Morland, Marianne Dashwood, Emma Woodhouse, and the rest. Her novels come to function as traps for undisciplined expectations, as Austen metes out restrictions with some of the serene sadism of Blake's Urizen. For such readers as Lewes and Tave, Austen is both the ingenious conceiver and the placid inmate of her restricted and complete universe, taking her pleasure from lack of risks. No voyages of discovery entice her.[5]

Jane Austen's artistic world does indeed call insistent attention to its own limitations, but not, I feel, in the spirit of contented resignation these critics define. Such recurrent devices as its hot, crowded rooms, its claustrophobic courtship and proposal scenes, its exacerbated sensitivity to banal, interminable talk and to the chafing imagination force the reader's awareness toward forbidden spaces, the 'worlds of passionate existence' Lewes evokes and denies. I think it would be helpful to look beyond the implicit virtue Tave finds in Austen's apparent refusal to 'fight for escape', seeing it as something more painfully complex, and more embedded in Austen's own Romantic age than an amiable adjustment to 'conditions' suggests.

For as I read Jane Austen, the pinched horizons that suggest forbidden spheres beyond themselves create a divided perspective like that of Keats' 'sick eagle looking at the sky', generating a torn awareness of spaces and powers denied. This awareness of inexorable denial mingles with the unimpeachable comfort of Austen's settings and, I believe, creates the unique tension that makes us keep returning to them. This continual tension between the security of a restricted world and its unrelenting imprisonment brings Austen into a special sort of agreement with her Romantic contemporaries.

It may still seem a desecration to some to place Jane Austen within a Romantic tradition, as if her perfection is somehow sealed off from time, or at least from the fluctuations of literary history. But definitions of 'Romanticism' may be as wide and various as were the concerns of its writers,[6] and the conjunction of Austen's severe limitations with the various Romantic quests for infinity may reveal new facets of both. The phrase from *Emma* that seems most resonantly to define both the quietly miraculous and the oppressive qualities of Austen's world—'a crowd in a little room' (249)—

may be kin to the pervasive 'shades of the prison-house' that fall over Romantic poetry with paradoxical effect.

Wordsworth's canon defines a childhood condition that is open to eternity, only to explore in mingled tones the ramifications of childhood's imprisoning recession. Blake's 'mind-forged manacles' determine the contortions of his best-known paintings, engravings, lyrics, and prophecies, a condition of imprisonment so fundamental that it alone can determine the intensity of release into visionary wholeness. Coleridge's psychic prison of dejection is the mental counterpart of the becalmed ship in *The Rime of the Ancient Mariner*, and perhaps the dark kin of the 'stately pleasure-dome' of 'Kubla Khan', with its later analogues, Keats' questionable 'paradise' of Madeline's chamber in *The Eve of St Agnes* and the delusive pleasure house in his *Lamia*. In all these works, closed-in space is the spirit's most appropriate, if most bitter, home.

All these states of incarceration are defined as intensely complex combinations of pleasure and pain, fulfilment and frustration, suggesting a fascination with gradations of imprisonment that is one ingredient of Romanticism: Prometheus unbound can be defined only by the mingled triumph and humiliation of Prometheus bound. Such diverse minor poems as Wordsworth's sonnet, 'Nuns Fret Not in their Convent's Narrow Room', and Byron's *The Prisoner of Chillon* recreate the ironic but intense satisfactions of accommodation to imprisonment, a complex loss and gain of selfhood that may illuminate both Jane Austen's already well-lit interiors and her refusal to 'fight for escape' from them. For even a cursory glance over Romantic poetry reveals its insistent awareness of states of imprisonment, as if from one point of view, the great lesson of Romanticism was not the fall of the Bastille, but its survival in perpetuity.[7]

Judging from her surviving letters and from irreverent mentions in the later novels, Jane Austen regarded the poetry of her Romantic contemporaries with a certain lofty and sardonic mistrust, if she regarded it at all; in *Persuasion*, its lingered-over regret is an emotional luxury a sane person cannot afford. We cannot know how much she read, how much she shielded herself from, how much simply bored her, but it is safe to surmise that the 'shades of the prison-house' that close over her fiction as well as their poetry come less from mutual influence than from a common cultural ambience.

One poem we know she did read, Byron's *The Corsair*,[8] rests on a structural irony which, as I will show, is very close to the imprisoning rhythms of Austen's own novels, and to one structural principle of Romantic narrative: the motif of the double prison, in which a journey of apparent liberation from captivity leads only to a more implacable arrest. In such a journey, 'Romantic' concepts of freedom become a deeply ironic snare, as they do in *The Corsair*, which opens, like the Ancient Mariner's tale and Mary Shelley's *Frankenstein*, with the sea voyager's boast of escape and transcendence: 'O'er the glad waters of the dark blue sea,/Our thoughts as boundless, and our souls as free,/Far as the breeze can bear, the billow foam,/Survey our empire, and behold our home!' (lines 1–4). But this rollicking possession of boundlessness is as empty a boast as the defiant elopements of such characters as Austen's Lydia Bennet and Maria Bertram, whose flights ensure only a more pervasive entrapment: Conrad, Byron's dashing hero, is soon taken captive by the Turk. After some languishing in prison, the movement from liberation to intensified captivity is repeated: Conrad is rescued by the passionate and bloodthirsty Gulnare, 'The Harem queen—but still the slave of Seyd!' As she has murdered the Seyd to effect Conrad's escape, Gulnare becomes invested with a horrible criminality that the men's casual and sporting homicide never approaches, but Conrad is ignominiously in her hands, having gone from free surveyor of a boundless empire to being the slave of a slave. His escape is thus at one with his most devastating captivity; he wilts out of life shortly after the death of the true love he has betrayed. The voyage to boundlessness has brought nothing but varieties of slavery.

Whether Austen adapted Byron's particular pattern or not, this ironic consummation of the Romantic quest is a suggestive gloss on, for example, Catherine Morland's sunny journey to Bath in *Northanger Abbey*, where she quickly falls captive to the mercenary stupidity of the Thorpes. Henry Tilney rescues her for a new liberation at Northanger Abbey, where she becomes a deeper prisoner of his father's tyranny, as it exists both within her imagination and without. Her last 'rescue' by Henry Tilney may be said to make her the slave of a slave of a slave, since the pedagogic Henry is ruled by the whim of his autocratic father, who is himself the slave of money and propriety. As in *The Corsair*, three journeys of escape lead to three more resounding imprisonments. As I shall discuss at length below, particularly in her early novels, Jane Austen shares the Romantic sense of pervasive and inescapable imprisonment. But their looming enclosures which are both seclusion and dungeon become for Austen not just a matter of setting and atmosphere, but a recurrent pattern in the structure of her narratives. The kinship between Catherine Morland's journey and Conrad's is part of a wider kinship they both share with a bizarre series of novels that flourished in the late eighteenth and early nineteenth centuries, which group loosely under the rubric of Romantic fiction.

It seems to me that the particular claustrophobia so many readers uncover in Jane Austen—beginning with Charlotte Brontë's recoil, 'I should hardly like to live with her ladies and gentlemen, in their elegant but confined houses'[9]—has been too easily disregarded as a mote in the eye of the beholder. As we have seen, the Romantic imagination is in large part an imagination of confinement. The prisons and imprisoning pleasure-houses we have noted in Romantic poetry become in Romantic fiction not only an obsessive series of examinations of the prison as setting, but a preoccupation with thematic and formal structures which themselves imprison both reader and protagonist, barring all escape from the confines of the novel's world. If, for the purposes of this essay, we place Jane Austen among this embarrassingly lurid school of her literary contemporaries who have received so little critical attention, I think we will find a convergence of vision and structure that brings to the surface the darkness that is part of her comic refusal to fight for her own or her characters' escape.

I am not defining 'Romantic fiction' as a purely chronological phenomenon.[10] Rather, I am struck by a group of common themes, motifs and structural devices in fiction ranging from the romances of Ann Radcliffe (*The Mysteries of Udolpho* was published in 1794) to the seemingly incoherent melange of cannibalism, demonism and torturing imprisonment in Charles Maturin's *Melmoth the Wanderer* (which was published in 1820), and the invisible border between spiritual possession and madness in James Hogg's *The Private Memoirs and Confessions of a Justified Sinner* (1824). In these extravagant novels, or anti-novels, all roads, even the most apparently open and winding, lead ultimately to some sort of prison.

In all of them, the journey to prison is presided over by a darkly ironic narrator. In all, the devil is in control, and like Melmoth, he is a laughing sardonic devil whose jocularity is corrosive. The joke he plays most often is the journey of the double prison we have traced in the *The Corsair*, where Conrad's liberation from the Turkish dungeon by Gulnare becomes a still more horrible captivity. More insidiously, the devil-author often uses as his material the most ecstatic and liberating images of Romanticism, such as its ultimate dream of escape from 'the prison-house' through the transfiguring marriage between the natural and the supernatural. Wordsworth defines this boundlessly expansive 'marriage' in his fragment from *The Recluse*: 'For the discerning intellect of Man/When wedded to this goodly universe/In love and holy passion, shall find these [journeys to Paradise]/A simple produce of the common day' (lines 52–5).

But these bonds of epithalamium that provide transfiguring release in Romantic visions are often a demonic bondage in Romantic fiction, as is the dark, carnivorous marriage between the supernatural Melmoth and the mortal child of nature, Immalee, whose issue is not renewed and transfigured life but imprisonment and a prisoner's death. Marriage in Romantic fiction is often a dark metaphor for the pursuit of the *doppelgänger*, or nightmarish anti-self; the dark prophecy of Frankenstein's monster—'remember, I shall be with you on your wedding-night'—echoes through all these works. Frankenstein's wedding night is a true, if diabolical, marriage, for after murdering his creator's bride as his own had been murdered, the monster is as indissolubly married to Frankenstein as was the demonic-divine murderer Falkland to Godwin's Caleb Williams. John Polidori's elegant vampire, Lord Ruthven, similarly marries the tale's narrator by 'glut[ting] his thirst' with his sister on their wedding night. In *Melmoth the Wanderer*, the lovers in 'The Parricide's Tale' and the intimate domestic unit in 'The Tale of Guzman's Family' literalise their bonds by eating each other under the pressure of starvation. The demonic marriage of the dead between Melmoth and Immalee is a recurrent pattern in Romantic fiction, whose weddings are almost invariably weldings of unnatural bondage and horror.

Many readers have been troubled by the shadowed epithalamia in Jane Austen's novels. In the early *Northanger Abbey*, 'Henry and Catherine were married, the bells rang and every body smiled' (252); in *Emma*, the narrator blandly consecrates 'the perfect happiness of the union' (484) between a vivid 'imaginist' (335), her heavily pedagogical guardian, and her parasitic father; and the epithalamium of the final *Persuasion* is inaugurated by a glimpse of 'quick alarm' (252). All these weddings seem to transmit dark signals beneath their comic reassurances. I think it will help us perceive them in their fullness if we recall the two faces of the Romantic epithalamium, the visionary bond and the unhuman bondage, the hope for liberty through transfiguration and the final reduction of aspiration to demonic cannibalism. Both manifestations of the spirit of her age are present in Jane Austen, troubling her marriages and enriching them.

In its twisting of other motifs as well, Romantic fiction appears a dark parody of Romantic visions, orchestrated by a laughing devil. In *Natural Supernaturalism*, his compendium of Romantic paradigms, M. H. Abrams defines as a frequent Romantic structure the 'circular or spiral quest', whose protagonist undertakes a pilgrimage gradually leading him back to his point of origin, which he perceives from a higher, often a transfigured plane of vision.[11] The ultimate coherence and transcendence of this circular quest in, for example, *The Prelude*, *The Rime of the Ancient Mariner* and *Prometheus Unbound*, carries the same hope we found in Wordsworth's fragment from *The Recluse* of a liberating journey to visionary clarity.

But Romantic fiction is typically a structural labyrinth, in which there is no freeing rediscovery of origin, but only a passage to deeper interiors. The rhythms of perception of Godwin's Caleb Williams, as he broods over Falkland's narrative, embody the typical structure of this fiction: 'I turned it a thousand ways, and examined it in every point of view. In the original communication it appeared sufficiently distinct and satisfactory; but, as I brooded over it, it gradually became mysterious.'[12] As with Frankenstein's scientific research, exploration results not in clarity, but in ever-intensifying mystery. The rationalistic documents with which James Hogg's *The Private Memoirs and Confessions of a Justified Sinner* begins soon lead us into the insane and miasmatic consciousness of the sinner himself, for whom all events and actions are inscrutable, he himself emerging as the most inexorable mystery of all.

The labyrinthine process of understanding is echoed in a typical device of Romantic fiction: the tale within the tale, collapsing into a series of increasingly claustrophobic vistas, a narrative series of dark passageways in which the reader recedes increasingly from the novel's point of origin. At one point in *Melmoth the Wanderer*, for instance, we are treated to a tale within a tale within a tale within a tale within a tale,[13] none of them providing the final closure that would allow us to return over the ground we have passed endowed with the higher, more perfect vision of the Romantic circular quest. The circular quest releases and completes us; the tale within the tale locks us in and away from transcendence.

Jane Austen's novels seem superficially removed from this endless series of dark passageways. They seem to end, like Abrams' circular quest, with perfect clarity; all but two of the heroines begin their novels with some degree of befuddlement, achieving illumination, marriage, and closure virtually in one burst, and in the cases of Fanny Price and Anne Elliot, who are fixed points of knowledge from the beginning, the movement from perplexity to illumination is taken over by the heroes. But the fascination and debate a novel such as *Emma* engenders suggests the presence of dark passageways of a particularly subterranean sort. A heroine like Emma, who, the first paragraph assures us, can be thoroughly 'known' by a judicious observer, becomes, like Godwin's Falkland, increasingly inscrutable the more she is brooded about. The many ways in which Emma can be seen (is she spoiled child, developing toward adult perfection? Is she insidiously powerful and deceitful woman? Is she dynamic victim of patriarchal rules and enclosures?) embody the essential movement of Austen's novel from clarity to obscurity, as she continues the tradition of Romantic fiction by enticing each reader to add another tale within a tale, no one of which can free us from Emma's essential mystery.

Romantic fiction, then, is the laughing denial of Romantic hopes for illumination. M. H. Abrams begins his guide to the latter by quoting from Shelley's *A Defence of Poetry*: 'The literature of England has arisen as it were from a new birth.' The hope for a new birth, for the perfect child who is symbol of the perfect human future, becomes in Romantic fiction a plenitude of abortions, miscarriages and clownish monsters, such as the twisted child Immalee bears Melmoth (looking forward to such contemporary demon children as that in *Rosemary's Baby*), or that ultimate abortion, Frankenstein's monster.[14] This swarm of twisted progeny, including such *doppelgängers* as Hogg's chameleon-like devil in *Private Memoirs*, who functions at one time or another as every character's deformed and parodic self, may provide one explanation for a certain horror of children that has troubled critics in Jane Austen.

Certainly, as an artist, Austen has little sympathy with the Wordsworthian child as 'mighty prophet', heralding a holy return to sanctified origins. But she does reveal a penchant for Romantic abortions, as in the following letter which has displeased so many

Janeites: 'Mrs Hall, of Sherborne, was brought to bed yesterday of a dead child, some weeks before she expected, owing to a fright. I suppose she happened unawares to look at her husband' (*Letters*, 24).[15] This unappealing tableau is as far from Wordsworth as it is from the Jane Austen many people want to see, but if we think of Romantic fiction, with its demon marriages that become claustrophobic bondages to the unnatural, its penchant for monstrous and aborted births, we can locate even Austen's seeming aberrations in the proclivities and fears of her time.

The prisons that pervade Romantic fiction are both a mockery of life's promises and life's ultimate reality. No escape is possible because in the corridors of these worlds no escape is available. The long frustration of 'The Spanish Tale', with which *Melmoth The Wanderer* begins, defines the ironic rhythms with which we and the protagonist are confronted. As the result of an elaborate plot against his family, the parents of the speaker have forced the Spaniard Monçada into a monastery, though he despises the niggling hypocrisy and institutionalised mediocrity of monastic life. The horror he perceives there is the threat behind all community, the horror of encroaching littleness. His tones are not alien to those of Marianne Dashwood confronting Mrs Jennings' evening parties, or of Emma Woodhouse surveying Highbury, as he excoriates '[t]he petty squabbles and intrigues of the convent, the bitter and incessant conflict of habits, tempers, and interests, the efforts of incarcerated minds for objects of excitement, the struggles to diversify endless monotony, and elevate hopeless mediocrity' (57). As Monçada perceives it, monastic life embodies all the distastefulness of the normal.

But a ray of hope enters: his loving brother has discerned the plot and sends word of a plan of escape. The promise held out here is that of fraternity as well as liberty, of a family bond that promises release rather than stagnation and bondage. Led by a figure known only as the parricide, Monçada descends into the bowels of the convent and they slip away. As they wind through an interminable series of dark corridors and fetid enclosures, the parricide whiles away time with a tale of illicit lovers imprisoned in one of the dungeons. In the crucible prison provides, the lovers confront the reality behind their tender bonds, 'the disunion of every tie of the heart': 'In the agonies of their famished sickness they loathed each other—they could have cursed each other, if they had had breath to curse. It was on the fourth night that I heard the shriek of the wretched female,—her lover, in the agony of hunger, had fastened his teeth in her shoulder;—that bosom on which he had so often luxuriated, became a meal to him now' (164–5).

The tale of imprisonment and cannibalism that embroiders their passage to freedom proves prophetic. Monçada's brother is killed, the plot has triumphed, and the tortuous dark journey leads only to the words quoted at the beginning of this essay: 'the Superior consented to your attempt to escape, merely that he might have you more in his power. . . . *You are in the prison of the Inquisition*' (174). The motif of the double prison, the painful journey from captivity that leads only to profounder bondage, is shown here in purest form. The narrative moves from the prison of others' mediocrity to a vision of the cannibalism inherent in all human bonds, and finally, to the prison of the mind itself.

As all these novels perceive, in a manner that looks forward to the twentieth-century political allegories of Kafka, Orwell and Koestler, the ultimate prison is acquiescence, even when acquiescence seems all life has to offer. In Jane Austen's two earliest novels, *Northanger Abbey* and *Sense and Sensibility*, I find a similar rhythm of a painful journey toward what looks like freedom but is in fact a deeper prison of the mind. Elizabeth Bennet, Fanny Price, Emma Woodhouse and Anne Elliot will learn in the course of their novels to keep a quiet corner of their minds to themselves; but Catherine Morland's adoring acquiescence in the rationalistic pedagogy of Henry Tilney, which leaves so much of his own household unperceived, and Marianne Dashwood's acquiescence in her mother and sister's prudential pressures, carry undertones of the sort of hopelessness only a Romantic vision can contain. In *Melmoth*, Monçada's bleak equivocation to his Superior forecasts the necessity of defeat: 'I am what they have made me' (131). In *Sense and Sensibility*, Marianne's penitential promise to her mother and Elinor prepares us for the lugubrious marriage she will make: 'I wish to assure you both . . . that I see every thing—as you can desire me to do' (349).

Like Monçada, Marianne begins her story in a prison of pervasive mediocrity and social lies. She adopts Willoughby as her guide in a journey to freedom from convention and the total honesty possible only between equals—metaphorically, the brotherhood for which Monçada also hopes—but his desertion abandons her to the deeper grip of convention, in the form of the damp presence of her ultimate husband, Colonel Brandon, whom even Elinor finds worthy but depressing. Like Monçada, the bruised Marianne adapts her identity to the vision of her conquerors and her aspirations to the illusory nature of her dream of escape. The prison of social lies becomes her ultimate truth.

This juxtaposition might seem incongruous when Jane Austen's sparse, commonplace interiors are compared to the grandiose settings of Romantic fiction. But this opulence of setting which tends to overwhelm even the central characters should not blind us to their ultimate similarities of structure. True, Austen's novels are not peopled by that personified Romantic liberator, Nature, which in Ann Radcliffe's *The Mysteries of Udolpho* and in Mary Shelley's *Frankenstein* provides the greatest snare of all: in both, the Alps, that traditional Romantic release for the soaring spirit, prove the nest of tyrants and dungeons (in Udolpho) and, in *Frankenstein*, of the monstrous anti-self, who seems the spirit of crevices and glaciers as he nimbly makes his way among them, using Percy Shelley's sublime Mount Blanc as an appropriate setting for his insistence to Frankenstein of their monstrous bond. Similarly, in James Hogg's *Private Memoirs*, stalwart young George, who 'could not endure confinement', escapes, like the Wordsworthian poet-climber, to the majestic peak of Arthur's Seat, only to be terrorised by the dreadful phantom of his murderous brother in a cloud. In all, like the pilgrimage of escape in *Melmoth*, communion with sublime Nature carries only the lesson of dark bondage. Jane Austen's nature, like her interiors, carries no such promises or threats; Marianne's effusions over the picturesque seem mannered and effete in contrast. But her quest, her vertigo and her ultimate incarceration echo those of our more intrepid Romantic mountaineers.

In all these works, terror lies in the reliability of sense. The dungeons and monsters are dreamlike, but insidiously, they are not dreams: they are implacably perceived, and cannot be made to vanish. In these worlds of terror and enclosure, the word 'sense' has a less cosy meaning than it does for most interpreters of Jane Austen. It indicates not repose on a steady commonality of perception which is opposed to the private turbulence of 'sensibility', but the most reliable organ of inescapable danger. William Godwin's *Caleb Williams* uses the word in this empirical, anti-Johnsonian fashion to verify the futility of escape from a world become a prison:

Escape from [Falkland's] pursuit, freedom from his tyranny, were objects upon which my whole soul was bent; could no human ingenuity and exertion effect them? Did his power reach through all space, and his eye penetrate every concealment? Was he like that mysterious being, to protect us from whose fierce revenge mountains and hills we are told might fall on us in vain? No idea is more heart-sickening and tremendous than this. But in my case it was not a subject of reasoning or of faith; I could derive no comfort either directly from the unbelief which, upon religious subjects, some men avow to their own minds, or secretly from the remoteness or incomprehensibility of the conception; *it was an affair of the sense*; I felt the fangs of the tyger striking deep into my heart. (240, my italics)

In Austen's novel, the 'sense' Elinor endorses and inculcates in Marianne seems less general wisdom than this acute perception of 'the fangs of the tyger'. Though its concrete, empirical meaning in *Sense and Sensibility* is usually ignored, it is less a medium of enlightenment than an organ of Romantic terror and confinement. For Austen as for these other novelists, 'sense' is the lens through which we perceive the terror within 'things as they are', the subtitle of Godwin's novel which could have been Austen's as well.

Like Jane Austen's art itself, the word 'sense' cuts both ways: it both assuages our terrors and verifies them. Reminding readers that 'the fangs of the tyger' are present in her world as well as those of her more extravagant Romantic contemporaries should not deny her geniality, her charm, her awareness of life's blessings; rather, I want to recall the persistent double vision that is the essence of Austen's and of all Romantic art. The *doppelgänger*, that persistent haunt of Romantic fiction, is our incessant reminder of literal doubleness, the fact that the Self with whom we live in intimacy can become deformed and a stranger; and a sobering reminder as well of the mask of commonality that passes for family happiness. In Romantic fiction by women, however, including that of Jane Austen, the sense of doubleness tends to take on a narrower focus. Its pervasive philosophic awareness of the self's potential self-betrayal becomes a more concrete, if ambiguously shifting vision, of the double face of male authority.

In Ann Radcliffe's *The Mysteries of Udolpho*, for example, which, in the tradition of Romantic fiction writers, Austen both absorbed and parodied, Emily St Aubert is endowed with twin fathers. The rule of her 'true' father is all benevolence; everything associated with him cloaks his power over Emily, as he weeps incessantly, travels obligingly, and languishes in a sickness consummated in saintly death. Almost immediately, Emily is dispossessed and imprisoned by her autocratic anti-father, her uncle Montoni, whose villainy lies less in his nature than in his awareness of the absolute power he may exercise over women: ' "You shall be removed, this night", said he, "to the east turret: there, perhaps, you may understand the danger of offending a man, who has an unlimited power over you." '[16]

Sense, as Caleb Williams uses it, endorses rather than minimises the villainy of Montoni in so far as it rests on a parodic extension of the unlimited rights of parent over child, male over female, much the same sort of power General Tilney coolly exercises in *Northanger Abbey*. In *Udolpho*, the doubleness of the male protector is never resolved. Emily escapes Montoni at last, hoping to recover her dashing lover Valancourt, only to learn of his supposed betrayal. Meeting him again, she perceives with irrevocable double vision the man who blends saintly father with diabolical anti-father:

> In these the first moments, . . . she forgot every fault, which had formerly claimed indignation, and beholding Valancourt such as he had appeared, when he won her early affection, she experienced emotions of only tenderness and joy. This alas! was but the sunshine of a few short moments; recollections rose, like clouds, upon her mind, and, darkening the illusive image, that possessed it, she again beheld Valancourt, degraded— Valancourt unworthy of the esteem and tenderness she had once bestowed upon him; her spirits faltered, and, withdrawing her hand, she turned from him to conceal her grief. (624)

Though the plot resolves her scruples, her double vision never clears as she accepts Valancourt's ambiguous protection.

Similarly, as much as he is Frankenstein's double and monstrous child, Mary Shelley's monster is the dominant father figure in her novel. Aside from assuming *droit de Seigneur* over Frankenstein's bride, his most heinous acts are the removal of patriarchs as benevolent and as full of sensibility as M. St Aubert—De Lacey and the 'indulgent' father of Victor Frankenstein—to replace them, as Montoni does, with his own tyrannical and regnant image. Monstrosity is less an emanation from within than it is an outgrowth of the double nature of all fathers and fatherly men.

Here we may remember the double eye Jane Austen casts upon

General Tilney, who simultaneously is and is not a Montoni, or upon even the good Mr Knightley, the vigorous benevolence of whose power finds its analogue in the clinging, denying nature of Mr Woodhouse's, both of whom Emma seems to marry at the end of her novel. Jane Austen, too, casts upon her protecting patriarchs a relentless double vision, though she is so deft an artist that she may lead us to think our own vision is slightly out of focus.

The novel that seems most to bridge the gap between Jane Austen and Romantic fiction, using the conventional settings of the genre for a specifically female indictment, is Mary Wollstonecraft's fragment, *Maria, or the Wrongs of Woman*, the unfinished legacy she left at her death, which Godwin published in 1798. Like much Romantic fiction, *Maria* is set entirely in prison, recalling the patriarchal dungeon/castle of Udolpho (Maria has been locked away from her child by her vengeful husband), but this prison is a madhouse as well, that is, a prison of the mind, looking forward to the monastery of *Melmoth the Wanderer*, where mediocrity institutionalised was at one with the prison of the Inquisition. This prison, then, is comprehensive—'Was not the world a vast prison, and women born slaves?' (27)—and Wollstonecraft is more explicit than our other authors about its allegorical nature. In a sketchy and unfinished preface, she makes clear her general intention, to use the trappings of Romantic fiction as an emblem of women's history within 'the partial laws and customs of society': 'In the invention of the story, this view restrained my fancy; and the history ought rather to be considered, as of woman, than of an individual.' This allegorical aim removes *Maria* from the usual mode of Romantic fiction, where the opulent setting dwarfs the human action. Wollstonecraft's conscious allegory brings her techniques close to Jane Austen's, whose imprisoning medium springs from our pervasive awareness of confinement rather than from its detailed, palpable representation.

Whatever structure we can discern in *Maria* seems to rest on the central irony of Romantic fiction: the existence of a double prison. Maria's incarceration is the result of her flight to escape the prison of her marriage. 'Marriage had bastilled me for life' (103), she writes, but her attempt to tear down the Bastille and flee to the continent leads her into this final trap of her husband's. Once she is in prison, the novel's central ambiguity rests on the nature of Henry Darnford, her adoring suitor there. Their romance grows from the books Darnford lends her; significantly, in view of Wollstonecraft's denunciation in *Vindication of the Rights of Woman*, they both palpitate to Rousseau; in fact, like Willoughby in *Sense and Sensibility*, Darnford seems to spring whole out of her feverish reading. Interestingly, at least in the Norton edition, the manuscript becomes patchy and fragmented every time Darnford enters the story, as if his identity and his role in the plot were a knot Wollstonecraft could not cut through. Darnford promises to free Maria under his protection, but in at least two projected endings (with three more hinted at), he abandons her to solitude and the ultimate prison of suicide. Like Emily St Aubert's dashing, reading Valancourt, Darnford seems simultaneously a redeemer and a jailer, Maria's guide from the Bastille of legally defined marriage to a profounder dungeon of romantic love.

Wollstonecraft creates her hero with the double vision we find so often in women's Romantic fiction. The fragmentary nature of the manuscript allows us to perceive more vividly the ambivalence with which she conceives him, a radical ambivalence which remains at the heart of Jane Austen's finished art, many of whose men can equally be perceived as redeemer/jailer, and whose gestures toward escape lead only to the ironic ubiquity of a double prison.

Seen in this context, it is possible to perceive Jane Austen's canon as one long, and always doomed, fight for escape. The early novels are most sharply aware of 'shades of the prison-house'. In its ambivalent parody of Romantic fiction, *Northanger Abbey* abounds in prison settings: not only the coach of John Thorpe's mock-captivity, or the ominous abbey itself, where, in true Romantic fashion, Catherine's greatest imprisonment is her humiliating expulsion thence, but what should be the fairy-tale glow of Catherine's first ball.

Catherine's first view of it from above seems a parody of the sublime ascents up Romantic mountains we have seen earlier: 'Here there was something less of crowd then below; and hence Miss Morland had a comprehensive view of all the company beneath her, and of all the dangers of her late passage through them. It was a splendid sight' (21). But, as in *Udolpho*, the splendour of ascent gives way to awareness of imprisonment: 'she was tired of being continually pressed against by people, the generality of whose faces possessed nothing to interest, and with all of whom she was so wholly unacquainted, that she could not relieve the irksomeness of imprisonment by the exchange of a syllable with any of her fellow captives' (21–2). Romantic ascent dissolves into a prison of pressing mediocrity, suggesting both Maturin's great and petty tyrannies and Wollstonecraft's prison of woman's history.

These slight verbal connections recur in the larger structure of the novel, as Austen toys with three variants of the Romantic double prison, while General Tilney shifts imperceptibly between ordinary father and monster, until the two come to resemble each other, and Henry takes on the ambiguous role of redeemer/jailer, 'torment[ing]' and 'instruct[ing]' Catherine simultaneously (109). The mechanical, even faintly zombie-like quality of the final epithalamium—'Henry and Catherine were married, the bells rang and every body smiled' (252), in which the smiles seem as non-human as the bells[17]—recalls the darker, enforced marriages of the unnatural in Romantic fiction, whose contrivance (as in *Frankenstein* or *Melmoth*) murders the living nature marriage claims to perpetuate.

With the exception of its title, and of Marianne's early effusions, literary language falls away in *Sense and Sensibility*. We have seen the dark construction the title's 'sense' can take on when aligned with William Godwin's appalled apprehension of the prison of 'things as they are'; Elinor Dashwood's sense is equally a seismographic awareness of danger, of the reality of others' power, from which Marianne's sensibility is initially, blithely free. Marianne's movement in the novel is one long fight for escape from the functional prison of Barton Cottage, symbol of a family cannibalism (embodied in the John Dashwoods) only less blatantly motivated than those of *Melmoth the Wanderer*. Like the parricide in *Melmoth*, Willoughby claims to inaugurate her to a freedom beyond the savagery of convention, but in the ambiguity of his motives and of his very identity, he is a perfect type of the redeemer/jailer we have seen so often. His consistent doubleness may explain the intensity of Elinor's reaction to his final confession, in their one, puzzling confrontation:

> She felt that his influence over her mind was heightened by circumstances which ought not in reason to have weight; by that person of uncommon attraction, that open, affectionate, and lively manner which it was no merit to possess; and by that still ardent love for Marianne, which it was not even innocent to indulge. But she felt that it was so, long, long before she could feel his influence less. (333)

The potent ambivalence of Elinor's response is often seen as a symptom of the fragility of her sense in the face of Willoughby's vividness and passion. But if we define 'sense' as Godwin does, this passage anatomises its strength: Elinor's profoundly double perception is painfully true to the dual identity of the hero, and, perhaps, to that of all heroes.

If we limit ourselves to the six Austen novels completed and published, the novels following *Sense and Sensibility* attempt in various ways to move beyond the double prison of Romantic structural irony by aligning the heroines with the sources of social power. Elizabeth Bennet in *Pride and Prejudice* is the simplest case: she assumes power by marriage to it, and the novel arcs with her comic rise. Unlike Catherine Morland and Marianne Dashwood, she falls back only in a muted, vicarious fashion through her sister's humiliating elopement. The double prison quietly persists, however, in Darcy's radically double character, his ambiguous affinity with his tyrannical aunt making him as suggestive a redeemer/jailer as Willoughby was. His humanisation is so undefined a process that we can see the 'shades of the prison-house' closing on Elizabeth forever at Pemberley.[18]

In *Mansfield Park*, Jane Austen solves the problem of the heroine rising to power through marriage, and thus remaining vulnerable to its vagaries, by dissociating Fanny's increasing power at Mansfield from her later union with Edmund in an unspecified future. Perhaps so many readers find this novel unpleasant because Fanny gains power in silence and solitude, keeping her own counsel in a most disingenuous and ungirlish fashion; only after she supplants his own children in the confidence of the head of the house does she marry the vacillating son. The influence Fanny gains over the estate enables her to exclude her enemies, such as Mary Crawford, from it, and to include her allies, such as her sister Susan, within its lush confines. She rises alone from being the prisoner of Mansfield to the status of its principal jailer.

This assumption by the lone woman of the hero's role of redeemer/jailer prepares us for the greater complexity of *Emma*, whose heroine, like Byron's Gulnare, is both queen and slave, prime mover and victim, of the confinements of Highbury and of her father's house. This tension between power and prison is so great that *Emma* is almost stationary, suggesting less a progress (even if illusory) through a double prison than an exploration, as

Wollstonecraft's *Maria* might have been, of the multitudinousness and richness of confinement.

For like the madhouse/prison of *Maria*, Austen's prisons are neither 'abodes of horror' nor 'castles, filled with spectres and chimeras, conjured up by the magic spell of genius to harrow the soul, and absorb the wondering' (*Maria*, 23). Austen's homely settings have no need for the exotic terrors of Maturin's Inquisition. But their inescapability is the same. Like Maturin's labyrinths, they are founded on the institutionalisation of mediocrity, a tyranny of the normal which the determined heroine can come to dominate, but which she cannot transcend. Austen's meticulous double vision transplants remote Romantic terror to the reassuring familiarity of the world we think we know.

In its imagination of a more seemingly open world and a cleansing, even a Utopian, society *Persuasion* is repeatedly dubbed Austen's one Romantic novel.[19] But as I hope I have shown, both Romanticism and Jane Austen express a profound awareness that the questing spirit is bowed down by indelible manacles, of its own and its society's making. When we read Austen among her Romantic contemporaries, the implacable reality of limitation leads neither to comfort nor complacency, but to the delicate desperation of Maria Bertram's complaint in *Mansfield Park*: 'I cannot get out, as the starling said' (99).[20]

NOTES

1. Mary Wollstonecraft, *Maria or the Wrongs of Woman* (1798; rpt New York: Norton, 1975), p. 27. Future references to this edition will appear in the text.
2. Charles Maturin, *Melmoth the Wanderer* (1820; rpt Lincoln, Nebraska: University of Nebraska Press, 1961), p. 174. Future references to this edition will appear in the text.
3. George Henry Lewes, 'The Lady Novelists', *Westminster Review* (July, 1852). Reprinted in *Jane Austen: The Critical Heritage*, ed. B. C. Southam (London: Routledge and Kegan Paul, 1968), p. 140.
4. Stuart M. Tave, *Some Words of Jane Austen* (Chicago: University of Chicago Press, 1973), p. 1.
5. A lively and flourishing critical school insists that Jane Austen's greatness springs not from her repose, but from the dynamic and unresolved tensions in her mind and her art. Among recent critics, see especially Tony Tanner's brilliant introductions to *Sense and Sensibility* and *Mansfield Park* (Harmondsworth: Penguin, 1969; 1966), pp. 7–34; 7–36; Bernard J. Paris, *Character and Conflict in Jane Austen's Novels* (Detroit, Mich.: Wayne State University Press, 1978); and Alison G. Sulloway, 'Emma Woodhouse and *A Vindication of the Rights of Woman*', *The Wordsworth Circle*, 7 (1976), 320–32.

6. See Karl Kroeber, 'Jane Austen, Romantic', *The Wordsworth Circle*, 7 (1976), 291–6. This fascinating issue of *The Wordsworth Circle*, devoted to an exploration of Jane Austen as a Romantic writer, was the first inspiration for my own chapter.

7. L. J. Swingle's rich study of the Romantic love of enclosures, 'The Perfect Happiness of the Union: Jane Austen's *Emma* and English Romanticism', *The Wordsworth Circle*, 7 (1976), 312–19, does not consider their imprisoning possibilities. Swingle's 'The Romantic Emergence: Multiplication of Alternatives and the Problem of Systematic Entrapment', *Modern Language Quarterly*, 39 (1978), 264–83, defines elegantly a spacious and flexible Romanticism that admits Jane Austen and other apparent dissenters.

8. 'I have read the Corsair, mended my petticoat, & have nothing else to do' (*Letters*, p. 379).

9. To George Henry Lewes, 12 January 1848. Reprinted in Southam, p. 126.

10. As, for example, Joseph Kestner does in 'Jane Austen: The Tradition of the English Romantic Novel, 1800–1832', *The Wordsworth Circle*, 7 (1976), 297–311.

11. *Natural Supernaturalism: Tradition and Revolution in Romantic Literature* (New York: Norton, 1971), p. 193. Abrams' book has been a useful source in crystallising Romantic paradigms, though it ignores some dark twists that are equally Romantic.

12. William Godwin, *Caleb Williams* (1974; rpt New York: Norton, 1977), p. 107. Future references to this edition will appear in the text.

13. 'The Tale of Guzman's Family' provides the final turn of the screw.

14. See Ellen Moers, *Literary Women: The Great Writers* (New York: Doubleday, 1976), pp. 91–9, for her influential discussion of Frankenstein as a female myth of childbirth. On p. 135, Moers mentions the divided image of the father in *The Mysteries of Udolpho*, on which I elaborate below.

15. For a more detailed discussion of Austen's dislike of children, see my 'Artists and Mothers: A False Alliance', *Women and Literature*, 6 (1978), 3–15.

16. Ann Radcliffe, *The Mysteries of Udolpho* (1794; rpt London: Oxford University Press, 1970), p. 305. Future references to this edition will appear in the text.

17. In *Melmoth the Wanderer*, bells are used to remind Monçada and the reader of the chillingly dehumanising non-humanity of the objects of religious ritual. Horrified by a dying monk's revelation of his hypocrisy, Monçada pleads, 'But your regularity in religious exercises . . .' only to be stopped by the bitter reminder: '*Did you never hear a bell toll?*' (p. 86. Maturin's italics.)

18. For a fuller discussion of Darcy's irreconcilable double nature, see my *Communities of Women: An Idea in Fiction* (Cambridge, Mass.: Harvard University Press, 1978), pp. 52–5.

19. See, most recently, my 'O Brave New World: Evolution and Revolution in *Persuasion*', *ELH*, 39 (1972), 212–28; William A. Walling, 'The Glorious Anxiety of Motion: Jane Austen's *Persuasion*' and Gene W. Ruoff, 'Anne Elliot's Dowry: Reflections on the Ending of *Persuasion*'. The latter two essays are both in *The Wordsworth Circle*, 7 (1976), 333–41; 342–51.

20. Profound thanks to my contagiously lively graduate students at the University of Pennsylvania in the spring 1978 semester. The vigorous Romantic fictions of English 751 honed and inspired my own efforts.

3 The Influence of Place: Jane Austen and the Novel of Social Consciousness

Ann Banfield

At the time when Jane Austen lived at Steventon, a work was carried on in the neighbouring cottages which ought to be recorded, because it has long ceased to exist.

Up to the beginning of the present century, poor women found profitable employment in spinning flax or wool. This was a better occupation for them than straw plaiting, inasmuch as it was carried on at the family hearth. . . . Some ladies were fond of spinning, but they worked . . . at a neat little machine of varnished wood. . . . I remember two such elegant little wheels in our own family.

It may be observed that this hand-spinning is the most primitive of female accomplishments, and can be traced back to the earliest times. Ballad poetry and fairy tales are full of allusions to it. The term 'spinster' still testifies to its having been the ordinary employment of the English young woman. It was the labour assigned to the ejected nuns by the rough earl who said, 'Go spin, ye jades, go spin'. It was the employment at which Roman matrons and Grecian princesses presided amongst their handmaids. Heathen mythology celebrated it in the three Fates spinning and measuring out the thread of human life. Holy Scripture honours it in those 'wise-hearted women' who 'did spin with their hands, and brought that which they had spun' for the construction of the Tabernacle in the wilderness: and an old English proverb carries it still farther back to the time 'when Adam delved and Eve span'. But, at last, this time-honoured domestic manufacture is quite extinct among us—crushed by the power of steam, overborne by a

countless host of spining jennies, and I can only just
remember some of its last struggles for existence in the
Steventon cottages.

J. E. Austen-Leigh, *A Memoir of Jane Austen*[1]

Writing in the period described in the retrospective opening of *Silas Marner*, 'in the days when the spinning-wheels hummed busily in the farmhouses—and even great ladies, clothed in silk and thread lace, had their toy spinning-wheels of polished oak',[2] Jane Austen's social experience was limited precisely in a way to make it representative of that experience formed by pre-industrial village life—by Raveloe or Steventon during the Napoleonic Wars. But elsewhere already the whir of spinning jennies was drowning the hum of the cottage wheels and the noise of the power loom was soon to obliterate the mysterious sound of Silas Marner's handloom. If domestic manufacture still survived in Steventon, it was struggling for existence. Austen did not record that struggle, but she felt its repercussions in the responses of the old landed families to the new sources of power brought by trade and manufacture. And her social vision became prophetic of that Victorian critique of the capitalist system which was to confront the effects of industrialisation with a set of principles formed by the experience of village life. For, however hierarchical the traditional village, the gulf between individuals of different classes was not based on a total ignorance of the other's experience; it had not yet been deepened by the exteriorisation of the labour process by one class and its location in another. 'Ladies did not disdain to spin the thread of which the household linen was woven', Austen-Leigh thought it important to record in a life of his aunt. 'Some ladies liked to wash with their own hands their choice china'; 'they took a personal part in the higher branches of cookery, as well as in the concoction of home-made wines, and distilling of herbs for domestic medicines'.[3] In *The Watsons*, Elizabeth Watson busies herself with the family's 'great wash' (321), while in *Silas Marner*, Nancy Lammeter's hands 'bore the traces of butter-making, cheese-crushing, and even still coarser work'.[4] Out of such an experience Austen judges the values brought from those places affected by the new social and economic relations of which the disappearance of the spinning wheel is one sign, values concentrated in the city and which lead Mary Crawford, newly arrived at Mansfield Park, to offend 'all the farmers, all the labourers, all the hay in the parish' by asking to hire a cart during the harvest. She 'could not be expected to have thought on the subject before', to 'see the importance of getting in the grass' (58), as those not completely divorced from the work that creates society would be.

Austen was the first great English novelist to create an appropriate formal expression for a critical vision of the new society. This is because in the experience of village life, with its arrangement of great houses, farms and cottages, and its relation to the distant city, she discovered a way to relate individual experience and the society it is formed in. Literarily, this meant bringing together and reshaping two distinct novelistic traditions. In Austen, the novel of consciousness, developed largely by Richardson, was integrated with the novel of place—the Gothic novel—to become the novel of consciousness of class and society. Unlike in Richardson or Burney, this consciousness of class is seen to limit any individual's point of view—the limitations of 'pride' and 'prejudice' can only be escaped through the self-conscious recognition Austen herself achieved, making social consciousness possible. The radically new conception which permits this fusion of two traditions is what Austen calls 'the influence of the place' (*Mansfield Park*, 88). This concept of influence allows place and self to be developed reciprocally, where either term may be alternatively agent or acted upon; the relation of place and self inherent in the notion of influence formally requires the distancing of the self in the social landscape and, stylistically, its presentation through a language representing consciousness that contrasts with the purely objective, narrative statement. Consciousness discovers itself in its alienation from the social landscape (which is the landscape socialised), just as the language of consciousness can only be grasped when it is distinct from a language in which subjectivity is absent.

The novel which most perfectly embodies the relation between consciousness and society expressed by 'the influence of the place' is *Mansfield Park*. This novel, which according to Lionel Trilling, 'Undertakes to discredit irony and affirm literalness'[5] is the one Austen novel whose style shows what George Eliot in *The Mill on the Floss* calls 'the emphasis of want', 'that tone of emphasis which is very far from being the tone of good society, where principles and beliefs are . . . of an extremely moderate kind, . . . no subjects being eligible but such as can be touched with a light and graceful irony'.[6] This change in tone is a response to a change in society and in the way it is perceived. That this tone of emphasis is self-consciously adopted as fitting for the novel's social concerns is apparent in Edmund's appreciation for Fanny's 'enthusiasm' (113) and in Austen's new tolerance for evangelicalism, evidenced by *Mansfield Park*'s defence of the clergyman's role unlike anything in her earlier novels and her admission to her niece in the year the novel was published that she was 'by no means convinced that we ought not all to be Evangelicals' (*Letters*, 410).

> If you could discover whether Northamptonshire is a country of Hedgerows I should be glad again.
> Letter to Cassandra Austen (*Letters*, 298)

Gothic Scenery versus the English Landscape

If the influence of place was a Gothic theme, Austen reconceived all the realisations of place, thereby transforming the Gothic romance into something more empirical—a realistic novel where setting is more than decor. 'Place' became not far-away and long-ago, not continental, medieval, Catholic and feudal, but domesticated, English, modern and, ultimately, bourgeois. The castle and the picturesque wasteland became the English country house and the English landscape—a term implying the land structured by the shaping hand or eye, nature made at once aesthetic and social, nature 'influenced', 'improved', conquered and nationalised. This is the 'sweet view' of 'English verdure, English culture, English comfort' presented by the Abbey Mill Farm in *Emma* (360).

The locus for Austen's own conception of this transformation, her formula for realism, is in Henry Tilney's lecture to Catherine Morland in *Northanger Abbey*:

> Remember the country and the age in which we live. Remember that we are English, that we are Christians. Consult your own understanding, your own sense of the probable, your own observation of what is passing around you—Does our education prepare us for such atrocities? Do our laws connive at them? Could they be perpetrated without being known, in a country like this, where social and literary intercourse is on such a footing; where every man is surrounded by a neighbourhood of voluntary spies, and where roads and newspapers lay every thing open. (197–8)

The landscape of fantasy is rejected; whatever ideal place

achieves must be consonant with a plausible conception of the real, must acknowledge and not ignore it. If part of Austen's antagonism to Repton's improving of estates rests on his destruction of the past in the landscape, part also follows logically from her rejection of an aesthetic which effaces the real, which arises from a class's unwillingness to confront the facts of work and the social world recorded in the landscape.

This denial of certain aspects of the landscape in the taste for the picturesque is what leads Catherine Morland to 'voluntarily [reject] the whole city of Bath, as unworthy to make part of a landscape', (111) just as Repton deletes from his 'View from my own cottage, in Essex' a one-eyed, one-armed beggar, ducks on the common and hams curing.[7] This intent to mask the realities of work and economic relations is also apparent in Henry Crawford's suggested improvements for Edmund's Thornton Lacey—'The farm-yard must be cleared away entirely, and planted up to shut out the blacksmith's shop' (242)—and in the general attempt to hide or find substitutes for fences under the pretence of eliminating them. The aesthetic aim masks a social one: to sever the empirical connection between landscape and social realities. In his lecture on the picturesque, Henry Tilney finds the association between landscape and politics inescapable, while Catherine's silent response betrays the Reptonian impulse to deny the latter: 'by an easy transition from a piece of rocky fragment and the withered oak which he had placed near its summit, to oaks in general, to forests, the inclosure of them, waste lands, crown lands and government, he shortly found himself arrived at politics; and from politics, it was an easy step to silence' (111). Fanny's wish to save the avenue at Sotherton in *Mansfield Park* is, according to this logic, not unrelated to her interest in discussing the newly abolished slave trade with her uncle on his return from the West Indies; the first position is consistent with the second interest and together they create a plausible character. The same relation between the felling of avenues and social issues is negatively embodied in John Dashwood's expenditures for improvements in *Sense and Sensibility*: 'The inclosure of Norland Common . . . is a most serious drain. And then I have made a little purchase within this half year; East Kingham Farm, . . . where old Gibson used to live. The land was so very desirable for me in every respect, so immediately adjoining my own property, that I felt it my duty to buy it. I could not have answered it to my conscience to let it fall into any other hands' (225). Elinor's sense can only 'censure'

(226) the economic philosophy behind these improvements, made explicit in Dashwood's vaunt 'I might have sold it again the next day, for more than I gave' (225), a speculation in real estate centrally satirised again in *Sanditon*. Austen's discomfort with the aesthetic of the picturesque is not quite Ruskin's, who 'could not help feeling how many suffering persons must pay for my picturesque subject'[8] but she shares with him the conviction that the subject of the landscape must lead to social questions.

For the author of *Northanger Abbey*, with a different aesthetic than Catherine Morland's, includes the city of Bath in her landscape. But it is the presentation of Portsmouth in *Mansfield Park* which most fully acknowledges the new relation of the city to 'the nation at large' (93). The contrast between places in *Mansfield Park* is not, however, the familiar one between country and city, as in *Sense and Sensibility*; it is a more complex triadic contrast between aristocratic Sotherton, petit bourgeois, if not proletarian, Portsmouth, and Mansfield Park, the country seat of a man with West Indian holdings, property in Woolwich and connections by marriage in Portsmouth.[9] The Portsmouth episode is striking in early sounding the modern themes which characterise the commercial or industrial city in the consciousness of social critics, whether those who looked with nostalgia toward a pastoral past or those who prophesied the decline of capitalism; it cannot be explained away as 'the low-life sequence' which was 'yet another cliché of the anti-jacobin novel'.[10]

Although the city itself is only briefly presented, through Fanny's experience of family life, there we derive the meaning assigned urban place. The descriptive terms applied to Fanny's original home, both city and house, arise from the experience of this new social world—bustle, noise, chaos, disorder, unrest, crowdedness and competition which the narrow streets and small house engender. The household activity is marked by 'interruption', 'sudden burst[s]' and 'sudden starts', 'thumping and hallooing', (383) and 'all talking together' (382); there Fanny hears 'the parlour door' 'slammed' (381) and can find no privacy, there the competition over a silver knife divides her sisters, making the house altogether the 'abode of noise, disorder, and impropriety' (388). Finally, the poverty of the surroundings—'the smallness of the house, and thinness of the walls' (382), 'the confined and scantily-furnished chamber' (387)—are seen as the cause of this disorder.

The combined force of these factors could be attributed to their being registered by the neurotically sensitive Fanny Price and so dismissed, if they did not also match the reactions of other less neurasthenic travellers in the city. The aspects of Portsmouth which are organised by Fanny Price's perceiving consciousness appear in similar configuration in Charlotte Brontë, Disraeli, Gaskell and Dickens, but they are perhaps most explicit in Engels' great description of the nineteenth-century city.

> The more that Londoners are packed into a tiny space, the more repulsive and disgraceful becomes the brutal indifference with which they ignore their neighbors and selfishly concentrate upon their private affairs. We know well enough that the isolation of the individual—this narrow-minded egotism—is everywhere the fundamental principle of modern society. But nowhere is this selfish egotism so blatantly evident as in the frantic bustle of the great city. The disintegration of society into individuals, each guided by his private principles and each pursuing his own aims has been pushed to its furthest limits in London. . . .
>
> What is true of London, is true of all the great towns, such as Manchester, Birmingham and Leeds.[11]

Portsmouth is no great town, but its expansion was tied to the expansion of trade and the British navy's role in it. There Dickens was born in 1812, two years before the publication of *Mansfield Park*, and as one of the eight children of a clerk in the Naval Pay Office, he could have been Fanny Price's brother. Thus, Portsmouth is already very far from the English society Henry Tilney portrays as 'a neighbourhood of voluntary spies' or what Raymond Williams calls 'a knowable community'.[12]

The 'disintegration of society into individuals' manifests itself not only in the anarchy of the Price household, where 'nobody could command attention when they spoke' (392), but also in that place which is its social opposite—Sotherton Court, whose cottages Maria pronounces 'a disgrace' (82). At Sotherton, the same discontent, restlessness and competition appear, the same lack of social cohesiveness in this world of the aristocratic past subjected to the new improving spirit, where 'every body likes to go their own way' (87), as in lower class Portsmouth. Although from the retrospective view of Portsmouth it seems to Fanny that 'in her uncle's house there would have been a consideration of times and seasons, a regulation of subject, a propriety, an attention towards every body which there was not here' (383), Mansfield at first shares in the social anarchy of Portsmouth and Sotherton, and, as we shall see, precisely because in all three Fanny is ignored.

The moral terms into which these descriptions of place are translated—making thereby possible the comparison of place on which the novel is structured—rest upon a partially conservative ideal of social order. Nevertheless, Austen 'provided the emphasis which had only to be taken outside the park walls, into a different social experience, to become not a moral but a social criticism', as Williams has argued,[13] a social criticism not necessarily in theory nor always in practice a conservative one. And she herself had already taken it outside the park walls in Mansfield Park, where all the features concentrated in the city make it the major model for the experience of social reality itself and its values those of the society at large.

> Charming as were all Mrs. Radcliffe's works, and charming even as were the works of all her imitators, it was not in them perhaps that human nature, at least in the midland counties of England, was to be looked for.
> *Northanger Abbey* (200)

The Influence of Place and Consciousness

More than the realisations of place are altered in Austen's transformation of the Gothic romance. The crucial change is in the relation of place to consciousness inherent in the notion of 'influence'. Place is no longer simply background or atmosphere; it interacts with and forms consciousness. In Fanny's conviction that 'there could be neither wickedness nor sorrow in the world; and there certainly would be less of both if the sublimity of Nature were more attended to' (113) and in Edmund's defence of the social importance of the chapel at Sotherton and his claim that 'the influence of the place and of example may often arouse better feelings than are begun with' (88), place is seen to educate its inhabitants. But the novel moves from education to investigate the modern notion of the formative role of social environment. The influence of place is lived experience, the lived reality through which consciousness is developed and character formed. Austen's concept of human nature is one which is not universal in that it is not free of time and place; it is, rather, modified by it—'human nature in the midland counties'. The sisters Mrs Price and Lady Bertram differ by the influence of place. The descriptions of the Price house explain the behaviour of those who live in it, just as the account of the formal gardens at Sotherton explains the feelings of restraint felt by the visitors there.

Characters, then, belong to one place, and they look at other places from the distance of their origins. In Austen, consciousness arises from a sense of the gulf between self and a society constituted by others with a different experience of place, and it develops as social consciousness through the recognition of the social limitations created by place for the individual. For place to be seen through consciousness, the self must necessarily be outside the scene perceived. The consciousness thus achieved becomes a consciousness of class, of the difference between Sotherton, Mansfield and Portsmouth, between the great house and the 'small house now inhabited by Mr. Price' (377).

But when a character from one place moves to another, the influencing of place also becomes possible—what in Austen's novels is called 'improvement'.[14] The social world conceived as an arrangement of different places is the arena of change; because changing places is possible, places too can change. While consciousness is formed by the confrontation with place, where prejudices and principles are acquired, place can be altered by consciousness, which imports the values of one place into another and precipitates social change toward an idealised place.[15]

Richardson is usually credited with the stylistic creation of consciousness confronting the social hierarchy in a plot dependent on social mobility. But in *Pamela*, although consciousness responds to class and place, the social milieu which characters are assigned by birth and fortune leaves untouched the self who is imprisoned in it. Social place and rank function only as a decor and costume because Pamela can become Lady B merely by changing place and dress. The fairy-tale motif is appropriately discovered here, because Pamela is the princess freed from servitude and rags. But Fanny Price is only Cinderella if the original tale is reinterpreted so that the features which qualify Cinderella for social advancement are seen as the result of her experience in poverty and servitude; Fanny has known the experience of want and oppression and so sees the world through another perspective. The popular desire underlying the Cinderella motif is transformed by a new insight into the relation between social background and character.

In *Mansfield Park*, then, one place is focused through a consciousness already influenced by another place. Mansfield and Sotherton are seen through Fanny Price's socially disadvantaged eyes, and then Portsmouth is seen through a Fanny shaped by Mansfield. *Mansfield Park* pleads her cause, with the emphasis of want. The critics who object to Fanny as a prude adopt Mary Crawford's socially superior perspective—she who only knew admirals, as she tells Fanny when Edmund enquires after William Price's captain, but 'very little of the inferior ranks' (60). (Mary's own background, we are to understand, is responsible for her values. Cf. p. 112.) The same failure to grasp the significance of Fanny's social position underlies the misinterpretation of her refusal to participate in social functions, including the amateur theatricals. For these critics, like the residents of Mansfield, Fanny's 'feelings' are 'too little understood to be properly attended to' (14).

From her arrival at Mansfield Park, Fanny is made conscious of the great gap between her and her cousins, for Sir Thomas is careful 'to preserve in the minds of my *daughters* the consciousness of what they are, without making them think too lowly of their cousin; and . . . without depressing her spirits too far, to make her remember that she is not a *Miss Bertram*. I should wish to see them very good friends, and would, on no account, authorize my girls the smallest degree of arrogance towards their relation; but still they cannot be equals' (10–11). Aunt Norris finds it 'desirable that there should be a difference' (19) between Fanny and her cousins. She is to be constantly reminded that her origins are elsewhere than at Mansfield.

Her social inferiority is underscored by an 'inferiority of age and strength' (17). And just as her 'delicate and puny' constitution 'materially' results from the poor air of Portsmouth (11), 'her faults of ignorance and timidity' (20) result from deficiencies in the place she comes from. When Fanny returns to Portsmouth, her health (411) and her looks suffer an 'alteration' (446) under the 'many privations, besides that of exercise, she endured in her father's house' (413), privations physical—Rebecca's puddings and hashes, for one—as well as mental. The influence of these privations of place explain, then, the Fanny who first arrives at Mansfield and the fact that, as Fanny later discovers, 'Susan had read nothing' (398).

Coming to Mansfield from the small house at Portsmouth, 'the grandeur of the house astonished, but could not console her. The rooms were too large for her to move in with ease; whatever she

touched she expected to injure, and she crept about in constant
terror of something or other' (14–15). Her sense of her smallness in
this great house is increased by the way she is ignored or patronised
by her rich relatives. Her cousin Tom, 'born only for expense and
enjoyment' (17), shows Fanny a kindness 'consistent with his
situation and rights; he made her some very pretty presents, and
laughed at her' (17–18). Most of the household share a 'mean
opinion of her abilities' (18). The sisters 'could not but hold her
cheap on finding that she had but two sashes, and had never learnt
French' (14). Lady Bertram finds her 'handy and quick in carrying
messages, and fetching what she wanted' (20), and Mrs Norris also
treats her as a servant (205). Perhaps even Edmund's forgetting of
Fanny beside Mary Crawford (113) has its roots in the kind of
attitude which leads Mr Elton in *Emma* to ask rhetorically: 'who can
think of Miss Smith, when Miss Woodhouse is near!' (131). On the
other hand, in Edmund's attentions toward Fanny, Austen draws a
connection between social consciousness and the profession of the
clergyman, whose social role, if it is not to 'head mobs' (92), as she
must be aware some have done in English history, must show a
sympathy for the poor.

This treatment of Fanny cannot help but have an effect on her,
despite Sir Thomas' intention not to depress her feelings. 'I can
never be important to any one,' she tells Edmund, because of 'my
situation—my foolishness and awkwardness' (26). Her situation—
that locative term—as a social outcast in the household makes of her
a silent observer and an unwilling participant. This is the source of
her timidity and her inertia, as it is also for Jane Fairfax's in *Emma*.
Fanny's social distance from the others puts her in the position of
social critic. Her consciousness of herself as apart, different, inferior,
transformed into a consciousness of class, makes her the judge of a
place in which she is banished to that invisible suburb reserved for
servants and all the lower classes, to those lower depths which
Margaret Hale in *North and South* sees only on her return from
Milton Northern: 'There might be toilers and moilers there in
London, but she never saw them; the very servants lived in an
underground world of their own.'[16] Austen notices Fanny, however,
because she observes, not with the eye of Mary Crawford failing to
see 'the importance of getting in the grass', but with an appreciation
of the contribution Fanny makes to the family's life.

Fanny's desire not to be noticed (26, 150, 164) is the counterpart
of the fashionable world's failure to notice her. To be the centre of

attention is the privilege of the rich. It is Mansfield Park's gradual noticing of Fanny and therefore of her class experience which changes Mansfield. Those who notice the poor cousin from Portsmouth can partcipate in the new society created at Mansfield; the others are banished.

For in *Mansfield Park*, class consciousness expands to social consciousness, to a distanced perspective on the society which condemns Fanny to a subservient condition and to a sympathy for others in her position. The stylistic requisite for this social distance presented at once through and beyond Fanny's limited perspective Austen had developed earlier when she freed herself from the first person form of her predecessors. She had used this epistolary form in *Lady Susan* and *Love and Freindship*, but exchanged it in the later work for that third person style I have elsewhere called 'represented thought'.[17] This style allows Fanny to be presented in her full interiority and yet remain the silent observer. Perhaps more important, her perceptions are often represented non-reflectively without suggesting that she fully assesses what she observes. We see through her eyes what she silently registers in the complexity of her response but at only certain moments reflects upon, while any observations recorded in the letter form would necessarily be present to full consciousness. Furthermore, the possibility of shifts from a character's point of view to pure narrative statements—a possibility excluded by the epistolary form, where the letter-writer's voice dominates all—means that the confrontation of consciousness and place is stylistically mirrored in the alternation of subjective represented thought and objective narration, or what the French linguist Emile Benveniste calls, significantly, *histoire*.[18]

Through represented thought, Fanny, 'so harmonized by distance' (152), is not the 'representative of . . . orthodoxy' Marilyn Butler thinks her to be,[19] but is one who struggles silently to reconcile the experience of Portsmouth with that of Mansfield Park. Her moral isolation is a factor of her social isolation. Like Charlotte Brontë's heroines, like all those who face the social world across the gulf of class differences, she has no one to consult but herself and the values of the world she is thrust into are unfamiliar and subject to interpretation.

Social consciousness requires the assertion of self, of equality, and requires crossing the gulf of class—an act which reveals the barriers of class in overcoming them. As long as her principles demand the negation of action, Fanny can resist: 'To be called into notice in

such a manner, to hear that it was but the prelude to something so
infinitely worse, to be told that she must do what was so impossible
as to act; and then to have the charge of obstinacy and ingratitude
follow it, enforced with such a hint at the dependence of her
situation' (15). This is why she is critical of her own behaviour
during the theatricals. Significantly, in one of the few places where
the representation of Fanny's point of view rises to full reflectiveness,
it is to record her uncertainty and inner turmoil:

> But she had more than fears of her own perseverance to remove:
> she had begun to feel undecided as to what she *ought to do*; and as
> she walked round the room her doubts were increasing. Was she
> *right* in refusing what was so warmly asked, so strongly wished for?
> what might be so essential to a scheme on which some of those to
> whom she owed the greatest complaisance, had set their hearts?
> Was it not ill-nature—selfishness—a fear of exposing herself?
> And would Edmund's judgment, would his persuasion of Sir
> Thomas's disapprobation of the whole, be enough to justify her in
> a determined denial in spite of all the rest? It would be so horrible
> to her to act, that she was inclined to suspect the truth and purity
> of her own scruples, and as she looked around her, the claims of
> her cousins to being obliged, were strengthened by the sight of
> present upon present that she had received from them. (152–3)

Fanny, in her inability to act, has already the lack of artificiality
associated in the nineteenth-century imagination with the lower
classes, and her hesitation to deny something requested by her
superiors is linked to her economic dependence.

What precipitates her defiance of the values her social superiors
represent is Crawford's proposal, which potentially elevates her to
his social level. Fanny's subsequent behaviour can be appreciated only in an interpretation of the novel which recognises the
influence of class on her relations with others. That Fanny should
refuse is unthinkable, because the proposal is 'an elevation' (332).
'She must have a sensation of being honoured' (328). She 'may', Sir
Thomas assures her, 'live eighteen years longer in the world,
without being addressed by a man of half Mr Crawford's estate'
(319). And all attempts to persuade one who had up till then seemed
to be malleable fail. Sir Thomas accuses her of 'wilfulness of temper,
self-conceit, and every tendency to that independence of spirit,
which prevails so much in modern days, even in young women'

(318), and of ingratitude, thereby recalling to her her dependent position. Fanny's defence hardly justifies interpretations of the novel as 'denigrating the individual's reliance on himself', and illustrating 'how dangerous it is to trust private intuition or passion in forming judgement of others'.[20] When Edmund urges that Fanny's refusal—'so very determined and positive!'—is 'not like yourself, your rational self' (347), she only argues her feelings: 'I *should* have thought . . . that every woman must have felt the possibility of a man's not being approved, not being loved by some one of her sex, at least, let him be ever so generally agreeable. Let him have all the perfections in the world, I think it ought not to be set down as certain, that a man must be acceptable to every woman he may happen to like himself' (353). Fanny's response is so outrageous in the eyes of the others because she does not humbly acknowledge the honour this man above her in rank and fortune does her by his proposal, does not show her characteristic gratitude. She too sees the situation through the consciousness of her class and her sex, and even her moral disapproval of Henry is tinged by this: 'he was taking, what seemed, very idle notice of me' (353). This estimation is based on her observation of his behaviour toward her cousins at Sotherton and during the theatricals. She is not merely prudish in hesitating to respond to him; she acts as her social superiors should expect: 'In my situation, it would have been the extreme of vanity to be forming expectations on Mr. Crawford' (353). Marriage would have been a presumption on her part. So her sense of injustice is understandable. 'How was I to have an attachment at his service, as soon as it was asked for? . . . The higher his deserts, the more improper for me ever to have thought of him' (353). The phrase 'at his service' spells Fanny's ultimate resentment of her treatment in Mansfield society; the impropriety she speaks of is not sexual but social.

That critics have largely ignored this episode is not surprising, given the consensus about Fanny's passivity and priggishness. But no other Austen heroine defies the combined opposition of her benefactors and superiors—not even Elizabeth Bennet against Lady Catherine. Through Fanny, Austen acknowledges social change from below and approves it. Having undergone many a 'strange revolution of mind' (393) as a result of her experience of the novel's three places, Fanny changes places and ultimately changes Mansfield Park. For in her novels formed by a consciousness of class, Austen's social ideal leads to a union of lovers where there is (except in *Emma*) some violation of social differences, some contamination of place. If Austen's sentiments are not quite Cobbett's—'Love is a great leveller; a perfect Radical'[21]—she does recognise with approval the potential catalyst for social change in sexual relations. 'Marriage is a great Improver', she wrote her sister Cassandra (*Letters*, 231). And, describing Mr Woodhouse as 'hating change of every kind', she observes in *Emma* that 'matrimony' is 'the origin of change' (7).

The revolution in Fanny's position consummated by her marriage to Edmund means that, with her experience of want, she has something to contribute to Mansfield which that place lacks. But she can only do this by subverting its traditional authority. Disobeying her uncle by refusing Henry Crawford, she asserts to Henry himself: 'We have all a better guide in ourselves . . . than any other person can be' (412), herself advising him on 'the welfare of the poor' (412) and her sister Susan on her reading. If, as has often been observed, Austen's novels demonstrate the moral chaos attendant upon the absence or weakness of the father, they also show the havoc wrought by the arbitrary and authoritarian father or parental figure: General Tilney in *Northanger Abbey* and Sir Thomas—or the bad advice of such a figure: Lady Russell in *Persuasion*, Edmund on the occasion of the theatricals and on Fanny's marriage. Sir Thomas is described as 'interfering' with Fanny's 'inclination', by advising her to go to bed; ' "Advise" ', we are told, 'was his word, but it was the advice of absolute power' (280). In ordering her in the presence of Mr Crawford, 'he might mean to recommend her as a wife by shewing her persuadableness' (281); but Fanny, who 'had known the pains of tyranny' in addition to those 'of ridicule, and neglect' (152), chooses Edmund, who has maintained, 'Let her choose for herself as well as the rest of us' (147).

Significantly, it is never that the father's return restores the traditional order;[22] instead, the daughter must create a new social harmony, in isolation and even in opposition. In *Mansfield Park*, the daughter creates a harmony out of the experience of oppression after defying the patriarch who is also her benefactor. In the teasing challenge with which Austen concludes *Northanger Abbey*—'I leave it to be settled by whomsoever it may concern, whether the tendency of this work be altogether to recommend parental tyranny, or reward filial disobedience' (252)—she records a 'modern' (a word decidedly not pejorative in Austen) dilemma. Austen's heroines make their own decisions because the truth about the social world is that a viable traditional order is absent. This is the shape—the anarchy—of the new order.

What Fanny brings eventually to Mansfield Park and to *Mansfield Park* is social consciousness, born of this experience of oppression; her view of place teaches people to be 'more carried out of themselves' (113), instead of seeing things only from the limited perspective of their own class and place, like those at Mansfield or Fanny's father, who 'had no curiosity, and no information beyond his profession; . . . he talked only of the dock-yard, the harbour, Spithead, and the Motherbank' (389). For Fanny's experience includes all the novel's places. Her own social consciousness is completed by her return to Portsmouth, when she finds she has something to give. It is exercised in her undertaking Susan's education. The effect of her influence on Crawford, who had once declared the subject of 'how to turn a good income into a better' the 'most interesting in the world' (226), is shown in his concern for the mill on his property and for 'the welfare of the poor' (412): 'He had introduced himself to some tenants, whom he had never seen before; he had begun making acquaintance with cottages whose very existence, though on his estate, had been hitherto unknown to him' (404). Fanny's response—'To be the friend of the poor and the oppressed!' (404)—has its counterpart in the novel's own social sympathy and vision, in its initial focusing on the family of the unfortunate Mrs Price. 'Poor woman! she probably thought a change of air might agree with many of her children' (11) is the sympathetic exclamation which closes the narrative exposition of the first chapter.

The acknowledgement that a change of air, of place, can be the crucial factor for the full development, physically, morally and intellectually, of the children of the poor, bases the novel's vision, from the start, on the recognition of the influence of place. Its plot makes this its theme through the gradual notice of Fanny and the eventual acceptance of her as a social equal by those characters who, with her, will reconstitute Mansfield Park. And throughout, characters are faulted for lacking Fanny's social consciousness: Rushworth for 'his zeal after poachers' (115) and Mrs Norris for 'the more than one bad servant . . . detected' (188), for suspecting the carpenter's son of stealing 'two bits of board' ('so good as your father is to the family, employing the man all year round!' [142]), for forcing the rheumatic old coachman out over rough roads on a snowy day (189). Against her belief that one of

Mrs Grant's faults is paying 'her cook as high wages as they did at Mansfield Park' (31) should be set the penitent Emma's sentiments to Miss Bates on the salary offered Jane Fairfax as governess: 'if all children are at all like what I remember to have been myself, I should think five times the amount of what I have ever yet heard named as a salary on such occasions, dearly earned' and Miss Bates' response: 'You are so noble in your ideas!' (382).[23]

Mansfield Park, then, is the first great English novel to confront the new society created by capitalism, with its deepening class divisions, its alterations of the social as well as the natural landscape, its growing ports and cities. The formal shape it gives this new experience is one which becomes representative for the experience of industrialisation throughout the nineteenth century. The contemplative gaze of a character whose social position imposes a distance between her and the social world and whose consciousness of this world is coloured by the awareness of this distance creates the point of view which interprets this world and orders it. The action of the novel requires that the central character leave her place of origin and confront this divided world from the vantage point assigned the outsider before choosing a new home. Having left, she finds she cannot return and so must change places, thereby effecting a change in social relations which unites the divided places through social consciousness—that is, the alienated consciousness of one who belongs to no one place. The place she longs for across the gulf of class differences is the utopia of Tory reform where the classes are united through an enlargening of sympathy brought by social consciousness.

> The road from Mansfield swerved round to the north.
> D. H. Lawrence, *Lady Chatterley's Lover*[24]

Jane Austen and the Novel of Social Consciousness

Austen's vision in this great novel, apparent again in *Emma* and *Persuasion*, holds for later generations of novelists; they rediscover, under the pressure of a social reality whose underlying features she had already intuitively grasped, her formal solutions. Austen's pattern is reapplied most explicitly in Elizabeth Gaskell's *North and South*, which opens as an Austen novel, in her South, first fashionable London and then pastoral Hampshire. There the heroine, Margaret Hale, like Austen the daughter of a village clergyman, receives a proposal of marriage from an Austen hero, Henry Lennox. Margaret refuses, her father has religious doubts and gives up his living, and the family moves to Milton Northern, an industrial city in the north. But Austen's form is only superficially rejected. For Margaret, like Fanny, confronts a new place as an outsider. *North and South*, like *Mansfield Park*, has a place name as a title, and the novel is built on the same contrasts of place, now seen on a larger scale. With the Austen heroine's weak father, Margaret finds she is on her own in Milton. Like Fanny, she discovers in returning home that she sees it from a different—an outsider's— perspective and she cannot stay. But the place of the novel's utopian future is reversed; it is the enlarged and industrialised city. The chapter 'Looking South' is a 'Looking Backwards'; the contrast it seems between industrial North and rural aristocratic South is one between present and an irrecoverable past.

We can discover Austen's social vision in other, less obvious, realisations. The social pariah as the judging consciousness becomes a common figure in Victorian fiction. Jane Eyre, Lucy Snowe, even Alton Locke, share Fanny's painful shyness, her aloofness, her physical weakness and inertia, her apparent prudishness. These features all accompany an acute consciousness of class. Margaret Hale, on the other hand, is not timid because she owes her position as outsider to her social superiority, but this is challenged and felt primarily as social distance. Some sense of difference is the crucial ingredient for the creation of social consciousness, for it must pass first through a consciousness of class. The outcasts can bring to the place which adopts them the harmony a wider sympathy makes possible; Margaret's entry into Milton has this effect, as does Sissy Jupe's into the Gradgrind household in *Hard Times*. Sissy, like Fanny, specifically brings the experience of oppression. Esther Lyons in *Felix Holt* and Eppie in *Silas Marner*, who like Fanny can exchange their humbler homes for a great house, reject this alternative because it does not derive from their lived experience, just as Eliot rejected the inheritance as a solution of a plot which develops 'what many yesterdays had determined'.[25] In this, she follows Austen, who never chooses this structural option which ignores the influence of place.

The world which meets this gazing consciousness is one which, like Mansfield, Sotherton and Portsmouth, increases the isolation of the central figure by its hostility and insouciance. This is a world ever more appropriately represented by the city or the industrialised village. Nor has the great house entirely disappeared from the landscape of the industrial novel; Fieldhead in *Shirley*, Transome Court in *Felix Holt*, adjust their position to the new mills and mines, as Henry Crawford's Everingham had to do.

Perhaps the last important novel to respond to industrial society with the novelistic form first developed in *Mansfield Park* is *Lady Chatterley's Lover*. Returning to the English landscape in this last work, Lawrence begins like Austen by rejecting another tradition, the fantastic and gothic landscape of the pornographic novel, the seraglio or Sade's castle, with its pseudo-aristocratic society, and places his lovers in the midland counties. The novel is organised around the same contrast of places, the constellation of industrial village, Tevershall, the great houses, Wragby, Chadwick Hall, Shipley and the collieries and mills which are now a settled feature of the landscape. Change is continuous, however. At Wragby, 'the avenue of yews was cut down',[26] going the way of Sotherton's and Transome Court's avenues. In this scenery, the improvement of estates under the logic of capitalism is carried to its ultimate conclusion: the Prince of Wales is reported to have said 'If there were coal under Sandringham, I would open a mine on the lawns, and think it first-rate landscape gardening.'[27] And, as in Austen's model, the stance of the novel's informing consciousness with respect to the social world is that of the distanced and judging outsider: Connie comes first to Wragby as outsider and then goes from there to Tevershall Village and Mellor's cottage and in *The First Lady Chatterley* to Parkin's lodgings in Sheffield. The harmony achieved at Mansfield can only be discovered, however, in Lawrence in a place outside society—in the woods which are themselves threatened by the noise and smoke of the collieries. Finally, the attack on industrial society is now delivered with the emphasis of want that is the tone adopted by the novelists of social consciousness. Lawrence could not avoid the tone of what he calls in *Lady Chatterley's Lover* 'the stream of gossip above Tevershall village. It was more than gossip. It was Mrs. Gaskell and George Eliot and Miss Mitford all rolled into one, with a great deal more that these women left out',[28] because he could not escape the society which was their social context as well as his.

The great changes separating Jane Austen from D. H. Lawrence which Austen-Leigh records in his memoir may have only been dimly understood from the perspective of Steventon. Nevertheless, Austen realised that the hope for some new social harmony lay with those who, like Fanny Price, came from the crowded districts of England's great towns. Austen shared with George Eliot's Nancy Lammeter a village life where ladies did not entirely excuse themselves from the demands of labour and so from a sympathy with those who laboured; she had also, as Nancy did not, the ability to overcome the prejudices of her limited experience and imagine the effect the adoption of a poor girl from beyond the village would have on that place. That imaginative act produced a work which pointed the direction the English novel would take in the context of industrialisation.

NOTES

1. J. E. Austen-Leigh, *A Memoir of Jane Austen* (London: Macmillan, 1906), pp. 39–40.
2. George Eliot, *Silas Marner, The Lifted Veil, Brother Jacob* (Edinburgh: Blackwood, 1913), p. 3.
3. Austen-Leigh, pp. 34–5. Austen reveals in a letter to her sister that she could use a spinning wheel: 'I cannot endure the idea of her [Mrs Knight] giving away her own wheel, & I have told her no more than truth, in saying that I could never use it with comfort;—I had a great mind to add that if she persisted in giving it, I would spin nothing with it but a rope to hang myself—but I am afraid of making it appear a less serious matter of feeling than it really is' (*Letters*, 285).
4. Eliot, *Silas Marner*, p. 142.
5. '*Mansfield Park*', *The Opposing Self* (New York: Viking Press, 1955), p. 208.
6. George Eliot, *The Mill on the Floss* (New York: Collier Books, 1962), p. 324.
7. From *Fragments on the Theory and Practice of Landscape Gardening* (London: J. Taylor, 1816), an illustration reproduced in Alistair Duckworth, *The Improvement of the Estate* (Baltimore, Md.: The Johns Hopkins Press, 1971).
8. *Modern Painters* (London: Smith, Elder, 1856), Vol. IV, p. 11.
9. For other discussions of place in *Mansfield Park* and, especially, its symbolic use of landscape gardening, see my 'The Moral Landscape of *Mansfield Park*', *Nineteenth-Century Fiction*, 26 (1971), 1–24; Tony Tanner, 'Introduction', *Mansfield Park* (Harmondsworth: Penguin, 1966), pp. 7–36; and Duckworth, *The Improvement of the Estate*. The interpretation of the novel given here is compatible with my earlier reading; the present essay may be said to put the earlier one 'in a social context'.
10. Marilyn Butler, *Jane Austen and the War of Ideas* (Oxford: Clarendon Press, 1975), p. 244.
11. Friedrich Engels, *The Condition of the Working Class in England*, trans. by W. O. Henderson and W. H. Chaloner (Stanford, Calif.: Stanford University Press, 1968), p. 31.
12. *The Country and the City* (St. Albans: Paladin, 1975), p. 202.

13. Williams, p. 146.
14. On the theme of 'improvement' in *Mansfield Park*, see Banfield and Duckworth.
15. When the landscape and the architecture on it come to be seen as the record of change, as Ruskin's Lamp of Memory, history itself takes on a place's influencing role. The process which Lukács (*The Historical Novel* [Harmondsworth: Penguin, 1969]), observes in the rise of the historical novel whereby novels 'historical only as regards their purely external choice of theme and costume' (15) are replaced by those where history is recognised as 'an uninterrupted process of changes' with 'a direct effect upon the life of the individual' (20) is seen first in the use of place. Lukács cites as an example of a novel where 'history is treated as mere costumery' (15) Walpole's *Castle of Otranto*, also seeing the Gothic novel as the origin against which the historical novel is defined. The transformation of the influence of place into the influence of history is supremely realised in George Eliot. In the retrospective coach trip through the midlands which opens *Felix Holt*, historical change is, however, presented first through the changes in the landscape.
16. Elizabeth Gaskell, *North and South* (Harmondsworth: Penguin, 1970), p. 458.
17. For a discussion of represented thought, see my 'Where Epistemology, Style and Grammar meet Literary History', *New Literary History*, 9 (1978), 289–314. Examples of the style in *Mansfield Park* can be found on pp. 156–7, 164–5, 218, 435–6, 438 and 441. For the distinction between reflective and non-reflective consciousness, see my 'The Formal Coherence of Represented Speech and Thought', *PTL*, 3 (1978), 289–314.
18. *Problèmes de linguistique générale* (Paris: Gallimard, 1966).
19. Butler, p. 247. Fanny's thoughts about the attempts to involve her in the theatricals (152–3), which I quote in the next paragraph of my text, should make it clear that it is not the case, as Butler contends, that Austen 'never allows the inward life of a character . . . to seriously challenge the doctrinaire preconceptions on which all her fiction is based' (293–4).
20. Butler, p. 101.
21. See Raymond Williams, *Keywords: A Vocabulary of Culture and Society* (New York: Oxford University Press, 1976), p. 210.
22. See Tanner, pp. 14, 16. 'In his [Sir Thomas'] absence Mansfield Park falls into confusion: after his return, order is re-imposed' (16).
23. Through Jane Fairfax, Austen delivers a criticism of the position of governess worthy of Charlotte Brontë. From it we can also deduce her hostility to slavery: Jane makes an analogy between the condition of governesses and that of slaves, speaking of 'the guilt of those who carry it on' (300).
24. *Lady Chatterley's Lover* (London: Heinemann, 1974), p. 86.
25. *Felix Holt the Radical* (Harmondsworth: Penguin), p. 277.
26. Lawrence, p. 210.
27. Lawrence, p. 208.
28. Lawrence, p. 147.

4 Disregarded Designs: Jane Austen's Sense of the Volume

Marilyn Butler

Of all the elements in a work of art, the form, or central principle of design, seems at face value one of the simplest and most communicable. It is tempting to suppose that the sense of form is fairly constant: that, within the same culture at least, the artist and the onlooker, the writer and the reader, will tend to see the same figure in the carpet. Yet it is a matter of common experience that, often within a short number of years, the same object can come to look quite different, and literary designs become overlaid as readily as any. We can now see, because scholars have shown us, that long Elizabethan poems were constructed with elaborate, indeed mathematical, refinement. At a point about halfway between the Elizabethans and ourselves, in the eighteenth century, notions of form became radically severe, and decorative detail submitted to line. When in this period Thomas Warton helped to lead the revival of interest in the literary Elizabethans, he did not commend them for their intricacies—that would have been no commendation—but as primitives, who hardly aspired to design at all. As schoolboys, Coleridge and Lamb absorbed Warton's view, and Coleridge could therefore write of the 'manly simplicity' of poets like Spenser and Donne.[1] In this context, his was surely an uneducated eye. A system forgotten looked to him like no system at all. Coleridge was arguably more completely mistaken on this question of form than he could ever be on other large literary topics, such as character, or language.

Modern ideas of shape in the novel have been influenced by movements of taste one might label late Romanticism, especially by the aestheticism of the latter part of the nineteenth century. Henry James, both as a novelist and as a critic, has been a presiding genius over taste in design. His own novels and tales often appear to have been planned according to an external, almost neo-classical notion of symmetry, but formal patterns are certainly not what James likes to discuss when he writes of fiction. He is an organicist. He wants a novel to appear to grow spontaneously from a single idea—what he calls the donnée—and this at its most typical occurs in the novels as an acute moment of perception, a discovery, of tragic implication, within the consciousness of a single character. Other people, a story, shapes, symbols, symmetries, are present in his fiction, but all, he claims, as ways of making us feel his large emotional truth. James' novel-criticism is often an exercise in resisting other men's attempts to separate out his work into component parts. 'The story and the novel', he says, 'the idea and the form, are the needle and the thread': distinct, certainly, but immobilised if taken apart. Analytical procedures remind him of the dissection of a living organism: 'The only classification of the novel that I can understand is into that which has life and that which has it not.'[2]

Jane Austen is perhaps the only novelist publishing before 1830 whose novels can be read as though Henry James had written them. A young girl is deciding whom to marry. There is our donnée, and nothing could seem more natural or more like ordinary life. And so Jane Austen's novels are art-ful in Henry James's sense, because they also appear artless, spontaneous and whole. While we are reading them this way, we are not likely to read them any other way. If it is hard to see an unfamiliar kind of pattern through an apparent jumble of detail, it is even harder to see it through a pattern that already appears distinct to us, and aesthetically satisfactory.

Nevertheless, it is a matter of record that Jane Austen, her immediate predecessors and her contemporaries, do not speak or write about organic form, the Jamesian notion of structure that becomes a seamless whole and is located, essentially, in the subjective experience of a central character. Naturalness and verisimilitude, qualities which relate the world of the novel to the actual world, are critical terms to conjure with before 1830; unity, which takes the novel to be self-sufficient, is not. About 1830, Jane Austen's contemporary, Maria Edgeworth, set out to write the last of her novels, *Helen*. She was out of practice: she had not published a novel since 1817, the year of Jane Austen's death. In the interval, new literary ideas had become current, the principles that novels should be built around characters rather than around didactic themes, and that they should have a strong unifying action. Maria Edgeworth's young step-sisters tactfully urged these fashions of the rising generation upon the novelist—who, having rather lost her nerve, was eager to listen to their advice: 'I quite feel all you say about the advantage of putting characters in action.'[3] But it was easier said than done, for a writer who by now had other notions in her bones. One senses, reading *Helen*, a new departure, not quite mastered, into a more sustained, continuous pattern of narrative.

What Maria Edgeworth's generation, and Jane Austen's, had been brought up to includes something quite prosy and literal: the solid physical presence of two books, or three, that weighed somewhat against the metaphysical notion of one novel. By the late 1820s, publishers began to aim at a mass market by producing books much more cheaply in a single volume. From the 1830s came the practice of serialisation in parts. It is clear that issuing a book in parts has a large influence upon its general design, and upon the way the story is told. When every episode has to be intrinsically interesting, but also to leave the reader wondering what happens next, a premium is put on eventfulness. Jane Austen would not have written as she did for publication that way. But she wrote as she did for publication in volumes. Isn't it reasonable to suppose that this affects the way she arranges her material, and, deeper, the very sense that she has of her own design?

It would be a matter for a different kind of investigation, why novels of Jane Austen's day came out in such a variety of forms, from Peacock's *Headlong Hall* in one volume to Fanny Burney's *Camilla* in five. This was a decision for the publisher, a commercial calculation. Prices of books were going up in the late eighteenth century, and after the nineties, in wartime, they went up again. In fact, in Jane Austen's day novels were relatively dearer than ever before or since. Purchasers had to pay five shillings a volume for *Sense and Sensibility*, and six shillings a volume for all the others, except *Emma*, which cost seven. How much to charge per volume, and how many volumes to issue a novel in, were professional questions, decided by the length of the text, and by the publisher's estimate of how much the public would wear. The more volumes, the greater the profit, if the novel sold. But if it did not sell, the publisher's costs, for labour and for paper, were likely to be high.

It is one matter how the publisher calculated; another, what supposition was in the author's mind when he or she wrote. It is my impression that the genteel author liked to be seen aiming at the shorter length, which looked less like profiteering. Perhaps this was less so in 1797, when the Rev. George Austen offered *First Impressions*, the future *Pride and Prejudice*, to Cadell as a novel in three volumes. But the price had gone up by 1811, when Jane Austen wrote *Sense and Sensibility*—and this looks uncommonly like a novel designed in two volumes, even though Thomas Egerton, the publisher, chose to bring it out in three. The same is also surely true of the revised *Pride and Prejudice*. Indeed, Jane Austen boasted in January 1813, 'I have lop't and crop't so successfully, . . . that I imagine it must be rather shorter than S. & S. altogether' (*Letters*, 298).[4] Her father estimated in 1797 that *First Impressions* was about the length of *Evelina*, which means, if correct, that the new version is only three-quarters of the length of the old. But the cutting did not induce Egerton to bring out *Pride and Prejudice* in two volumes. Once again, he preferred three.

A possible insight into the Author's thinking is provided by another gentlewoman who disliked being thought of as a professional writer. Maria Edgeworth had to handle her own business decisions for the troublesome last novel, *Helen*. At the time of writing, she might have been glad of money to help her financially embarrassed family, but she was also bent on cutting her manuscript down to make a two-volume novel, and felt awkward when her publisher offered her an extra £200 to publish it in three: 'You find that I did not swear or kick but behaved like a reasonable woman & a lady moreover & pockets my £200 with a very good grace. . . . I know that far from having stretched a single page or a single sentence to *make out* a third volume—I have cut away as much as ever I could—cut it to the quick—and now it matters not whether it be printed in 2 or 3 volumes.'[5] It mattered somewhat to her, however; a lady did not like to feel greedy. She liked the smaller scale, not only for aesthetic reasons—the two inches of ivory—but also the modest, reasonable call upon the public purse. For Jane Austen, who published anonymously, and pushed the sheets under the blotter when visitors called, to plan for two volumes came as naturally as it did for Maria Edgeworth. At any rate, the internal evidence suggests that, with one significant exception, she generally did so.

If Jane Austen went on thinking, despite her publisher, that she was a two-volume novelist, Scott knew that he would come out in three. When he turned to the novel in 1814, he was already a phenomenonally successful poet. *Waverley* might be anonymous; but Scott himself had all the self-confidence, the professionalism, the open concern for financial success, that Jane Austen and Maria Edgeworth shrank from. Scott thought in large subjects, what he called the big bow-wow strain, and he also thought in three or four volumes, for which the public was charged from the first a steep price—seven shillings a volume for *Waverley*, going up to ten for *Ivanhoe* and ten and six for *Kenilworth*. Scott worked closely with his publishers, often delivering the text to them volume by volume. In other words, he conceived his novels in the actual volume-format in which they appeared, rather than having the pattern imposed by his publisher. I do not think anyone has followed up the implication of this for Scott's novels. The volumes are designed, often quite elaborately designed, as volumes; his novels are three books in one. Later readers, finding them rearranged into two volumes apiece in a Collected Edition, or crammed into one volume in abominable print, have tended to conclude that Scott's volumes are badly designed or perhaps not designed at all. On the contrary, he has, I think, a sophisticated sense of structure, of a kind new in the novel. Even Fielding, a meticulous planner, has nothing quite resembling Scott's imaginative, often near-symbolic, use of design motif. In *Old Mortality*, each volume is planned around a battle or skirmish. In *The Antiquary*, three gentlemen, Jonathan Oldbuck, Sir Arthur Wardour, the Earl of Glenallan, are seen against the settings of their ancestral homes, in which they all take great pride. But largely by means of the beggar, Edie Ochiltree, who moves on foot between the houses, the reader comes to visit homes which are the focus of very different ways of life and livelihood: the fisherman's hovel at the foot of the cliff, the Fairport post office. He is also taken, with sardonic effect, to the ruined abbey of St Mary's, where deception is practised on Sir Arthur, and to the mound which Oldbuck mistakes for a Roman fort. Within each volume, the 'houses' are arranged in a pattern like counterpoint. By parallel and contrast, Scott means to undercut the pride of house. This kind of elaborateness was possible only when an author felt confident of his control over the publication process, as few but Scott did.

The lack of co-operation between most authors and their publishers strikes one in retrospect as a curious business. The better novelists write with consistent awareness of division into volumes. Their work breaks into blocks of approximately suitable length.

Often there is a change of scene, or the passage of time, at a point where a new volume would probably be required. And the new volume does not follow on from the old in a simple linear development, but to some extent runs parallel with it, repeating, or challenging, its ideas. Yet, as often as not, authors who have written their books this way find them bound up differently. With all their forethought they did not, apparently, use the covering letter—or, if they did, scant notice was taken at the printing-house.

To take two examples from the 1790s, Jane Austen's formative years as a novelist. Elizabeth Inchbald published her *Simple Story* in four volumes in 1791. This was in a sense two simple stories. The first half, written many years earlier as a complete short novel, is the story of a spoilt heiress, Miss Milner, who falls in love with her guardian, Dorriforth, a Catholic priest. Halfway through Miss Milner's story, Mrs Inchbald, an experienced dramatist, has worked a climax. Miss Milner's friend, knowing of her passion for Dorriforth, threatens to tell him unless Miss Milner voluntarily leaves his house. At this point, with the distressed heroine's journey to Bath, the second volume correctly begins. The start of the third volume is right again: it begins what is in effect a new plot, the story in the next generation of Matilda, the daughter of Miss Milner's ill-starred marriage to Dorriforth. But the printer has spoilt the break at the end of the third volume. Mrs Inchbald had contrived another climax there, meant to echo the end of Volume I. Matilda has been living in the same house as her father, but he refuses to see her. After they have met accidentally, he sends her away. The third volume was obviously meant to end poignantly, with Matilda's carriage rolling away from Dorriforth's house, just as her mother's did a generation earlier. Mrs Inchbald's nicely contrived curtain is lost, by a printer who begins the last volume at an insignificant point, one chapter too soon.

Mrs Radcliffe is even worse served in *The Mysteries of Udolpho*. She has designed a novel of four volumes, the first and last to be set in Languedoc, the middle two in Italy. The printer ends the first volume correctly, with Emily's farewells to the hero, Valancourt; the next volume has her setting out to cross the Alps. But Mrs Radcliffe clearly meant that this volume, which describes the heroine's imprisonment in the castle of Udolpho, should end with a brief interpolated chapter telling of Valancourt's dissipation at the French court. This digression would have had the effect of intensifying Emily's plight, making the reader fully aware that she is not only imprisoned by Montoni but, for the time being, abandoned by her lover. Unfortunately the printer chooses to squeeze a further four chapters into the second volume, and he does the same at the end of the third, so that one of Mrs Radcliffe's real skills as a novelist, her architectural sense of structure, is obscured.

Authors who clung to their amateur status were at a disadvantage when dealing with those avowed professionals, the publishers. This was probably true for gentlemen authors: certainly Thomas Love Peacock would seem not to have had his way with *Melincourt*, 1817, a work which is planned with careful symmetry for three volumes— and issued in three, divided up with the usual indifference to authorial logic.[6] But the problem was surely exacerbated for gentlewomen, who were doubly obliged, by notions both of sex and of caste, not to be seen to take their writing too seriously. Female authors emerged from a narrower band at the upper end of the social scale than their male counterparts, since other women (with scarce exceptions, like Ann Yearsley, the Bristol Milkwoman) were unlikely to have the requisite education. Very probably the upper-class women drawn to writing were more inclined than many male litterateurs to work at their craft; to polish and burnish, as the Edgeworths put it; and thus to see the design possibilities of the volume. At the same time, their lines of communication to their publishers were liable to be vulnerably long. Often, where anything is known of this crucial relationship—certainly in the cases of Jane Austen and Maria Edgeworth, though not in Charlotte Smith's—a male relative acted as intermediary. One hopes that even ladies were capable of feeling a certain ire at the indifference to their own wishes that this situation encouraged.

R. W. Chapman seems to have assumed that the volume-divisions in Jane Austen's first editions do match the author's intentions, but it is not clear why he thinks so.[7] It is true that Jane Austen does not try to round off her volumes with the same drama and point as Mrs Inchbald, or the same grave formality as Mrs Radcliffe. Quite often the Austen chapters just seem to stop, and this can be true even when one guesses that she has mentally reached the end of an entire volume. At first sight this will appear paradoxical. Her mode of thought seems profoundly influenced by her notion of volume. In her three shorter novels—*Northanger Abbey*, *Sense and Sensibility* and *Persuasion*—she uses one of the most emphatic methods of distinguishing between her two parts, a complete change of location. But she seems to have little faith that the printer will hit a

particular spot, and with reason. Though her novels came out as
sixteen volumes, there is only one instance—in *Persuasion*—where the
division looks as though it was selected with an eye to literary effect,
rather than convenience—or accident.

A design which Jane Austen herself did not round off as formally
as the other writers I have mentioned rounded theirs, and which the
printer consistently ignored, sounds as though it might not be of
much lasting interest. I want to imagine what it would be like if we
could hold the novels in our hands as volumes—not, that is, the
sixteen volumes which emerged from the printing house, but the
units which appear to have taken shape in the author's own mind. If
these volumes were allowed a certain integrity, an expressive power
of their own, would reading Jane Austen be an altered experience?

Northanger Abbey was the first of the novels to be sent to a
publisher, as *Susan*, in 1803. In the end it was among the last to be
published, coming out in 1818 as half of a four-volume set with
Persuasion. It is worth beginning with, because from the point of view
of volume-arrangement it is the most naïve of the novels: a typical
two-volume story, set out with a kind of blunt symmetry. Volume 1,
chapter 1, which has Catherine at home with her parents, is roughly
balanced by her return to them three chapters from the end.
Otherwise the plan is of course to show Catherine's adventures in
the world, at Bath in the first volume and at Northanger Abbey in
the second.

What is the significance of this? Two volumes, one weighed in
either hand, make, notionally, two parallel stories. But usually we
do our best to read *Northanger Abbey* as a single, unitary action.
Catherine is deceived—this, we are told, is where the interest lies—
first by sentimental fiction, and then by Gothic fiction. The book, in
true Jamesian style, is about her seeing through both deceptions,
and growing up. But *is* she deceived by sentimental fiction while she
is at Bath? She is taken in by the Thorpes, which is not the same
thing. The Bath section of the novel reads—if read without
preconceptions—more like an imitation of the Burney type of novel,
in which the heroine encounters a series of embarrassments, than
like any sort of literary burlesque. Because Catherine makes her
celebrated mistake at Northanger, a too literal application of Mrs
Radcliffe to real life, the modern reader feels tempted to bring the
first half of the book into line, and above all to see it consistently,
even rather grandly, in terms of the heroine's progress towards
maturity.

The successive titles are no help. In 1803, the novel was to have been called *Susan*; by 1817, it had become *Catherine*; both titles, Jane Austen's presumably, do certainly imply a story about a heroine's progress. The posthumous title *Northanger Abbey* quite visibly throws the book off balance by focusing attention on the allusions to the Gothic—which leads us back, in turn, to the heroine's folly. But what if some kind of Trades Descriptions Act had been in force, whereby a book's title had to reflect its contents? What if, unimaginably, it had come out into the world as *Bath and Northanger Abbey*?

The design after all seems to give a rough notional equality to the two locations—even if Bath gets nearly twice the number of pages. Once the reader perceives this, he may also find significance in the way the two actions are matched. The Thorpes and the General are very modern, modern in being mercenary. They are peculiarly acquisitive about possessions, especially the flashy kind that impress other people: Isabella acquires clothes, John horses, the General a house and garden full of the latest consumer goods. Because of this common taste, they become tangled together in the plot, to a degree which in real life would not be entirely probable for people of such different social status. Isabella pursues Frederick Tilney, while John misinforms the General about Catherine—who, as a supposed heiress, becomes their common quarry.

The effect of seeing the two-volume design as important to Jane Austen is to turn the emphasis around. When Catherine comes out into the world, at Bath and at Northanger, the Thorpes and the General are in effect the world that she meets. They are the novel's most active characters, its schemers. Catherine's conversations with Henry and Eleanor Tilney, which the romantic approach takes to be central, could alternatively be seen as reflective interludes, throwing light upon the satirical sketch of the world. From this point of view, the novel does not need its Gothic burlesque, which is indeed a distraction. Giving too much weight to the Gothic idea, in its few chapters at Northanger, means interpreting the entire action as Catherine's awakening from a world of illusion to something better, the world of reality. One objection to this is that the text of the novel does not often concern itself with Catherine's fantasy life. Another is that though Jane Austen does seem interested in portraying reality, she does not present it as desirable, or capable of contributing positively to Catherine's moral education. If the Thorpes and General Tilney represent the real world—and the novel's symmetrical arrangement suggests that they do, that there are many more like them—then the world is an unpleasant place, vain, cold and greedy. An endearing goose of a heroine is there as a contrast, and a consolation, for a sharp little vignette about society. *Susan*, or *Northanger Abbey*, might strike us as the comic romance of such a heroine. *Bath and Northanger Abbey* is a satirical novel which reflects on Southern England rather than on the pretend-Pyrennees.

A novel in two balancing parts need not necessarily be a novel primarily directed at describing the outer world, but its patterns of symmetry and recurrence do give special opportunities to the social novelist. With *Sense and Sensibility* Jane Austen seems fully aware of this. The first chapter, with its memorable vignette of the financial arrangements of Mr and Mrs John Dashwood, is conscientiously matched by a last chapter which deals with the policy of John, Fanny and Mrs Ferrars towards the various marriages. In the first volume, Elinor and Marianne are at Barton Cottage, the country; in the second they are in London, the town. Events in each repeat themselves with an elaborate symmetry not attempted in *Northanger Abbey*. The two sisters have each to decide whether their lovers love them; when they conclude that they do not, they have to bear up under the strain in order not to upset everyone else. In the country, light is thrown on the state of each young man's heart by his attitude to staying at Barton Cottage; in the town, each appears to settle the matter by becoming engaged to someone else. The knife is turned in Elinor's heart in each volume by the malicious triumphing of Lucy Steele; Colonel Brandon comes in on cue to hold out the hope of future comfort to Marianne. Such a catalogue makes the book sound excessively schematic; it is, though, not nearly as bad to read as uncovering the skeleton of the plot makes it sound. Considering that the book is planned to make the same things happen to two girls in each of two volumes—which means that every significant point is made four times—*Sense and Sensibility* is surprisingly natural. The scheme is always in practice being quietly softened, even in the too summary and didactic last chapter. Bringing back Mr and Mrs John Dashwood throws the reader's mind back to Norland Park, where the girls lost their childhood home. It is a reminder of the transition from girlhood to maturity, a hint of the emotional cost by which maturing is achieved, even though the surface of the writing deals with none of these things.

And yet the symmetries are there, and presumably for a purpose.

It is a striking feature of the way in which the two complementary volumes are conceived that the two societies, country and town, seem representative. The scale is panoramic, where in *Northanger Abbey* it was more intimate and domestic. Though Catherine Morland goes to the well-known public rooms at Bath, and walks and rides down real, named streets, Jane Austen does not attempt a sketch of Bath society. The great fictional representations of Bath are Smollett's in *Humphry Clinker* or Fanny Burney's in *Evelina*, but even *Persuasion* gives a much clearer sense of an observed real world, with its different degrees of fashion—the exclusiveness of Camden place, where Sir Walter has taken the best house, the heterogeneity of the public rooms, where Sir Walter keeps snobbishly to his own circle. There are no such social gradations in the Bath of *Northanger Abbey*, nor the same sense that, when Catherine leaves it, she leaves Town for Country.

But *Sense and Sensibility* deals in just these generalities. The Middletons, who rule social life at Barton, are typical country gentry, with the appropriate vices and virtues. Sir John has an old-fashioned sense of hospitality, and a genial passion for field sports, but the tone of his family circle is dull and uncultivated. His kindness mitigates his wife's insipid formality, just as Mrs Jennings' vulgar warmth offsets the hard rapacity of Mrs Ferrars' ambience. The nouveau-riche London world in *Sense and Sensibility* is Jane Austen's most sustained general social satire, and it is unrelieved by any quiddity in the individual lesser characters, or humour in their dialogue. Perhaps Jane Austen drew her City circle so black because she had little experience of anything like it, outside the pages of a Burney novel. The impression of a universal nastiness, east of Hounslow Heath, becomes all the more emphatic.

There cannot be any one way to read a novel by a great writer. But we hear so much about the two heroines of *Sense and Sensibility*, especially Marianne, that we are in danger of thinking it has to be read as a story about two sisters, when it is palpably designed at the same time as a story about England. Elinor, with her more sophisticated intellectuality, understands more about the outer world than Marianne does, and what happens to her has a more continuous social point. It is Elinor who is placed in direct competition with the anti-heroine, Lucy Steele, for the same man, Edward Ferrars. Elinor's ideal of civility is more poignantly challenged than is Marianne's unsociability by Lucy's parody of ᵛcivility, her obsequious currying of favour. The outcome in this competition is pointed, even a little bitter: the immaculately behaved Elinor gets Edward, but Lucy the status, the income, the family approval. Elinor's choice is in the author's eyes the better part—a modest competence and independence in a country vicarage—but Lucy's success in achieving *her* aims is meanwhile a decided comment on the state of the rest of the nation.

Pride and Prejudice, *Mansfield Park* and *Emma* are the great central sequence of Jane Austen's career, written when she was already a published author, and before the shadow of her final illness. The design of them reflects her growing confidence in her own powers, although only *Emma*, the last of three, looks like a bold plan for three volumes rather than for two. At some stage *Pride and Prejudice* has certainly been conceived as a novel in two parts: a volume of Elizabeth hating Mr Darcy, and ending by refusing him, has been balanced by a volume of Elizabeth falling in love with Mr Darcy, and ending by accepting him. Conceptually, *Mansfield Park* also falls into two, as plainly as any of the novels. Part 1 deals with the Bertram sisters' entry into the world, and the bad job they make of it: their defective education, their ambition to marry money, their readiness at the same time to be tempted by Henry Crawford. Then Fanny tries, for all the world like the youngest child in the fairy tale; and of course like so many boys called Jack, or girls like Cinderella, she meets the same adventures as her unsuccessful seniors. But Fanny copes with ballrooms the better for still clinging to the schoolroom, and her youngest-child's caution and shrewdness and inner resource make her healthily suspicious of those bad fairies, the Crawfords.

It has been a pity, for Fanny's credit with many readers, that her heroine-ly qualities have been obscured by the publisher's re-arrangement. If the first volume had ended with Maria's marriage to Mr Rushworth, we should have been prompted to see Maria as the protagonist, or anti-heroine, of volume one, and Fanny as the true heroine of volume two. As it is, volume one ends *in medias res*, with Sir Thomas' return from Antigua: the reader is free to compare Fanny not with Maria but with Mary, which is not nearly so much to her advantage. But how much it says about Jane Austen's growing subtlety that, though she did evidently have a use for a symmetrical structure in *Mansfield Park*, it scarcely resembles the way she used the device in *Sense and Sensibility*. *Mansfield Park* is a reflective novel, which works through the experience of its characters. The portrayal of the Bertram family incidentally tells us a great deal about the English gentry in 1814—more indeed than the Middletons and Ferrars put together—but it does so in a personal way. There is neither an attempt at a panorama, nor a claim to representativeness. When the scene moves to Portsmouth, it does so in order to complicate Fanny's predicament, especially the pressure on her to marry Henry. It would be perverse to read this sequence as an excursion to see how the other half lives. For *Mansfield Park* nowhere deploys the technique to which the two-volume format perhaps more obviously lends itself, the direct, objective comparison of contrasting social worlds. It is a novel of interiors, about families and their houses. Sotherton, gutted since its chapel ceased to be a chapel. Mansfield Park, where the sons and daughters of the family, aided by aunt Norris, turn their father's study into a theatre. The Parsonage, whose occupants seem to have been preoccupied, in their very different styles, with housekeeping. Portsmouth, nominally Fanny's home, but proving no home to her in practice. A motif of hollowness repeats itself: houses put to frivolous or materialistic use, families without family feeling, professionals without vocation. This is a much more complex way of novel-building, localised, suggestive, innovatory. It has a great deal to do ultimately with Jane Austen's perception of the state of the gentry in her day, but the means are indirect—as they will be with *Emma*—more truly than elsewhere the two or three families in a village.

To say that with *Persuasion* we return to externality may seem on the face of it perverse. Anne Elliot is the most feeling and introspective of the heroines, and her consciousness is the medium through which the story is told. Hers is the most moving of Jane Austen's narratives. And yet, *Persuasion* has also been planned as a two-volume novel, with all the old clear-cut symmetries of Jane Austen's relatively novice performances.

Each volume is more rounded and complete than ever before. *Persuasion* is built upon two distinct 'stories': in volume I Wentworth appears to fall in love with Louisa, while Anne looks on; in volume II she is courted by Mr Elliot, while Wentworth looks on. But Jane Austen was by now an experienced author, who knew all too well that no plan, however clear-cut, would necessarily be carried out. With *Sense and Sensibility* she designed a novel in two locations, but her publisher has Elinor and Marianne set off for London at volume II, chapter iv. (He was similarly to delay Catherine's departure for Northanger Abbey until chapter v of the second volume.) It may be a sign of Jane Austen's growing familiarity with the ways of publishers that she creates a buffer zone of two chapters between her two main locations. After her visit to Uppercross, before her departure for Bath, Anne goes to stay with Lady Russell at Kellynch Lodge. The publisher begins volume II immediately before this sequence, just after the day at Lyme; but it would clearly have suited the author's scheme equally well, or disarranged it as little, if he had delayed for two chapters. Apart from this instance of prudent flexibility, the novel is formally planned. As in *Sense and Sensibility*, volume I is set in the country (among the Musgroves at Uppercross); volume II in the town (among the Elliots at Bath)— with the additional refinement, that the first volume is prefaced by five chapters with Sir Walter Elliot at Kellynch, and the second concluded by three chapters with the Musgroves at Bath. When, in his book on *Jane Austen's Literary Manuscripts*, B. C. Southam discussed her changes to these last chapters of *Persuasion*, he showed how the new version is much more introspective than the first one.[8] This is indeed true; but the revised ending is also more formal and symmetrical, in terms of the two-volume scheme. Might it not be a concern for elegance rather than for inward interest that prompted Jane Austen to make the change?[9]

For here in *Persuasion*, even more than in *Sense and Sensibility*, is a most careful design, surely intended to be noticed, and itself expressive of a significant part of Jane Austen's meaning. Like the Middletons, the Musgroves are typical country people. They are more precisely specified than the Middletons, because Jane Austen observes that at the end of the Napoleonic Wars the manners of the gentry are in a state of transition, between old ways and new:

> To the Great House accordingly they went, to sit the full half hour in the old-fashioned square parlour, with a small carpet and shining floor, to which the present daughters of the house were gradually giving the proper air of confusion by a grand piano forte and a harp, flower-stands and little tables placed in every direction. Oh! could the originals of the portraits against the wainscot, could the gentlemen in brown velvet and the ladies in blue satin have seen what was going on, have been conscious of such an overthrow of all order and neatness! The portraits themselves seemed to be staring in astonishment.
>
> The Musgroves, like their houses, were in a state of alteration, perhaps of improvement. The father and mother were in the old English style, and the young people in the new. Mr. and Mrs.

Musgrove were a very good sort of people; friendly and hospitable, not much educated, and not at all elegant. Their children had more modern minds and manners. . . . Henrietta and Louisa, young ladies of nineteen and twenty, . . . had brought from a school in Exeter all the usual stock of accomplishments, and were now, like thousands of other young ladies, living to be fashionable, happy, and merry. (40)

At Bath, just as the fashionable world is analysed in its gradations, so too its seedy underside is allowed to appear. Parvenus and adventurers like Mrs Clay and William Walter Elliot are parasites upon the aristocracy. It is a town world which rivals in its distastefulness the London of *Sense and Sensibility*, while seeming much more closely observed. The general nastiness is clearly intended. There is a social dimension in the unpleasant behaviour of Sir Walter Elliot; Sir Thomas Bertram and Mr Bennet matter almost wholly in the domestic sphere, as heads of their respective families. Sir Walter's abandonment of Kellynch for self-indulgence at Bath is not seen primarily in terms of its effect on Anne, but as a point of general principle. Anne is not so much his victim, as the dispassionate observer who notices that Admiral Croft is a more manly and practical occupant of Kellynch than her father had been. Equally, Captain Wentworth was a more effective guardian to poor Dick Musgrove than were Dick's kind but muddle-headed parents.

There is nothing in the least revolutionary about this critique of the existing gentry. Jane Austen is arguing that the true gentleman is a paternalist, and that is no levelling doctrine. She of course also shows that he is properly the head of a loving family, for the family is the microcosm of the landed estate, the village community, the nation at large. It is not radical, but it is social, and critical. However poignant the love story, and sweetly disordered Anne's consciousness, the issues conveyed to us through her awareness of them have not to do with her love story only.

Yet if this is true, *Persuasion* remains the most puzzling of the novels. Jane Austen had become immensely subtle in her ways of representing the inner life; in her last three novels, her art had become increasingly introspective and complex in the way it was organised. Why should she then seem to fall back upon a structure which, however useful and effective, is also blunt—and indeed induces her to create lesser characters, and dialogue, as simplified and bitterly unfunny as any outside *Sense and Sensibility*? One can only speculate. Jane Austen's health is a possible factor. But it is also surely significant that while she was writing *Persuasion* in 1816, the condition of England was widely felt to be giving cause for alarm. Jane Austen's last novel, *Sanditon*, begun in January 1817, promises to be the most thorough-going social satire yet, a story about more gentry who have abandoned their homes and estates for fashion or speculation or a feverish search for novelty. It is hard to pass a critical judgement on *Sanditon*, which is so incomplete, but it looks as though imaginative visual effects were to have been grafted on the relatively crude techniques of eighteenth-century satire. The desire to comment on modern life was taking Jane Austen back to certain simple, expressive devices—typed characters, identifiable by exaggerated peculiarities of speech, together approximating to an impression of a whole community. Where all these are appropriate, so too are the contrasting volumes, together representing a social panorama.

Jane Austen sent Maria Edgeworth, whom she admired, a complimentary copy of *Emma*. As would often happen in the early nineteenth century, it was read aloud to the family circle, and at the end of the first volume came the time for taking stock. The Edgeworths decided to pass it on to friends, the last two volumes unread, since, as Maria Edgeworth said, 'there was no story in it, except that Miss Emma found that the man whom she designed for Harriet's lover was an admirer of her own . . . and *smooth, thin water-gruel* is according to Emma's father's opinion a very good thing & it is very difficult to make a cook understand what you mean by smooth thin water-gruel!'[10] That first volume ends slightly awkwardly, after a chapter in which Frank Churchill's coming visit is discussed. Would the Edgeworths have reacted so unfavourably if what they had just read ended well, almost immediately after the scene in the carriage in which Mr Elton proposes? Perhaps not. Not even *Emma* merely aims to imitate by its easy flow the naturalistic life of a village, though Victorians like Mrs Gaskell were soon writing this kind of episodic, desultory novel, and assuming that their predecessors wrote them too. In the case of *Emma*, Jane Austen had surely designed a plan to point up her heroine's tendency to make mistakes. The first two volumes should each end with a proposal from the wrong suitor, comically compared: Mr Elton, really proposing to Emma, though she expects him to speak of Harriet; Frank Churchill, actually revealing his love for Jane, though Emma takes him to be making love to her. Both these lesser climaxes anticipate the grand one, when Emma longs for Mr Knightley to propose, and thinks he will not because he is in love with Harriet.

With the shorter novels, Elinor, Anne and even Catherine Morland are observers, gazing at a representation of the wider world which symmetry in arrangement helps to order for us. The obscured designs might well have suggested concerns that were not merely personal, or parochial; just as a more faithful first section of *Emma* would have drawn attention to something other than the recipe for water-gruel. A complete novel will always be more than the sum of its parts. But, when the parts are volumes, it may be that as well.

NOTES

1. *Biographia Literaria* (1817), ed. J. Shawcross (London: Oxford University Press, 1907), Vol. I, p. 4.
2. 'The Art of Fiction' (1884), *Henry James: Selected Criticism*, ed. Morris Shapira (London: Heinemann, 1963), p. 59.
3. Maria Edgeworth to Fanny Wilson, 1 November 1831. (Quoted, Marilyn Butler, *Maria Edgeworth: A Literary Biography* (Oxford: Clarendon Press, 1972), p. 459.)
4. The same letter alludes to the appearance of *Pride and Prejudice* in terms which seem to hint at the mild embarrassment felt by both Jane and Cassandra at the business side of publication: 'it might be unpleasant to you to be in the neighbourhood at the first burst of the business. The Advertisement is in our paper to-day for the first time 18s. He shall ask £1.1s for my two next & £1.8s for the stupidest of all' (*Letters*, 297).
5. Maria Edgeworth to Honora Edgeworth, 2 November 1833. (Quoted in full, Butler, p. 465.)
6. See my *Peacock Displayed: A Satirist in his Context* (London: Routledge and Kegan Paul, 1979), p. 84.
7. 'Introductory Note' to his edition of *Pride and Prejudice*, xii.
8. *Jane Austen's Literary Manuscripts* (London: Oxford University Press, 1964), pp. 86–99.
9. For a fuller analysis of the design of *Persuasion*, see G. J. F. Kilroy, 'Ironic Balance in *Persuasion*', *Downside Review*, 96 (1978), 305–13. An early view of this article first attracted my attention to the subject of Jane Austen's symmetrical structures.
10. Maria Edgeworth to Sneyd and Harriet Edgeworth, n.d. [1816]. (Quoted Butler, p. 445.)

5 Sex and Social Life in Jane Austen's Novels

Jan S. Fergus

The definitive twentieth-century opinion of sexuality in Jane Austen's novels was uttered at one of Gertrude Stein's parties in Montparnasse: ' "You are talking of Jane Austen and sex, gentlemen?" said a tweedy Englishman with a long ginger moustache. "The subjects are mutually exclusive." '[1] The subjects exclude one another, however, only when 'sex' is narrowly defined as explicit, exhaustive detail about what people do and feel in bed. Austen's own understanding of sexuality is much less narrow. She is interested in dramatising sex in everyday social life—in the drawing room rather than the bedroom. The courtship plots she creates allow her to explore the relations between sex and moral judgement, sex and friendship, sex and knowledge—that is, between sex and character. In this sense, there is no escaping sexuality in Austen's novels. It is always present, treated with a variety and freedom that most modern readers overlook and that the novels of most of her contemporaries were unable, for various reasons, to achieve.

Austen's contemporaries were constrained both as readers and as writers of didactic domestic fiction by their own social context: by literary and social conventions that established very elaborate codes of behaviour for relations between the sexes. These conventions do not constrain Austen in the same way. Similarly, readers who share the tweedy Englishman's opinion are limited by a modern social context: by conventions which define sex as sexual intercourse and dictate explicitness. These notions have prevailed long enough to provoke a reaction. Recent works by critics like Michel Foucault and George Steiner convey a sense of fatigue with sexual explicitness itself.[2] To different ends, both Foucault and Steiner are prepared to

66

insist that sexuality may be more freely and powerfully expressed privately and tacitly than explicitly. Perhaps the shift in sensibility these writers may be anticipating, if it does occur, will make Austen's own broader vision of sexuality more accessible. But even Steiner, who identifies the 'sexual turbulence' Austen conveys below the surface of polite conversation, underestimates the extent and depth of her rendering of sexuality; he concludes that in Austen's novels sex is a 'limited terrain', confined by a 'necessarily public'[3] idiom. On the contrary: the very publicity of sex in Austen's novels—the constant awareness, the relentless dramatisation—is what makes her examination of it in social life so extensive and powerful.

A thorough study of Austen's treatment of sex in social life would have to address and answer several questions. What were some of the literary and social conventions governing sexuality during the time Austen composed her novels? What relations did these literary and social conventions have to one another and to documented sexual attitudes or sexual behaviour during this period? And finally, how does Austen render sexuality, and how does her treatment compare to the sexual conventions, attitudes and behaviour of her time. Although the first of these questions can be readily answered, the second is highly problematic. Human behaviour is, after all, frequently at odds with the codes or conventions that are supposed to govern it. Private sexual behaviour, and even private sexual attitudes, are notoriously likely to diverge from publicly proclaimed norms and are, for this reason, rarely documented and very hard to establish.[4] The best sources are private journals and letters, but even these are unsatisfactory: they are scarce and unrepresentative, for usually only those of aristocratic, political or literary figures survive; and these journals and letters are often uncandid or censored—by friends, by nineteenth-century editors, or by the author himself. Sources which publicly proclaim ideal sexual conduct are, on the other hand, endless, and the accepted norms themselves remarkably stable, from the mid-eighteenth through the nineteenth century. Courtship, however, because it is the one publicly approved form of sexuality, is fully documented by both public and private sources during this period. Courtship is also the focus of didactic novelists and of Austen herself.

Publicity is not merely sanctioned in courtship but required. A secret engagement like that between Frank Churchill and Jane Fairfax in *Emma* is felt to be reprehensible because it defies or mocks 'the world'; properly, Highbury should be aware of their relation and Enscombe should endorse it. All available eighteenth-century records—journals, letters, sermons, conduct books, essays and novels—insist that every possible stage of courtship must be reached in full view of the public eye. These stages—initial attraction, flirtation, infatuation and love—develop within a social world and are subject to intense social scrutiny. Moreover, the public eye is readily offended by any deviation from the various courtship conventions which operate, to some extent, both in life and in literature; at least, so we are told in conduct books written by a clergyman like Thomas Gisborne or by moralists like Hester Chapone, Hannah More and Jane West, in the didactic novels of writers like Samuel Richardson, Fanny Burney, Maria Edgeworth and Elizabeth Inchbald, and even in some contemporary journals and letters. Such moralists make it their business to articulate the conduct appropriate to every stage of courtship, often by taking a grim and detailed view of misconduct. Only by contrast with their frequently absurd attitudes toward attraction, flirtation, infatuation and love can the freedom, wit and good sense of Austen's treatment be fully appreciated.

Initial attraction between the sexes is a subject of many warnings, for example, in conduct books addressed to young women. Love at first sight is particularly reprobated. The likely consequence—a marriage based on 'mere personal liking, without the requisite foundation of esteem, without the sanction of parental approbation'—can produce only 'misery and shame', as Mrs Chapone, among others, affirms.[5] But oddly enough, despite the dazzling beauty enjoyed by nearly all heroes and heroines, surprisingly little attention is paid in didactic novels to the attractive power of good looks, upon women at any rate. A reference to 'person' is conspicuously absent when a character in Edgeworth's *Patronage*, Rosamund Percy, praises Colonel Hungerford as having 'Temper, manners, talents, character, fortune, family, fame, every thing the heart of woman can desire.'[6] And indeed, most heroines scrupulously attribute their interest in a hero to his estimable qualities, not to his personal charms. Amusingly enough, male novelists are rather more prepared to permit their heroines, the 'angelic' Sophia Western and Clarissa Harlowe among them, to respond to male beauty—but never without the illusion, at least, that other virtues attend it. And although in all his novels Richardson attests the attractive power of 'person', he invariably regards it as inferior to the attractions of 'mind'. The moral turn typically given by Richardson and his contemporaries to the subject of initial attraction is especially emphatic in Anna Howe's lament to Clarissa that 'our likings and dislikings, as I have often thought, are seldom governed by prudence or with a view to happiness. The eye, my dear, the wicked eye has such a strict alliance with the heart, and both have such enmity to the understanding!'[7]

Although the conduct books only rarely warn young women against the seducing effects of good looks in men, such works continually put them on their guard against the seducing effect of their own charms on themselves, that is, against the 'consciousness of being distinguished by personal attractions'.[8] This consciousness makes women particularly susceptible to the elaborate compliments of flirtation, known also as gallantry, coquetry and polite raillery. Although women are adjured in the strongest terms not to coquet, much more frequent are exhortations to close their ears to compliments. Gisborne, for example, blames them for encouraging men to 'intoxicate the head, and beguile the heart, by every mode and every extravagance of compliment'.[9] A woman's vanity is always seen as her weakest, most vulnerable point. Hannah More, citing '*vanity, selfishness,* and *inconsideration,* that triple alliance in strict and constant league against female virtue', is severest against vanity. It is the most insidious and incurable of vices: it is 'diffused through the whole being, alive in every part, awakened and communicated by the slightest touch', and 'those persons know little of the conformation of the human, and especially of the female heart, who fancy that vanity is ever exhausted' by anything other than a properly rigorous education.[10] In conduct books and novels, then, vanity is the likeliest source of a woman's misconduct or undoing; all Richardson's heroines are betrayed in some way by their vanity. This extreme vulnerability prompts Dr Gregory to conclude that 'Male coquetry is much more inexcusable than female, as well as more pernicious', but he adds with comfortable Podsnappery, 'it is rare in this country'.[11]

Infatuation, not often mentioned by name, is clearly proscribed for women in the maxim Dr Gregory (among others) promulgates: 'love is not to begin on your part, but is entirely to be the consequence of our attachment to you'.[12] Here, indeed, the conduct books reach heights of virtue that daunt even the didactic novelists—except Edgeworth, whose Belinda Portman is such a model of prudent reserve to her suitors that Edgeworth was herself later 'provoked with the cold tameness of that stick or stone'.[13] Other novelists resort to making their heroines unconscious of their affections as long as possible: Clarissa Harlowe and Evelina Anville are good examples. The rule that a woman must not love until she is beloved is, of course, wholly contradicted in life, as private journals and letters witness. But even there, women are usually determined to conceal their love from 'the world' if not from themselves. When Burney finally reveals her unrequited 'regard' for George Cambridge to her dear friend Mrs Locke, having determined that she cannot 'any longer, conceal from her any thing', her candour still has limits. She writes to her sister, in a passage later crossed out, 'Nothing upon Earth will I palliate but the depth of the Wound which has so long been kept open, & the unmerciful heedlessness with which it has so often been probed.'[14] Burney's letters corroborate Dr Gregory's view that a modest woman will always feel 'shame', or even that 'violence' has been done 'both to her pride and to her modesty', if she harbours love with any doubt 'of a return'.[15] An even higher standard of delicacy is expected from heroines in novels, who are so often proposed as exemplars that contemporary readers expect perfection and are offended by any deviation from it. Austen records in her collected 'Opinions of *Mansfield Park*' that her cousin Mary Cooke 'Admired Fanny in general; but thought she ought to have been more determined on overcoming her own feelings, when she saw Edmund's attachment to Miss Crawford' (*Minor Works*, 432–3).

A woman's love, according to the conduct books and many novels, is founded on gratitude and esteem and does not vary; a man's love is acknowledged to be more capricious, but esteem should be its foundation also. In her recorded 'Opinion' of *Mansfield Park*, Fanny Knight, Austen's niece 'could not think it natural that Ed[mund should] be so much attached to a woman without Principle like Mary C[rawford]' (*Minor Works*, 431). Love unfounded on esteem never prospers in didactic novels. And for women, other initial sources of love are usually ignored. Before Austen's novels, the possibility that antagonism can include a form of sexual attraction or grow into love is not recognised, except perhaps by Richardson in *Clarissa* and by Inchbald in *A Simple Story*. Similarly, the mentor relation, enjoyed by so many eighteenth-century heroes and heroines, and even enjoined by the conduct books, is not initially seen as sexually charged, though it often ends in marriage (as, for example, in *Evelina*, *Camilla* and *Pamela*).

The prescriptions for courtship in conduct books and didactic novels may differ slightly, but both sources emphatically agree that any violation of the elaborate and unreasonable conventions that they prescribe will be punished. Austen's freedom from the constraints imposed by these social and literary conventions was first noticed, with a sense of enormous relief, by Richard Whately in 1821:

> Her heroines are what one knows women must be, though one never can get them to acknowledge it. As liable to 'fall in love first', as anxious to attract the attention of agreeable men, as much taken with a striking manner, or a handsome face, as unequally gifted with constancy and firmness, as liable to have their affections biassed by convenience or fashion, as we, on our part, will admit men to be.[16]

Austen subjects all the conventions of courtship to the scrutiny of irony and commonsense as part of her attempt to dramatise the relations between character and sexuality within everyday social life. Informing this scrutiny in all the novels is a favourite perception: that good looks and charm inevitably create favourable responses and biased judgement. Such bias is at work when Elizabeth Bennet honours Wickham for his sentiments toward Mr Darcy's father and thinks him 'handsomer than ever' (80) as he utters them, or when she reflects that Wickham's 'very countenance may vouch for [his] being amiable' (80–1). This simplest and most instinctive sexual response is always taken for granted in Austen's novels, not criticised or investigated. Bingley is immediately attracted to Jane Bennet, 'the most beautiful creature I ever beheld!' (11), as Jane is to Bingley, although her account is rather less candid:

> 'He is just what a young man ought to be', said she, 'sensible, good humoured, lively; and I never saw such happy manners!— so much ease, with such perfect good breeding!'
> 'He is also handsome', replied Elizabeth, 'which a young man ought likewise to be, if he possibly can. His character is thereby complete'. (14)

Willoughby and Marianne Dashwood are also attracted to one another at first sight; they discover in their first conversation that

'The same books, the same passages were idolized by each—or if any difference appeared, any objection arose, it lasted no longer than till the force of her arguments and the brightness of her eyes could be displayed' (47). Catherine Morland becomes attracted to Henry Tilney because he is good looking and charming, although his greatest charm is, quite simply, that he pays attention to her.

Such attentions lead, however, to the more complicated forms of sexuality in Austen's novels—flirtation, infatuation and the mentor relation, all of which may precede but need not necessarily lead to courtship. Of these, flirtation is by far the most complex. As Austen treats it, flirtation is often indistinguishable from courtship. In the beginning, the same behaviour—attention, admiration, teasing, flattery, even professions of devotion—may be appropriate to both. But the two cannot be confused in the end, for courtship 'means' something—marriage—and flirtation nothing. Henry Tilney cannot strictly be said to flirt with Catherine in the early chapters of *Northanger Abbey*, for it takes two to play that game and Catherine is altogether too direct and naïve to participate. Isabella Thorpe, on the other hand, is one of Austen's favourite kinds of flirt—mindless, vain and predatory, but too stupid to fool anyone long. Though few of Austen's major characters pursue flirtation as strenuously as Isabella, all the novels dramatise the loose, free-floating sexual energies that lead characters like Kitty and Lydia Bennet, Harriet Smith, and even Louisa and Henrietta Musgrove to attach themselves to anyone available. Unlike her contemporaries, then, Austen is capable of a number of attitudes toward flirtation. As practised by Frank Churchill at first with Emma or by Henry Crawford with Maria Bertram, flirtation is dangerous: one character, who is no fool, is deliberately fooling another. In such cases Austen's moral judgement is adverse; but as a rule she delights in flirtation as a form of sexuality, for example when she describes Elizabeth Bennet dressing for a ball 'with more than usual care', preparing 'in the highest spirits for the conquest of all that remained unsubdued of [Wickham's] heart, trusting that it was not more than might be won in the course of the evening' (89).

Flirtation shades easily into infatuation, and distinctions can be difficult: is Elizabeth flirting with Wickham or infatuated? Although she is deceived in him, Elizabeth's interest in Wickham is never strong enough to be labelled infatuation. Moreover, for Austen infatuation often involves attraction to a consciously predetermined ideal. Emma Woodhouse, for example, creates

Frank Churchill's attractions and her own response to them long before she meets him, just as she manufactures Mr Elton as the ideal spouse for Harriet Smith. In both cases, a kind of sexual fantasy is at work, filling the 'many vacancies' (183) which exist in Emma's mind as well as Harriet's. Marianne Dashwood's requirements for a lover—'He must have all Edward's virtues, and his person and manners must ornament his goodness with every possible charm' (18)—seem to be met by Willoughby. Because his 'person and air were equal to what her fancy had ever drawn for the hero of a favourite story' (43), Marianne takes his goodness for granted, allowing attraction to grow into a love that, in the end, she must call her 'own folly' (352). Austen always distinguishes infatuation from more solid but not stronger sexual attraction in this familiar way: when upon better knowledge the object of one's feelings proves unworthy or unreal—a creature of one's own imagination, as Edmund Bertram finally says of Mary Crawford (458)—then the feelings are labelled infatuation, very much after the fact. Greater knowledge always transmutes infatuation into dislike, indifference or genuine affection: in the end, Edmund Bertram dislikes Mary, Emma Woodhouse is indifferent to Harriet Smith, and Catherine Morland loves Henry Tilney. Infatuation is, then, misdirected or untested sexuality just as jealousy, another important subject in the novels, is frustrated sexuality.

Infatuation can begin as an attraction between what seem to be either opposite or like energies. Marianne's infatuation with Willoughby arises partially because she perceives him as her counterpart. But in Austen's novels, infatuation more frequently operates through the attraction of opposed energies, that is, through the fantasy of becoming complete by association with something that one feels oneself to lack and that one (rightly or wrongly) attributes to another. It is in this sense that Emma and Harriet are mutually infatuated, Emma by Harriet's soft blonde beauty and mindless yielding, Harriet by Emma's charm, wit and social position. Austen is well aware of the sexuality inherent in the relation, for she perceives that where the senses exist, sex exists. We could label her awareness a bisexual one, but to do so would certainly be to attach more importance to it than she would; again, she takes sexuality in social life for granted.

The attraction of opposing personalities usually takes a far stronger and more complex form than is exhibited in the relation of Harriet and Emma. This form of attraction—sexual antagonism—

is most clearly dramatised in *Pride and Prejudice*. Undercurrents of sexual attraction and challenge accompany the antagonism expressed in the early exchanges between Darcy and Elizabeth, an antagonism based on differences in manner and style. Just as flirtation tries to make sex a game, antagonism makes it a combat, a contest, a power play. *Mansfield Park* displays Austen's most thorough examination of the sexual attraction that arises from opposition or antagonism and becomes a contest for dominance: Austen's charming characters, Henry and Mary Crawford, are attracted against their expectation or will to the good characters, Fanny Price and Edmund Bertram, who find themselves responding in turn against their better judgements. Goodness and charm are conceived as opposites in this novel, and Austen dramatises the way these qualities can fascinate or challenge one another. Mary Crawford regards Edmund as a challenge; she wants her charm to overcome his goodness and rejoices when 'his sturdy spirit' (358) so yields to her attractions that he takes part in 'Lovers' Vows' against his will. Henry Crawford is just as challenged sexually by Fanny's initial aversion; his desire to make 'a small hole in Fanny Price's heart' (229) has equally ugly sexual and moral implications.

Although Austen does not endorse the drive for conquest that is at work in this form of sexuality, neither does she dismiss sexual antagonism as a means of making characters known to one another. Darcy and Elizabeth come to know each other despite (and partly because of) early misjudgement and conflict. One reason Darcy is attracted to Elizabeth is that she is always teasing or challenging him, not flattering him like Miss Bingley. Darcy and Elizabeth's conflicts are resolved because both can move from misjudgement, testing and conflicts of will to those fundamental likenesses in principle and perception that so often give rise, paradoxically enough, to antagonism.

It is in knowledge and intimacy, however, that Austen prefers to locate the most enduring sexual responses; she trusts sexual attraction to last only when it is based on knowledge. Here she is farthest from Dr Gregory, for instance, who warns young women that 'satiety and disgust' will be 'the certain consequence' if a wife confesses 'the full extent' of her love to her husband.[17] In Austen's novels, however, sex, love and knowledge reinforce one another. All the novels are structured to move toward knowledge through testing and misjudgement. But in the last three novels, Austen chooses to deepen and complicate that knowledge by making the central characters intimately known to one another before the movement of the plot begins. In *Mansfield Park* and *Emma*, she solves the problem that ensues—the problem of keeping the characters unmarried for three volumes—by placing Edmund Bertram and Mr Knightley in what seem to be fraternal relations to Fanny Price and Emma Woodhouse. And, further, she makes them mentors to the heroines; that is, they can care for and interest themselves in Fanny and Emma without questioning the sources of their concern. Austen seizes on the mentor relation, a dissatisfying plot convention of eighteenth-century didactic fiction, as a convenient means to dramatise the conscious or unconscious sexual attraction that can develop over time in conjunction with intimate knowledge. She varies the relation endlessly; for example, Fanny is as much Edmund's mentor as he is hers, Emma congratulates herself on being Harriet's teacher, and Elizabeth corrects Darcy despite herself and himself too. In recognising and dramatising throughout her work the sexuality inherent in the student–teacher relation, Austen gives the clearest expression to her conviction that knowledge and intimacy are forms of sexuality. In all her novels, sex is one of the ways men and women come to know each other, and sexual attraction consummated by sexual union in marriage is the highest form of intimacy that the characters achieve.

Austen's most profound studies of sexuality occur, as one might expect, in *Mansfield Park*, *Emma* and *Persuasion*. These novels may be misread by readers insensitive to Austen's interest in sex in social life. Much will be missed, for example, by the reader of *Persuasion* who fails to recognise that the plot turns in part on Anne Elliot's recovery of her own sexuality. When the novel opens, she is 'faded and thin', for 'her bloom had vanished early' (6). Her broken engagement to Captain Wentworth has been the cause: 'Her attachment and regrets had, for a long time, clouded every enjoyment of youth; and an early loss of bloom and spirits had been their lasting effect' (28). In this state of lowered spirits or depression, Anne is forced to encounter Captain Wentworth again, a conjunction that deeply stirs her, reawakening feelings of attraction and loss that she has suppressed for years. When she goes to Lyme, then, she has been to some extent reanimated by being made to feel pain, regret, attraction and jealousy. At Lyme, although she has to 'struggle against a great tendency to lowness' (98) at the thought that the Harvilles would have been her friends, although she has grown 'so much more hardened to being in Captain Wentworth's company than she had at first imagined could ever be' (99), that is, although she is still generally in a state of reduced or depressed feeling, Anne is able to interest herself in Captain Benwick, drawing him out and giving relief to 'feelings glad to burst their usual restraints' (100). On the next day, she is looked at by William Elliot 'with a degree of earnest admiration, which she could not be insensible of'. And Captain Wentworth too looks at her, giving her 'a glance of brightness, which seemed to say, "That man is struck with you—and even I, at this moment, see something like Anne Elliot again"' (104). Much is expressed in this novel by blushes and looks. A little later, Mr Elliot shows once more by his 'looks, that he thought hers very lovely' (104), and Anne responds: 'Anne felt that she should like to know who he was' (105). Similarly, when Anne learns that Captain Benwick apparently wishes to visit her after she has left Lyme, she 'boldly acknowledged herself flattered' (131)—and she, like Lady Russell, thinks of his coming. Anne undergoes, then, a kind of sexual reawakening, feeling herself once again a sexually attractive woman.

What is remarkable in *Persuasion* is Austen's willingness to depict a heroine decidedly revived by a stranger's admiration, so revived that she takes an interest in him and in another admirer, even though she is in love with yet another man. The extreme openness of all these events is equally remarkable and (with the partial exception of *Mansfield Park*) typical of the novels. Sexual attraction always occurs in public, it is always scrutinised and speculated on, it is always a part of social life. Thus, Captain Wentworth witnesses Mr Elliot's and Captain Benwick's interest in Anne. Captain Harville praises Anne for her attentions to Captain Benwick. Mary and Charles Musgrove—himself once Anne's suitor—debate the degree of Benwick's interest in Anne before her and Lady Russell. Even more astonishing here and elsewhere in the novels than the publicity of sexual attraction is its sheer fluidity, almost promiscuousness.[18] Captain Benwick, having lost Fanny Harville, is attracted to Anne, then to Louisa Musgrove; Captain Wentworth, having lost and rejected Anne, is pleased by Henrietta and Louisa's attentions, then seeks Anne once again; Mr Elliot admires and then loves Anne, but elopes with Mrs Clay; and Anne herself briefly fantasises marriage to William Elliot at a time when she is in love with Captain Wentworth.

In *Persuasion*, then, social life can readily accommodate the fluid and pervasive sexuality that Austen takes for granted in all her novels. In *Mansfield Park*, however, sexuality becomes covert, uncontained by social life. Austen examines in this novel the consequences of divorcing sexuality from the protection social conventions afford. This inversion of a characteristic theme is typical of Austen's practice in *Mansfield Park* as a whole, a practice that may account for its mixed reception among her critics. Although the novel is generally much better received now than it once was, its readers still tend to be troubled by the 'Lovers' Vows' episode and to ask why so much fuss is made over the theatricals. What, in fact, makes the play so wrong? This question, posed also by Tom and Maria Bertram, receives far too many answers in the text. None of these precisely defines the real issue, which is sexual. Instead, we are told first that the theatricals are wrong because they are inappropriate and insensitive on several counts: all amateur acting is undesirable; Sir Thomas is in danger at sea; Maria's position is delicate (her engagement lacks Sir Thomas' final sanction); Sir Thomas himself would disapprove of acting by his 'grown up daughters' (127); and Sir Thomas would condone neither the disturbance to his room nor the expense. Second, we are told that the theatricals are wrong because 'Lovers' Vows' is itself offensive. And finally, we are told that the theatricals will 'do away all restraints' (154) among the actors.

To give a variety of inconsistent arguments against a particular action is always suspect. Any one of these lines of argument, including the feeblest, could carry more conviction if Austen's treatment were different, that is, if the argument were proposed more consistently. Even Fanny, opposed to the theatricals from the beginning, becomes anxious—'Was she *right* in refusing what was so warmly asked, so strongly wished for?' (153)—and apparently inconsistent (she consents at last to read the part of Cottager's Wife). Even Fanny is slightly implicated in that general anxiety and inconsistency which persuade us that the real issue is being avoided. Only if this issue is identified as a sexual one can conviction follow that, in these particular circumstances, the theatricals are indeed dangerous and wrong. Austen intends this issue to be identifiable, but with difficulty. The reader is intended, as often in Austen's novels, to experience at first the same confusion that besets the characters.[19] We are to acknowledge, slowly, the support and comfort afforded by an ordered social world—a world whose demands are in many ways tyrannical but whose conventions rescue us from the problems and anxieties of continual choice. In *Mansfield*

Park we come to feel that no human feelings, qualities or virtues—
not judgement, sympathy, passion, principle, wit, charm, love,
selfishness, self-sacrifice, goodness—can make for individual satisfaction apart from 'The elegance, propriety, regularity, harmony—
and perhaps, above all, the peace and tranquillity of Mansfield',
(391) even though Mansfield alone does not satisfy either.

The theatricals pose a sexual threat to the order of Mansfield
largely because the 'young people' have been in unstable sexual
relations to one another since the visit to Sotherton. There the
amorphous sexuality excited in the Bertrams by their introduction
to the Crawfords hardens into several ugly or painful triangles. Mr
Rushworth, provisionally engaged to Maria, is jealous of Henry
Crawford. Julia, infatuated with Henry, is jealous of Maria. Fanny,
in love with Edmund, is jealous of his increasing interest in and
attentions to Mary. The Crawfords themselves are, at this point,
unpleasantly immune. Henry prefers Maria to Julia but is amusing
himself with both, and Mary is only beginning to be attracted to
Edmund. The flirtations conducted at Sotherton, however, although highly charged, are not 'unsafe amusements' (188) like the
theatricals, for at Sotherton and elsewhere, social conventions
operate to discharge some of the sexual tension. By contrast, to act in
'Lovers' Vows' is to divorce sexuality from social life, from the
protection and restraints that social conventions ordinarily supply.
When Edmund claims that the theatricals will 'do away all
restraints' among the actors, he comes closest to articulating the
problem. The only real sexual danger is to Maria, however; Julia is
eliminated from the cast, and Edmund and Mary are actually
falling in love with one another, so that their play-acting hurts only
Fanny.

At Sotherton, the highly stylised conventions of flirtation and
courtship offer Maria some protection from her own feelings and
from Henry's 'attack' (160). Because flirtation is inherently ambiguous in Austen's social and sexual world—it can be a prelude to
serious courtship, it can be merely playful, or it can be mocking or
self-serving (like Henry's)—convention dictates 'safe' responses: all
gallantry should be treated as if it were playful or mocking. One
prolongs the game either by a response in kind or by disbelief and
denial, which disarm mockery. In her exchanges with Henry at
Sotherton, Maria shows that she is fully in command of these
conventions, although not entirely in command of her feelings. She

treats his whispered 'I do not like to see Miss Bertram so near the altar' as a pleasantry:

> Starting, the lady instinctively moved a step or two, but recovering herself in a moment, affected to laugh, and asked him, in a tone not much louder, 'if he would give her away?'.
> 'I am afraid I should do it very awkwardly', was his reply, with a look of meaning.
> Julia joining them at that moment, carried on the joke. (88)

The alternative defence of denial is exercised in another exchange, although again with some difficulty; Henry begins:

> 'And to tell you the truth', speaking rather lower, 'I do not think that *I* shall ever see Sotherton again with so much pleasure as I do now. Another summer will hardly improve it to me.'
> After a moment's embarrassment the lady replied, 'You are too much a man of the world not to see with the eyes of the world. If other people think Sotherton improved, I have no doubt that you will'. (98)

Henry's claim to be telling the truth, his lowered voice, and his oblique profession of regret at Maria's engagement under the guise of a comment on Sotherton are part of the game of 'liking to make girls a little in love with him' (363); Maria's denial, which keeps up the pretence that Sotherton is the subject, is also part of the game. Such exchanges can be suggestive and exciting but need not be dangerous, for disbelief and denial protect the players to some extent. Maria's embarrassment and uneasiness, however, show that her disbelief is only coy; she is not wholly playing a game. She does have genuine feelings for Henry which, with her vanity, make her wish to think him in earnest. Nevertheless, the conventions which prescribe disbelief prevent her, to some degree, from taking Henry seriously. To take compliments, flattery, and gallantry for courtship is, after all, precisely the sort of vanity that every young woman is constantly warned against. Fanny later seizes on this conventional admonition as a convenient although disingenuous means to account to Edmund for her indifference to Henry:

> He took me wholly by surprise. I had not an idea that his

behaviour to me before had any meaning; and surely I was not to
be teaching myself to like him only because he was taking, what
seemed, very idle notice of me. In my situation, it would have
been the extreme of vanity to be forming expectations on Mr.
Crawford. I am sure his sisters, rating him as they do, must have
thought it so, supposing he had meant nothing.(353)

Maria has just enough discretion and pride to counteract this sort of
vanity, that is, to keep her from believing that Henry is serious, until
rehearsals begin.

The social conventions that govern Henry's behaviour (again,
until the theatricals) also help to prevent Maria from taking him
wholly seriously. He is restrained by 'the world' or public opinion;
his attentions cannot be too marked. He must take care that his
manners to both Maria and Julia stop just 'short of the consistence,
the steadiness, the solicitude, and the warmth which might excite
general notice' (115). But once 'Lovers' Vows' begins, Henry can do
what would have brought his game to an abrupt end before: he can
declare love for Maria as often as they rehearse. Social convention
permits a declaration of love only in the context of courtship. If no
offer of marriage follows, the context is clearly seduction or
mockery, both of which call for indignant repudiation.[20] But
convention takes no account of and offers no defence against a
declaration of love in a play. In the role of Frederick, Henry can
safely proclaim his devotion—and not merely in words and looks.
He can also touch Maria, and because any physical contact is so
rare in the social world Austen describes, it has the greater sexual
and emotional power. In *Persuasion*, for example, Anne Elliott
nearly faints when she feels Captain Wentworth remove the child
who is clinging to her neck; Mr Knightley, loving Emma and
fearing that she has loved and been hurt by Frank Churchill, draws
her arm within his and presses it 'against his heart' (425). Thus both
Maria and Julia find it especially significant that when Julia bursts
into the last rehearsal with the news of Sir Thomas' arrival,
'Frederick was listening with looks of devotion to Agatha's narrative, and pressing her hand to his heart, and as soon as [Julia] could
notice this, and see that, in spite of the shock of her words, he still
kept his station and retained her sister's hand, her wounded heart
swelled again with injury' (175). The 'heart' and the 'hand' signify
love and marriage in the conventional eighteenth-century formulation evoked earlier, with multiple irony, by Henry: 'I think too

well of Miss Bertram to suppose she would ever give her hand
without her heart' (45–6) to Mr Rushworth. To Maria, then,
Henry's unconventional behaviour after Julia's announcement is
'the sweetest support'. The gesture seems to her unequivocal:

> Henry Crawford's retaining her hand at such a moment, a
> moment of such peculiar proof and importance, was worth ages of
> doubt and anxiety. She hailed it as an earnest of the most serious
> determination, and was equal even to encounter her father. (176)

Much later in the evening, Maria is 'still feeling her hand pressed to
Henry Crawford's heart, and caring little for any thing else' (182).
The power of this touch to move her is underlined when, two days
later, Maria learns that Henry has been as much 'at treacherous
play with her' (135) as he had been with Julia:

> He might talk of necessity, but she knew his independence.—The
> hand which had so pressed her's to his heart!—The hand and the
> heart were alike motionless and passive now! Her spirit supported
> her, but the agony of her mind was severe. (193)

Certainly Maria's vanity and her infatuation have assisted her to
believe Henry Crawford in earnest in 'Lovers' Vows'. But his words,
looks and touches of love in the play do allow her an intensity of
passionate response that ordinary social life and social convention
would prevent until an engagement or a marriage; that is, his play-
acted devotion increases the sexual tension, allowing Maria's
infatuation to become the sexual passion that takes Edmund, Sir
Thomas, and even Henry by surprise at the end. Their blindness is
central to one of the major themes in the novel. In *Mansfield Park*,
Austen investigates the costs, for social conduct and for moral
judgement, of either underestimating the power of passionate
feeling or being excessively vulnerable to it, as Fanny is; and these
costs are exacted from principled and unprincipled characters alike.

The costs to Fanny are clear; the costs of neglecting or ignoring
passion may be less obvious. Sir Thomas, Edmund and Henry all
underestimate and fail to allow for the nature and strength of
Maria's feelings, as she herself does, and all suffer from the
consequences—the elopement—in proportion as their conduct
deserves. Edmund, who is 'not at all afraid for' Maria, despite
Fanny's hints, 'after such a proof as she has given [by engaging

herself to Mr Rushworth], that her feelings are not strong' (116), cannot see Maria's love for Crawford and does not prevent its consequences, either at Mansfield or at London. Her father sanctions her marriage despite perceiving her indifference to Mr Rushworth:

> Sir Thomas was satisfied; too glad to be satisfied perhaps to urge the matter quite so far as his judgment might have dictated to others. It was an alliance which he could not have relinquished without pain . . .; and if Maria could now speak so securely of her happiness with [Mr Rushworth], speaking certainly without the prejudice, the blindness of love, she ought to be believed. Her feelings probably were not acute; he had never supposed them to be so. (201)

Henry Crawford, however, unprincipled and more selfish than either Edmund or Sir Thomas, loses the most by having 'put himself in the power of feelings on her side, more strong than he had supposed' (468).

That the intensity of Maria's passion for Henry can be traced to 'Lovers' Vows' is made explicit at the end of the novel, when Tom Bertram feels himself 'accessary' to the elopement 'by all the dangerous intimacy of his unjustifiable theatre' (462). Here the sexual objection to the play receives its most direct formulation. The 'Lovers' Vows' episode recalls, in fact, the masquerades used as set pieces in so many eighteenth-century novels (*Sir Charles Grandison, Cecilia* and *Amelia* among others) to reveal character or to introduce a sexual threat. Austen domesticates this convention, thereby transforming and intensifying it. The Mansfield theatricals are no frenzied one-night stand but a sustained sequence in which sexual tension and threat accumulate, to be discharged only by the elopement of Maria and Henry at the end.

In *Emma*, sex is less threatening but equally pervasive. The sexuality of Emma and particularly of Mr Knightley has often been denied. He is thought too stuffy, she too father-fond (to use Lovelace's term) for sexuality to flourish. But only wilful misreading can ignore the sheer vitality of both characters or can overlook passages like Mr Knightley's early description of Emma, full of open and unconscious sexual response: he praises Emma's looks, saying 'I have seldom seen a face or figure more pleasing to me than her's' and then, much more powerfully, 'I love to look at her' (39).

Sexuality is as fluid in *Emma* as are Harriet's infatuations. An awareness of sexual energy is forced on the reader in nearly every page by Mr Knightley's jealousy, Emma's jealousy, Jane Fairfax's jealousy, Emma's delight in matching wills with Mr Knightley, her sexual game with Frank Churchill, and his with her and Jane. This sexual energy is channelled into social forms but not contained by them, and during the famous climactic scene at Box Hill all the teased, frustrated sexuality of the various characters explodes at last. Emma's much-cited insult to Miss Bates is buried in far more obviously ugly interaction, notably Frank Churchill's declaration to Emma that when he returns from abroad, 'I shall come to you for my wife' (373). This flirtatious remark is designed to torment Jane Fairfax, but torments Mr Knightley with equal success; both take it as serious courtship of Emma while Emma detects a 'commission' (373) to groom Harriet for the post.

Hereafter, of course, the novel moves quickly from frustration and misjudgement to satisfaction in every sense. Every page of Austen's novels is charged with emotional, moral and social as well as sexual conflicts, and all are resolved in the end. What distinguishes Austen's treatment of sex in social life distinguishes all her concerns equally: she gives us resolutions in which sexuality is as tested and satisfied as is morality or any other aspect of character. Between major characters, the mentor relation, sexual antagonism, flirtation and infatuation give way to or even lead to full knowledge and intimacy between equals. Though separate sexual roles are certainly adopted by Austen's married couples, her conclusions tend to disregard (without denying) the social conventions that make wives submissive to husbands. Instead, the endings celebrate an equality as complete as differences between the characters themselves allow. A witness to and model for this equality is the compromise that resolves *Emma*: out of respect for the conditions of Emma's life, Mr Knightley gives up his own home to live at Hartfield.

The social roles and activities Austen explores are the modes of sexuality in daily life, and they pervade the emotional, moral and intellectual lives of Austen's characters perhaps even more than they do our own; in this sense, her novels may have too much sex rather than too little. Austen's rendering of everyday sexuality takes for granted in ways unthinkable to her contemporaries and often ignored by moderns that every relationship can carry a sexual charge. Sexual response and excitement are, in Austen's novels, so much a part of ordinary social life that in significant ways social intercourse is sexual intercourse. By dramatising the interplay of character and sex in ordinary life, then, Austen gives us the unavoidable and complicated sex of our social lives, seen with a persuasiveness and wit that ought not to surprise us, knowing Austen, and with a relentlessness that does not surprise us, if we do know her.

NOTES

1. John Glassco, *Memoirs of Montparnasse*, selections rpt *Gertrude Stein: A Composite Portrait*, ed. Linda Simon (New York: Avon, 1974), p. 174.
2. See Foucault, *The History of Sexuality*, Vol. 1, trans. Robert Hurley (New York: Pantheon, 1978), and Steiner, 'Eros and Idiom', in *On Difficulty and Other Essays* (New York: Oxford University Press, 1978), pp. 95–136.
3. Steiner, pp. 97, 131.
4. Lawrence Stone's *The Family, Sex, and Marriage in England 1500–1800* (New York: Harper and Row, 1977) is the most provocative recent work to document actual sexual behaviour during Austen's lifetime. But his work has only limited application to a study of sex in Austen's novels, for he does not really focus on courtship. The findings that do bear on courtship—e.g. that 'among the squirarchy, the median age at first marriage coincided with the median age at inheritance' (51)—cast only doubtful light on the novels. Do we conclude, for example, because the fathers of Austen's heroes have usually died, leaving Willoughby, Darcy, Bingley, Crawford, Mr Knightley and Captain Wentworth free to choose wives without parental opposition, that Austen has a sure grasp of the social world that Stone is describing or that she is merely attached to a convenient eighteenth-century plot convention?
5. Hester Chapone, *Letters on the Improvement of the Mind* (1772; rpt with Dr John Gregory's *A Father's Legacy to his Daughters*, 1774 [London: Suttaby, Evance and Fox, 1820]), *Letter* (5, p. 60). These two works were frequently reprinted together. Dr Gregory's section in this edition, pp. 141–80, will hereafter be cited as *Legacy*.
6. *Patronage*, 4 vols (London: J. Johnson, 1814), Vol. 11, p. 122.
7. *Clarissa or, the History of a Young Lady*, intro. John Butt, Everyman's Library, 4 vols (1932; rpt London: Dent, 1968), Vol. 11, pp. 116–17.
8. Thomas Gisborne, *An Enquiry into the Duties of the Female Sex* (London: T. Cadell, 1797), p. 36.
9. Gisborne, p. 102.
10. *Strictures on the Modern System of Female Education* (1809), Ch. 2, rpt *The Works of Hannah More*, 2 vols (New York: Harper, 1835), Vol. 1, pp. 322, 323.
11. *Legacy*, p. 171.
12. *Legacy*, p. 165.
13. Quoted by Marilyn Butler in *Maria Edgeworth, A Literary Biography* (Oxford: Oxford University Press, 1972), p. 494.
14. *MSS Diary and Letters*, Vol. 11, 1950–1951, sheet 5, 2^r. These suppressed journal-

letters, written between 8 January–22 February 1785, are not numbered consecutively with the rest of the MSS (located in the Henry W. and Albert A. Berg Collection of The New York Public Library, Astor Lenox and Tilden Foundations). I am grateful to the Library for permission to read the MSS and to make this quotation from them.

15. *Legacy*, p. 161.
16. Unsigned review of *Northanger Abbey* and *Persuasion* in *Quarterly Review*, 24 (January 1821), 352–76; rpt in *Jane Austen: The Critical Heritage*, ed. B. C. Southam (London: Routledge and Kegan Paul, 1968), p. 101.
17. *Legacy*, p. 167.
18. Irvin Ehrenpreis has recently offered his own reading of 'Austen's earthy view of passion and courtship. Given proximity, familiarity, and persistence, a set of good qualities on one side will respond to a set of good qualities on the other, so long as an impulse begins somewhere' ('Jane Austen and Heroism', *New York Review of Books* [8 February 1979], p. 41). True enough, but Austen's view is even earthier, as I have tried to suggest: proximity alone is often sufficient, and good looks almost always create immediate sexual attraction.
19. Lionel Trilling's ingenious attempt to identify the issue is well known but somewhat off-centre, perhaps because he fails to recognise that the issue is at first intentionally clouded. For him, the theatricals are wrong because play-acting, in *Mansfield Park*, seems to betray 'the integrity of the self as a moral agent' (*The Opposing Self* [New York: Viking, 1955], p. 219). Trilling does note that 'Some of the scenes of the play permit Maria Bertram and Henry Crawford to make love in public, but this is not said to be decisively objectionable'. This silence leads him to conclude that 'What is decisive is a traditional, almost primitive, feeling about dramatic impersonation' (218). But Austen has no inherent objection to 'sexuality as a game', as Trilling claims (221); she objects only when the game is not mutual or when it is unrestrained by social convention.
20. Clearly, I cannot share Mary Lascelles' view that Austen 'closed her imaginative consciousness against' the act of seduction (*Jane Austen and her Art* [1939; rpt. London: Oxford University Press, 1963], p. 75); rather, Austen's focus on social life excludes that private and anti-social activity. The 'Lovers' Vows' sequence makes perfectly clear how Maria seduced and was seduced at London and Twickenham.

6 'Real Solemn History' and Social History

Christopher Kent

To the social historian, the apparent preoccupation of literary critics with the historical dimensions of Jane Austen's canvas suggests limitations in their conception of history more than limitations in her art.[1] It reflects a 'big bow-wow' view of history, to adapt Sir Walter Scott's phrase, in which certain epic events—the French Revolution, the Industrial Revolution—tower over all others. It is a view fostered by traditional large-scale text-book emphases, but it gets significant ratification from the pervasively determinist and providential historical views of such classic theorists of literary realism as George Lukács, Erich Auerbach and Arnold Hauser. Auerbach, for instance, defined realism as 'a serious representation of everyday social reality against the background of a constant historical movement'.[2] That historical movement is forever tending in Auerbach, as in other Marxist-oriented literary critics, to become reified, 'history' and 'historical forces' being invoked as if they were independent entities. The novelist is in danger of being judged chiefly by the degree to which he fits retrospectively prescribed emphases and directions into the historical background of his work. Notoriously, Jane Austen fails these tests. Quite unashamedly she seems to flout Fanny Burney's Law: that it is 'impossible to delineate any picture of human life without reference to the French Revolution'.[3]

One of the earliest examples of this line of criticism is provided by the eminent Victorian historian Goldwin Smith, who was no Marxist, but as an exponent of the Whig interpretation of history almost as committed to the providential approach. He closes one of the earliest full-length studies of Jane Austen by solemnly remarking that in commending her works he does not mean to detract from

those who have written on 'nobler or more entrancing themes': 'Few
sets of people, perhaps, ever did less for humanity or exercised less
influence on its progress than the denizens of Mansfield Park and
Pemberley, Longbourn and Hartfield in Jane Austen's day. As they
all come before us at the fall of the curtain we feel that they, their
lives and loves, their little intrigues; their petty quarrels and their
drawing room adventures are the lightest of bubbles in the great
stream of existence.'[4] 'They contributed nothing to Progress'—
what epitaph could be more damning?

It is significant that this trend in Jane Austen criticism opened in
the mid-Victorian period. While earlier commentators had emphasised the verisimilitude of her world – Scott, Whately and Macaulay
were unanimous in praising the accuracy of her portrayal of
society—by 1870 Richard Simpson, in an article which has since
come to be regarded as the point of departure for modern Austen
criticism, cast doubt upon the historicity of the novels. In part this is
simply an illustration of Dr Johnson's dictum: 'all works which
describe manners require notes in 60 or 70 years'[5] if they are to be
understood. But in addition to the gap of two generations, there was
the gap between two notions of what a novel should be and do.
Austen's novels did not measure up to Simpson's standards which at
the time represented orthodoxy on one point at least—the novel's
relation to history.

This is a matter rooted of course in the very origins and early
development of the novel when the novelist, to evade the Platonic
accusation of lying, sheltered under the legitimising aegis of history.
But novelists were quick to appreciate the further advantages of the
historical genre—the scope for ambiguity and experiment in
narrative techniques and even the opportunities to challenge the
pretensions of History herself. Henry Fielding provides a notable
early example of this tendency. His great work is significantly titled
The History of Tom Jones, A Foundling, and in it he remarks at one
point, *à propos* of the contingencies of the plot, 'I am not writing a
system but a history', thereby emphasising the superior narrative
self-consciousness of the novelist who was, after all, no more
arbitrary than the historian so-called in shaping and guiding his
narrative.[6] Fielding questioned whether the pattern which historians claimed to *find* in history was really there.[7] As a novelist
Fielding proclaimed himself the historian of the private lives of
ordinary people who, unlike the great public figures of conventional
history, left behind none of the documents by which conventional

historians were able to prove the truth of their statements. For this reason, he argued, the novelist had to keep strictly within the bounds of probability to ensure that his story would be believed.[8] Probability meant verisimilitude, which meant accurate observation on particular matters which readers could judge from their own experience. But by a sort of paradox, these particulars, by their conformity to general expectations, achieved a sort of generality or typicality which made such history superior according to the Aristotelian doctrine of the superiority of the general to the particular—the superiority of the universal truths of the poet to the specific history of the historian. The novelist could thus have his cake as historian, and eat it is as poet.

By the nineteenth century this line of argument was well developed as the novel and history entered into open competition for the attention of the fast-expanding reading public. However, it was a competition that saw considerable borrowing on both sides. The historical novel came into its own with Scott, and many historians were not too proud to learn from him, notably Thomas Macaulay, who praised Scott for using 'those fragments of truth which historians have scornfully thrown behind them in a manner which may well excite their envy. He has constructed out of their gleanings works which, even considered as histories, are scarcely less valuable than theirs. But a truly great historian would reclaim these materials which the novelist has appropriated.'[9] Macaulay himself tried such a reclamation and was richly rewarded, by the public at least, if not by the opinions of other historians. Charles Kingsley the historical novelist was chosen Regius Professor of History at Cambridge (though admittedly the appointment was widely considered to be scandalous even at the time) and a future Regius Professor, James Anthony Froude, saw the first volume of his *History of England* reviewed in *Blackwoods* not as history but as a novel to be compared with Harrison Ainsworth's.[10]

Amidst such confusion the great Victorian novelists further consolidated Fielding's claim that the novelist was the true historian of society, and not merely by default. Its most striking formulation comes not from an English novelist but from Balzac, who declared: 'The historian of manners obeys harsher laws than those that bind the historian of facts. He must make everything plausible, even the truth; whereas in the domain of history properly so-called, the impossible is justified by the fact that it occurred.'[11] Balzac considered himself a social historian, and his claims were upheld by historians as notable as Marx and Engels. The latter claimed that he learned more about Louis Philippe's France from Balzac than 'from all the books of historians, economists and statisticians of the era put together'.[12] The harsh law of verisimilitude did not, however, constrain Balzac from the grotesque, nor did it Dickens, who hotly defended the bizarre death by 'spontaneous combustion' of Krook in *Bleak House* against the claim of G. H. Lewes that it was scientifically impossible, by claiming that, however improbable, such events had happened.[13] Neither novelist was in fact happy with the full implications of verisimilitude, which naturally tended towards the average, the typical. Dickens particularly did not conceal his scorn for such statistical creations. Neither novelist was a scientific historian of society, for they would not fetter their imaginations with such dehumanising abstractions.

George Eliot was more tractable, however. In the first of her *Scenes from Clerical Life* she answers a hypothetical objector to such a subject as the Rev. Amos Barton, a man 'very far from remarkable', by declaring: 'But, my dear madam, it is so very large a majority of your fellow-countrymen that are of this insignificant stamp. At least eighty out of a hundred of your adult male fellow-Britons returned in the last census neither extraordinarily silly, nor extraordinarily wicked nor extraordinarily wise.'[14] Here speaks the voice of the modern social historian, for George Eliot was not intimidated by the new dispensation of social sciences and political economy, of statistics and averages. Significantly, this very passage is quoted by G. H. Lewes in an essay of 1859 comparing her work with Jane Austen's. While admiring Austen's artistic economy and dramatic skill, he deprecates her scale: 'Miss Austen's two-inch bit of ivory is worth a gallery of canvas by eminent R.A.s, but it is only a bit of ivory after all.' George Eliot, by comparison, is praised for her greater 'reach of mind', her larger scale and loftier theme—Society itself.[15]

Some ten years later Richard Simpson, in the article alluded to earlier, developed Lewes' point in what seems almost certainly an implicit comparison of Jane Austen with Eliot, who provided his standard of what a novel should be. It is pretty damning:

> Of organized society she [Jane Austen] manifests no idea. She had no interest for the great social and political problems which were being debated with so much blood in her day. The social combinations which taxed the calculating powers of Adam Smith

or Jeremy Bentham were above her powers. She had no knowledge how to keep up the semblance of personality in the representation of a society reckoned by averages and no method of impersonating the people or any section of the people in the average man.[16]

The gravamen of Simpson's charge is remarkable less for its wrongheadedness than for its longevity, since Jane Austen is still taxed with not providing her readers the self-consciously comprehensive social vision that mid-Victorian novelist social historians felt it their duty to provide.

In this century, and particularly since the 1930s, the question of what literature can or should tell us about society has been greatly complicated by the enormous growth in the academic profession of literary criticism, which has applied much serious thought and ingenuity to the matter. Jane Austen became, as David Lodge has remarked, one of the earliest battlegrounds in the war between the literary historians and new critics on the issue.[17] As the latter encouraged a new sensitivity to the ironies, ambiguities and other formal excellences of her art (some first hinted at in Simpson's essay), they also tended to neglect the historical dimension, quite intentionally, since such temporal accidents were felt to be a distraction from a timeless verbal icon which was effectively self-defining, as well as being an obstacle to undergraduates, especially in North America, who could hardly be expected to know anything of Regency England (this latter, being a practical point, was not dwelt on however). An additional complicating factor was that the traditional historical expositors of Jane Austen were rather an embarrassment to academic professionals. These were the dreaded Janeites, amateur enthusiasts who revelled in the social minutiae of her novels, asking 'How many servants had Lady Bertram?' and indulging in the escapism alluded to in E. C. Bentley's clerihew: 'The novels of Miss Austen/Are the ones to get lost in.'

The case for Jane Austen's historicity was taken up particularly by Marxist and Marxisant literary critics suspicious of the sterile élitism of the new critics, and convinced of certain historical laws which enabled them to put her novels in the correct historical perspective and to demonstrate their continuing social relevance. Thus, calling attention to the emphasis on money and material possessions in her work, David Daiches remarked that Jane Austen was 'in a sense, a Marxist before Marx' (which is reminiscent of

W. E. Gladstone's discovery that Homer was a Christian before Christibefore
Christ).[18] Arnold Kettle has presented *Emma* as an unintentional indictment of the author's own society, which emerges despite her vision being 'limited by her unquestioning acceptance of class society'. But it is also this limited vision which exonerates her from not writing about Waterloo or the Industrial Revolution. Size of canvas is not a criterion of artistic merit; only depth and truth are, Kettle urges. Thus, Hartfield is the truth; it is not a symbol of something else, but a narrow, class-bound Surrey town circa 1814. Where Jane Austen fails is in not recognising that there was Something Wrong: fortunately we do.[19]

Another able critic in this vein is Graham Hough who repeats Kettle's exoneration, but then diverges quite sharply: 'It would be foolish', he writes, 'to complain that a quiet lady living in the country had no very comprehensive view of the political and social stresses of her time. But it would be equally foolish to suppose that the structure of her world is that of any actual segment of society in Regency England. That would be to suggest that pastorals are written by shepherds.'[20] This recalls Lionel Trilling's remark in his essay on *Emma* that 'the world of Highbury . . . is the world of the pastoral idyll', and his warning to readers that 'the impulse to believe that the world of Jane Austen really did exist leads to notable error'. 'Any *serious* history will make it sufficiently clear that the *real* England was not the England of her novels. . . . All too often it is confused with the actual England, and the error of the identification ought always to be remarked',[21] he solemnly states (my italics).

Trilling's heavily reinforced caution to the reader is understandable perhaps as a warning to those who might assume that Jane Austen conscientiously undertook to provide an accurate portrayal of a typically early nineteenth-century town—a regency version of the sociologists' 'Middletown' (or George Eliot's Middlemarch, for that matter). The historian may be somewhat dismayed that so eminent a literary critic should think it necessary to caution a sophisticated readership against such an egregious error. After all, few would think of appealing to the 'real England' of the present against the novels of, say, Anthony Powell; but the past inevitably tends to contract and homogenise itself in our minds and admit these abstractions, though the historian's task is to resist this. It can be argued that early nineteenth-century England was much more diverse, regionally, economically, socially and culturally than it is today, and that to talk of the 'real England' of that time, therefore, is even less admissible.

Lurking behind Trilling's phrase, one suspects, are the two 'missing' revolutions, and their attendant figures, the missing Manchester cotton-spinner and the missing Paineite cobbler. The explanation for their absence—the suggestion the society portrayed in Jane Austen's novels is an idyll—affords an example of one of the strategies by which literary critics have tried to overcome the problem of the novel's historicity. This has been done by striking a sort of compromise between the ahistoricism of new critical formalism and the contextual density of history. The compromise consists of finding myths and symbols and other para-historical entities that do not carry such a burden of fact, which are more malleable to interpretation and generally have a more timeless quality. The notion that Jane Austen's world is a bourgeois idyll belongs to this genre: it attempts to escape the problem of the author's mimetic intentions, and of the novel's specific temporal and physical reference by elevating her whole landscape into idea. Thus the historical component of the novels becomes essentially intellectual history—the branch of history which has the closest affinity to literary scholarship and indeed was largely created by literary scholars as a separate field. The most striking manifestation of this development is the 'American Studies' school of literature and history, wherein a whole 'American mind' has been sythesised out of the myths, symbols and imagery extracted by scholarship from authors that the vast majority of Americans know nothing about.[22] That no similar school has developed in England is perhaps because like most Europeans, the English have a firmer sense of their nation's historical identity. And perhaps they feel they have quite enough history without inventing more.

Graham Hough has observed that 'literary critics often derive their information about historical situations almost entirely from works of fiction, and in talking about the truthfulness of such works are often therefore arguing in a circle'.[23] The remark helps to make Trilling's warning more understandable, because many novelists have worked hard to foster this tendency and, in default of an adequate social history by historians, have established a firm position. There can be no doubt that the popular image of nineteenth-century England owes for more to Austen, Dickens and Galsworthy than it does to historians. But it is worth recalling that Jane Austen did not regard herself as an historian of her society in the way, for instance, that Eliot, Meredith or Hardy did. This gives her novels a peculiar interest and value to the historian as historical evidence, as historical documents, precisely because they are not self-consciously 'historical'. Because she has not tried to do the historian's work, to mediate and shape her world into something recognisably historical, she deserves the historian's attention and respect, even if she may mislead some critics.

This is not to suggest that Jane Austen was unaware of history. Quite the opposite. Her decision not to write history was a conscious one; not to write history as she understood it, not 'real, solemn history'. It is evident that she was much interested in history from a very early age, witness her precocious 'History of England' (1791), a hilarious and quite sophisticated parody of 'partial [and], pre-judiced' (*Minor Works*, 139) historians whose history was chiefly a vehicle for their social and political beliefs. She caricatures a number of errors which, in less blatant form, have been committed by very eminent historians. For instance, she goes right to the heart of the presentist fallacy, which tends to confuse the recovery of history, which must move backwards, with the living of it, which is of course done forwards, when she chides the English for the double folly of allowing Mary Tudor to succeed Edward VI to the throne, since she died childless: 'They might have foreseen that as she died without children, she would be succeeded by that disgrace to humanity, that pest of society, Elizabeth' (144–5). She was equally sensitive to the subjectivity of history, as her shamelessly obtrusive narrator makes clear, and to its selectivity in determining the 'principal events' to be narrated.[24]

This saucy disrespect for history, one assumes, was not entirely gained from reading Goldsmith and Hume. Some of it must have come from the schoolroom where undertrained governesses mechanically catechised their students with lists of historical facts such as those set down by Miss Mangnall in her *Historical and Miscellaneous Questions*. This approach to history is later evident in *Mansfield Park* when the young Bertram sisters smugly exclaim at the ignorance of their newly arrived cousin Fanny compared to themselves, who can 'repeat the chronological order of the kings of England, with the dates of their accession, and most of the principal events of their reigns!' (18). *

That history is what historians write and teachers teach, is also the view of Catherine Morland. Her discussion with Eleanor Tilney on the subject of history provides another occasion for Jane Austen to develop her views. Miss Morland is a dissatisfied consumer of what she understands to be history—'real solemn history':

> I read it a little as a duty, but it tells me nothing that does not either vex or weary me. The quarrels of popes and kings, with wars or pestilences, in every page; the men all so good for nothing, and hardly any women at all—it is very tiresome: and yet I often think it odd that it should be so dull, for a great deal of it must be invention. The speeches that are put into the heroes' mouths, their thoughts and designs—the chief of all this must be invention, and invention is what delights me in other books. (108)

Miss Tilney on the other hand is 'fond of history—and . . . very well contented to take the false with the true. . . . If a speech be well drawn up, I read it with pleasure, by whomsoever it may be made— and probably with much greater, if the production of Mr. Hume or Mr. Robertson, than if the genuine words of Caractacus, Agricola, or Alfred the Great' (109). There is at least a hint of Fieldingesque subversion in this derogation of the historian's pretensions to superiority on the grounds of truthfulness. It picks again at the theme introduced earlier in the novel when the author makes her celebrated intervention in defence of novels, their readers and writers, and indignantly compares the low prestige of the novelists' creative activity with the eulogy that customarily greets 'the abilities of the nine-hundredth abridger of the History of England' (37).

'And hardly any women at all', Catherine Morland's legitimate objection to 'real solemn history', finds an echo in *Perusuasion* when at the critical point in the plot Anne Elliot defends the constancy of women against Captain Harville, who replies that 'all histories are against you'. Her rebuttal is simply that the histories are written by men—'the pen has been in their hands' (234). With the pen in her own hand Jane Austen did not, apart from these fairly gentle pinpricks, openly challenge the historian by presenting herself as a rival, as a Fieldingesque historian of female private life. Such inflated declarations of intent were not her style—and moreover she was seemingly confident enough of the merits of her work not to feel the need to borrow the honorific of History.[25]

What then does the historian do with Jane Austen's novels? That they were praised by her contemporaries for their accuracy is a good warrant for reading them as vivid views of gentry life in the southern counties during the late Georgian period seen through the eyes of a clever woman. The language, the moral tone, the social concerns, the recreations, the basic rhythms of life are there to be shared by the reader, who is invited to enter the communities of Hartfield, Longbourne or Meryton. This talent of Jane Austen for 'sharing rather than judging', in John Bayley's words, affords the historian peculiar opportunities for the kind of re-enactment which R. G. Collingwood believed to be the essential process in the recovery of the past.[26] In no other novelist does this experience have so rich a texture; though others may have more systematically salted their works with the sort of physical and public detail which might at first sight seem more useful to the historians, these can usually be found elsewhere. What is unreplaceable is the exact pace of domestic events and weight of personal relationships which are so economically conveyed that the reader feels confident that in his own re-enactment he can share the exact criteria appropriate to the time and place without fear of anachronism. It is this sense of participation, rather than having it all packaged and labelled that is perhaps most satisfying to the historian who enters Jane Austen's world.

That she was herself a dissatisfied consumer of history, and that in her novels she consciously chose to avoid the public frame of reference that most readers associate with 'real solemn history' might seem to justify the sort of comment that is still made about her work, as for instance by George Steiner: 'At the height of political and industrial revolution, in a decade of formidable philosophic activity, Miss Austen composes novels almost extra-territorial to history.'[27] And yet, the social historian asks, if Scott, Whately and Macaulay were right in praising her truthfulness and accuracy, and if the great revolutions of her time did in fact have anything like the impact they are supposed to have had, that in our lectures we claim they *did* have, then surely they must be there in her novels, even among the gentry of Hampshire. And of course they are. But not surprisingly, they are not labelled. After all the industrial revolution was itself not named until well into the nineteenth century, and historians still differ very strikingly over just what, and when, it was. (By contrast the French Revolution was so named virtually at its outbreak—this was one of its most portentous features.) Moreover, since the locus of neither revolution coincided with Jane Austen's world, one must look for the ways in which they impinged upon it. One should adopt, so to speak, a consumer's perspective—as a consumer not of histories, seeking some phenomenon to coincide with *ex post facto* reifications of complex events, but of history itself, of events being lived.

The Industrial Revolution was a protean phenomenon, of complex causation, but one of its most important features was that it was a consumer revolution. Traditionally the emphasis has fallen on the production side, with its spinning jennies, water frames, steam engines and power looms, all shrouded by a pall of factory smoke, through which limp the stunted proletariat—man, woman and child. Less emphasis has been placed on the demand side, the consumption side, partly perhaps because it is rather less dramatic and less idealogically loaded. But mass production entails mass consumption and the great bulk of Britain's expanding industrial output was consumed at home rather than exported. In *Mansfield Park* that disagreeable busybody, Mrs Norris, mentions *en passant* her approval of the strict housekeeper at Sotherton who 'has turned away two housemaids for wearing white gowns' (106). Behind this casual remark lies a whole transformation in textile technology that brought the price of cotton cloth down so spectacularly in the late eighteenth century that what was once the prerogative of the well-to-do—a white gown (only cotton could be easily washed so that it could be kept white)—came within the reach of servant girls. Mrs Norris' view of the matter was not unique: a writer in the *London Magazine* lamented 'the luxury in the dress of our female servants and the daughters of farmers and many others in inferior stations who think that a well-chose cotton gown shall entitle them to the appellation of young ladies, is highly prejudicial both to the land owner, the farmer and the public'.[28] Social confusion was an obvious consequence of the insubordinate manners of dress promoted by cheap fabric and a socially precarious person such as Mrs Norris would be particularly sensitive to this threat. Servants were an important channel by which fashion and the taste for luxury were communicated downward in society, since they were peculiarly exposed to it. But what appeared to some moralists as a malignant social disorder was for others the very motor of progress. It has been very persuasively argued that 'at bottom the key to the Industrial Revolution was the infinitely elastic home demand for mass consumer goods. And the key to that demand was social emulation'.[29]

One of the places where this mechanism of emulation worked most feverishly in the late eighteenth century was the town of Bath.

Once again a crucial aspect of the industrial revolution lies behind the vapid chatter of idle women in *Northanger Abbey* over 'the spotted, the sprigged, the mull or the jackonet' (74). These are all varieties of fancy muslin, of different weave and figure, which represented the most profitable part of the cotton trade. This area only opened up in the mid-1780s when mechanised spinning technology enabled the English at last to rival the Indians in producing the very fine-spun thread necessary to weave muslin, a cloth that became suddenly very fashionable at this time as women's dress style adopted more flowing classical lines (which also conveniently required more yards of material than the previous style).[30] A fierce commercial battle was fought by English manufacturers against the imported muslin which they could now undersell, though, by a familiar paradox, the higher priced Indian cloth acquired additional snob appeal by virtue of its greater cost. When Mrs Allen fears a tear in her gown, which is a favourite 'though it cost but nine shillings a yard' she is thus able to advertise the fact that it is imported stuff, as Tilney, to her gratification, notices by remarking that he recently was able to buy a gown for his sister in 'true Indian muslin' for the bargain price of five shillings a yard (28). English manufacturers produced a bewildering variety of muslins—sprigged, spotted, striped, tamboured, etc.—to capture the all-important, high-fashion market where competition for novelty was intense—as indicated by the following business letter from a Scottish weaver in 1788:

As the muslin trade depends principally on fancy goods, it is absolutely necessary that the manufacturers go to London to see Fashions and get new patterns. It is necessary that they be on the spot themselves to see which way the whims of the moment point, and be enabled to form new things that will hit the varying taste of the times.[31]

The success or failure of cotton manufacturers, at the leading edge of the Industrial Revolution, in fact depended to a very large extent on their ability to capture the whims of women like Mrs Allen, who in places like Bath set in train the chain of fashionable emulation that led down to the village girl who, as a 'Lady of Distinction' complained in 1810, could buy a 'pretty muslin gown' for ten shillings, 'while a robe of the same material, but of finer quality, cannot be purchased by a lady of rank for less than as many guineas'.[32] High profit margins at the top of the line, high volume at the bottom: it is the familiar formula of the mass market.

Northanger Abbey provides yet another example of consumer history, another significant aspect of the demand side of the Industrial Revolution, in the shape of the mysterious General Tilney. He is, *par excellence*, the pre-Veblenesque conspicuous consumer, proudly showing off all the expensive gadgets and modern improvements installed at his seat in Gloucestershire. These include a fuel-efficient Rumford fireplace on the one hand, and on the other a 'village of hot-houses' which consume large quantities of coal to indulge the General's fashionable taste for pineapples (162, 178). But perhaps most telling is the elegant breakfast set which Catherine Morland notices approvingly:

> He was enchanted by her approbation of his taste, confessed it to be neat and simple, thought it right to encourage the manufac-ture of his country; and for his part, to his uncritical palate, the tea was as well flavoured from the clay of Staffordshire, as from that of Dresden or Sève. But this was an old set, purchased two years ago. The manufacture was much improved since that time; he had seen some beautiful specimens when last in town, and had he not been perfectly without vanity of that kind, might have been tempted to order a new set. (175)

The breakfast set in question, though not identified, is almost certainly Wedgwood. Josiah Wedgwood, more commonly re-membered for his innovative managerial practices such as extreme division of labour and strict worker discipline in order to ensure the absolute uniformity and high quality essential in pottery manufac-ture, was also one of the most astute marketers in the annals of English entrepreneurship. He played every card in promoting his product, including patriotism, against his German and French rivals; but above all he promoted and profited from snobbery. Wedgwood sedulously cultivated the aristocratic arbiters of taste and succeeded in turning them virtually into a claque, praising and publicising his ware and setting a fashion for it which emulation spread widely. Intensely snobbish, boastful (though by transparent inversion) and a zealous neophiliac, General Tilney is almost the embodiment of Wedgwood's marketing strategy. Wedgwood sold his ware at prices far above his competitors' in elegant showrooms selling nothing else. Here the latest pieces were exhibited with great éclat, and new lines introduced with carefully orchestrated fanfares of publicity, and special viewings by ticket only for the 'Nobility and gentry'. One particularly successful set showed the country seats of a select group of these, who naturally attended the exhibition to bask in the glory thus conferred on them by a tradesman, and to buy.[33] The Wedgwood showrooms on Milsom Street in Bath were of course a place of fashionable resort. They were in fact managed by a Mr William Ward, the father of Anne Radcliffe.[34] It has never been noticed, I believe, that General Tilney, Jane Austen's parody of Montoni, the villain of *Udolpho*, would have bought his Wedgwood from the father of the original Montoni's creator—a neat juxtaposition of fact and fiction.

All this may seem rather a weight of history to place on a few slender passages from Jane Austen's novels, but of course the point is that the novels are not *about* the Industrial Revolution: only that being realistic representations from the time and place of the Industrial Revolution, they cannot avoid it, and it is in fact right where it should be. But what of the French Revolution? 'It never occurred to Jane Austen', writes Harry Levin, 'that the young officers who figure as dancing partners for the heroines of her novels were on furlough from Trafalgar and Waterloo.'[35] This breathtaking assertion of ignorance and condescension hardly deserves refutation, since the most cursory reading of *Persuasion* alone, even of its last paragraph, explodes the suggestion that the Jane Austen was ignorant of the navy's military, as opposed to its social, role. But while much has been written about the importance of the navy in her novels—and her life—less attention has been given to the army, concerning which Levin's remark might be taken by some to be at least not quite so wrongheaded.

The army figures prominently only in *Pride and Prejudice*, though characters in the other novels are significantly connected with it. For instance, Jane Fairfax is an orphan because her father, a soldier, died in action (163). Colonel Brandon, a gentry younger son, went off to serve in India to forget a thwarted love affair, and, though generally felt to be rather a stick, adheres to the military code of honour to the extent of fighting in the only duel mentioned in the novels (206–7, 211). But the army as it figures in *Pride and Prejudice* is not the regular army; it is significantly the militia. This was a highly localised and rather amateur body raised solely for the defence of Great Britain. There were indeed riots in 1796 when it was suggested by the government that the militia might be forced to serve abroad, even in Ireland. So far was it from being 'on furlough from Waterloo'. With its purely defensive role the militia was particularly visible in the South of England because of French invasion threats from across the Channel. And because it had considerable leisure, awaiting an invasion that never came, it is not surprising that this army appeared to Mrs Bennet and her younger daughters chiefly as an incentive to visit the local lending library (apparently a popular meeting place), an agency of dances and a market for husbands.[36] Such a consumer view was quite appropriate in the circumstances. It is appropriate also that Mr Wickham, a militia officer, should be the major disruptive force in the plot since the militia was itself a somewhat irregular and, potentially at least, radical organisation, being an eighteenth-century English version of the citizen army. It was originally intended as a sort of counterpoise to the regular standing army of the king.[37] Because militia commissions were not purchased, it was much less exclusive than the regular army and consequently lacked the latter's social prestige. The militia had difficulty in attracting suitable officers however, which explains the presence of George Wickham, ne'er do well son of an estate steward. However, Wickham ends up in the regular army, thanks to Darcy's paying his debts and buying him a commission. Such is the rather precarious regularisation of Wickham and his marriage in the new social equilibrium established at the novel's end.

Even as a regular soldier, Wickham is not sent abroad, but to Newcastle in the turbulent industrial North. This recalls another point: that the army was not simply for use against foreign enemies. In the almost complete absence of effective police forces in England the army was central to the maintenance of public order at home.[38] Thus, while war raged on the continent considerable detachments of regulars had to be kept at home for use particularly in the frequently troubled industrial areas, for the years of the French Revolution were of course years of great political and social unrest in England. Even in rural Hampshire Jane Austen was aware of this; her brothers after all served in the navy, which suffered serious mutinies in 1797 which were widely thought to be inspired by Jacobin agitators. So when Eleanor Tilney, sheltered in rural Gloucester, hears Catherine Morland talk of 'something very shocking' (112) soon to come out in London, she assumes that the mob is about to riot and her brother, a cavalry officer, will be called in with his regiment to quell it at great risk. The perils of Waterloo could be found much closer to home as Jane Austen—and her contemporary readers—knew.

Trafalgar and Waterloo do finally make their appearance in Jane Austen's work, but in a context which gives a new twist to the consumer's view of history. Mr Parker, the bouncing promoter of Sanditon—and as great a neophiliac as General Tilney—names his modern residence, which commands the new seaside town, 'Trafalgar House—which by the bye, I almost wish I had not named Trafalgar—for Waterloo is more the thing now. However, Waterloo is in reserve—& if we have encouragement enough this year for a little Crescent to be ventured on—(as I trust we shall) then, we shall be able to call it Waterloo Crescent' (*Minor Works*, 380). Thus the names of England's two most glorious victories over the French Revolution are harnessed to one of the Industrial Revolution's most significant offspring—the leisure industry. The detail perfectly captures the optimistic entrepreneurial spirit which capitalised on patriotic sentiment, and presciently foreshadows the hundreds of pubs, lodging houses and streets in English coastal resort towns that still bear these stirring names and preserve them for the common memory at least as well as history books do. This is worth far more, for instance, than a messenger reining in his frothing horse to announce the defeat of Napoleon to the gaping villagers of Uppercross.

To conclude, the reader of Jane Austen should listen not so much for history's 'big bow-wow', but, following the advice of Sherlock Holmes, listen for the dog that did not bark. If the French Revolution does not loom so visibly in her novels as it does in the history texts, one should perhaps reflect on the significance of that absence. The great French historian Elie Halévy, his ears accustomed to the din of revolution in the history of his own country, did a great service to the study of English history when he seriously addressed the question of why England escaped revolution at the turn of the nineteenth century. The answer he suggested was that the religious revival, and particularly the Methodist movement, generated a sort of antibody to revolution in the English body politic. There has since been considerable debate over the 'Halévy Thesis', and social historians, as they refine their techniques for recovering the largely undocumented lives, attitudes and activities of the ordinary people, will be able to come closer to answering such questions.[39] Although social historians are currently somewhat preoccupied with the working classes, it is perhaps to the 'middling classes', Jane Austen's own province, that one should look for an answer to Halévy's question. They emerge from her novels as a confident group who could insouciantly borrow a dance from the French Revolution (the Boulanger) and dance it at the Meryton Assembly, who had strength of nerve in their economic endeavours and faith in their own values and standards. They were by no means a homogeneous stratum, as the contemporary phrase 'middling classes' suggests; indeed, their relative fluidity was ultimately a source of social stability in that it left fewer opportunities for the dangerous accumulation of social frustrations. Read from this point of view Jane Austen's novels are not about history, not self-conscious substitutes for, or rivals to it. They are themselves the very evidence of social history.

NOTES

1. A notable exception is Donald Greene's excellent 'The Myth of Limitation', *Jane Austen Today*, ed. Joel Weinsheimer (Athens, Georgia: University of Georgia Press, 1975), pp. 142–75.
2. *Mimesis: The Representation of Reality in Western Literature* (Princeton, NJ: Princeton University Press, 1968), p. 518.
3. Dedication to *The Wanderer* (1814) cit. Mary Lascelles, *Jane Austen and Her Art* (Oxford: Oxford University Press, 1939), p. 124.
4. *Life of Jane Austen* (London: Walter Scott, 1890), p. 191.
5. James Boswell, *Life of Johnson* (Oxford: Oxford University Press, 1953), p. 509.
6. *The History of Tom Jones, A Foundling*, eds M. C. Battestin and F. Bowers (Middletown, Conn.: Wesleyan University Press, 1975), Vol. 11, p. 651.
7. Cit. Leo Brandy, *Narrative Form in History and Fiction* (Princeton, NJ: Princeton University Press, 1970), pp. 135–45.
8. *Tom Jones*, Vol. 1, pp. 395–407.
9. 'History' (1828), cit. Fritz Stern, ed., *The Varieties of History from Voltaire to the Present* (New York: Vintage Books, 1973), pp. 86–7.
10. James C. Simmons, 'The Novelist as Historian: An Unexplored Tract of Victorian Historiography', *Victorian Studies*, 14 (1971), 299.
11. Balzac cit. George Watson, *The Study of Literature* (London: Allen Lane, 1969), pp. 180–1. Incorrectly attributed here to the Preface of *Les Paysans*; I have not identified the source.
12. Friedrich Engels to Margaret Harkness (April 1888) cit. George J. Becker, ed., *Documents of Modern Literary Realism* (Princeton, NJ: Princeton University Press, 1963), p. 485.
13. Michael Harrison, *Fire from Heaven: A Study of Spontaneous Combustion in Human Beings* (London: Pan Books, 1977), p. 268.
14. Quoted in G. H. Lewes 'The Novels of Jane Austen', *Blackwood's Edinburgh*

Magazine (July 1859) cit. Brian Southam, ed., *Jane Austen: The Critical Heritage* (London: Routledge and Kegan Paul, 1968), p. 156.

15. Southam, p. 155–6.
16. *North British Review* (April 1870) cit. Southam, pp. 250–1.
17. 'Crosscurrents in Modern English Criticism', *The Novel at the Crossroads and Other Essays on Fiction and Criticism* (Ithaca, New York: Cornell University Press, 1971), pp. 269–70.
18. 'Jane Austen, Karl Marx and the Aristocratic Dance', *American Scholar*, 17 (1948), 289.
19. *An Introduction to the English Novel* (London: Hutchinson, 1967), Vol. I, pp. 93–5.
20. 'Narrative and Dialogue in Jane Austen', *Critical Quarterly*, 12 (1970), 226.
21. '*Emma*', *Encounter*, 8 (Summer 1957), 57, 59.
22. On these matters see Gene Wise, 'The Contemporary Crisis in Intellectual History Studies', *Clio*, 5 (Fall 1975), 57–63 especially, and R. Gordon Kelly, 'Literature and the Historian', *American Quarterly*, 26 (1974), 141–59.
23. *An Essay on Criticism* (London: Duckworth, 1966), p. 118.
24. This is not to dismiss Brigid Brophy's ingenious reading of the *History of England* as an implied threat by its young author: 'If you force me to become a governess, *this* is what I will teach my pupils.' 'Jane Austen and the Stuarts' in *Critical Essays on Jane Austen*, ed. B. C. Southam (London: Routledge and Kegan Paul, 1968), p. 35.
25. 'Plan of a Novel, according to hints from various quarters' (*Minor Works*, 428–30), demonstrates how consciously (and effortlessly) she abstained from writing the sort of 'historical romance' that the engregious James Stanier Clarke urged her to undertake (Jane Austen, *Letters*, pp. 430, 444–5, 451).
26. John Bayley, 'The "Irresponsibility" of Jane Austen', in Southam, *Critical Essays on Jane Austen*, p. 8; R. G. Collingwood, *The Idea of History* (Oxford: Oxford University Press, 1946), pp. 218, 244–9, 282–302.
27. *After Babel: Aspects of Language and Translation* (Oxford: Oxford University Press, 1975), p. 9.
28. Cit. Anne Buck, 'Variation in English Women's Dress in the Eighteenth Century', *Folk Life*, 11 (1971), 20.
29. Harold Perkin, *The Origins of Modern English Society, 1780–1880* (London: Routledge and Kegan Paul, 1969), p. 140.
30. Michael M. Edwards, *The Growth of the British Cotton Trade, 1780–1815* (Manchester: Manchester University Press, 1967), pp. 34–5.
31. Edwards, p. 149.
32. Edwards, p. 48.
33. Neil McKendrick, 'Josiah Wedgwood: An Eighteenth Century Entrepreneur in Salesmanship and Marketing Techniques', *Economic History Review*, 2nd ser. 12 (1960), 408–33. Jane Austen's *Letters* refer several times to the purchase of Wedgwood ware by her family (pp. 268, 290, 328).
34. Aline Grant, *Ann Radcliffe* (Denver, Col.: Alan Swallow, 1951), pp. 29–35.
35. *The Gates of Horn: A Study of Five French Realists* (New York: Oxford University Press, 1966), p. 79.
36. J. R. Western, *The English Militia in the Eighteenth Century: The Story of a Political Issue 1660–1802* (London: Routledge and Kegan Paul, 1965), pp. 397–403.
37. Western, pp. 438, 440–2.
38. Malcolm I. Thomis, *The Luddites: Machine Breaking in Regency England* (New

York: Schocken Books, 1872), pp. 144, 152.

39. Elie Halévy, *History of the English People in the Nineteenth Century*, Vol. 1: *England in 1815* (London: Ernest Benn, 1961), p. 387ff. See also E. J. Hobsbawm, 'Methodism and the Threat of Revolution in England' in his *Labouring Men* (New York: Anchor Books, 1967), pp. 27–40; E. P. Thompson, *The Making of the English Working Class* (New York: Pantheon Books, 1964), pp. 41–6, 367–70, 375–82, 385–94; Gertrude Himmelfarb, *Victorian Minds: A Study of Intellectuals in Crisis and Ideologies in Transition* (New York: Harper Torchbooks, 1970), pp. 292–9; B. Semmel, 'Elie Halévy, Methodism and Revolution', introduction to Elie Halévy, *The Birth of Methodism in England* (Chicago: University of Chicago Press, 1971), pp. 1–29.

7 Jane Austen and the Position of Women

David Monaghan

Women can rarely have been held in lower esteem than they were at the end of the eighteenth century. We might, for example, find the following statement, made in 1794, outrageous: 'You must first lay it down for a foundation in general, that there is inequality in the sexes; and that for the better œconomy of the world, the men, who were to be the lawgivers, had the larger share of reason bestowed upon them.'[1] Nevertheless, as the speaker's tone of dogmatic certainty suggests, it is completely in tune with the spirit of the age, and it is not hard to discover echoes of its sentiments. Thus, James Fordyce observes that 'Nature appears to have formed the faculties of your sex for the most part with less vigour than those of ours',[2] and Hannah More claims that women 'do not so much generalize their ideas as men, nor do their minds seize a great subject with so large a grasp'.[3] The notion that women not only are but should be the intellectual inferiors of men was so fundamental to Dr Gregory's thinking that, in all seriousness, he advises any woman who might have offended against nature by cultivating her mind to conceal the fact: 'But if you happen to have any learning, keep it a profound secret, especially from the men, who generally look with a jealous and malignant eye on a woman of great parts, and a cultivated understanding.'[4]

The kind of education offered to girls during this period was such that few women could have had need of the stratagems advised by Gregory. Most governesses and academies for young ladies sought to avoid overtaxing the limited minds of their charges by substituting accomplishments such as piano-playing, drawing and dancing for intellectual pursuits. And even more ambitious educational schemes, including those proposed by the Evangelicals, discriminated sharply between what was proper for boys and for girls. Fordyce, for example, while disapproving of the emphasis placed on accomplishments, nevertheless asserts that 'I do not wish to see [the female world] abound with metaphysicians, historians, speculative philosophers, or Learned Ladies of any kind. I should be afraid, lest the sex should lose in softness what they gained in force.'[5]

As adults women found their opportunities for self-assertion severely restricted. According to Hannah More, 'to women moral excellence is the grand object of education; and of moral excellence, domestic life is to a woman the appropriate sphere'.[6] For Gisborne, too, a woman's life must be centred on the home, and according to him her main responsibilities involve 'contributing daily and hourly to the comfort of husbands, of parents, of brothers and sisters . . . in the intercourse of domestic life'.[7] Even within this narrow domestic world women were, of course, expected to be subservient to their husbands. According to Lady Pennington 'A woman can never be seen in a more ridiculous light, than when she appears to govern her husband' because to do so 'invert[s] the order of nature, and counteract[s] the design of providence'.[8] Outside the family the only role offered to the woman was that of arbiter of manners. Gisborne argues that she should be concerned with 'forming and improving the general manners, dispositions, and conduct of the other sex, by society and example',[9] and Mrs West that 'To these domestic duties and obligations, may be added what belongs to us in the aggregate, as the refiners of manners, and the conservators of morals.'[10]

Since recognition of her inherent inferiority and suppression of whatever abilities she might possess were such integral parts of the woman's role, it is hardly surprising that at this time meekness was considered the major feminine virtue: 'One of the chief beauties in a female character, is that modest reserve, that retiring delicacy, which avoids the public eye, and is disconcerted even at the gaze of admiration.'[11]

Demeaning as these views may appear to us, few women expressed any dissatisfaction with their lot in the final years of the eighteenth century, and Mary Wollstonecraft's call for the assertion of the Rights of Woman[12] went almost entirely unheeded. It is tempting to argue that this was simply because women were so oppressed that they were not conscious of their situation. However, such a line of reasoning is not entirely satisfactory because it fails to account for the fact that, while she rejected many of her society's feminine stereotypes, so intelligent and sensitive a person as Jane

Austen appears to have been almost entirely satisfied with the restriction of women to domestic and polite functions. It will be the aim of this chapter to establish why this was so.

Jane Austen's disagreements with the prevailing attitudes of her time are fairly apparent. Indeed, as Lloyd Brown argues, perhaps too forcibly, she often appears to be closer to Mary Wollstonecraft than to James Fordyce or Thomas Gisborne.[13] Like Mary Wollstonecraft, for instance, Jane Austen operates on the assumption that women are inherently as intelligent and rational as men. The fact that, in the pedagogic relationship into which her lovers usually enter, the woman is as likely to be the instructor as the man, is indicative of Jane Austen's belief in female intelligence.[14] Whereas in *Northanger Abbey* and *Emma* it is Henry Tilney and Mr Knightley who teach Catherine Morland and Emma Woodhouse, in *Mansfield Park* and *Persuasion*, it is Fanny Price and Anne Elliot who provide guidance to Edmund Bertram and Captain Wentworth. Even Darcy, in *Pride and Prejudice*, whom Jane Austen describes as clever, learns as much from Elizabeth Bennet as she does from him.

The rationality of women is demonstrated by the Cobb incident in *Persuasion*. Louisa's startling fall robs even Wentworth and Charles Musgrove, the senior males in the party, of their self-control and the task of creating a semblance of order out of the prevailing panic is left to a woman. Anne Elliot is called upon not only to supervise the resuscitation of Louisa, but also to look to the needs of the despairing Wentworth. She handles her formidable task with such decision that, in relation to her companions, she appears as an adult amongst helpless children.

Only slightly less radical than her faith in the power of the female mind is Jane Austen's belief that intellectual abilities are as desirable in the woman as in the man. This re-evaluation of standards of female worth informs the treatment of some of the main female characters in *Pride and Prejudice*. Jane Bennet and Miss Bingley both have qualities which were regarded as marks of feminine excellence in an age which advised women to conceal any mental accomplishments. Jane has a benevolent attitude towards the world, and hers is a soft and yielding temperament; Miss Bingley is accomplished, elegant and physically attractive. Yet neither is judged the equal of Elizabeth Bennet because they lack her 'quickness of observation' and 'judgment' (63). This standard of excellence is made explicit by Darcy, who comments that while a woman should cultivate accomplishments such as 'music, singing, drawing, dancing and the modern languages . . . , to all this she must add something more substantial, in the improvement of the mind by extensive reading' (85).

'Improvement of the mind' is in fact so important to Jane Austen that in considering how girls should be educated she grants rather less importance to accomplishments than does Darcy. Almost all of her heroines are deficient in the superficial virtues. Elizabeth Bennet and Emma Woodhouse both neglect their piano practice and hence are no more than moderate performers; Catherine Morland learnt the piano for only a year before ceasing to play altogether and has little taste for drawing; and Fanny Price has no knowledge of either music or drawing. Yet none of them is called upon to improve in these areas. Their education is complete so far as Jane Austen is concerned once they have corrected certain failings in judgement and/or feeling.

Jane Austen's view of marriage is also at odds with the mainstream of contemporary thought. For her, the proper marriage is one in which the two parties operate on a basis of mutual respect. The reader is offered a symbol of this ideal in the description of the way in which Admiral and Mrs Croft handle their carriage:

> But by coolly giving the reins a better direction herself, they happily passed the danger; and by once afterwards judiciously putting out her hand, they neither fell into a rut, nor ran foul of a dung-cart; and Anne, with some amusement at their style of driving, which she imagined no bad representation of the general guidance of their affairs, found herself safely deposited by them at the cottage. (92)

What Jane Austen suggests here is that the Crofts manage to stay upright, in their married life as much as in their carriage, because, rather than blindly obeying her husband, Mrs Croft corrects his faults and supports his endeavours. Whenever a wife is over-indulgent towards her husband in Jane Austen's novels we get the kind of imbalance that characterises the Palmers' relationship in *Sense and Sensibility*. The more Mrs Palmer remains good-natured in the face of her husband's displays of childish bad temper, the more excessive and self-indulgent his conduct becomes. The full implications of such an unevenly weighted marriage are made clear in *Mansfield Park*. Lady Bertram is virtually a parody of Lady

Pennington's ideal wife in that she is entirely without a will of her own and turns to Sir Thomas for guidance in every situation, even going so far as to consult him as to whether she can do without Fanny for an evening (217). As a result of Lady Bertram's abnegation of responsibility, Sir Thomas is forced to bear an impossible burden. He is, for example, provided with no assistance in deciding whether Rushworth would be a desirable husband for Maria, even though at the time he is called upon to make the decision he is preoccupied with the poor fortunes of his estate. The consequence is a hasty and ill-judged decision which allows Maria to embark on an unsuitable marriage which ends in elopement and disgrace.

Jane Austen is equally hostile to the view that meekness is the major feminine virtue. So far as she is concerned, Elizabeth Bennet behaves far more admirably when she ignores decorum and tramples across muddy fields to visit the sick Jane, than does the young Fanny Price when she creeps timidly around Mansfield Park. Indeed, in *Mansfield Park* Jane Austen goes so far as to argue that meekness is a fault rather than a virtue. For much of the novel Fanny is, by Fordyce's standards, the ideal woman in that she is religious, morally upright and, above all, subservient to others.[15] However, for Jane Austen, Fanny's lack of self-assertion constitutes a serious deficiency because it ensures that she is unable to exercise any influence and hence to do anything to halt the gradual corruption of the Bertram family. This is particularly evident during the Sotherton excursion. Throughout the day Fanny behaves impeccably, but she is ignored by those around her, and at its conclusion Mary Crawford has inveigled herself deeper into Edmund Bertram's affections and Henry Crawford has advanced his dual flirtation with Maria and Julia. It is only when Fanny begins to involve herself in the world by attending dinners and balls and when she acquires a little charm that she is able to make her presence felt. Henry Crawford is so attracted to this new Fanny Price that he falls in love with her. Fanny is thus at last given the opportunity to grapple actively with the forces of evil. By resisting his attempts to make her marry him, Fanny eventually exhausts Henry's patience and compels him to reveal his own and, indirectly, his sister's moral turpitude. As a result they are both discredited and Mansfield Park is saved.

Yet, for all Jane Austen's sense of female worth, nowhere in her novels, with the significant exception of *Persuasion*, to which I will return later, does she follow Mary Wollstonecraft in expressing discontent at the woman's restricted role. None of her heroines has any ambition to be admitted into the professions, to manage an estate or to join the army. Instead, they concentrate their energies into the world of manners until, at the conclusions of the novels, they add to this the concerns of marriage. Only one of Jane Austen's major characters, Jane Fairfax in *Emma*, is faced with working for a living, and the prospect is viewed with horror: ' "I did not mean, I was not thinking of the slave-trade", replied Jane, "governess-trade, I assure you, was all I had in view; widely different certainly as to the guilt of those who carry it on; but as to the greater misery of the victims, I do not know where it lies" ' (300–1). A paradox thus seems to emerge. However, it can be resolved once we realise that, for Jane Austen, the restrictions imposed on the woman's social role do not diminish its importance. Rather, basing her case on contemporary conservative philosophy, she argues that those who control manners and the home have a crucial role to play in preserving the *status quo*.

The conservative vision sprang from the assumption that society is a divine creation in which things are so beautifully ordered that each person living in it is a microcosm of the whole. Thus, although some have larger roles to play than others, the conduct of every member has a direct bearing on the health of the total organism. Consequently, we find in the eighteenth century a great interest in the individual's moral performance, which, since this was a very formal society, frequently manifested itself ritually in a display of manners. By behaving politely, the individual was considered to be carrying out the single most important social function of demonstrating an awareness of, and an ability to serve, the needs of others. The act of opening a door for a lady was thus, in a sense, as vital to the preservation of English society as serving in Parliament or administering justice. Indeed, since the demands of the code of politeness were subtle, unremitting and entered into every aspect of life, it could be argued that displays of good manners were more important than the performance of the larger social duties, which made infrequent and obvious demands. The link between manners and social stability is made explicit by Edmund Burke:

> Manners are of more importance than laws. Upon them, in a great measure, the laws depend. The law touches us but here and there, and now and then. Manners are what vex and soothe,

corrupt or purify, exalt or debase, barbarise or refine us. . . . They give their whole form and colour to our lives. According to their quality, they aid morals, they supply them, or they totally destroy them.[16]

Granted this link, considerable prestige should have accrued to women from their role as preservers of manners. And, even though they did not seem aware of the contradictions inherent in admitting that people they regarded as second-class citizens were of importance to society, the conduct-book writers frequently praised women for performing such a function. Mrs West says of women as 'the refiners of manners' that, 'in these cases every judicious statesman readily allows our relative importance. No nation has preserved its political independence for any long period after its women became dissipated and licentious'.[17] In a similar vein, Mrs Priscilla Wakefield asserts:

Women are prohibited from the public service of their country, by reason and decorum; but they are not excluded from promoting its welfare by other means, better adapted to their powers and attainments. The gradual and almost imperceptible, though certain influence, of forming the opinions and improving the manners of their countrywomen, by their conversation and their practice, is the undisputed prerogative of our female nobility.[18]

And *The Lady's Monthly Museum* claims that:

Female worth . . . expands and purifies the heart by a thousand nameless refinements, is a fertile source of excellence in every pursuit, and polishes the public taste, which forms our manners, fashions, our preferences . . . .
    For these reasons, the conduct and qualities of women are of the highest moral and political consideration to social welfare. It is from the peculiar cast of their character, public opinion takes its complexion and bias.[19]

This microcosmic view of society also, of course, embraced larger social units, including the family. Mary Wollstonecraft, here echoing the assumptions of the very conservatives she wished to overthrow, states: 'A man has been termed a microcosm; and every family might also be called a state.'[20] Consequently, the woman's domestic function was granted a significance similar to that of her polite role. By concerning herself with the early education of her children, by commanding the servants and by ensuring the comfort of her husband she was considered to be engaged in creating a sense of order and harmony, the implications of which extended far beyond the single household. The conduct-book writers, although again unaware of the ramifications of what they were saying, were equally ready to point out the importance of the woman's role in the family.Mrs West, for example, argues:

> In our relative situation, as mothers and mistresses of families, we possess so much influence that, if we were uniformly to exert it in the manner which the times require, we might produce a most happy change in the morals of the people.[21]

Because her novels are primarily concerned with young, single heroines rather than with married life, Jane Austen tends to place her main emphasis on the part played by women in preserving manners and morals. Nevertheless, she is also very much concerned with demonstrating the larger social consequences of their familial functions.

Of the various duties of women as wives and mothers, Jane Austen singles out the education of young children for particular attention. This is because she perceives direct links between the child's ability to effect the transition into adulthood and the kind of training she has received from her mother. Mrs Morland in *Northanger Abbey*, for example, has a sound enough theoretical knowledge of proper values but, living as she does in a rather secluded village, she fails to realise how complex and deceitful the world can be. As a result her daughter Catherine is not properly prepared for what she encounters in Bath society and her progress towards maturation is hindered by her naïve confidence in the essential benevolence of mankind. All of the Bennet sisters suffer from their mother's deficiencies. Lydia and Kitty simply learn her silliness and concern for the surface of life; Jane remains uncorrupted by Mrs Bennet, but, lacking any positive direction, ends up with an untrained and undiscriminating mind; and Elizabeth and Mary, in trying to compensate for this absence of maternal guidance, are forced to pursue programmes of self-education based in the first instance on Mr Bennet's cynicism and in the second on his books. The result is complete failure to achieve maturity on the part of Kitty, Lydia and Mary, and a difficult period of initiation for Jane and Elizabeth. The importance of the mother's early influence on the child is demonstrated perhaps most clearly in *Persuasion*. Although the excellent Lady Elliot died when her second daughter was fourteen, nevertheless she stamped her values so firmly on Anne that, in spite of an adolescence spent with a foolish and arrogant father, they provided her with the model according to which she shaped her adult self: 'Lady Russell loved them all; but it was only in Anne that she could fancy the mother to revive again' (6).

The implications of household management, the other main aspect of the woman's domestic role, are stressed less frequently, but become very clear if we examine the symbolic use of houses in *Mansfield Park* and *Persuasion*. Mansfield Park represents English society at a time when its rural ideal of order and repose is being threatened by new values brought in from effete aristocratic circles by Yates and from the city by the Crawfords. The disruption that this causes first manifests itself tangibly in the literal disordering of the Bertram household which derives from Lady Bertram's failure to exercise authority during the theatricals. Thus, for the sake of proper rehearsal space, book cases and billiard tables are moved, scenery is erected and a floor is ruined by paint. Sir Thomas' return ensures a restoration of order and eliminates the immediate danger. Nevertheless the forces of corruption continue to exercise a strong influence on the Betram family with the result that it temporarily casts out Fanny Price, the only member of the household who has retained a firm grasp on traditional Mansfield ideals. The kind of chaos which would result should what is effectively a separation of Mansfield from its moral code become permanent is suggested by the nature of the household Fanny encounters during her exile in Portsmouth. Under the guardianship of Mrs Price, who has yielded completely to the moral apathy and lack of principle which are rapidly infiltrating Mansfield Park, the Portsmouth house is characterised by 'noise, disorder, and impropriety' (388).

Persuasion opens with an account of domestic problems at Kellynch Hall. So long as Lady Elliot lived the Kellynch estate was run with 'method, moderation, and economy' (9). However, since her death Sir Walter Elliot has given free rein to his natural extravagance until, burdened with debt, he is finally forced to rent out his estate and retire to Bath. Because the country house is the centre of the landed gentleman's life, the source from which his duties spring, Sir Walter has lost all function once he abandons Kellynch. As the novel develops it becomes clear that Jane Austen is not taking Sir Walter Elliot as an isolated case, but is, rather, suggesting that the entire established order is ceasing to be useful. Anne, the only fully worthy member of the gentry in the novel, and the only one of the Elliots cognisant of the intimate links between household management and the preservation of Kellynch (12), and hence of social order, is compelled to transfer her allegiance to the 'new men' of the navy, who seem to offer the best chance of a general revival of worthwhile values. The capabilities of this group are suggested by another symbol of household management. Despite the fact that he has little to work with, Captain Harville, through 'ingenious contrivances and nice arrangements', has managed to make out of his lodgings a 'picture of repose and domestic happiness' (98).[22]

In both novels, then, Jane Austen is saying, symbolically, that those who order their houses well are securing the health of the nation, while those who neglect them are damaging it. However, what we must recognise is that she is not simply employing household management as a convenient symbol, but is also expressing her quite literal belief in the domestic environment as a microcosm of the nation. It is not just the Mansfield Parks and Kellynch Halls of her novels that take on larger implications, but all households. Hence, every housewife has a crucial role to play in preserving the *status quo*.

This should help us to understand why Jane Austen reserves some of her sharpest irony in *Sense and Sensibility* for Mrs Dashwood's deficiencies as a household manager: 'In the mean time, till all these alterations could be made from the savings of an income of five hundred a-year by a woman who never saved in her life, they were wise enough to be contented with the house as it was' (29–30). Were it not that Elinor introduces some method into her dealings, Mrs Dashwood would be guilty of damaging the fabric of English society, and thus deserves to suffer the lash of Jane Austen's tongue.

The kind of importance that Jane Austen attaches to manners is made quite clear in 'Catharine', one of her earliest stories:

> 'But I plainly see that every thing is going to sixes & sevens and all order will soon be at an end throughout the Kingdom.'
> 'Not however Ma'am the sooner, I hope, from any conduct of mine, said Catherine in a tone of great humility, for upon my

honour I have done nothing this evening that can contribute to overthrow the establishment of the kingdom.'

'You are Mistaken Child, replied she; the welfare of every Nation depends upon the virtue of it's individuals, and any one who offends in so gross a manner against decorum & propriety is certainly hastening it's ruin. You have been giving a bad example to the World, and the World is but too well disposed to receive such.' (*Minor Works*, 232–3)

It is, of course, impossible to demonstrate very explicitly this link between individual manners and the moral health of the nation, since the equation is an almost indefinable one, depending as it does on an infinite number of tiny gestures. However, in some of her novels Jane Austen is able to show very precisely what function manners play in the life of the village, which is, for her and her age, a microcosm of the larger society.

The village of Highbury in *Emma* serves as an excellent example. Life is so pleasant and well-ordered in this community that it has become moribund. Nothing happens there, and nothing changes. Balls have long been defunct and formal social intercourse is so limited that it is two years since the Woodhouses have been to Donwell. Mr Woodhouse, the arch-enemy of change, for whom visits even to his closest neighbours are severe trials and marriages disasters, is a suitable patriarch for the community. What saves Highbury is the intrusion of new forces in the shape of Emma Woodhouse demanding admittance into the adult world, the Coles claiming the right to move in the highest circles, and Mrs Elton and Frank Churchill pushing in from the outside. In order to accommodate these newcomers Highbury is compelled to revive its social life. Frank Churchill inspires the Crown Ball; the Coles invite the leading families to dinner; Emma feels obliged to hold a dinner for Mrs Elton; and Mrs Elton generates the visit to Donwell and the Box Hill excursion. On each occasion influences are at work which are strange to Highbury society, and it has to consider once again the finer points of manners, which had previously been reduced to little more than reflex gestures. Only thus can it test and perhaps assimilate the newcomers. The Coles, for example, are found to be worthy because, in making the arrangements for their dinner, they pay special attention to Mr Woodhouse's comfort. Similarly, by taking heed of Mr Knightley's comments on the implications of her rudeness to Miss Bates at Box Hill, Emma comes to recognise the limitations of her egocentric approach to experience, and finally achieves the maturity necessary for full admittance into Highbury society. Others fail the test. Mrs Elton frequently demonstrates her unworthiness by making presumptuous claims to social precedence and Frank Churchill is guilty of repeated indiscretions, particularly in his dealings with Jane Fairfax. Highbury is so regenerated by these changes that the novel inevitably concludes with the replacement of Mr Woodhouse by more effective leaders in the shape of Emma and Mr Knightley. Manners thus play an integral part in the process by which Highbury regains its vitality, and, by including some and excluding others, at once reaffirms and strengthens its moral position.

The larger implications of manners can be similarly perceived if we examine some of the symbolic aspects of Elizabeth Bennet's relationship with Darcy in *Pride and Prejudice*. The differences which keep Elizabeth and Darcy apart for much of the novel have social roots. He assumes that anyone with middle-class associations must be unworthy, while she believes that the aristocracy are merely snobs. Both, of course, are guilty of misunderstanding a central tenet of conservative social philosophy, which is that all ranks have a common interest and are motivated by the same ideals of duty and respect for others. In each case, this deficient social outlook manifests itself in bad manners. Elizabeth is consistently pert and rude towards Darcy, while he acts arrogantly towards the inhabitants of Meryton. Repeated displays of bad manners by both parties serve only to widen the gap between them and, symbolically, to create a rift between the aristocracy and the gentry-middle-class which threatens the structure of English society. The union of ranks necessary for the continuing health of society is achieved only after Darcy and Elizabeth come to understand the worth of each other's groups and correct their manners. Elizabeth learns respect for the aristocracy as a result of her experiences at Pemberley and Darcy is made to realise the limitations of his outlook by the gentlemanly behaviour of the tradesman, Mr Gardiner. As a result, Darcy politely invites Elizabeth and the Gardiners to dine at Pemberley, and Elizabeth, who now recognises the great honour involved in such an invitation, accepts graciously. Such proper manners guarantee that society will flourish, and the harmonious relationship thus established between the ranks is represented symbolically by the marriage between Elizabeth and Darcy.

In *Emma* Jane Austen further indicates that for her manners are not only important, but are at least as important as any of the social functions reserved for men. Mr Knightley is assiduous in the management of his estate, concerned about the needs of his community and attentive to the administration of justice. Yet he falls short of being the ideal English gentleman because, as a result of an emotional immaturity which causes him to withdraw from involvement with women, he has failed to complete himself through marriage. In the ritual version of life constituted by manners, Mr Knightley declares his ineligibility by refusing to engage in the courtship ritual of the dance: 'There he was, among the standers-by, where he ought not to be; he ought to be dancing—not classing himself with the husbands, and fathers, and whist-players' (325). Effectively, then, in spite of all his professional virtues, Mr Knightley is judged inadequate because he will not dance, that is, because his manners are defective. He does not win Jane Austen's full approval until he corrects his manners and takes part in the dance. Only then can he move towards maturity and marriage. The direction in which dancing will take Mr Knightley is clearly suggested by the conversation which precedes his first excursion onto the ball-room floor with Emma:

'Will you?' said he, offering his hand.
'Indeed, I will. You have shown that you can dance, and you know we are not really so much brother and sister as to make it at all improper.'
'Brother and sister! no, indeed'. (331)

The lives of Jane Austen's heroines, who spend much of their time at balls, dinners and on extended visits, should not, therefore, be considered trivial. Essentially they are engaged in receiving an education in manners, the subtleties of which can be fully explored only in the context of the formal social occasion, and are thus being prepared for their role as arbiters of manners and preservers of morals. By undergoing this process, and by eradicating the deficiencies in manners from which all but Elinor Dashwood and Anne Elliot suffer, the heroines eventually become as useful to society as any politician, soldier or clergyman.

We may take the case of Catherine Morland as an example. Throughout *Northanger Abbey* Catherine is anxious to behave correctly. However, because of her excessively benevolent view of the world she tends to accept people for what they claim to be rather than for what they are. As a result she is frequently unable to perform her polite duty. For instance, although she is aware of the importance of adhering to the convention of the prior invitation, Catherine is easily tricked by John Thorpe's lies into breaking an engagement with the Tilneys, and accepting instead his offer of a trip to Blaize Castle. Thus, while the more active heroines like Marianne Dashwood, Elizabeth Bennet and Emma Woodhouse offend against the first aspect of the eighteenth-century moral code in that they are not sufficiently concerned with the needs of others, Catherine, like Fanny Price, offends against the second in that she is unable to serve these needs.

However, at the same time that Catherine fails in the world of manners, so she is educated by it, and gradually learns that by studying the polite performances of those around her she can uncover their true selves. John Thorpe's rudeness at balls, which is made to appear even worse by Henry Tilney's impeccable behaviour, soon forces Catherine to come to what is, for her, the bold conclusion that, even though he is the brother of her friend and the friend of her brother, she does not like him. Catherine remains blind to Isabella's faults for much longer, but even here, the seeds of knowledge are sown early by the contrast between her manners and Eleanor Tilney's. Similarly, it is manners that teach Catherine the truth about General Tilney. Having been misled for a considerable time by her Gothic fantasies, Catherine is finally brought to a true understanding of the General by his rudeness in dismissing her from his house on the pretext of a prior invitation. By the end of *Northanger Abbey*, then, Catherine has learnt how to make moral discriminations by reading the language of manners. Therefore, although she is far from being Jane Austen's most sparkling and intelligent heroine, from her vantage point as the wife of Henry Tilney and a member of the Woodston community she will be able to play her part in preserving national standards of morality, and must be considered a full and useful member of society.

Lest there be any temptation to suspect that Jane Austen's acceptance of conventional female roles was simply a rationalisation of her unwillingness to mount the challenge to the *status quo* which her perception of women's innate equality with men might seem to indicate as appropriate, we must turn finally to *Persuasion*. By the time she wrote this novel, Jane Austen, as I have already suggested, had begun to realise that the old order of things was breaking down. Two aspects of this breakdown were particularly significant for women. First, manners were ceasing to function as a source of moral communication. For the decadent old order, as represented by the Elliots and the Dalrymples, they were becoming little more than vehicles for empty display and the emerging naval classes were as yet too unsophisticated to understand the intricacies of polite codes. Second, the home and the family were declining in importance. The Elliots have come to regard the family unit as a source of prestige rather than of love and duty, and are quite willing to yield up their permanent home at Kellynch in exchange for lodgings at Bath. Family feeling is much stronger amongst naval people like the Harvilles but their lives as yet lack the stability needed for them to put down firm roots, and they must make do with a series of temporary accommodations.

The woman's *raison d'être* is thus seriously undermined. By the standards established in the earlier novels Anne Elliot is perhaps the most perfect of all Jane Austen's women—she possesses an 'elegant and cultivated mind' (41), is an excellent surrogate mother to Mary's children, is highly accomplished, and has impeccable manners—and yet she is 'nobody' (5) to the Elliots, the Musgroves or the naval characters. The fact that she eventually becomes an important member of the Musgrove/naval group in no way invalidates Jane Austen's point. The incident which gives Anne the chance to prove her worth—Louisa's fall from the Cobb—is a freakish accident and leads to the conclusion that her ultimate success is the result of good fortune rather than the inevitable consequences of personal virtue.

Jane Austen responds to this new set of social facts by making some tentative proposals for a redefinition of the female role. Deprived of their function the 'quiet, confined' (232) lives to which women have traditionally been limited are transformed into sources of frustration rather than of fulfilment. In such circumstances a woman's 'feelings prey upon' (232) her, and she becomes subject to 'all manner of imaginary complaints' (71). What she needs, then, is a new arena of 'exertion' (232), and through her presentation of Mrs Croft Jane Austen suggests that it will be found in fields of endeavour previously reserved for men. When Admiral Croft goes to sea, his wife accompanies him (70); when it comes time to rent Kellynch Mrs Croft 'asked more questions about the house, and terms, and taxes, than the admiral himself, and seemed more conversant with business' (22); and when the Admiral talks to his naval friends, Mrs Croft joins in 'looking as intelligent and keen as any of the officers around her' (168).

If Mrs Croft is anything to go by such a redefinition of the area of feminine activity will produce a completely new type of woman. Physically she will be more robust and her complexion will be less soft. Thus, Mrs Croft possesses 'vigour of form' and her face is 'reddened and weather-beaten' (48). She will be more active and demand less in the way of creature comforts. Mrs Croft, for instance, enjoys a rather dangerous form of carriage riding (84) and regards anything more than the amenities that can be provided on board ship as 'idle refinement' (69). In conversation she will assume the blunt and assertive style previously felt to be appropriate only for men, as Mrs Croft does in response to Captain Wentworth's objection to allowing women on board ship: 'Oh Frederick!—But I cannot believe it of you.—All idle refinement!—Women can be as comfortable on board, as in the best house in England' (69).

Given her admiration for Anne Elliot, Jane Austen no doubt regrets that she can no longer provide the model for womanhood. Nevertheless, the affection with which she portrays Mrs Croft suggests that what is important to her is not some *a priori* definition of the proper female, but that women should seek out a role in society that will allow them to be fulfilled as 'rational creatures' (70). Control of manners and the family satisfy Jane Austen only because she regards these as being functions of crucial importance to society and not because they are in any absolute sense suitable occupations for women. Thus, once the society begins to change and the importance of manners and the family is diminished, then the woman must move into other areas of activity and must adopt a personal style appropriate to her new role, however 'unfeminine' this style may be.

Jane Austen's attitude to women, then, while growing directly out of the social and philosophical environment in which she lived reveals the workings of a keen individual intelligence. She may be committed in general to the *status quo*. Nevertheless, she is not prepared to go along with prevailing views about innate female intelligence and abilities. The fact that her contemporaries' view of women was demeaning does not, however, tempt her to follow Mary Wollstonecraft in demanding a complete reorganisation of society. Instead, she takes a clearsighted look at the functions performed by women and finds that, regardless of the very low esteem in which their sex is held, they are given a role substantial enough to satisfy the needs of such intelligent and capable people as Elinor and Marianne Dashwood, Elizabeth Bennet, Fanny Price and Emma Woodhouse. Only when the society changes does Jane Austen look for a change in the woman's area of activity.

NOTES

1. 'Lord Halifax's Advice to his Daughter', *Angelica's Ladies Library or Parents and Guardians Present* (London: J. Hamilton, 1974), pp. 339–40.
2. *Sermons to Young Women* (London: Millar and Cadell, 1767), Vol. I, pp. 271–2.
3. *Strictures on the Modern System of Female Education* (London: Cadell and Davies, 1799), Vol. II, p. 25.
4. 'Dr Gregory's Legacy to his Daughters', *Angelica's Ladies Library*, p. 12.
5. Fordyce, Vol. I, pp. 201–2.
6. More, Vol. II, p. 149.
7. *An Enquiry into the Duties of the Female Sex* (London: Cadell and Davies, 1797), p. 12.
8. 'Lady Pennington's Advice to her Daughter', *Angelica's Ladies Library*, p. 148.
9. Gisborne, pp. 12–13.
10. *Letters to a Young Lady* (London: Longman, 1806), Vol. I, p. 56.
11. Gregory, p. 10.
12. In her famous, *A Vindication of the Rights of Woman* (1792).
13. 'Jane Austen and the Feminist Tradition', *Nineteenth-Century Fiction*, 28 (1973), 321–9.
14. Juliet McMaster offers an excellent study of this topic in 'Love and Pedagogy', *Jane Austen Today*, ed. Joel Weinsheimer (Athens, Georgia: University of Georgia Press, 1975), pp. 64–91.
15. Marian E. Fowler, 'The Courtesy-Book Heroine of *Mansfield Park*', *University of Toronto Quarterly*, 44 (Fall 1974), 32–46, demonstrates in some detail how Fanny Price lives up to the standards of the courtesy books. However, Fowler ignores Fanny's later acquisition of more active qualities.
16. 'First Letter on a Regicide Peace', *The Works of Edmund Burke* (London: George Bell, 1906), Vol. V, p. 208.
17. West, Vol. I, p. 56.
18. *Reflections on the Present Condition of the Female Sex* (London: Darton, Harvey and Darton, 1817), pp. 77–8.
19. (London: Vernor and Hood, 1798), Vol. I, p. 1.
20. *A Vindication of the Rights of Woman*, ed. Carol H. Poston (New York: Norton, 1967), p. 264.
21. West, Vol. II, p. 484.
22. The fact that it is Captain rather than Mrs Harville who is credited with organising their household is perhaps symptomatic of Jane Austen's tendency in *Persuasion* to challenge traditional roles.

8 Jane Austen and the Problem of Leisure

Jane Nardin

At the time of his death, Lionel Trilling left an unfinished essay called 'Why We Read Jane Austen' in which he mentioned the difficulty students taking his Austen course had experienced in understanding novels set in a society radically different from their own. One aspect of the culture which Trilling's students found especially perplexing was its lack of emphasis on sustained work as a means of achieving fulfilment. 'We remarked', Trilling notes, 'on the circumstance that no one in the novels sought personal definition through achievement . . .; the "work ethic" was still under a cloud, yet I could not fail to see that . . . the students expected the interest of life to be maintained by some enterprise requiring effort.' The society Austen depicts, however, Trilling and his students found to be one in which 'most persons naturally thought that life consisted not of doing, but only of being'.[1] The distinctions Trilling seems to be suggesting here are very important if we are to understand Austen's attitudes toward leisure. The sort of 'work ethic' which Trilling failed to find in Austen's novels has two distinct, indispensable characteristics. The worker must derive his sense of identity from achievements that are socially valuable and not merely from activities that are primarily intended to improve or amuse himself as an individual. And, in addition, the enterprise in which the worker engages must require sustained effort. These two traits need not always accompany each other: a socially valuable act, like the donation of a large sum to charity, may be accomplished without much effort, and a great deal of effort may go into activity, like learning Italian in order to read literature in that language, which will benefit no one but the learner.

Trilling's contention seems to be that both aspects of the 'work ethic' are absent from Austen's novels; that her characters do not typically put much effort into any activity and that the activities they do engage in are undertaken from a desire for pleasure or self-cultivation ('being'), rather than from a desire to accomplish something that is socially valuable ('doing'). Trilling's generalisations about the absence of a thoroughgoing work ethic are applicable, at any rate in a modified form, to *Sense and Sensibility*, *Pride and Prejudice* and *Northanger Abbey*, the three novels Austen drafted before 1800. However, they really do not fit the works she began after 1811. *Mansfield Park*, *Emma*, *Persuasion* and *Sanditon* all give serious consideration to the possibility of achieving fulfilment through sustained, socially useful labour and to the difficulty of achieving fulfilment in any other way. In her first novels, Austen seems to have been influenced by conventions about leisure which she discovered in earlier eighteenth-century novelists. But in her later novels many of the ideas about work and leisure which she employs reflect those of her favourite moralist, Samuel Johnson, a writer who consistently stresses the importance of useful labour in the achievement of self-definition, sanity, contentment, and even salvation.

For many eighteenth-century novelists, the ideal human being is necessarily a person of leisure. Richardson, Fielding, Fanny Burney, Mrs Radcliffe, Maria Edgeworth and their imitators, all tend to draw major characters whose innate excellences and acquired accomplishments are intended as their passports to the reader's favour, and who demonstrate those excellences through their pursuit of leisure time activities: socialising, reading, giving casual charity, drawing and making music. Such characterisations imply a justification for the leisure class as a whole. If the aristocracy and gentry can use their leisure to acquire good-breeding and culture, to make themselves into patterns of human excellence, then the entire society will benefit and learn from their very existence. Lord Orville, the ideal aristocrat of Burney's *Evelina*, is a fine example of this sort of hero. As far as the reader can see, Orville is not personally involved in the management of his estates and spends all his time in London and other places of pleasure, going from concert, to opera, to tea party, to ball. It is precisely in this round of somewhat trivial activities that a man like Orville can, in Burney's view, be of use to society at large by the example of good breeding he sets. At various balls, Orville defends the unsophisticated Evelina from the impertinence of rakes and fops; at the opera, he rebukes the inattention of others by listening avidly; at Cox's museum, where marvels of jeweller's work are displayed, he laments the absence of cultural or social content in the exhibits. In short, Orville keeps the best moral, artistic and literary standards of his civilisation alive in his own person and helps those who admire him to fulfil their human potential. No harried worker could possibly hope to achieve Orville's level of culture and hence of human excellence. Like many eighteenth-century novelists, Burney would not accept as absolute the distinction Trilling makes between activities undertaken for self-cultivation and those undertaken to produce social benefit, for she feels that the self-cultivation of the aristocracy is their way of serving society. In Trilling's terms, however, Lord Orville is not a worker.

To say that Orville and his peers in the eighteenth-century novel devote themselves almost entirely to self-cultivation is not to say that they are inactive or lazy. Readers found them worthy of admiration precisely because of their ability to fill up immense tracts of leisure time with constructive activities that made them better people. The yawning fops and vapourish ladies who cannot dispose of their leisure hours, and who pursue pointless amusements like cards while neglecting more improving activities, receive snubs and censure from both the novelist and his admirable characters. 'How in the world can you contrive to pass your time?' a dissolute young aristocrat asks Evelina. 'In a manner which your Lordship will think very extraordinary', answers Evelina's friend, 'for the young lady *reads*.'[2] Frequently we are invited to marvel at the self-discipline which enables a heroine to fill every moment with difficult, self-improving activity. Richardson's Clarissa, with her elaborately formalised schedule of devotions, study, correspondence and good works, is perhaps the most striking example of an eighteenth-century ideal: the conversion of leisure into human distinction.

Austen's juvenilia and early novels approach leisure in ways that are deeply conditioned by this novelistic tradition and the social values which underlie it. From the beginning of her writing career, Austen shows herself to be highly conscious of the dullness which characterises the daily routines of her heroes and heroines, who are mostly gentlefolk residing in the country, and whose lives lack the sort of sustained, socially useful labour to which Trilling refers. Even a clergyman, like Henry Tilney in *Northanger Abbey*, can be a non-resident whose curate performs most of the parish work, without eliciting authorial surprise or disapproval. The absence of work is not compensated by a stimulating social life, for most neighbourhoods are very small and the general cultural tone is depressing. 'The insipidity of the meeting', says Austen of a fairly typical dinner party, 'was exactly such as Elinor had expected; it produced not one novelty of thought or expression, and nothing could be less interesting than the whole of their discourse both in the dining parlour and the drawing room' (143). Strong words these—and they suggest how seriously Austen takes the problem of leisure which faces her intelligent characters. In such a society, without necessary labour, the individual is indeed thrown upon his own resources.

Because she sees the lives of the gentry as offering few challenging activities, Austen's juvenile parodies tend to mock the mechanical ease with which the problem of leisure is handled by earlier novelists. In 'Lesley Castle', a semi-parodic fragment written while she was in her teens, Austen makes fun of the convention, now clichéd from overuse, which has the heroine demonstrate her superiority by the good use she makes of her time. 'Matilda and I continue secluded from Mankind in our old and mouldering castle, which is situated two miles from Perth on a bold, projecting rock', the well-born Margaret Lesley writes a friend, 'But tho' retired from almost all the World . . . we are neither dull nor unhappy; on the contrary there never were two more lively, more agreable, or more witty girls, than we are; not an hour in the Day hangs heavy on our Hands. We read, we work, we walk, and when fatigued with these Employments releive our spirits, either by a lively song, a graceful Dance, or by some smart bon-mot, or witty repartee' (111). Part of the fun of this passage comes from the fact that the reader simply does not believe it. To generate wit from all that emptiness seems virtually impossible, and the ultra-conventional descriptive language employed casts doubt on the reality of the amusements being described. The passage asks us to wonder whether it is really so easy to dispose of total leisure happily and constructively as the novelists whose work is being parodied would like us to believe.

Margaret Lesley's characterisation mocks the heroines of many eighteenth-century novels by exaggerating their already extreme characteristics. But the convincing ordinariness of Catherine Morland and Elizabeth Bennet, the heroines of *Northanger Abbey* and *Pride and Prejudice*, suggests that the typical heroines who are their opposites in so many ways lack life and truth. Like many another heroine, Catherine is an innocent girl who has been raised in rural retirement of the least stimulating sort. But Catherine lacks the discipline to avoid boredom by employing her leisure time in satisfying works of self-cultivation. She reads for pleasure, but her tastes run to books that are 'all story and no reflection' (15). She is often inattentive in the schoolroom, refuses to practice the spinet, and has no talent for painting. Comparing her country pursuits with the 'busy idleness' of her visit to Bath, Catherine says, 'I, who live in a small retired village in the country, can never find greater sameness in such a place as this, than in my own home. . . . I walk about here, and so I do there;—but here I see a variety of people in every street, and there I can only go and call on Mrs. Allen' (78–9). Thus, Catherine undercuts the heroines who never suffer a moment's ennui, though sustained work is absent from their lives. Her characterisation demonstrates that a sensible and well-intentioned young woman might well lack the resolution necessary to prevent leisure activities from degenerating into a mere search for elusive amusement.

And as Catherine undercuts the fictional convention of satisfying, well-used leisure, so Elizabeth Bennet undercuts the closely related convention of the supremely cultured, exemplary heroine. Unlike Catherine, Elizabeth is not often bored or restless, but she certainly does not set standards of cultivation for the society at large to imitate. Her musical performance is 'pleasing, though by no means capital' (25), for, as she herself says, she will 'not take the trouble of practising' (175). Elizabeth plays for pleasure, not for show, and since her interest in music is not consuming, she has not tried to achieve excellence. Early in *Pride and Prejudice*, Darcy, the hero, helps define the 'really accomplished' woman for Elizabeth, and the staggering list of attainments enumerated—'a thorough knowledge of music, singing, drawing, dancing, and the modern languages . . . and . . . the improvement of her mind by extensive reading' (39)—could describe many eighteenth-century heroines. Elizabeth replies that she no longer doubts Darcy's assertion that he knows only six truly accomplished women—she is now surprised that he knows *any*. The point is clear. Elizabeth, like most intelligent women, is not highly cultured and fritters away much of her leisure. Further, Austen suggests that there is something ostentatious and suspect in the 'exhibitable' culture idealised in characters like Lord Orville.

But if there is a sense in which *Pride and Prejudice* and *Northanger Abbey* take exception to the way the problem of leisure was often treated, there is also a sense in which these novels adopt the very

conventions they criticise. Catherine's unheroic laziness and boredom are real, yet Catherine is definitely less lazy and bored than
her friends Isabella Thorpe and Mrs Allen. Catherine does not read
systematically to acquire information, but she is moderately well
read in serious fiction and belles-letters—a significant achievement
which she underrates because of the low repute of fiction at the time.
Further, Catherine's indifference to pictorial art evaporates when
she finds the interesting, lovable Henry Tilney willing to act as her
tutor, and the restlessness country dullness once inspired in her is
much abated when she visits the secluded Northanger Abbey in his
society. Henry and his sister Eleanor are much closer to the standard
cultivated hero and heroine than Catherine. They draw, show an
interest in the niceties of the English language, follow public affairs,
and read history as well as novels. Although Henry is a clergyman,
Austen conceives him in the mould of earlier genteel heroes, gives
him a curate to do most of the work, and allows him to fill his time
with activities that result solely in improvement of his own mind.
Henry and Eleanor are Catherine's chosen friends and companions
and, by the end of the novel, they have clearly taught Catherine to
use her time as constructively as they do theirs. Since they do not
suffer from boredom, we can be fairly sure she will also cease to do
so.

Elizabeth Bennet, too, turns out to resemble the standard
eighteenth-century heroine more closely than at first appears to be
the case. Her level of artistic attainment, education and moral
commitment though not staggeringly high, is, like that of the typical
heroine, far superior to the average and sought for the right reasons.
Therefore, though in a more muted way than Orville or Evelina, she
does represent an ideal of well-used leisure. And in the characterisation of Darcy, Austen uses ideas from earlier novels even more
straightforwardly. Darcy's great pride is responsible for a stiffness of
manner verging on the ill-bred—a flaw Austen sees as serious
because in *Pride and Prejudice* she accepts the view that one social
function of the aristocracy is to set standards of politeness. But
except for this flaw, Darcy is a pattern aristocrat out of the classic
mould. His estate is a model of good taste from which visitors can
learn. Darcy, a highly cultured man himself, is extremely serious
about his responsibility to maintain the family library as a sort of
cultural foundation, is careful to use his powers of patronage in the
church wisely, is fair to his tenants, and does good among the poor.
His family pride is excessive, but in so far as it is a motive for much of

his good conduct, it is not totally reprehensible, and his very
existence is a blessing to society at large. Darcy's good conduct is of
great social importance, but he does not need to expend a great deal
of effort in order to perform his social duties adequately. Austen
conceives Darcy as she does Henry Tilney—as a character whose
vocational responsibilities (in this case as a landowner) do not
interfere with his leisure. And if, early in *Pride and Prejudice*, Darcy
seems to be having some trouble killing time, it finally becomes clear
that this is because he is waiting for the right woman to come along.
Elizabeth and Darcy's married life will be all 'comfort and
elegance' (384)—and the absence of sustained absorbing work will
not be mourned.

Thus Austen, after ridiculing conventions about leisure, culture
and boredom in *Northanger Abbey* and *Pride and Prejudice*, is forced,
perhaps for want of an alternative, to fall back on modified versions
of the very conventions she has mocked. She realises that it is not
always easy for a decent individual to discipline himself to use
leisure well and she suspects that a self-serving, ostentatious element
taints the idea that accomplishment is the main duty of the leisured
classes. But Austen still believes that self-discipline is the only
possible protection against idleness and ennui, and that self-
cultivation is the most useful course of action open to the
aristocracy. For superior people, at any rate, these things provide a
practicable solution to the problem of total leisure.

In *Northanger Abbey* and *Pride and Prejudice* Austen both mocks and
uses ideas about leisure characteristic of earlier novels. But in *Sense
and Sensibility*—the only one of Austen's novels drafted before 1800
which we have yet to discuss—the notion that the self-disciplined
individual can convert leisure into human distinction, and make
himself happy in the process, is quite simply and uncritically
employed. Here superior people can be easily distinguished from
their less admirable fellows by the way they use their time. One
reason the reader is sure that Marianne Dashwood, in spite of her
adherence to the pernicious cult of sensibility, will turn out well, is
the energetic, constructive use she makes of leisure. Marianne's
extensive reading, her serious interest in music, and even her love of
exercise, associated as it is with a love of natural beauty, are
guarantees that her mind is healthy and expanding. We can wait
fairly confidently for her to outgrow her youthful follies—and she
does. When Marianne finally admits her errors, she plans a scheme
of reform based on the ultra-disciplined use of her leisure hours for

self-improvement: 'we will take long walks together every day. . . . I mean never to be later in rising than six, and from that time till dinner I shall divide every moment between music and reading. I have formed my plan, and am determined to enter on a course of serious study' (343). No matter that we smile at the characteristic 'literary' excess Marianne's virtuous zeal here displays—clearly Marianne *will* use her time in future to become a better person. And her mature sister, Elinor, has been using her leisure in this way all along. Elinor's interest in drawing parallels—rather mechanically—Marianne's interest in music and gives a sense of purpose to her days. When they are not suffering from disappointments in love, the girls, like earlier heroines, find their leisure pursuits of self-cultivation totally satisfactory. They certainly do not need socially valuable achievements to give themselves a sense of identity or importance.[3]

So Austen's early work does fit Trilling's generalisation that in her novels there is no real 'work ethic', that the individual is judged for what he is, not for what he does, and that provided he can use his time to make himself a decent, cultured person, he is neither expected to do sustained, socially valuable work, nor expected to be unhappy because he has little work to do. These ideas Austen derived in part from her reading in eighteenth-century novels. But her attitudes changed after the appearance of *Sense and Sensibility* in 1811 ended a ten- or twelve-year period in which, discouraged by her failure to get her first three books published and by family troubles, she did little writing. In the books Austen drafted after this time, novelistic commonplaces about the individual's responsibility to use leisure well are replaced by a highly Johnsonian complex of ideas about the importance of sustained work.

What caused this change? Austen certainly knew Johnson extremely well from an early age, so if she began to draw more heavily on his ideas in her later novels, we must look for the origin of this alteration in the personal and intellectual influences affecting her thinking during the period between the drafting of the first three novels and the commencement of *Mansfield Park* in 1811. In personal terms, we might hypothesise that Austen's almost total loss of professional involvement and ambition during the decade from 1800 to 1810—followed as it was by her highly satisfying experience of the pleasures and rewards of successful authorship in the productive years after 1811—might be responsible for her willingness, in her later novels, to take work as seriously as Johnson took it. But it is also true that the place of work in the life of the individual and society was being discussed in a variety of intellectual contexts during the later part of Austen's writing career.

From the 1790s on, the Evangelical Revival generated a great deal of public controversy concerning the relationship between works and faith and the need for a Christian to justify himself by useful activity. In addition, during the decades following the French Revolution, the role of labour in an ideal society was often debated by philosophical and literary theorists. And beginning in the 1780s, English novelists, responding to the social changes brought about by the growth of manufacturing, increasingly rejected the convention that heroes and heroines ought to come from the highest social ranks and began to include exemplary characters of humble origin in their novels. These developments—along with the gradual spread of middle-class values during her lifetime—may have started Austen thinking more seriously about the problem of leisure as she grew older and she seems to have concluded that of all the writers who had treated the subject, Johnson came closest to what she now wanted to say.

Johnson suggests that there are two ways in which a person can express the altruism that is a basic, though not a compellingly strong, human motive: indirectly, through useful labour, and directly, through charity. And these, in Johnson's scheme, are the most important Christian virtues. Johnson defines labour as socially beneficial activity and holds it to be a religious duty. 'No man', he writes, 'ought to be so little influenced by example . . . as to stand a lazy spectator of incessant labour; or to please himself with the mean happiness of a drone, while active swarms are buzzing about him.'[4] Thus for Johnson the obligation to labour is as important for the financially secure members of the gentry and aristocracy as it is for those who must work or starve. It involves nothing less than the salvation of their immortal souls. On the dial-plate of Johnson's watch were engraved the first words of Christ's admonition that we must make good use of the time allowed us to prepare for eternity: 'the night cometh, when no man can work'.[5] Johnson—and indeed the work-oriented Protestant tradition which produced him—does not fit Trilling's description of a temper of mind which judges people by what they are, rather than what they do, since for Johnson you are what you do for others. Virtuous hermits, he notes censoriously, 'are happy only by using useless',[6] and therefore are not truly virtuous.

The religious obligation to work, then, is clear and unambiguous in Johnson's thought; to define the psychological status of work is a more complex problem. As the remarks about drones and hermits quoted above suggest, Johnson sometimes talks as though ease, idleness and isolation do produce happiness of a sort. Certainly he feels that most people are naturally lazy. Throughout his life he tormented himself with reproaches for his own idleness. A typical Johnson prayer runs: 'Impress upon my soul such repentence of the days misspent in idleness and folly, that I may, henceforward, diligently attend to the business of my station in this world.'[7] Johnson understands the natural human impulse toward sloth, but he also realises that sustained labour, even if it is not interesting in itself, prevents ennui, gives a sense of purpose, and thus promotes happiness and self-esteem. In *The Idler* essays, Johnson repeatedly analyses the manifold miseries of total leisure. One imaginary correspondent of independent fortune, Dick Linger, complains of listlessness resulting from 'a want of something to do'.[8] And this association between moneyed idleness and the whole range of psychosomatic ailments denominated spleen or the vapours, is a commonplace of eighteenth-century thought and is frequently mentioned by both Pope and Swift. After discussing listlessness, Dick Linger describes his shame that his life is neither 'useful or agreeable' and laments the difficulty of living actively when financial necessity is not present as a motive for working hard. 'Twenty years have passed since I have resolved a complete amendment, and twenty years have been lost in delays.'[9] Johnson's *Idler* essays suggest that sustained work is a blessing, but that most people lack the strength of character to seek this blessing if they are not forced to do so. Thus leisure, financial independence, and the social status that goes with them—those most valued blessings of Johnson's era—are really curses in disguise, undermining happiness, sense of self, and ultimately acceptability to God.

Idleness, in Johnson's view, can have psychological consequences that go far beyond listlessness. Too much leisure threatens sanity itself. Like many of his predecessors and contemporaries, Johnson believed the human mind to be involved in a ceaseless struggle between reason—the mental faculty that takes cognisance of facts—and imagination—the mental faculty which reshapes reality according to the dictates of hope or fear. At several points in his life Johnson feared for his own sanity and he regards the dominance of reason over imagination in any individual's mind as a precarious achievement. 'Of the uncertainties of our present state, the most dreadful and alarming is the uncertain continuance of reason',[10] he writes. And two conditions which tend to strengthen the imagination at the expense of the reason are idleness and solitude—associated conditions, for work generally involves a person with others and thereby prevents solitude; and solitude removes social sanctions against idleness, while it denies even the minimal possibilities for activity arising naturally from social intercourse. In solitude and idleness, the individual lacks the corrective to his own delusive imagination that comes from contact with other viewpoints, he lacks the constant stream of useful factual information that practical activity affords, and he suffers from an excess of free time in which he has nothing to do but indulge his imagination. 'It is certain', Johnson writes, 'that any wild wish or vain imagination never takes such firm possession of the mind as when it is found empty and unoccupied. The old peripatetick principle that "Nature abhors a Vacuum", may be properly applied to the intellect, which will embrace anything, however absurd or criminal, rather than be wholly without an object.'[11] Johnson's remedies for madness are hard work and social intercourse.

This cluster of Johnsonian ideas about the value of sustained, useful work—work as a religious duty, work as a means to satisfaction, idleness as seductive, yet debilitating, work as necessary to the maintenance of mental balance—appears repeatedly in Austen's last three novels and the fragment she left at her death. In these works Austen seriously questions the premises of her early fiction, that it is the individual's own responsibility to use leisure well, that leisure used for self-cultivation *is* leisure well used, and that the ability to use leisure in this way is one quality a really admirable person must possess. Like Johnson, Austen now rejects the idea that devotion to self-improvement can give members of the aristocracy a sense of purpose and social utility. And so she begins, in her later work, to turn her thoughts to the importance of professional commitment.

The question of choosing a profession is central in *Mansfield Park*, the novel Austen began immediately after the publication of *Sense and Sensibility* reanimated her own professional commitment to writing. Fanny Price, the heroine, is Austen's only full-dress portrait of a working woman. First as the oldest girl among the ten children of an impecunious family, then as poor relation and unpaid semi-servant at Mansfield Park, Fanny works hard and continuously.

Fanny's profession is not terribly rewarding and she herself is not very happy, but the novel clearly suggests that the necessity to work hard and renounce pleasure has had a good effect on Fanny's moral character, helping her to apply her religious principles to everyday life. Fanny's professional duty to be useful to her relations has given her habits of self-exertion and good conduct and a highly Christian sense of herself as one whose function in life is to serve others.[12] She may be harried, but she is never bored and her moments of free time are all the sweeter for their rarity. Indeed, she uses her free time well precisely because the habits of application she has been forced to learn influence her choice of leisure activities and make her uneasy at the idea of wasted hours. Similar points could be made about Fanny's siblings—all of whom are saved from purposelessness and turn out well because necessity has forced them to do socially useful, sustained work—and about her cousin Edmund, who has no fortune and therefore must earn his living as a clergyman. It is perhaps indicative of the change in Austen's attitude to work that Edmund, unlike Henry Tilney, feels he has a duty to reside in his parish, without a curate, even at the expense of considerable family inconvenience. In choosing the church, Edmund chooses not merely a secure income, but a vocationally oriented way of life. Austen was only partly in jest when she wrote that the subject of *Mansfield Park* would be 'ordination' (*Letters*, p. 298)—for the novel does deal with the moral value of professional commitment in Johnsonian terms.

The lives of those young characters in *Mansfield Park* who are sufficiently well-off to have no reason to labour form a striking and consistent contrast with the purposeful, active lives of the worker characters. Tom, Maria and Julia Bertram, and Henry and Mary Crawford are all intelligent and talented, yet none has been able, in the customary manner of the intelligent characters in the earlier novels, to turn his leisure to good account. They need a sense of achievement, but their situation offers them only hobbies— activities of self-cultivation which cannot satisfy this need. And so their very talents, ambitions and energies involve them in a restless, self-destructive search for pleasure, challenge and variety. The stupid, vegetable-like Lady Bertram is the sort of person who, in *Mansfield Park*, can be content with a totally inactive existence which destroys people of greater potential. Lacking the sense of commitment which a profession gives, the idle young characters have no fixed sense of who they are and feel free to experiment with a variety of roles, of selves. It is partly for this reason and partly because they really do long for activities involving sustained application and producing demonstrable results, that these characters throw themselves so eagerly into the work of amateur theatricals. But this experimentation with new identities proves dangerous and ultimately it becomes clear that all these characters (though in varying degrees) lack the stability which is gained from early habits of vocational application. Their pathetic fates constitute a sadly ironic commentary on the idea that total leisure can be the means by which human excellence is achieved—for the absence of work from their lives has helped to destroy them.

In Austen's early novels it was the weak, unintelligent characters like Mrs Bennet, Lydia Bennet or Lady Middleton, who failed to deal with the problem of leisure, sought harmful or silly distractions, or grew restless or petulant. But in *Mansfield Park* Austen no longer sees leisure as an individual problem which the intelligent individual can solve—here the life of leisure is a social problem which most people cannot solve by their own unaided efforts and which takes a particularly heavy toll of the strongest and best. The tragedy of even a totally destructive character like Mrs Norris is that given a situation in which she had plenty of useful work to do, her great energies could never have become so evil and perverse in their expression as a life of enforced idleness has made them. As an impoverished hard-pressed mother of nine, Mrs Norris could have been respectable, as Fanny realises. But as a prosperous, childless wife her energies and her ambition to achieve and to affect the lives of others express themselves in snobbish cruelty, unwarranted interference, and the purposeless accumulation of money. Austen makes a similar point in *Sanditon*, through the character of the wealthy, able, energetic and well-meaning Diana Parker, a hypochondriac of an unusually vigorous sort. In her search for excitement and variety, Diana persuades her sister Susan to have three teeth pulled, herself applies leeches for Susan's headaches, and decocts her own physic. The spectacular 'achievements' of pulled teeth, nearly fatal fainting spells, and miracle cures satisfy Diana's desire to shine and be of use to others far better than the conventional leisure activities, which are all her situation offers, possibly could. As in *Sanditon*, so in *Mansfield Park*, the Johnsonian idea that work is beneficial, but that it is nearly impossible for even the most able people to seek out and make themselves do sustained, constructive work, is central. Thus, it is no accident that Fanny, the character who needs it least, is seen reading *The Idler* in her leisure moments.

Austen's next novel, *Emma*, also deals with idleness in Johnsonian terms. Emma Woodhouse sees herself as the typical eighteenth-century heroine who uses her leisure to become an admirable, accomplished, exemplary woman, and who never suffers a moment's ennui for lack of something to do. She plays, she sings, she draws in a variety of styles, she is vain of her literary attainments and general information, she does the honours of her father's house with style, and confers charitable favours on a variety of recipients—in her own eyes, in fact, she is a veritable Clarissa. But Emma's claims to Clarissahood are hollow. Blessed—or cursed—with money, status, a foolish father and a pliant, though intelligent, governess, Emma has earned admiration too easily. She has not had to apply herself to earn the praise her vanity demands and in fact she has not applied herself. Her music is 'just good enough to be praised' (232) for she is too lazy to practise. Her drawings have 'merit', (44) but it is undeveloped. She makes lists of improving books to read and then does not read them. Her charity is infrequent and yet ostentatious. Further, though she sees herself as a self-reliant woman of resources, who does not need a husband or children to add interest to her life, her indisciplined imagination and her interference with other people's affairs suggest that really she is bored and needs both excitement and a sense that she is accomplishing something. So Emma, who thinks her life demonstrates her ability to use leisure for self-cultivation and the sort of social benefit that comes when a cultured woman uses her good sense to influence others, in fact demonstrates the inability of a talented individual to make herself work when there is no real encouragement to do so.

And Emma's closely related belief, so typical of eighteenth-century novels, that those who lack leisure cannot acquire culture or the highest forms of human excellence, proves equally invalid. Emma is sure that Robert Martin, because he is a farmer whose 'business engrosses him' (33) most of the time, must also be 'full of the market, . . . illiterate and coarse' (34). But the novel makes it clear that Robert's business has been enlarging and educative, rather than confining, that he is highly literate, and if not very cultured, is probably as cultured as Emma herself. Both are engaged in reading the frivolous *Elegant Extracts*, but Robert also reads *The Vicar of Wakefield*, which is more than can be said for Emma. The Johnsonian idea that it is habits of hard work, rather than leisure combined with self-discipline, which enable people to use time well, is important in *Emma*, as it was in *Mansfield Park*.

Emma's blindness to these truths suggests another destructive effect of excess leisure: self-delusion. Johnson's belief that constant vocational and social contact is necessary to the maintenance of sanity is relevant here. Emma has no work to bring her into contact with others or to occupy her mind and her high status forces her to live in something of a social vacuum. Her very small circle is composed mostly of social inferiors to whom Emma's word is law. Her idleness and laziness stimulate her imagination—for imagination is one way to produce variety and a sense òf achievement without actually taking the trouble to do anything.[13] And since Emma is alone a lot and gets little valuable criticism from her cowed acquaintances—Mr Knightley is the only real exception here—she has difficulty realising how often she is mistaken in her opinions. Emma's hypochondriacal father points up the dangers to which she is exposed. Mr Woodhouse, who lives on the income of safe investments, has never been forced to be active or useful and his life, though he is a basically kind man, has been marked by his increasingly sterile preoccupation with protecting his health. Cut off from all but the most minimal contact with others, basing all his ideas on his own preferences and sensations, Mr Woodhouse lives in a world that bears little resemblance to ordinary reality. Thus when a friend tells him that a 'thoughtless young person', overheated from dancing, has been known to open the window in a ballroom to get a breath of air, this reported disregard of health shocks Mr Woodhouse deeply: 'Bless me! I never could have supposed it. But I live out of the world, and am often astonished at what I hear' (252). Like her father, Emma lives out of the world of ordinary people and it is probably not too strong to say that her sanity would be in danger were it not for the corrective Mr Knightley provides.

Mr Knightley is the ideal landowner of Austen's later novels, as Mr Darcy is of her earlier. Both men are intelligent, cultivated, conscientious, and devoted to their families and estates. The most noteworthy difference between them is that Darcy, though responsible, is primarily an absentee landlord, while Knightley lives on his estate and works constantly at a multitude of duties. In the course of *Emma* we see Knightley engaged in minute details of estate management—discussing practical farming, advising his tenants, consulting his lawyer-brother over difficult legal questions encountered in his activities as a Justice of the Peace, and attending meetings in his capacity as an official of the parish. Probably it is because Knightley is not as wealthy as Darcy—we are told that he has 'little spare money' (213)—that he has been forced to involve himself so actively in estate management. In any case, absorbing, socially valuable work was there for Knightley, along with some incentive to do it—advantages few of Austen's wealthy characters enjoy. Constant activity has made Knightley hardy, constant involvement with others has taught him the pleasure of altruism. Where the humanity of Mr Woodhouse and Emma, rich, idle and uninvolved, shows signs of atrophying from disuse, Knightley's human potential has clearly been developed by his vocational involvements. Where they live locked in worlds created by imagination, he is well-informed and pre-eminently sane. The reader's most convincing guarantee that Emma, at the end of the novel, will become a better woman, derives not from her disillusionments and consequent resolutions—for we have seen her, like characters in *The Idler*, make good resolutions before—but rather from the fact that, as Knightley's wife, she will enter his life of activity and involvement. It is these, and not the individual's resolutions, that are guarantees of sanity and even happiness in the world of *Emma*.

Sir Walter Elliot, the proud and stupid father of *Persuasion*'s heroine, Anne Elliot, makes himself ridiculous by his failure to realise that professional distinction is the best claim to admiration any man can possess. Sir Walter counts only birth and physical beauty as criteria of human excellence and thus finds the Navy, which has just saved England from Napoleon, to be merely 'offensive. . . . First, as being the means of bringing persons of obscure birth into undue distinction . . . ; and secondly, as . . . a sailor grows old [in appearance] sooner than any other man' (19). By the time she writes *Persuasion*, Austen takes the great value of professional service so completely for granted that she can use Sir Walter's inability to see this point as a source of broad comedy. Totally satisfied with himself and seeing distinction as something that is born, not earned, Sir Walter lives uselessly and fails to perform even the minimal duties of his station. The characters in the novel who are naval officers, on the other hand, have all acquired vocational habits of hard work and service which make them extraordinarily active and useful even on shore. For example, Captain Harville, whose 'lameness prevented him from taking much exercise', nonetheless manages to occupy himself indoors: 'He drew, he varnished, he carpentered, he glued; he made toys for the children, he fashioned new netting-needles and pins with improvements; and if every thing else was done, sat down to his large fishing-net at one corner of the room' (99). That this catalogue of practical, useful occupations goes far beyond the genteel, self-improving or amusing ones—reading, drawing, music, sport—which the heroines and heroes of Austen's early novels were allowed to indulge in, suggests how far in the direction of a real work ethic her thought has moved.[14]

The characterisation of *Persuasion*'s heroine also emphasises the value of labour in a new way. Anne Elliot, voracious reader of poetry and works of serious moralising, accomplished musician and linguist, approaches the stereotype of the self-disciplined, highly cultured heroine more closely than any of her predecessors in Austen's work. Yet, unlike earlier cultivated heroines such as Elinor Dashwood, Anne is deeply dissatisfied with her life, in spite of the constructive use she makes of her leisure: And the reason for this is not solely that she has been disappointed in love—it is also that she longs for the sense of purpose and clearly demonstrable usefulness to others that leisure-time activities of self-cultivation cannot furnish. Anne is constantly seeking out work and duty: doing all the little jobs her hopeless father ought to have done on leaving his estate to reside in Bath, devotedly nursing her sister through an autumn of imaginary ailments. Anne's desire to serve is shown to be pathetic indeed when she eagerly embraces even this phantom, unsatisfying opportunity to be 'of some use' (33). Anne's belief in the psychological value of hard work is so great that she tells Captain Harville that, in her opinion, the satisfactions and distractions of useful labour can cure a broken heart. Unlike the energies of leisured characters in *Mansfield Park* and *Sanditon*, Anne's pent-up energies have not become evil or self-destructive, but with all her abilities, she has not been able to find a way to make her existence consistently useful or satisfying—though the opportunities for real usefulness she does occasionally find provide her deepest satisfactions.[15] At the end of *Persuasion*, Anne gains a sense of community and purpose as the wife of a naval officer. Since naval wives in the novel share their husband's professional activities in an unusually intimate way, often living for long periods on shipboard, we can conclude that for Anne, as for Mrs Croft, satisfaction and interest will be found, in part, through involvement in her husband's profession.

Persuasion is also notable for the way it treats the questions of ambition and earning money. Characters in Austen's earlier novels regard a sufficient and assured income as one prerequisite of a good life, but that income need not be large. Elinor Dashwood receives Austen's approval for her ability to settle down on a rather small income. The early novels suggest that sensible people live within their means and give money no further thought. To show too much interest in money—as a vulgar acquaintance of Marianne Dashwood's does when she tries to find out how much Marianne spends on her laundry—or to care a great deal about getting more money than you have, is simply ill-bred. This is in striking contrast to the attitudes about money expressed in Austen's correspondence, where prices and economical expedients are discussed endlessly. And in the early novels it is the unattractive characters, like Lucy Steele or Mr Collins, who stress getting ahead financially and professionally at the expense of more human values.[16] The early heroes and heroines, as Trilling says, do not seek personal definition through achievement. But in *Persuasion*, the attitude toward money has changed, though this change was perhaps heralded in *Emma*, with its details of Knightley's small economies. *Persuasion*'s naval characters all show a keen interest in success and rank and earning not merely comfortable incomes, but large fortunes. They know the joys of achievement and of earning the financial reward which proves that society recognises achievement. 'Ah! those were pleasant days when I had the Laconia!' says Wentworth of an early command, 'How fast I made money in her' (67). These admirable characters are unabashed in their ambition for distinction and wealth—ambitions which the early novels usually equated with greed and a desire to get something for nothing—because they associate the fulfilment of these ambitions with a proven ability to serve the nation. In *Sandition*, too, we find a financially secure character, Tom Parker, whose get-rich-quick ambitions are clearly linked with a desire to accomplish something useful to humanity. In his attempt to turn the village of Sanditon into a prosperous resort, Tom is thinking of the welfare of the population in general, as well as of his own profit. His sincere wish to 'have done something in my Day' (383) has prompted his involvement in this ill-conceived, visionary project.[17]

Perhaps because, by the time she came to write *Persuasion* and *Sanditon*, Austen had herself experienced the joys of earning money and fame, and because these motivations had gained in social acceptability, she has grown less suspicious of them. *Persuasion* even includes a genteel woman, Mrs Smith, who engages in the extremely ungenteel activity of working for money. It is true that Mrs Smith saves her amateur status by using her earnings for charity—but Austen's admission that a lady can enjoy earning and spending small sums is a new departure. This new interest in working women can also be seen in the character of Nurse Rooke, a woman who has had little formal education, but whose profession has afforded her such a wide variety of broadening experiences that her conversation can even be of interest to sensible gentlewomen like Mrs Smith and Anne. In fact, it is only in *Emma* and *Persuasion* that Austen examines the possibility that a mutually satisfying relationship—almost a friendship—might arise between an intelligent, genteel person and a worker whose mind has been developed by his vocational experiences. Mr Knightley genuinely respects and enjoys talking to both the farmer, Robert Martin, and his steward, William Larkins—a contrast with the early novels where only stupid and restless gentry, like Mrs Bennet and Lydia who make a friend of their housekeeper, derive pleasure from fraternising with members of the lower classes.

From the starting point of Johnsonian ideas about labour, Austen, in her later books, re-examines and rejects the conventions about the value of leisure on which her early works are premised. In the late novels, leisure is by no means a prerequisite to the acquisition of culture and human excellence—for now work is seen as having its own educative value. The activities work provides are learning experiences, and help to maintain mental balance, while the habits of application workers must learn make them more likely to use their free time well than many non-workers, like Emma or Tom Bertram, who have gained only habits of laziness from their leisure. The assumption of the early novels that the superior individual can and will use his free time for self-cultivation, is replaced in the late novels by the view that people of ability, whose situations give them no opportunity to do sustained, valuable work, may find leisure activities of self-cultivation unsatisfying, and hence may be unable to devote themselves to such activities. These individuals may, like Anne Elliot, grow quietly miserable, or, like Henry Crawford, or Diana Parker, they may substitute for the sense of achievement work can bring, accomplishments of a more dangerous or destructive sort. An important premise of both *Persuasion* and *Sanditon* is that doing useful labour and proving that one has done so by earning money and professional success can give direction and purpose to a life—a possibility which the early novels ignore. The insights of Austen's later years, that personal definition is most easily found through a life of sustained effort in a socially valuable enterprise and that it is difficult to separate what a person is from what he does, are among the innumerable ways in which her fiction moves beyond the work of the eighteenth-century novelists who provided her initial inspiration.

NOTES

1. *TLS*, 5 March 1976, p. 251.
2. *Evelina: or the History of a Young Lady's Entrance into the World* (New York: Norton, 1965), p. 257.
3. It might be objected that the ability to use time well is not a reliable clue to the worth of the major male characters in *Sense and Sensibility*: for Willoughby, the villain, seems cultured and energetic, while the two heroes, Edward Ferrars and Colonel Brandon, are aimless and depressed. But this is more apparent than real. Willoughby is not as interested in poetry and music as he seems to be: he has merely 'caught [Marianne's] enthusiasm' (47) for them, because he is attracted to her. Sport is his real passion. Willoughby's pique when a party of pleasure is cancelled suggests that he is too dependent on trivial socialising. The aimlessness of Edward and Brandon turns out to be as superficial as Willoughby's dedication to culture. Edward's ambitious mother will neither make him financially independent, nor aid him in becoming independent as a clergyman, the profession he prefers (though, interestingly, this is less for the occupation it would provide, than for the fact that it would *not* interfere with quiet domestic life as more active professions would). Further, in his early youth, Edward foolishly engaged himself to a poor woman whose unworthiness he soon discovered. So Edward is on the horns of a dilemma: should he achieve financial independence, he will be bound in honour to make an unhappy marriage. He has no motive for activity, therefore, and his depression is situational. Once he is free to marry the woman he loves, Edward quickly becomes active and cheerful. Similar points could be made about the heartbroken Brandon. Though situational depression prevents them from appearing to advantage, both men have used their time to acquire much solid information.
4. *The Works of Samuel Johnson*, LLD (Oxford: Talboys and Wheeler, 1825), Vol. IV, pp. 43–4.
5. James Boswell, *The Life of Samuel Johnson* (New York: Modern Library, 1952), p. 152.
6. Johnson, Vol. IV, p. 204.
7. Johnson, Vol. IX, p. 215.
8. Johnson, Vol. IV, p. 210.
9. Johnson, Vol. IV, p. 212.
10. Quoted in Max Byrd, *Visits to Bedlam: Madness and Literature in the Eighteenth*

Century (Columbia, South Carolina: University of South Carolina Press, 1974), p. 96.

11. Samuel Johnson, *Selected Essays from the Rambler, Adventurer, and Idler*, ed. W. J. Bate (New Haven, Conn.: Yale University Press, 1968), p. 145.

12. I am not asserting, however, that Fanny is perfect—either as a woman or as a Christian. A nearly loveless childhood has made her insecure and the high standards of conduct by which she has been forced to live make her very censorious in her judgement of others. She is not a perfect Christian in terms of her ability to forgive, but only in terms of her utility to others.

13. For a very illuminating discussion of the role played by imagination in Emma's life, see Stuart M. Tave, *Some Words of Jane Austen* (Chicago, Ill.: University of Chicago Press, 1973), pp. 205–55.

14. It also suggests a significant difference between admirable worker characters in the later novels, and admirable workers in the earlier ones, such as Mr Gardiner in *Pride and Prejudice*. Gardiner is a merchant and a very estimable man, but estimable precisely because his trade has *not* influenced his manners or interests—because he is just like any other gentleman in spite of being in trade, as Elizabeth reflects with satisfaction when she introduces him to Mr Darcy. But in later novels, worker characters whose interests and personalities have been formed by their work are admired precisely for this reason. No one could mistake Admiral Croft for anything but what he is: a sailor.

15. The opportunity of nursing her injured nephew alone gives 'sweetness' to the months she spends in Uppercross (93).

16. The character in the first novels who places greatest stress on the value of professions is, significantly, the villain of *Northanger Abbey*, General Tilney. General Tilney is a wealthy landowner, yet he has insisted that his heir adopt the army as a profession. The general protests that he believes young men need employment, but clearly his real motive is ambition. He is a name-dropper and very conscious of all sorts of titles.

17. The stock character of the mad projector—so often met in the work of eighteenth-century writers like Pope and Swift, or artists like Hogarth—is obviously relevant to Austen's conception here, ominously darkening the reader's estimate of the projector Tom Parker's prospects for the future.

9 *Mansfield Park*: The Revolt of the 'Feminine' Woman

Leroy W. Smith

No other novel of Jane Austen's has stimulated such diverse interpretations as *Mansfield Park*, her deepest probe into family relations, and no other heroine such divergent responses as Fanny Price. Recently, however, critics have tended to develop one or the other of two emphases—the novel is about the threat to an existing order and its reform or vindication,[1] or it is about a heroine of principle[2]—and they have been led, in Joseph Wiesenfarth's apt summary, to ask the following question: 'Does or does not *Mansfield Park* show that a meaningful personal freedom and integrity are viable within a traditional pattern of morals and manners?'[3]

Professor Wiesenfarth answers the question affirmatively. The central issue of *Mansfield Park*, he says, is 'the threat to the integrity of the self that comes from an easy life lived without principle'. The central conflict thus is within the self rather than between the self and a threatening family or society. Fanny 'refuses not to be free within the bonds of duty, and duty does not direct her to sacrifice herself either to the consequence or to the convenience of others'.[4] However, a number of other critics who admire the heroism of Fanny Price regard it as demanded of her in a battle with her family and social environment.[5] In this view Fanny embodies the self's desire to preserve its independence, and the family and society seek to subject her to their authority.[6]

At issue also among the admirers of Fanny is Jane Austen's purpose in writing *Mansfield Park*. In Clyde L. de Ryal's opinion, she wished to examine 'what it means to have formed a central core of self' in a 'modern *Zeitgeist* . . . destructive of individual integrity and wholeness of being'.[7] At the other extreme, Robert Donovan suggests that Jane Austen wished to set herself 'the most difficult artistic challenge': could she 'deprive her heroine of all the outward graces and . . . command our admiration for strength of character alone?'.[8]

How should one view Fanny Price? Is the main concern of the novel the welfare of the social order or the welfare of the heroine? What moved Jane Austen to write *Mansfield Park*?

To answer these questions one must first define the relationship between Fanny Price and the society of Mansfield Park. The essential fact is that in this novel, as in all Jane Austen's novels, the society is patriarchal in character. Ownership of property is vested in the male and transferred from father to son. More emphasis is placed on property rights than on human rights. In the family patriarchalism encourages the deification of the parents, a high evaluation of the father's role, suppression of the child's aggressive and sexual impulses, and the fostering of dependency in children. It is supported by the artificial polarisation of human qualities into sexual stereotypes. The masculine stereotype derives from the image of the person in authority: the male is hyper-rational, objective, aggressive, and possesses dominating and manipulative attitudes toward other persons and his environment. The feminine stereotype is the opposite: the 'feminine' woman is tender, genteel, intuitive rather than rational, patient, unaggressive, readily given to submission. Her essential characteristic is passivity.

The women of Jane Austen's novels live in a male-dominated society in which they are inferior and dependent. This standing is imposed upon them by education and social tradition. From infancy a girl is taught to revere the male; in adolescence she discovers the economic and social foundations of male superiority. She is brought up to be subordinate, praised for being 'feminine', and offered 'advantages' for acquiescing. Playing the 'feminine' role, she finds herself in a vicious circle: the less she exercises her freedom to understand, the fewer resources she discovers in herself and the less she dares to affirm herself as a subject. Marriage is her chief means of support and the chief justification of her existence. As a result, getting a husband is her most important undertaking, and the disposition she makes of herself in marriage is the most critical event in her life.

What Jane Austen found in the parlour was the drama of woman's subjugation and depersonalisation. But whereas in *Pride and Prejudice* the emphasis is on the problem of making a desirable marriage in a patriarchal society, in *Mansfield Park* it falls on the broader problem of how the patriarchal system affects the personality and destiny of its members, presented, specifically, in terms of how it works to stifle the potential for selfhood of Fanny Price. This emphasis is manifested by several features of its plot: *Mansfield Park* is the only one of Jane Austen's novels to follow the heroine's history over a period of years; it gives as much attention to the relations of parents and children as to the relations of the sexes; it shows more interest in the making of wrong marriages than of right ones; and it dares, as a proof of its honesty, to feature a heroine whose most celebrated trait is her passivity.

⌈Mansfield Park, home of the Bertram family, is a model of the patriarchal order. Sir Thomas is master at the Park and the principal patriarchal figure: grave, Olympian, seeing only what he wants to see. His eldest son Tom enjoys a favoured place among his children. Although Sir Thomas reminds the reader of General Tilney of *Northanger Abbey*, he is more broadly and positively conceived. His acts proceed, we are told, from a concern for himself and society and a wish to do right. He first appears as the guardian of what is good and proper, but soon reveals defects: a narrowly conceived plan of education, a moral blindness and vulgarity, and a smug authoritarianism.⌋

The females at the park are subordinate figures whose fates are decided by the marriages they make. Lady Bertram is an extreme example of the reduction of the female to virtual non-being by the patriarchal system. Having achieved a fortunate marriage, she has no further sense of purpose in life. She is helpless without masculine support, totally selfish and self-centred, too indolent even to enjoy her daughters' social success. She thinks more of her dog than of her children and misses her husband only when his return reminds her that he has been gone.

Maria and Julia Bertram are the female offspring of patriarchalism: 'remarkably fine' in appearance and in cultivation of drawing-room graces; raised in idleness and without purpose except to marry well; selfish, vain and insensitive. Although both girls outwardly comply with the process of their dehumanisation, they strive to escape the boredom and the constricted life of their society. Marriage seems to offer attraction for them as a means to gain freedom from parental control as well as to achieve status and economic security, but they find that it is an exchange of one confinement for another. A girl such as Maria Bertram, in Simone de Beauvoir's eyes, is fated for adultery: as a married female, the 'sole concrete form her liberty can assume'[9] is infidelity. Maria's final disgrace exhibits both society's double standard (468) and the greater danger to the female in a sexist society of succumbing to sexual temptation (a point made more fully in *Sense and Sensibility*).

In *Mansfield Park* the abuses of the patriarchal system, not the transgressions of individuals, are Jane Austen's main subject. All the characters, with the possible exception of Mrs Norris, possess the potentiality for suitable behaviour were they to live in a different setting. Even the system's champion, Sir Thomas, is no villain. His intentions are good, and at the conclusion he not only acknowledges his errors but modifies his behaviour. Faulty upbringing—the inculcation of faulty values and selfish attitudes—accounts for the behaviour of both parents and children. The emphasis on wealth and position has a debilitating effect on the personality of both those who possess them and those who do not. No one is as independent or assertive as Elizabeth Bennet or possesses as strong a sense of self.

Jane Austen stresses four principal faults of the patriarchal system: the failure of female education; the absence of love and understanding between parents and children; the cultivation of shallow goals and inadequate moral standards; and the perversion of courtship and marriage.

Whether or not one accepts Professor Wiesenfarth's statement that the education of Fanny Price is the subject of *Mansfield Park*, the failure of female education in a patriarchal society is an important issue. In Denis Donoghue's view, 'the sins of Julia and Maria have been prefigured, from the beginning of the novel, by instances of their defective education';[10] and the faulty upbringing of the Crawfords is cited as the source of their failures in principle and judgement.[11] Patriarchal education prepares young women only to carry out their limited function, which is to add lustre to a family while a part of it and to add to its greatness when they leave it by marriage. Sir Thomas saw his daughters 'becoming in person, manner, and accomplishments every thing that could satisfy his anxiety' (20).

But for all their promising talents and early acquired information the Bertram sisters (and their brother Tom and the Crawfords as well) are deficient in self-knowledge, generosity and humility. At issue is the difference between an education that emphasises 'accomplishments' and that models behaviour on social example or other-directedness and one that emphasises the interiorisation of values. Although Fanny escapes her cousins' formal schooling, she does not escape the broader educating effects, the social conditioning, of being brought up as a dependent female in a patriarchal society. She receives as little preparation as her cousins and Mary Crawford to act as a free and responsible individual.

A second fault of the patriarchal society—the absence of love and understanding between parents and children—is a principal cause of the misbehaviour of the Bertram children. Sir Thomas' view is that members of a patriarchal family exist for the sake of its advancement. He is not outwardly affectionate, and his reserve represses the flow of his children's spirits toward him (19). Having placed them under the care of a governess, with proper masters, he believes that they could need nothing more. As a result 'their father was no object of love to them, he had never seemed the friend of their pleasures, and his absence was unhappily most welcome. They were relieved by it from all restraint' (32).

Jane Austen's third criticism is that patriarchalism cultivates shallow goals and inadequate moral perception. All the prominent adults are self-centred and guided by materialism. The society encourages self-gratification in young males with little concern for consequences, since they are protected by their favoured position; and it turns young females away from any substantial activity in favour of an interest in appearance, manners, accomplishments and admiration.

The fourth principal fault—patriarchalism's corruption of courtship and marriage relationships—is as important an issue as the failure in education. One observes the same materialistic attitude toward the making of marriages as in *Pride and Prejudice*. Since Maria Bertram regards her happiness as assured by Mr Rushworth's large fortune, she regards it as her duty to marry him if she can (38–9). Marriage is also Mary Crawford's object, provided she can marry well. Sir Thomas expects his daughters' marriages to produce alliances advantageous to the family, and Lady Bertram is stirred for almost the only time in the prospect of Fanny's marrying a man of such good estate as Henry Crawford. Mary Crawford sums up the view of marriage in her society: it is the transaction in which people expect the most from others and are themselves the least honest; one should marry as soon as it can be done to advantage. From observation she can see that it is a 'manoeuvring business' (46).

The plot of *Mansfield Park* turns on two events: an abortive revolt against the restraints of patriarchalism by its favoured offspring and a successful revolt against its constraints by Fanny Price. In the first revolt the 'corrupted' children of patriarchy seek independence in order to indulge their whims, but their rebellion tends toward moral chaos. In the second revolt, however, Fanny Price, seeking to preserve her moral integrity and selfhood from the depersonalising demands of the patriarchal order, rehabilitates the moral order.

The cause of the first revolt is the upbringing of the Bertram children (and of the Crawfords and Mr Yates). They put personal pleasure and gratification of vanity above all else. The occasion is Sir Thomas' absence. The means is a private theatrical performance. In the opinion of Edmund and Fanny, to stage it in their father's house while he is absent and in some danger would show 'great want of feeling' (125). They also believe that he would regard it as unfit for home representation (140) and a danger to the privacy and propriety of the house (158). Edmund at first stands firm with Fanny as an upholder of the authority of Sir Thomas and a defender of decorum. When he enters into the activity, however, Fanny is left alone as the defender of the patriarchal order, wretched in her personal predicament. The first revolt collapses with Sir Thomas' unexpected return. It was shallowly conceived and lacked substance; the 'corrupted' children could only offer behaviour that would destroy both the system and what remained of their own selfhood. However, with Sir Thomas reinstated as master, nothing changes and nothing is learned.

In the second revolt the morally mature, responsive and sensitive Fanny Price seeks to protect her freedom to choose a husband in accord with personally defined criteria. Forced upon her and fully provoked, her revolt is the ultimate response of a morally mature person to a concerted and uncompromising attack by the parents and children of patriarchy on her integrity and selfhood.

Fanny Price first appears to be the model of a passive and submissive female, formed for and created by a patriarchal society. She is gentle, affectionate, desirous of doing right, and possessing great sensibility. Her disposition and lowly circumstances encourage timidity and very low self-esteem. Unlike her cousins she does not place personal pleasure above other considerations (131), values 'fond treatment' (365), and is concerned to please and do her duty. In the eyes of the representatives of the system, Fanny perfectly fits the stereotype of female and wife (276, 294).

Jane Austen gives special attention to Fanny's relationship with

Sir Thomas. The two figures appear to carry to an extreme the types of the dominant patriarchal father and the submissive patriarchal daughter. Fanny's awe and fear of Sir Thomas' opinion and her desire to please him are emphasised (321). She regarded him as 'so discerning, so honourable, so good' (318). His advice is that of an 'absolute power' (280). She is afraid that she will not appear properly submissive.

Thus, prior to her revolt, Fanny's behaviour exhibits much of the 'false' humility, the psychological paralysis, and the emotional dependence rooted in low self-esteem that Mary Daly describes as the by-product of the internalisation of masculine opinion brought about in the female in an androcentric society through social conditioning.[12] She appears to be a partner in what Elizabeth Janeway describes as the collusion of weakness and power to preserve subordination by the withdrawal of the weak from the possibilities of action.[13] Fanny's case seems almost a perfect illustration of Simone de Beauvoir's representation of the formation of the 'feminine' woman.[14]

However, Fanny's personality is more complex than those around her perceive. Her taste is strong (337), she is responsive to natural environment and to anything that warms her imagination with scenes of the past (85–6), and she is clever and has a 'quick apprehension' as well as 'good sense' (22). She is perceptive and reactive to those around her, as is shown particularly by her disgust at what she believes to be Henry Crawford's want of feeling (329). She is not to be won by gallantry and wit or without the assistance of sentiment and feeling and seriousness on serious subjects. But Fanny can feel temptation, can unconsciously adapt her attitude to circumstances, and can, at least momentarily, temper moral considerations with personal concern. She has all the heroism of principle and determination to do her duty, but she also has many of the feelings of youth and nature.

During the first revolt Fanny has the fineness of feeling to recognise her debt to the patriarchal society, to appreciate its values, to be loyal, to be cautious about self-assertion, and to keep her poise between the claims of judgement and the heart. She has, in fact, come to embody the order's potential virtues more satisfactorily than its more favoured members. Edmund tells his father that only Fanny had judged rightly throughout, and she is embraced by the latter as his sole faithful and upright child.

Subsequently, Sir Thomas treats Fanny with a new kindness. Her health and beauty markedly improve, as she seems to have earned a place in the patriarchal order. But the happy outcome is only temporary. The aborted theatricals were only a dress rehearsal for the later, more reprehensible breakaway of the Bertram sisters and the Crawfords. Furthermore, Fanny's recognition and promotion only follow upon her appearing to fill, as Sir Thomas' natural daughters did not, the role of a model patriarchal child. In fact, as Fanny's worth is recognised, the patriarchal order moves to appropriate her will and exploit her gifts. In the remainder of the novel her integrity and selfhood come under attack by three males whose goal is her submission. The response is Fanny's revolt.

Henry Crawford authors the first attack on Fanny's integrity and selfhood. Attracted by her new spirit and improved appearance, he decides to amuse himself by making her fall in love with him. As his thoughts turn from flirtation to marriage, two themes emerge: the increase of his interest as he perceives how well Fanny fits the patriarchal idea of a model wife; and the inconceivability to all that Fanny can refuse his offer. Henry ticks off her qualifications: strong affections, a dependable temper, a quick and clear understanding, manners that 'were the mirror of her own modest and elegant mind', and strong principles, gentleness and modesty. He especially praises 'that sweetness which makes so essential a part of every woman's worth in the judgment of man, that though he sometimes loves where it is not, he can never believe it absent' (294). Mary Crawford assures him that Fanny 'is the very one to make you happy' (295). Crawford, of course, cannot believe that he can ask Fanny in vain. When he is understood, he must succeed. Mary Crawford seconds him with the arguments of convention: Fanny's upbringing must influence her to accept, and her gentle and grateful disposition would assure her consent even if he were less pleasing (293). To these constraints upon Fanny are added her gratitude to Crawford for William's promotion and her sense of the improvement in his own behaviour (328).

But Fanny's objection to Henry Crawford is deeply rooted. She refuses him because she perceives an absolute incompatibility of personality and attitudes. She has often been oppressed by his spirits. Still more does she object to his character. She has seen him behaving 'very improperly and unfeelingly' (349). Her most serious charge: 'And, alas! how always known no principle to supply as a duty what the heart was deficient in' (329).

The attack from Sir Thomas is even more serious and oppressive because it brings the patriarchal father and daughter into direct conflict. The encouragement Fanny has received from Sir Thomas and her own increased affection for him only add to the pressure upon her. She appears doubly ungrateful because she has received a genteel upbringing beyond her expectations. Upon her refusal of Crawford, Fanny is thrust back into her former fearful relationship, augmented by an increase in guilt. She feels almost ashamed for not liking Henry Crawford (316).

The scenes between the two illustrate how the patriarchal system demands the female's submission and self-effacement. For all his merits Sir Thomas represents the parent as tyrant. In accord with his notions of marriage and the relations of parents and children, he believes that after his sanction nothing remains but Fanny's acquiescence. Consequently, he is dumbfounded by her assertion that she cannot return Crawford's 'good opinion'. Three times Sir Thomas asks if she refuses Crawford, uncomprehending. His displeasure mounts as he finds no explanation for her behaviour (318). Finally, he addresses her with the cold accents of the patriarchal father whose authority and wishes have been defied (the accents of Richardson's Mr Harlowe); his words reflect the assumptions that support the patriarchal family structure:

It is of no use, I perceive, to talk to you. We had better put an end to this most mortifying conference. Mr. Crawford must not be kept longer waiting. I will, therefore, only add, as thinking it my duty to mark my opinion of your conduct—that you have disappointed every expectation I had formed, and proved yourself of a character the very reverse of what I had supposed. . . . I had thought you peculiarly free from wilfulness of temper, self-conceit, and every tendency to that independence of spirit, which prevails so much in modern days, even in young women, and which in young women is offensive and disgusting beyond all common offence. But you have now shewn me that you can be wilful and perverse, that you can and will decide for yourself, without any consideration or deference for those who have surely some right to guide you—without even asking their advice. . . . The advantage or disadvantage of your family—of your parents—your brothers and sisters—never seems to have had a moment's share in your thoughts on this occasion. How *they* might be benefited, how *they* must rejoice in such an establishment for you—is nothing to *you*. You think only of yourself; and because you do not feel for Mr. Crawford exactly what a young, heated fancy imagines to be necessary for happiness, you resolve to refuse him at once, without wishing even for a little time to consider of it . . ., and for really examining your own inclinations—and are, in a wild fit of folly, throwing away from you such an opportunity of being settled in life . . . as will, probably, never occur to you again. (318–19)

Understanding the import of Sir Thomas' speech is crucial to understanding the basic relationship between Fanny Price and the society of Mansfield Park. The words are those of the dominant patriarchal male parent. Sir Thomas expresses the system's intolerance of any independence of spirit and identifies as wilful and ungrateful any concern for self that opposes the parents' wishes. He places the interests of the family above those of its individual members. He places material values and a concern for status and security in the society above personal aspirations and emotional happiness. He finds any deviation from its standards more reprehensible in the female than in the male. Fanny is a subverter of the patriarchal order, to a worse degree even than the 'corrupted' children.

Sir Thomas decides that kindness may be the best way of working with such a gentle-tempered girl. But his retreat from a dogmatic and demanding position is only tactical. He still intends to manipulate her, and he hopes for a resolution in accord with his wishes. In encouraging Crawford's departure, he hopes that Crawford will be missed and that the loss of consequence will cause regret in Fanny's mind (366). And his prime motive for sending Fanny to Portsmouth is the hope that abstinence from elegance and luxury will induce a juster estimate of the value of Crawford's offer (369).

Fanny too hopes that time will favour her. She

trusted . . . that she had done right, that her judgment had not misled her; for the purity of her intentions she could answer; and she was willing to hope . . . that her uncle's displeasure was abating, and would abate farther as he considered the matter with more impartiality, and felt, as a good man must feel, how wretched, and how unpardonable, how hopeless and how wicked it was, to marry without affection. (324)

Fanny here identifies the basic concern prompting her revolt: her right to make a marriage choice in accord with her own view of what would constitute her happiness or welfare. At issue is the question of location of authority over the self. The individual who seeks self-fulfilment is in conflict with the patriarchal order that would subordinate the individual to the group. As in all of Jane Austen's novels, the clash occurs in most striking form in the choice of a spouse, where the pressure of the patriarchal society to conform is most severe and potentially traumatic.

The attack from Edmund Bertram is the most dangerous of the three. It occurs when Crawford's behaviour is attracting favourable response from Fanny and when Sir Thomas has substituted siege for assault. Edmund is Fanny's first and principal friend, toward whom she has a respectful, grateful, confiding, tender feeling (39). Since he casts himself in the role of a kind of mediator and seeks to provide a rationale for surrender, his attack comes in insidious form.

Although at the outset Edmund is the protector and mentor of Fanny, as the story develops one observes an ironic reversal of roles: the pupil becomes the teacher. Edmund reveals two deficiencies in moral development: his powers of moral discrimination are not as fine as Fanny's and his adherence to what he believes is right is less firm. As a result he lapses twice in behaviour: he joins in the revolt of the 'corrupted' children and in the attempt to coerce Fanny into a bad marriage. Despite his attractive qualities, his kindness to Fanny, and the affinity of feeling and principles that they possess, Edmund is susceptible to the same impulse for self-indulgence and the pursuit of selfish goals that guides the others.

Edmund too is a scion of patriarchalism. His sexism is not as aggressive or overt as Crawford's or Sir Thomas', but well engrained. For example, his use of stereotyping is implicit in his criticism of Mary Crawford: 'No reluctance, no horror, no feminine—shall I say? no modest loathings!' (455). His attitudes concerning marriage are also in perfect accord with those of his patriarchal society. He is entirely on Sir Thomas' side and hopes for a match (335).

At first Fanny is reluctant to talk to Edmund because she assumes that they think too differently, but when he professes his objection to marriage without love, especially where her happiness is at stake, he appears to be wholly on her side (347). However, in Edmund's words, 'the matter does not end here'. Since Crawford's is no common attachment, he perseveres with the hope of creating that regard which has been lacking. His gentle admonition is as firmly patriarchal as Sir Thomas' bluster: 'let him succeed at last, Fanny, let him succeed at last. You have proved yourself upright and disinterested, prove yourself grateful and tender-hearted; and then you will be the perfect model of a woman, which I have always believed you born for' (347). Briefly he tries to explain away the problem of their different tempers. Finally, he summons up the traditional arguments for woman's submission. There are, first of all, his assumptions about the difference between marriage roles. Henry Crawford will be 'a most fortunate man . . . to attach himself to such a creature—to a woman, who firm as a rock in her own principles, has a gentleness of character so well adapted to recommend them. He has chosen his partner, indeed, with rare felicity. He will make you happy, Fanny, I know he will make you happy; but you will make him every thing' (351). Then there are his assumptions about her obligations of duty and gratitude and her need to be rational (meaning practical or prudent): 'I cannot suppose that you have not the *wish* to love him—the natural wish of gratitude' (348). Finally, because he cannot shake himself free from traditional assumptions about woman's nature, he assumes that her resistance must be due to the force of her attachment to the Park (347–8). If she can get used to the idea of Crawford's being in love with her, a return of her affection should follow (356). Edmund has completely missed the point of Fanny's objection.

Fanny's devotion to principle and sense of duty to self is as unyielding to Edmund's attack as it was to Sir Thomas'. Her anguish is even greater: 'Oh! never, never, never; he never will succeed with me' (347). Her justification is the same: one should not marry without love; she cannot love where she does not admire (349). To his suggestion that when Crawford's love becomes familiar to her it will become agreeable, and to the charge, conveyed by Crawford's sisters, that a woman who would refuse such an offer must be out of her senses, Fanny makes the fullest and most forthright defence of the independence and power of woman's feeling and of woman's right to choose for herself and the most direct attack on sex-role stereotyping to be found in Jane Austen's novels. In context Fanny's sense of self, honesty, and directness are remarkable:

I *should* have thought . . . that every woman must have felt the possibility of a man's not being approved, not being loved by some one of her sex, at least, let him be ever so generally agreeable. Let him have all the perfections in the world, I think it ought not to be set down as certain, that a man must be acceptable to every woman he may happen to like himself. . . . In my situation, it would have been the extreme of vanity to be forming expectations on Mr. Crawford. . . . How was I to have an attachment at his service, as soon as it was asked for? His sisters should consider me as well as him . . .—we think very differently of the nature of women, if they can imagine a woman so very soon capable of returning an affection as this seems to imply. (353)

Fortuitously, all ends well for Fanny. The Crawfords' misbehaviour frees her from Henry's suit and opens Edmund's eyes to Mary's unsuitability. Sir Thomas discovers his own errors of belief and judgement. Edmund is loved by Fanny, and reasonably soon after his disappointment he discovers where his true interest lies.

From close examination of the contention between Fanny Price and the patriarchal social order of Mansfield Park, one answers the questions cited at the outset with confidence: Fanny Price is a 'heroine of principle'; the main concern of the novel is her welfare; the patriarchal society at the Park is the 'enemy'; the contention springs from the latter's attempt to dictate Fanny's marriage choice; and Fanny's ordeal and triumph provide the dramatic centre of the novel. One also perceives that Fanny is originally a victim of the social order, never its foe; that the society is on trial; that any advantage she receives from it is accidental; that she becomes its preserver; and that the threat to the social order results from its own shortcomings. To the question identified by Professor Wiesenfarth—is a meaningful personal freedom and integrity viable within a traditional pattern of morals and manners?—the answer would appear to be a cautious 'yes'. The needs of the self and of the society are not incompatible. But an equilibrium is reached only after a very painful ordeal for the heroine and a difficult lesson painfully learned by the leaders of the established order.

One question remains: what was Jane Austen's purpose in writing *Mansfield Park*? At the heart of the matter Jane Austen is concerned about the threat to selfhood of a social order that subordinates the needs of the individual to those of the society;

specifically, in *Mansfield Park* she depicts what for her would be the most pressing and disturbing form of this danger—the victimisation of the female in a male-dominated society.

Jane Austen's treatment of Mary Crawford confirms the point. In the eyes of many readers the charming and gifted Mary far outshines the presumably dull heroine. Yet Fanny enjoys a final 'triumph' and Mary a 'defeat'. The most common explanation is that Jane Austen's didactic intention inhibited or deflected her personal preference and artistic judgement.

Unquestionably the presentation of Mary Crawford serves the author's intellectual and moralising purpose. But to assume that these purposes are adequately served by the trite association of charm with moral obtuseness and dullness with moral discernment discounts Jane Austen's artistic capability and possibly her intelligence. What is important to recognise is that Fanny and Mary are both raised in a patriarchal society and thus are both potentially 'victims' of the society. The divergence in their fates is a result of the differences in their relationships to that society. Their personality differences accentuate the irony of the contrast in their fortunes. Despite her apparent subjugation, Fanny's position as 'outsider' both helps her to develop the capability to take a moral stand (a moral education in reverse) and it shields a natural capacity for moral judgement from corruption, whereas Mary's favourable position, along with the pressure of positive reinforcement, both subverts an inborn moral capacity and encourages only pragmatic, materialistic and cynical attitudes, hallmarks of the 'privileged' female and the 'corrupted' child in the patriarchal society.

Mary Crawford is an actual victim of the patriarchal order, just as Fanny is a potential victim. She is rich, beautiful, gifted with wit, good humour and musical skill, and courageous. Nevertheless, the faults of her upbringing display themselves quickly. These defects, we are repeatedly told, are the product of her exposure to a selfish, materialistic and sexist society. The point is made most forcefully by Edmund, following his breaking off from Mary:

> This is what the world does. For where, Fanny, shall we find a woman whom nature had so rightly endowed?—Spoilt, spoilt!— . . . No, her's is not a cruel nature. I do not consider her as meaning to wound my feelings. The evil lies yet deeper; in her total ignorance, unsuspiciousness of there being such feelings, in a perversion of mind which made it natural to her to treat the

subject as she did. She was speaking only, as she had been used to hear others speak, as she imagined every body else would speak. Her's are not faults of temper. She would not voluntarily give unnecessary pain to any one. . . . Her's are faults of principle, Fanny, of blunted delicacy and a corrupted, vitiated mind. (455–6)

(He had spoken earlier of her mind being 'tainted' [269].) In corroboration, the narrator says that Miss Crawford had 'shewn a mind led astray and bewildered, and without any suspicion of being so; darkened, yet fancying itself light' (367). For Mary the victim, as for Louisa Gradgrind of *Hard Times*, there is no happy ending. Though discontented with her life, she cannot free herself from the warping of her nature by her environment (469). It is a bitter ending for Mary Crawford, caught between two worlds and essentially undeserving of her fate.

An understanding of the relationship between Fanny Price and the environment at Mansfield Park discourages the view that the novel is cautious and conservative or nostalgic and fearful of the future, in favour of the view that it challenges convention and the *status quo* and looks toward the future. It favours those interpretations that see the novel as examining selfhood,[15] condemning a decaying environment that relegates women to a state of subjection,[16] and expressing the importance and difficulty of being free[17] and the need to preserve order by partisan commitment to action[18] over those interpretations that see it as exposing the dangers of individuality or counselling a retreat to a life of art, ritual and imposed form.[19] Finally, this perception supports the belief that there is a 'feminist' element in Jane Austen's fiction. Jane Austen presents Fanny Price as representative of an oppressed sex. Unaware of the conflict between herself and the family structures that have provided a crippling security, she is forced by necessity to speak from the self. But in defending her integrity and her personal freedom to choose, an effort that is more moving in that she makes a stand, alone and weak, against the patriarchal family and the world, Fanny Price defends the birthright of everyone.

NOTES

1. Douglas Bush, *Jane Austen* (New York: Macmillan, 1975), p. 109; W. A. Craik, *Jane Austen: The Six Novels* (London: Methuen, 1966), p. 92; Joseph M. Duffy.

Jr, 'Moral Integrity and Moral Anarchy in *Mansfield Park*', *ELH*, 23 (1956), 73–9; Alistair M. Duckworth, *The Improvement of the Estate: A Study of Jane Austen's Novels* (Baltimore, Md.: The Johns Hopkins Press, 1971), p. 31; David Lodge, 'The Vocabulary of *Mansfield Park*', *Language of Fiction* (London: Routledge and Kegan Paul, 1966), p. 97; Avrom Fleishman, '*Mansfield Park* in its Time', *Nineteenth-Century Fiction*, 22 (1967), 1–18; Joseph Wiesenfarth; *The Errand of Form* (New York: Fordham University Press, 1976), pp. 86–108.

2. See Robert Alan Donovan, '*Mansfield Park* and Jane Austen's Moral Universe', *The Shaping Vision* (Ithaca, NY: Cornell University Press, 1966), p. 150; Lionel Trilling, '*Mansfield Park*', *The Opposing Self* (New York: Viking, 1955), pp. 221, 230; Joseph W. Donohue, Jr, 'Ordination and the Divided House at Mansfield Park', *ELH*, 32 (1965), 171, 178.

3. Wiesenfarth, p. 86.

4. Wiesenfarth, pp. 107, 90.

5. See Donovan, pp. 153, 171; Trilling, pp. 225–30; Donohue, pp. 171, 178.

6. See Janet Burroway, 'The Irony of the Insufferable Prig: *Mansfield Park*', *Critical Quarterly*, 9 (1967), 135–8. Stuart M. Tave describes Fanny as redeeming her society by her insistence on personal integrity in making a marriage choice ('Jane Austen and One of Her Contemporaries', *Jane Austen: Bicentenary Essays*, ed. John Halperin [Cambridge: Cambridge University Press, 1975], p. 73); D. D. Devlin says that by not submitting Fanny threatens the society and proves that she alone is free ('*Mansfield Park*', *Ariel*, 2 [1971], 35).

7. 'Being and Doing in *Mansfield Park*', *Archiv*, 206 (1970), 346, 359.

8. Donovan, p. 150.

9. *The Second Sex*, trans. and ed. by J. M. Parshley (New York: Bantam 1970), p. 176.

10. 'A View of *Mansfield Park*', *Critical Essays on Jane Austen*, ed. B. C. Southam (London: Routledge and Kegan Paul, 1968), p. 50; see also Kenneth Moler, *Jane Austen's Art of Allusion* (Lincoln, Nebraska: University of Nebraska Press, 1968), pp. 111–45.

11. Norman Sherry, *Jane Austen* (London: Evans, 1966), p. 98.

12. *Beyond God the Father: Toward a Philosophy of Women's Liberation* (Boston, Mass.: Beacon, 1973), pp. 50–4.

13. *Man's World, Woman's Place* (New York: Morrow, 1971), pp. 107–9.

14. de Beauvoir, pp. 261–2, 267–9, 337.

15. Ryals, *op. cit.*

16. Madeline Hummel, 'Emblematic Charades and the Observant Woman in *Mansfield Park*', *Texas Studies in Language and Literature*, 15 (1973), 251–65.

17. Devlin, *op. cit.*

18. Burroway, *op. cit.*

19. D. W. Harding, 'Regulated Hatred: An Aspect of the Work of Jane Austen', *Scrutiny*, 8 (1940), 346–62; Duckworth, op. cit.; Duffy, op. cit.

10 Muted Discord: Generational Conflict in Jane Austen

Patricia Meyer Spacks

In a 1977 article in the *Boston Globe*, Patrick Moynihan designates adolescents as 'barbarians', 'invaders' confronting beleaguered adult 'defenders' of society's values. 'There is much to be said for barbarians', he acknowledges. 'These are the years when people do wonderful things: Run the fastest, dance the longest.' His view, resting on the assumption of necessary and fundamental conflict between the generations, embodies a common, deeply felt attitude of our time. At least equally common is the opposite definition of necessary conflict, given respectability by Edgar Friedenberg and his followers among others: adolescents, natural aristocrats, potential saviours of society, meet desperate opposition from their benighted elders, who feel concerned only to protect a decaying *status quo*. Both positions assume natural enmity between young and old; they differ only in the values assigned to each.

Consider, in this context, a summary of *Persuasion*, Jane Austen's last completed novel. A nineteen-year-old girl loves and is loved by a young man with his fortune still to make. Her father and her main female advisor join to oppose the match. Accepting their prudential arguments, the girl remains unmarried until, eight years later, her lover reappears, they reach an understanding, and she welcomes his renewed proposal. Even then, she believes herself right in having yielded to an older woman's judgement, although she would not, she says, herself offer similar advice in a situation comparable to her own.

This plot hinges on generational conflict, but the assignment of values suggests a more complicated system of assumptions than

Moynihan or Friedenberg reveals. Anne Elliot, the protagonist of
Persuasion, with a more highly developed moral sensibility than her
advisor, Lady Russell, paradoxically attests her worth by yielding to
the persuasion of a moral inferior. The principles that govern her at
twenty-seven reverse those appropriate for nineteen. As a girl, she
declares her virtue by accepting the hegemony of even misguided
elders; as a woman, she must assert her independence. In girlhood,
she demonstrates manifest superiority to those whose authority she
acknowledges, but their right to that authority remains un-
questioned. If conflict between the young and the old seems
inevitable here too, one does not immediately know what hierarchy
of values governs it. Nor is it clear where Austen's point of view
derives from, how it fits with beliefs about the relations between
generations held by her contemporaries and predecessors. I want to
explore these matters: to try to define more precisely what view of
the interchange between young and old emerges in the structure
and the detail of Austen novels, to describe the fictional functions of
the view, and to look at how it correlates with attitudes expressed by
other thinkers and imaginative writers of the late eighteenth and
early nineteenth centuries.

Not all of Austen's young people demonstrate the moral per-
ceptiveness of Anne Elliot. At one point in *Mansfield Park*, Julia
Betram finds herself forced to accompany an older woman in whom
she feels no interest at all. The narrator summarises,

> The politeness which she had been brought up to practise as a
> duty, made it impossible for her to escape; while the want of that
> higher species of self-command, that just consideration of others,
> that knowledge of her own heart, that principle of right which
> had not formed any essential part of her education, made her
> miserable under it. (91)

Anne Elliot's superiority to those around her consists in her
possession of precisely the qualities Julia lacks. The heroines of
Northanger Abbey, *Sense and Sensibility*, *Pride and Prejudice*, *Emma*,
Mansfield Park, all have or develop self-command, self-knowledge,
consideration of others, right principle which converts politeness to
an expression of feeling rather than duty. The terms comprise a
familiar moral litany. Yet each novel contains at least one unworthy
female contemporary of the heroine, frivolous, insensitive or foolish.
Virtue does not necessarily inhere in adolescents, nor are its sources

readily apparent. The quotation from *Mansfield Park* implies that Julia's inadequacies derive from poor education, but the diversity of siblings in Austen's novels suggests a less facile interpretation. Elinor Dashwood and Marianne, daughters of the same mother, demonstrate opposite moral positions; the Bennet sisters, the Bertram brothers, the Price children—all exemplify the problematics of pedagogy. Bad training does not guarantee moral insufficiency; thoroughly good training for the young is never directly described in Austen's novels.

Within the confines of the fictional world, assertions of causality abound; characters readily and insistently explain one another's actions in terms of hidden or apparent causes. Charlotte Lucas marries Mr Collins *because* at her age she could hardly hope to do better; Emma is spoiled, according to Knightley, *because* she has always been the cleverest in her family; Lydia Bennet elopes with Wickham *because* her undisciplined upbringing has left her responsive only to impulse. Occasionally, however, a narrator raises questions about such impositions of logic on the social universe. Sensible Elinor Dashwood, for instance, blames Edward Ferrars' peculiarities on his mother; the narrator comments 'it was happy for her that he had a mother whose character was so imperfectly known to her, as to be the general excuse for every thing strange on the part of her son' (101). Ignorance, fantasy and wish contribute heavily to the structures of causality erected by the actors in Austen's dramas. The reader in turn can manufacture comparable structures on similar grounds, or on the grounds of knowledge the novel has supplied, or on the basis of his or her understanding of how things work in the world of direct experience; in crucial instances Austen herself (or her narrator) supplies no adequate causal explanations. The characters exemplifying moral excellence by and large comprise such instances. Often the novels suggest a general association between adolescence and a disposition to folly. At nineteen (and yet more at fifteen or sixteen), little can be expected of anyone. Edward Ferrars, for instance, may be forgiven his youthful infatuation with Lucy Steele, but four more years, 'years, which if rationally spent, give such improvement to the understanding, must have opened his eyes to her defects of education' (140). Elinor similarly counts on time alone to improve the quality of her seventeen-year-old sister's thought and perception, finding foolish romanticism appropriate to her age but much inferior to opinions settled 'on the reasonable basis of common sense and observation' (56). But though the novels reiterate the view of folly as adolescent norm, they depict youthful characters who unaccountably evade it, making mistakes of judgement and action but possessing even in girlhood the essential virtue of right feeling.

For such virtue the parental generation can rarely claim responsibility. Austen's fictional mothers and aunts seldom offer much to admire. They bear a comfortable relation to the society they inhabit, supporting that society's assumption that young women exist to marry and young men to be married: 'a single man in possession of a good fortune, must be in want of a wife' (*Pride and Prejudice*, 3). They understand also the social connection of love and money and feel no shame at attempting to further prosperous matches for young people they care about. Even the sentimental mother of *Sense and Sensibility* allows her fantasy to play about a young man eligible because wealthy, although she professes not to care about money; and that man has a mother whose protectiveness merges with social and financial ambition. Mrs Bennet worries about money and status, not about feeling; so does Lady Catherine de Bourgh. The selfish and superficial Aunt Norris fills an equivalent role in *Mansfield Park*; *Emma* provides the background figure of Mrs Churchill to exemplify the same attitude. Fathers as well as mothers may concern themselves with wealth and status; those in *Northanger Abbey* and *Persuasion*, exemplars of capitalistic morality and of triumphant narcissism, actively interfere with the course of young love. More characteristically, fathers absent themselves, literally or metaphorically. Mr Bennet avoids the central concerns of his family in *Pride and Prejudice* until events demand his participation; even then, others become the agents of rescue for erring Lydia. He wishes to be left alone in his library, aware of his younger daughters' inadequacies, reluctant to involve himself in remedying them. Although he supports Elizabeth in her rejection of Mr Collins, he provides her with little help. Sir Thomas Bertram, in *Mansfield Park*, exemplifies sound principles and good sense, but his prolonged absence expresses his psychic distance from his family. Emma's father focuses her loving attention but supplies her no guidance, enclosed as he is in his infantile self-concern. By their exemplification of meretricious values or their failure actively to represent sound ones, the fathers as well as the mothers in these novels effectively interfere with their daughters' progress toward genuine maturity.

The admirable daughters, then, owe relatively little that we can see to their parents. Unlike their mothers, they do not consciously pursue marriage as life's goal. Only Emma explicitly declares her intent of remaining unmarried, but even those who recognise their emotional entanglement with a man (Fanny Price, Elinor Dashwood, Catherine Morland) seek other modes of personal fulfilment first: imaginative excitement in Catherine's case, service to others for Fanny and Elinor. These heroines feel more or less surprised when they discover in a man their reward. Their less admirable contemporaries—such figures as Harriet Smith or the Bertram sisters—pursue marriage with single-minded intent, but this fact helps to measure their moral insufficiency. Unlike their fathers, however, the adolescent heroines do not separate themselves from their social context; they live by its rules without allowing those rules to corrupt the heart.

The gap between the generations I have been describing does not manifest itself in the same way, let me emphasise once more, for all young people and adults. Some of the young prove prematurely corrupt, some merely silly; a few grown-ups (the Bennet sisters' sensible aunt Mrs Gardiner, Knightley in *Emma*) possess moral clarity and integrity. Moreover, the measure of the admirable involves more than moral criteria. Jane Bennet, Elizabeth's elder sister, excels her in altruism but interests the reader far less and receives in the novel the reward of a less complicated, less compelling, less wealthy young man than her sister wins. Elizabeth has more vitality, courage and charm—qualities she shares with other youthful Austen heroines, and qualities associated particularly with the young in these novels, never granted in any conspicuous way to adults, and never explained by any sequence of causality. The novels provide means of defining what makes these heroines good and attractive, but not of accounting for how they got that way.

So one is tempted to speculate that the responsiveness which generates moral capacity and which marks energetic involvement in life amounts to a native gift which cannot guarantee moral achievement but which alone makes it possible. Bad environment, bad education may threaten the individual's development, but, given the will to self-awareness, she can triumph over such obstacles. The action of Austen novels acknowledges in detail the necessities of social actuality, but the 'good' characters do not simply sink into compromise. Their marriages, by no means the goal of their previous existence, testify to their ability to live within the system but also to their capacity for self-definition; their submerged conflicts with their elders have the same double meaning.

The idea that self-sustenance depends on innate and mysterious power which allows its possessor to grow through experience links Austen with her 'Romantic' contemporaries. Eighteenth-century novels, especially novels about women, explained youthful virtue as largely the consequence of adult guidance. The picaresque tradition generated a literature about young male wanderers—Tom Jones, Roderick Random—who achieve adulthood as a result of painful experience; such young men clearly possess a natural goodness which needs only appropriate channels for expression. Tom's warm impulse makes him the moral superior of many adults he encounters. But Tom and Roderick need adult mentors in order to learn. The image of Squire Allworthy remains always in Tom's mind, more powerful than the guidance of such unwise adults as Thwackum and Square; his elders provide for him a means of growth as well as of rescue. Young women in eighteenth-century novels on the whole, although they too change through experience, do not enlarge the moral perceptions which they have acquired through early adult instruction. Pamela's goodness, derived from good parents, remains undeviating, although it finds increasingly complex modes of expression; Evelina's depends on her training by a virtuous clergyman. She learns more about the world and its demands, but never alters her judgements: although she acquires new reasons for disliking the cad Willoughby, she knew enough to disapprove of him from the beginning. Camilla, the youthful heroine of Fanny Burney's third novel, gets in trouble every time she attempts independent action and learns the safety of relying always on adult advice. Clarissa differs from most of her fictional sisters in her utter rejection of what her elders have to offer, but in fact the bitter lessons of her experience substantiate her parents' rightness in disapproving of Lovelace (although not, of course, their advocacy of Solmes) and corroborates the moral doctrine she learned at her grandmother's knee. The unusual complexity of Richardson's fictional imagination expresses itself in the complications of his protagonist's inner life, but the 'virtue' she achieves and perfects derives from received tradition—passed down through the generations—more than from individual perception: just as one would expect in an eighteenth-century narrative. Although the twentieth-century reader may recognise Clarissa's inadequate self-knowledge, Richardson supplies little evidence that self-awareness, in Austen's complicated sense, concerns him as a central moral issue.

In the eighteenth century's less important novels, evidence multiplies for the common fictional assumption that young women achieve appropriate selfhood mainly by heeding advice from those older and wiser than themselves. Eliza Heywood's Betsey Thoughtless, for instance, has a four-volume career of mistake-making before she comes to accept the instruction of her elders; then she gives up vanity for sobriety and finds security in marriage. Many plots lend themselves to similar summary, although occasionally (as in *The Memoirs of Miss Sidney Bidulph*, a work much admired and imitated) virtue learned from adults ensures the earthly sadness rather than the happiness of its female practitioner. The dreary predictability of the mass of female novels derives partly from their restrictive moral assumptions: young women guarantee disaster for themselves if they try to discover new modes of perception or action.

The literature of advice, explicitly intended to inculcate the society's values, promulgates yet more insistently the doctrine of youth's necessary moral dependency. Of course the flourishing phenomenon of advice literature itself implies the view of publishers and readers as well as writers that adults have something of value to offer the young. Often advisors direct their wisdom to parents rather than children, but whether they write for fellow-adults or for adolescents they assume that moral growth depends on incorporating the views of a previous generation. 'The moral architect who builds a man', Vicesimus Knox writes—'great from internal qualities—good at heart—meaning nothing but what is generous and beneficent, and able to accomplish his purposes—is surely as well employed as he who forms a heap of stones into a palace, beautiful in its symmetry, magnificent in its size.'[1] A fantasy of himself as moral architecture clearly dictates the content of his book on 'personal nobility': the young, he believes, infinitely malleable, can be formed into any desirable shape, glory accruing to the elders who do the shaping. His language, even in the single sentence quoted above, betrays startling confusion about precisely what can be imagined as subject to change. He sounds as though he believes it possible for the moral architect to create great internal qualities as his more mundane equivalent might create a palace.

Less grandiose versions of the same fantasy abound, even very late in the century. John Aikin's two-volume collection of letters to his son deals with landscape gardening, ruins, the ancients and the moderns, the nature of truth—everything that crosses his mind. A doctor himself, he wishes to instruct a teenage boy who plans to enter the church; his awareness that the young will not necessarily listen to the old only intensifies his determination to make himself heard. Thus he comments that parental advice about marriage has 'peculiar propriety' because the advisors possess experience unavailable to their offspring. On the other hand, such advice may have little effect, for 'passion commonly takes the affair under its management, and excludes reason from her share of the deliberation'. Such a conclusion, however, does not long deter him; youthful passion, he feels, will yield to wisdom properly delivered. 'I am inclined to think', he concludes, 'that the neglect with which admonitions on this head are treated, is not unfrequently owing to the manner in which they are given, which is often too general, too formal, and with too little accommodation to the feelings of young persons.'[2] Carefully calculated literary style, in other words, will resolve all difficulties.

Parents, this stress on advice-giving implies, bear absolute responsibility for the moral welfare of their children. Even Mary Wollstonecraft seems inclined to think so, suggesting that children end up 'neither wise nor virtuous' because their parents have mistakenly tried to protect them. She believes in the value of self-knowledge and knowledge of others, both of which derive—as Jane Austen thought too—only from experience; but unlike Austen she declares parents responsible for their offspring's inadequacies of experience.[3]

An early nineteenth-century review of a work by Elizabeth Hamilton (*Letters Addressed to the Daughter of a Nobleman*) observes—with incalculable proportions of naïveté and irony—that 'the rising generation ought to be much better than that which is passing away, since so many more endeavours have been made to promote their improvement'. A view of the young as ideal passive recipients of moral instruction still prevailed. 'Youth is not the season for discussion and examination', the review continues, 'and therefore the object should be rather to store than critically to exercise the mind.'[4] So books of advice multiplied, for parents and children alike. Parents received repeated warnings about their immense responsibility: 'the mistakes and follies of those to whom the nurture of youth is committed, even of such as are on the whole truly respectable, leave ill impressions which are not easily worn out, and have been productive of great and lasting evils'.[5] The young were subject to emotional blackmail, reminded of a parent's anxious feelings 'on the occasion of a beloved son's first removing from the safe shelter of the parental roof' as justification for a three-volume discourse on religion and manners;[6] reminded constantly of their emotional obligations, as in this sentence by the father-daughter team of Maria and Richard Edgeworth: 'A desire in some degree to repay the care, to deserve the esteem, to fulfill the animating prophecies, or to justify the fond hopes of the parent who has watched over his education, is one of the strongest motives to an ingenuous young man; it is an incentive to exertion in every honourable pursuit.'[7] A wish to prolong the subservience of young to old echoes through many moral utterances of the early nineteenth century as of the century preceding. Internal and external forces alike might threaten such subservience. Isaac Taylor, an unusually thoughtful theorist, in his *Advice to the Teens* takes a rather testy tone about the inner life of adolescents:

> If you are arrived at that point which undervalues the wisdom of age, and sets up the self-conceit of ignorant youth as a better guide, there is little hope of self-cultivation effecting much with you. No rules which can be given will appear to you so proper as your own notions. It is in hopes you know yourself better, that I proffer to you my assistance.[8]

Hannah More joins many contemporaries in attacking a familiar external enemy, the morally ambiguous genre of the novel:

> Mrs Stanley lamented that novels, with a very few admirable exceptions, had done infinite mischief, by so completely establishing the omnipotence of love, that the young reader was almost systematically taught an unresisting submission to a feeling, because the feeling was commonly presented as irresistible.[9]

Submission to one's own feelings, as opposed to submission to the presumably rational guidance of adults, will lead the young astray.

One does not expect opposition to feeling as a literary theme in the first quarter of the nineteenth century, and a counter-strain indeed developed, in reflective prose as well as fiction and poetry. Taylor himself, in a later work (*Home Education*, 1837) raised the possibility that 'the unwarped reason' of youth might rightly, although always dangerously, resist the imposition of 'prejudices . . . authoritatively forced upon the young'[10] under the guise of rationality. In *The Friend*, Coleridge provided a full statement of the doctrine that the insight of the young might exceed that of the old. Those who have had 'some intercourse with nature', he explains, even if educated under the prevailing system, 'when they pass from the seclusion and constraint of early study, bring with them into the new scene of the world, much of the pure sensibility which is the spring of all that is greatly good in thought and action'. The danger such young people face in the world, he continues, is not 'the seduction of its passions, but of its opinions'. They will find about them many eager to function as guides but offering 'little else than variety of danger'; far more dependable is the steady 'inward impulse' of the youth whose environment has enabled his 'speculative opinions' to 'spring out of [his] early feelings'.[11] Feelings, in other words, provide the source of wisdom; all other claims to authority remain suspect.

Well into the nineteenth century, such authors as Mary Brunton continued to flourish, their novels bearing titles like *Self-Control* and *Discipline* (Jane Austen described *Self-Control* as 'an excellently meant, elegantly-written Work, without anything of Nature or Probability in it' [*Letters*, 344]). But from the late eighteenth century on, many works of fiction covertly or openly declared the high value of youthful feeling, even when such feeling generated insubordination. The unhappy protagonist of Mary Hays' *Memoirs of Emma Courtney* (1796) attributes her subsequent misfortunes partly to the loss of her aunt when she was barely seventeen—'at that critical period of life', she elaborates, 'when the harmless sports and occupations of childhood gave place to the pursuits, the passions, and the errors of youth'. The aunt's affection and persuasive powers, Emma believes 'might have checked the wild career of energetic feeling'.[12] Such feeling only causes her trouble; she warns her son against it; yet the account of her career conveys her superiority to her contemporaries and her elders, based entirely on her emotional capacity and expressiveness. Similarly, the male hero of Mary Robinson's *Walsingham* (1797) describes himself:

Mine have been the errors of a too vivid imagination; the miseries of sensibility, acute, but not indiscriminate. It is not from the multitude that I derive my anguish; the senseless throng, and the gaudy ephemera of prosperous days, never had power to sting me—for they were not my associates! Cold and cheerless sorrow has been my companion; and the shaft which pierced my bosom was winged by a resistless hand—the hand of nature.[13]

The adolescent sensibility is virtually indistinguishable from the Romantic sensibility; many protagonists of late eighteenth-century novels belong to both categories.

Robert Bage's *Hermsprong; or, Man as He is Not* (1796) provides a particularly influential example of the Romantic impulse in fiction. Its eponymous hero, reared among North American Indians, conveniently proves to be the son of a baronet; previously, however, he has demonstrated such virtues as a preference for walking over riding, distaste for dinner parties, and unfailing truthfulness. He courts teenage Caroline Campinet, daughter of an irascible and unreasonable father, partly by urging her to disobey her father and follow her own sense of right. When she returns to live with her parent, she receives a reproachful letter from Hermsprong which causes her 'to doubt whether the step she had lately taken, was as meritorious as she wished to have thought it'.[14] Having learned the moral limits of filial obedience, she becomes worthy of her suitor, whom she ultimately marries with paternal approval, the novelist hedging his bets at the last minute. But the hopeful message that natural goodness will lead the young to embrace truth and justice, their elders lingering meanwhile in a morass of conventional expediency, emerges clearly.

Jane Austen's work does not fit readily into a context of novels based on the assumed virtue of youthful feeling any more than it belongs to the line of fiction in which young characters learn to welcome the guidance of their elders. Unlike the minor fiction to which I have referred, Austen's novels rarely offer explicit advice to their readers, and neither the advice-book tradition which warns that the young must protect their intuitive resources nor that which tells youth to heed the wisdom of age accounts for her fiction's implicit moral doctrine. If Austen learned something of technique from Fanny Burney and Maria Edgeworth, she did not learn from them any relevant theory of the relation of generations. Investigation of her social, intellectual and literary context provides little insight into the sources of her moral doctrine about this matter, and even less help in understanding her mode of moral instruction through fiction.

The problem of how novels inculcate morality attracted the attention of at least one literary critic among Austen's contemporaries, an anonymous commentator in *Blackwood's Magazine* who explains that novels, however virtuous their intent, necessarily fail to engage the will and therefore cannot achieve true moral effects: 'Mastery over our feelings is gained by exerting the will in the course of our personal experience; but, in reading a novel, the will remains totally inactive.'[15] The assumption that only through exercise of the will can one achieve moral advancement of course characterises much eighteenth- and nineteenth-century thought; it does not, I think, characterise Jane Austen, who relies instead, I will argue, on an unstated conviction that significant growth takes place through involvement of the imagination. Both the content and the fictional structures of her novels reiterate that 'mastery over our feelings' involves more than an exercise of will. The intricate conflict of generations, as rendered in her fiction, focused a large range of moral as well as psychological issues; as a novelistic subject it enabled her to celebrate the capacity for imaginative development uniquely characteristic of the young.

Even one of the earliest and simplest of the major novels, *Northanger Abbey* (probably written about 1798), supports this point. The book's final clauses call attention to the generational issue: 'I leave it to be settled by whomsoever it may concern, whether the tendency of this work be altogether to recommend parental tyranny, or reward filial disobedience' (252). Establishing several parental figures, and several modes of conflict with them, the novel proceeds by a rhythm of generational interchange corresponding to the action's spatial shifts. The opening summary account of Catherine's childhood and early adolescence in Fullerton defines her relationship with her own parents. Although both, by the narrator's account, exemplify admirable qualities, the mother of ten children can give little attention to any one of them; Catherine consequently prefers 'cricket, base ball, riding on horseback, and running about the country, at the age of fourteen, to books—or at least books of information' (15). A tomboy as well as a romantic ('from fifteen to seventeen she was in training for a heroine' [15]), she expresses in both roles unconscious defiance of maternal values and expectations—a point made vivid at the novel's conclusion, with its stress on Mrs Morland's contrasting commitment to commonsense and domesticity. During the trip to Bath, Mr and Mrs Allen fill parental roles, their inadequacy making itself apparent even to naïve Catherine. Mrs Allen feels genuine interest only in clothes, unable to focus or sustain attention on other matters;

Mr Allen, although sensible enough, like other adult males in Austen's work most often absents himself psychically or physically from Catherine and her problems. Of course Northanger Abbey supplies the formidable General Tilney, at once ingratiating and tyrannical, whose will must finally yield to that of his juniors. Catherine finds happiness after her ignominious return to Fullerton and her mother when her lover arrives, having defied his father; but the young couple must wait to marry until Henry wins paternal consent for his match.

Of the cast of parental characters, only General Tilney possesses obvious direct importance for the novel's action. Yet Catherine's relations with each parental figure direct her growth. Despite the signs of independence implicit in her roaming about the country-side, her reading of romances, in Bath she seems a girl at the mercy of circumstance. Henry Tilney invites her to dance; that fact alone makes him fascinating. Isabella Thorpe offers friendship; no penetration into the other girl's character impedes Catherine's acceptance. John Thorpe insists on wooing her; she has too much self-doubt, too little experience, even to acknowledge to herself his inability to please her. But she learns to value Henry for better reasons, to reject Isabella and John on the basis of their conduct. Her reproach to Mrs Allen for failing to warn her about the impropriety of excursions with John signals her increasing aware-ness. Mr Allen's comment has alerted her to the issue; she feels relieved by his approbation of her behaviour 'and truly rejoiced to be preserved by his advice from the danger of falling into such an error herself' (105). But she also feels conscious that Mrs Allen has failed in her obligation, and is able directly to say so. Her declared dependence on advice coexists with her realisation that she has not received advice she needed; in the future, she will make more independent decisions.

Soon, of course, she finds herself inhabiting General Tilney's establishment, subject to the vagaries of a man whom at first she feels obliged to believe flawless because of her attachment to his children. She expresses her anger at him in her fantasy of his responsibility for his wife's death; eventually she allows herself to know that anger directly. Her moral superiority to her friends' father becomes apparent finally even to her; by the time he drives her away, she does not doubt his wrongness. She can feel no such conviction about her mother's gentler sway, enforcing the doctrine of useful work and no repining as General Tilney supports the gospel of self-interest. Although Catherine has learned, and the reader with her, the possible corruption of the grown-up world, she has little effective recourse against it, and even less against adult moralism, which must also be combated for the sake of self-realisation.

Catherine's commitment to Gothic romance suggests misdirected imaginative energy. In the course of the action it yields to an increasing desire and capacity for understanding the actual, a capacity issuing from her redirected imagination. Not so her elders. In the parental figures she depicts in detail, Austen reveals significant separation from important truths of experience. Mrs Allen consistently ignores the essential for the non-essential, blind to the feelings or the needs of others because of her preoccupation with a fantasy-world dominated by patterns of muslin. General Tilney lives in a dream of his own importance, equally out of touch with reality, unable to distinguish John Thorpe's visions of grandeur or squalor from the facts to which they obliquely refer. Even Mrs Morland, an admirable representative of middle-class female values, inhabits a world of her own: her theories about what is wrong with her daughter derive not from perception but from a pre-existent set of ideas and assumptions altogether unrelated to the immediate situation. Catherine, on the other hand, having used her derivative fantasies to express hostility and rebellious impulse, surmounts her need for them. By the novel's end, she knows what she really wants, the admirable moral qualities which Henry has perceived in her all along now less obscured by inexperience, uncertainty and isolating fantasy, her imagination refocused on the possibilities of life with a real man.

Another parody of Gothic romance from the same period, Eaton Barrett's *The Heroine* (1813), a work in the tradition of Charlotte Lennox's *The Female Quixote*, illuminates the special importance of Austen's contrast of generations. A lively and entertaining novel, heavily reliant on farce, *The Heroine* supplies as central character fifteen-year-old Cherry Wilkinson, who, believing herself to be Cherubina de Willoughby, engages in a series of Quixotic adventures in pursuit of her true inheritance. She acquires a set of loyal followers, as well as a dangerous suitor, defends a ruined castle as her family seat, appears in public in the guise of romantic heroine. Finally an attack of brain fever and the advice of a good clergyman teach her the error of her ways; she accepts her mundane position in life and a stable suitor.

This novel too expresses abundant hostility toward parents. Cherry actually confines her father in a madhouse, convinced that he has usurped the parental function; she cannot tolerate being his child. She encounters in a dungeon an enormously fat, loathsome personage with a toad in her bosom who declares herself Cherry's mother. The resulting conflict between duty and inclination causes Cherry to decide that she will 'make a suitable provision' for her mother but never 'sleep under the same roof with—(ye powers of filial love forgive me!) such a living mountain of human horror'.[16] But of course Cherry is mistaken in both instances—she rejects her father only because she does not believe in his paternity, the mother she loathes is not her mother—and utterly wrong, as she abjectly confesses, in allowing herself to be seduced by romance. Catherine Morland employs her fantasies to express her feelings, grows through them, and rejects them; only once does someone else need to tell her of her mistake. Cherry uses romance quite deliberately to separate herself from reality ('Oh, could I only lock myself into a room, with heaps of romances, and shut out all the world for ever!' [II, 216]; she requires enlightenment by others; her indulgence in fantasy, although it has allowed her to claim active independence, facilitates no growth and eventuates in her total submission to the judgement of others. Her father has no faults beyond his inability to cope with her; her challenge to received opinion meets utter defeat. Her involvement with romance emphasises the stereotypical young person's incapacity to understand the world without guidance from her elders.

Catherine too displays incapacity and needs guidance, but the fable which reveals her nature emphasises her ability to use what experience she has, an ability greater than that of many of her elders. The conjunctions of old and young through which the action progresses convey a subversive message: value does not inhere automatically in maturity or conventionality. Austen, in short, uses the assumed conflict of generations as she uses the convention of parodying Gothic romance: to explore the ambiguities and potentialities of growth.

Northanger Abbey lends itself readily to my thesis; *Mansfield Park*, on the other hand, seems less clearly related to the generational issue. Alone among Austen's heroines Fanny Price lacks both self-confidence and assertive force; she lacks, in fact, the kind of attractiveness the others display. She possesses instead considerable powers of passive resistance, through which she substantiates her moral superiority to most of those around her. The moral opposites of the novel—although they may not sound like opposites—are 'selfishness' and 'tranquillity'; both words recur frequently. 'Tranquillity' both reflects and encourages lack of selfishness; it represents an ideal condition of living with others. Although Fanny yearns for this state as her natural environment, she rarely achieves it for long, the selfishness of others creating endless obstacles. In the two events which most vividly threaten her tranquillity, the excursion into amateur theatricals and the visit to Portsmouth, she discovers the limits of passivity as self-defence. Both episodes provide abundant displays of self-interest. As the others contend over the choice of a play, Fanny watches and listens, 'not unamused to observe the selfishness which, more or less disguised, seemed to govern them all, and wondering how it would end' (131). It ends, of course, badly, with Fanny herself at least apparently implicated. The visit to her family involves her among noisier and more blatant clashes of selfishness, the chaos of the domestic scene echoing the disorder of opposed private interests. Fanny acts to moderate the discord, an important gesture of self-assertion. Her *learning*, unlike that of most Austen heroines, involves coming to understand her responsibility to act in relation to others without their direct request. For this learning she does not depend on Edmund, whom she considers the source of her previous knowledge of right principle. Indeed, Edmund himself—unlike Austen's other lover-mentors—makes mistakes, misled, as he explains, by fantasy— which he calls, confusingly, imagination: 'it had been the creature of my own imagination, not Miss Crawford, that I had been too apt to dwell on for many months past' (458).

The propensity of the imagination to recreate the world to its liking, as Dr Johnson had pointed out, represents a constant moral danger. This characteristic of what he calls imagination belongs to what I am calling fantasy, using the word in its psychoanalytic sense to designate a private form of mental activity which represents an attempt at the fulfilment of a wish. Austen's dramatisations of fantasy's dangers organise much of the action in all her novels. Amateur theatricals provide an obvious symbol of fantasy's power, and both Henry and Mary Crawford significantly regret the loss of their theatrical fantasy-world. The marriages and love affairs of the Bertram sisters reflect their capacity to transform reality by ignoring its incorrigible unpleasantness in favour of dreams of social power or romantic freedom. Aunt Norris inhabits a realm entirely of her own creation and tries to impose it on others. Similarly, in other novels, Emma's fantasies lead to Harriet's disillusion and her own; Elizabeth Bennet reconstructs Darcy's character on the basis of her 'prejudice', which generates its own fantasies; Marianne Dashwood perceives her experience as a romance of a different genre from Catherine Morland's. Education, in every case, is education in reality, the only source of tranquillity; selfishness both generates and is supported by private fantasy. Fanny, less susceptible than others to the temptations of self-romanticising, must yet learn how properly to assess her own importance, given as she is to under-estimate rather than to overestimate her place in the scheme of things.

Her capacity for this significant learning marks her specialness, as her sister Susan's propensity to learn marks hers. In different ways from *Northanger Abbey*, *Mansfield Park* dwells on the problem of what enables some to grow, while others remain immobile. Both the novel's narrator and, finally, Sir Thomas Bertram attribute the deficiencies of the Bertram sisters to failures of adults in arranging their upbringing. Edmund blames Mary's moral inadequacies on other people, corrupting influences in her environment. On the other hand, the clumsily integrated Portsmouth episode provides the younger Price boys and Betsy, the youngest girl, as evidence of the damaging effects of environment, but also presents Susan Price to demonstrate that the naturally good may escape significant danger. Fanny ponders at length the mystery of Susan:

> Her greatest wonder on the subject soon became—not that Susan should have been provoked into disrespect and impatience against her better knowledge—but that so much better know-ledge, so many good notions, should have been hers at all; and that, brought up in the midst of negligence and error, she should have formed such proper opinions of what ought to be—she, who had no cousin Edmund to direct her thoughts or fix her principles. (397–8)

Once more, the novel demonstrates in the very structure of its plot—the good progressing through increasing self-knowledge to their reward, the misguided suffering the consequences of their selfish separation from reality—the mystery and the high import-ance of the human capacity for goodness.

In evoking this mystery, *Mansfield Park* too relies on the conflict of generations, emphasising that virtue is not distributed on the basis of seniority. Aunt Norris helps to make Fanny's life miserable by her aggressive selfishness, Lady Bertram's passive selfishness provides no succour, Fanny fears Sir Thomas as his children do. The reader feels conscious of Fanny's moral superiority, in action and in feeling, to her elders; but not until her refusal of Henry Crawford does she come into direct conflict with parental figures other than Aunt Norris. The issue of marriage of course has special symbolic importance for generational conflict. As John Aikin had pointed out, parents necessarily have first-hand experience of the institution which their children necessarily lack; parents therefore draw on powerful sanctions in asserting their authority in the matter. On the other hand, marriage for the young represents escape from parental supervision; youthful lovers thus often feel powerfully impelled to defy their elders at this point. The most significant, sometimes the *only* significant choice available to a woman, the selection of a life-partner, may provide her single moment of independence—unless she allows her father to pre-empt it. Austen's juvenile fictions reiterate with crude and insistent, although ostensibly comic, emphasis the theme of parental tyranny and youthful defiance, both focused on issues of young love. Defiance mutes itself in the mature novels, but even meek Fanny Price, bathed in tears at the very thought of displeasing Sir Thomas, feels no doubt of her absolute right to determine her own marital destiny, or at least to reject a man of whom she disapproves. Julia Bertram, of course, claims a similar right, on different grounds. Fanny knows the correctness of her moral judgement; Julia knows the authority of her will to social power. Julia—unlike Anne Elliot in *Persuasion*—asserts her pre-rogative to choose; Fanny, only her need to refuse. Both demonstrate the strength of youthful will; and Fanny, like the other heroines, embodies the possible superiority of youthful discernment to that of the old and experienced.

Such embodiment implies no ideological programme, no specific recommendations about conduct. Austen's heroines guide themselves by principled morality, functioning as ethical Christians, but the novels do not finally suggest that morality, in the sense that matters most to Jane Austen, can be taught at all, though it can be learned. Good conduct and politeness are matters for teaching; 'right principle', although teachers may inculcate it, develops often without conscious instruction: in Susan Price, for example, in Anne Elliot, in Elinor Dashwood. The action of Austen's novels, the patterns of aspiration, conflict, reward and nemesis, reiterate the value of capacity to learn through experience. The middle-aged, in these books, seldom posssess it: if Mr Bennet briefly sees the error of his ways, he does not change his life as a result; Sir Thomas learns to regret the past and changes his style, but he is unique in Austen's novels; no middle-aged woman in Austen's fiction changes in any significant respect at all.

So the young provide—as they often do in fiction of every period—the nexus of social hope. They epitomise as characters a truth of possibility, although the novels they inhabit also carefully reiterate alternative possibilities. The 'realism' of Austen's fiction depends partly on its refusal merely to accept the limitations of assumed social actuality. Meticulous in its rendition of speech and custom, it depicts with equal exactitude different modes of human development and dramatises their implications. Other reflectors of the social scene had not previously done so much. Didactic texts about the young and how they may or should behave describe simpler versions of 'reality' and reflect simpler standards of conduct. Constructing plots which turn on moral conflicts between accurate young and muddled old, yet basing those plots on *mores* which assume the authority of society's elders, Austen expands her readers' perceptions. Her mode of fictional embodiment enlarges the meaning of generational conflict, placing it in the context of a poetics as well as a morality of personal growth. The idea of growth shapes the novelistic structures: Catherine moves from the restriction of a mind shaped by fanciful reading to the freedom of real relationship; Fanny proceeds from moral and psychological confinement to an enlarged life which she has earned by her comprehension of it. Imagination must join with will, may sometimes even replace will, the novels suggest, as means of education. People—especially young people—learn by exploring possibilities never realised in actuality, by attending to their own inner life, and by rigorous investigation of the relation of inner and outer. Fantasy, the undisciplined production of the mind, separates from reality those who indulge in it; imagination, involving the capacity to enlarge experience by conjuring up alternatives to the given, involves, in Austen's world, a discipline which returns one to the real. The fictions instruct their readers by inviting their vicarious—that is, imaginative—participation in social and psychological dilemmas involving moral as well as emotional issues. They manipulate their characters in comparable ways, demonstrating how imagination provides the means of change: through the romances Catherine uses as guides to conduct before rejecting them as inadequate moral mentors; through Fanny's sympathetic and increasingly disciplined imaginative identification with the needs of others.

In all respects, Jane Austen appears to believe, the young prove more educable than the old, and are often possessed of more accurate intuition. On the other hand, the moral point of *Persuasion* is reiterated in other novels: the young who understand their own necessarily inadequate knowledge of the world must assume and defer to the wisdom of their elders; willingness to do so defines their educability. Adults, however, seldom justify their trust. Adult modes of dealing with experience often involve hardened commitment to alienating fantasy—in Mrs Bennet, for example, Aunt Norris, Mr Woodhouse—and such fantasy finds abundant social support.

Some young people—the Bertram sisters, John Thorpe in *Northanger Abbey*—indulge in the sort of fantasy which will turn them into just such adults; others accept the rigorous task of training the imagination for growth rather than restriction. The reader has the same alternatives, warned by the text of the dangers of false attributions of causality, selfish acceptance of limited goals, but also offered examples of the growth that derives less from conscious will than from unconscious capacity and depends on the ability to acknowledge the limits of a single sensibility as means of grasping reality. Like Dr Johnson, Austen acknowledges the imagination's danger; like Wordsworth, she recognises its moral potential. The opposed possibilities often express themselves in the clash between generations, the generational issue in its fictional representations exposing with particular clarity the novelist's capacity to articulate through action complicated moral truths and the degree to which Austen's fiction embodies values of the eighteenth and nineteenth centuries alike.

NOTES

1. *Personal Nobility; or, Letters to a Young Nobleman* (London: Charles Dilly, 1793), preface, pp. xxxiii–xxxiv.
2. *Letters from a Father to a Son*, 2 vols (New York: Garland, 1971), Vol. 1, pp. 330–1. [Vol. 1 written 1792–3, pub. 1796; Vol. 11 written 1798–9, pub. 1800.]

3. *A Vindication of the Rights of Woman*, ed. Carol H. Poston (New York: Norton, 1975), p. 112. [First published 1792.]

4. *Monthly Review*, 54 (1807), 17.

5. Notice of J. Taylor, 'A Summary of Parental and Filial Duties', *Monthly Review*, 54 (1807), 320.

6. Review of *Letters Addressed to a Young Man on His First Entrance into Life* . . ., by Mrs West, *Gentleman's Magazine*, 90 (1801), 735.

7. Maria Edgeworth and Richard Lovell Edgeworth, *Practical Education*, 2 vols . (London: J. Johnson, 1798), Vol. II, p. 515.

8. *Advice to the Teens, or, Practical Helps Towards the Formation of One's Own Character* (Boston, Mass.: Wells and Lilly, 1820), pp. 26–7. [First published 1818.]

9. *Coelebs in Search of a Wife, Works of Hannah More* (London: Bohn, 1853), Vol. VIII, p. 131. [First published 1809.]

10. *Home Education*, 7th ed., revised (London, 1867), p. 163.

11. S[amuel] T[aylor] Coleridge, *The Friend: A Series of Essays*, 3 vols (London: Rest Fenner, 1818), Vol. III, pp. 2–3.

12. *Memoirs of Emma Courtney*, 2 vols (New York: Hugh M. Griffith, 1802), Vol. I, p. 30.

13. *Walsingham; or, The Pupil of Nature*, 4 vols (London: T. N. Longman, 1797), Vol. I, pp. 7–8.

14. *Hermsprong; or, Man As He Is Not*, 3 vols (London: William Lane, 1796), Vol. III, p. 241.

15. 'Thoughts on Novel Writing', *Blackwood's Magazine*, 4 (1819), 395.

16. Eaton Stannard Barrett, *The Heroine, or, Adventures of Cherubina*, 1st American, from 2nd London edn, 2 vols (Philadelphia, Pa.: M. Carey, 1815), Vol. II, p. 16.

11 In Between—Anne Elliot Marries a Sailor and Charlotte Heywood Goes to the Seaside

Tony Tanner

The figure of the young girl who does not have a secure or defined position in society is familiar in Jane Austen's work, in which her heroines tend to be either overprivileged like Emma, or under-privileged like Fanny Price. The overprivileged think that they know their place, as we say, but they have to learn to redefine it; the underprivileged know that they do not have a place and they have to find one. This figure we may call the girl on the the threshold, existing in that limboid space between the house of the father which has to be left and the house of the husband which was yet to be found. No longer a child and not yet a wife this threshold heroine is, precisely, in between, and she lives in betweenness. In this, I think, for Jane Austen these girls incorporated or reflected on the level of individual biography some problematical aspects of the England of her day as she perceived it, which was not what it was, nor yet what it was to become, as it were. You will remember the Musgroves in *Persuasion*: 'The Musgroves, like their houses, were in a state of alteration, perhaps of improvement. The father and mother were in the old English style, and the young people in the new' (40). Note the hesitation in that 'perhaps'; Jane Austen is not taking sides. There is no malice in the text directed against the new young people: 'Their dress had every advantage, their faces were rather pretty, their spirits extremely good, their manners unembarrassed and pleasant; they were of consequence at home, and favourites abroad' (40–1). They live to be 'fashionable, happy, and merry'

(40) and this frankly hedonistic commitment is not attacked by Jane
Austen, for just as she knew there was a stability which preserved
and transmitted values, so she knew there was an empty repetition
of habit which was stagnation, and while she showed very clearly
that there was a self-gratifying appetite which led to dissoluteness
and destruction (as in the figures and fates of the Crawfords), so she
recognised that there was a frankly self-delighting energy which
engendered those innovations and renovations—those *differences*, as
we say—which keep society alive. But Anne Elliot is no longer of the
old nor yet does she belong to the new. She does not disapprove of
the Musgrove children but 'she would not have given up her own
more elegant and cultivated mind for all their enjoyments' (41).
Nor can she find self-realisation in her father's house. She is in
between.

Her position is in many ways exemplary and I want to look at it a
little more closely—I will be coming back to her father's house later.
Persuasion opens in a rather remarkable way:

Sir Walter Elliot, of Kellynch-hall, in Somersetshire, was a man
who, for his own amusement, never took up any book but the
Baronetage; there he found occupation for an idle hour, and
consolation in a distressed one; there his faculties were roused into
admiration and respect, by contemplating the limited remnant of
earliest patents; there any unwelcome sensations, arising from
domestic affairs, changed naturally into pity and contempt, as he
turned over the almost endless creations of the last century—and
there, if every other leaf were powerless, he could read his own
history with an interest which never failed—this was the page at
which the favourite volume always opened:
'ELLIOT OF KELLYNCH-HALL'. (3)

Jane Austen opens her book with the description of a man looking
at a book in which he reads the same words as her book opens with—
'Elliot, of Kellynch-hall'. This is the kind of teasing regression which
we have become accustomed to in contemporary writers but which
no-one associates with the work of Jane Austen. It alerts us to at least
two important considerations—the dangers involved in seeking
validation and self-justification in book as opposed to life, in record
rather than in action, in name as opposed to function, and the
absolutely negative 'vanity' (her key word for Sir Walter) in looking
for and finding one's familial and social position, one's reality, in an

inscription rather than in a pattern of behaviour, in a sign rather than the range of responsibilities which it implicitly signifies. We know how fond Sir Walter is of mirrors and how hopelessly and hurtfully unaware of the real needs and feelings of his dependents he is. This opening situation poses someone fixed in an ultimate solipsism gazing with inexhaustible pleasure into the textual mirror which simply gives him back his name. The opening of Jane Austen's text—a title, a name, a domicile, a geographic location—implies a whole series of unwritten obligations and responsibilities related to rank, family, society and the very land itself, none of which Sir Walter Elliot, book-bound and self-mesmerised, either keeps or recognises. He is only interested in himself and what reflects him—mirrors or daughters. Thus he likes Elizabeth because she is 'very like himself'—this is parenthood as narcissism—and Mary has 'acquired a little artificial importance' because she has married into a tolerably respectable family—'but Anne, with an elegance of mind and sweetness of character, which must have placed her high with any people of real understanding, was nobody with either father or sister: her word had no weight; her convenience was always to give way;—she was only Anne' (5). Only Anne—no rank, no effective surname, no house, no location; her words are weightless, and physically speaking she always has to 'give way'—that is, accept perpetual displacement. She is a speaker who is unheard; she is a body who is a 'nobody'. I emphasise this because the problems of the body who is, socially speaking, a nobody, were to engage many of the great nineteenth-century writers.[1] We might recall here that in one of the seminal eighteenth-century novels, *La Nouvelle Heloise*, Julie's father refuses even to listen to the idea of her marrying Saint-Preux because Saint-Preux is what he calls 'un quidam' which means an unnamed individual or in dictionary terms 'Person (name unknown)'. This is to say that as far as the father is concerned, Saint-Preux exists in a state of 'quidamity'. As far as her father is concerned Anne also exists in that state of quidamity—she was nobody, she was only Anne: 'He had never indulged much hope, he had now none, of ever reading her name in any other page of his favourite work' (6). Until she is, as it were, reborn in terms of writing in the Baronetage she does not exist—not to be in the book is thus not to *be*. We may laugh at Sir Walter but Jane Austen makes it very clear what kind of perversity is involved in such a radical confusion or inversion of values whereby script and name take absolute precedence over offspring and dependents: or, to put it another way, when you cannot see the body for the book.

Anne, then, is perpetually displaced, always 'giving way' as opposed to having her *own* way—it is worth emphasising the metaphor. The story of her life consists precisely in having had her own way blocked, refused, negated. One might almost think of the book as being about dissuasion, for she is not urged or forced into doing something which she does not want to do, but into *not* doing something which her whole emotional being tells her is the right way (that is, marry Captain Wentworth at a time when he had no fortune). Her words carry no weight. So when it comes to their early engagement (and they are said to fall 'rapidly and deeply in love') Sir Walter—and Jane Austen could not have chosen her words better—'gave it all the negative', the negative of 'great astonishment, great coldness, great silence' (26) but the important point is in the generic 'negative'. He is a father who in every way negates his daughter—gives her all the negative. Now I am not here going into the whole matter of to what extent Jane Austen might seem to approve or disapprove of the 'persuasion' exercised by Lady Russell; there is rich ambiguity there, hesitation as I called it, and phrases like the 'fair interference of friendship' (27) in their poised ambivalence indicate that Jane Austen knew all about the multiple motivations which are at work in the impulse to exert some apparently beneficent control over a person in a weaker position. There is no point at which you can clearly distinguish persuasion from constraint or constraint from coercion, and quite properly she leaves it a blur, a confusion if you will—for it is out of just that confusion that Anne the nobody has somehow to remake her life. What Jane Austen does say is this: 'She had been forced into prudence in her youth, she learned romance as she grew older—the natural sequence of an unnatural beginning' (30). Most of Jane Austen's heroines have to learn some kind of prudence (not Fanny Price who has suffered for her undeviating dedication to prudentiality!). Anne, born into repression and non-recognition, has to learn romance, a deliberate oxymoron surely, for romance is associated with spontaneous feelings. But in Anne's case these had been blocked; her father gave it all the negative. To find her own positive she has, as it were, to diseducate herself from the tutoring authorities who, whether by silence or disapproval or forceful opposition, dominated that early part of her life when she was—in relation to Captain Wentworth—becoming somebody. I want to stress the rather unusual process that Jane Austen is embarking on in starting her novel in this way. The whole story of Anne's first romance with Mr Wentworth is recounted in the first paragraph of Chapter 4—that is to to say, what could and did make up the basic lineaments of her other novels—how the unattached young girl finally finds the most appropriate man who proposes because of her personal qualities and not for reasons of social advancement or whatever—is here reduced to a summary paragraph. It is a novel in brief. But the marriage is blocked by the father and others so Anne has to start on a long and arduous second life, which is based on loss, denial, deprivation. This is the 'unnatural beginning' to her life, and to Jane Austen's novel which differs quite radically from her previous works in which, as I said, her heroines tend to graduate from romance to prudence. And because of what she has lost and regretted losing (again an unusual condition for the Jane Austen heroine, who has usually not yet had any significant romance when the book opens) Anne undergoes a new kind of trial and tribulation since any reference to Captain Wentworth offers 'a new sort of trial to Anne's nerves' so that she has to 'teach herself to be insensible on such points' (52). Among other things Anne Elliot has to combine sense and *in*sensibility, again a change from Jane Austen's earlier work.

In all this I believe it is worth thinking a little more about Captain Wentworth's profession. If we recall the husbands of previous Jane Austen heroines—Knightley, Darcy, Edmund Bertram and so on—we are usually confronted with responsible landowners or an intending clergyman. But Captain Wentworth is of course a sailor and in writing about sailors Jane Austen identifies in that brotherhood a range of values which obtain there more obviously and sincerely than they seemed to do in society. Thus, when Anne is in the party with Captain Harville and Captain Benwick and their friends, she experiences 'a bewitching charm in a degree of hospitality so uncommon, so unlike the usual style of give-and-take invitations and dinners of formality and display' (98). And Louisa is allowed to expound 'on the character of the navy—their friendliness, their brotherliness, their openness, their uprightness' (99) and warmth and so on. Society in the form of Sir Walter Elliot is all empty self-regarding form and display—he has no sense of responsibility to his position, to the land, and it is significant that he rents his house to go and participate in the meaningless frivolities in Bath. This matter of renting his house is worth pausing over for a moment. The notion—'Quit Kellynch-hall'—is initially horrendous to Sir Walter. But he would as he says 'sooner quit Kellynch-hall' (13) than undertake any economies or constraints on his unrestricted pursuit of pleasure. His relation to his house is not a responsible one—he does not see his house as part of a larger context, an interrelated rural society, an ecology, if you will; it is more like a pleasure dome or a three-dimensional mirror which flatters his vanity. So he agrees to quit it if he cannot have those pleasures. But note that 'Sir Walter could not have borne the degradation of being known to design letting his house—Mr. Shepherd had once mentioned the word "advertise"—but never dared approach it again' (15). I will come back to 'advertising' but here again we note that Sir Walter wants the profits of 'renting' while still pretending to belong to an aristocracy which did not contaminate itself with contact with any kind of 'trade' or commerce. This is the self-deception of a figure no longer sensible of the significance of his social rank. When he does consider renting it he thinks of it in terms of 'a prize' (17) for the fortunate tenant—'a prize'; he has no appreciation of the real value of his inherited house. And I will just note the areas to which he does not really want the new tenant to have access: 'The park would be open to him of course . . ., but what restrictions I might impose on the use of the pleasure-grounds, is another thing. I am not fond of the idea of my shrubberies being always approachable' (18). Funny of course—but again there is no sense of the importance and significance of the house of his fathers, the house in which he so signally fails in *his* paternal duties. To abandon it in exchange for money for mere pleasure rather than 'economise' is a very notable dereliction of his duties. This is an alteration which is most definitely not 'perhaps an improvement' but indisputably a degradation.

If society in the form of Sir Walter has sacrificed responsibility to egoism, vanity and pleasure, society in the form of Mr Elliot the cousin is unmitigatedly evil. Hence the importance of the testimony of poor Mrs Smith, a victim of the inequities of the social system and again a rather new kind of character for Jane Austen to introduce into her world. She tells Anne that 'Mr. Elliot is a man without heart or conscience; . . . who, for his own interest or ease, would be guilty of any cruelty, or any treachery, that could be perpetrated without risk of his general character' (199). This description is not challenged but endorsed by the book.

It would seem then, that to find a locus and image of true values Jane Austen was turning from the landed society to a group whose responsibilities are to each other and to the country but not to the existing social structure (thus the naval figures may not have exquisite manners, they may lack 'polish', but they are authentic, open, generous, loyal and so on). In Sir Walter's world of mere rank and mirrors Anne is nobody; she gains her identity by marrying effectively *out* of society. You will remember that at the end her one regret is that she has 'no relations to bestow on him which a man of sense could value . . . no family to receive and estimate him properly' (251). Her new family is precisely the brotherhood of the sea and for a brief moment one is oddly close to Conrad and his sense of the hypocrisies of society on land and the values of fidelity within the ranks in the navy. The conclusion of the book is worth quoting as it is quite unlike the conclusions to her previous novels: 'His profession was all that could ever make her friends wish that tenderness less; the dread of a future war all that could dim her sunshine. She gloried in being a sailor's wife, but she must pay the tax of quick alarm from belonging to that profession which is, if possible, more distinguished in its domestic virtues than in its national importance' (252). The possibility of war introduces a note of potential insecurity and uncertainty into the usual concluding felicities, and, perhaps even more interesting, the new location for the true practice of the 'domestic virtues' has been moved out of conventional society into a group whose commitment is to the nation rather than this or that parish or village, and whose character values are developed not out of devotion to the land but engagement with the sea. We have come a long way from Mansfield Park and Pemberley.

I want to return briefly to Anne's situation as what I have called a threshold figure, the nobody in the house who always has to 'give way'. One consequence of this position is that she is literally moved about or displaced quite frequently and in the course of this she learns something which indicates once again Jane Austen's uncanny alertness to the operations of society: 'Anne had not wanted this visit to Uppercross, to learn that a removal from one set of people to another, though at a distance of only three miles, will often include a total change of conversation, opinion, and idea. . . . She acknowledged it to be very fitting, that every little social commonwealth should dictate its own matters of discourse' (42–3). This awareness that within the one common language—English—there can be innumerable discourses according to group, place and so on is a very crucial one. It is not the same thing as a dialect but what the

French critic Roland Barthes calls an 'idiolect'—'the language of a linguistic community, that is of a group of persons who all interpret in the same way all linguistic statements'.[2] This is not the arid point it may sound since a great many problems in Jane Austen's world, or our own come to that, stem from the fact that people within the same language can very often not really hear each other because they are operating within different discourses or idiolects. It is characteristic of many of Jane Austen's heroines that they are aware when people are operating within different discourses—an awareness which is an aspect of their sense and very often a consequence of their detachment or isolation. If you are 'in between' then you have no settled discourse of your own and are made aware of differences in the discourses around you. No one is more aware of this than Anne Elliot and it teaches her another painful but salutary lesson—'the art of knowing our own nothingness beyond our own circle, was become necessary for her' (42). Just as the one language is in fact made up of many discourses, so the one society is made up of many 'circles' and in many of these circles one is a nothing just as in some discourses one is inaudible. Anne's word carried no weight precisely because she is a nobody within the circle of her own family. Her speech can take on its full value only when she is taken into a new circle—the navy. In between she is, well—in between.

The question of circles and discourse is taken up again in *Sanditon* where in fact there are so many intersecting 'circles' that a certain kind of comical vertigo is one of the characteristic effects of this marvellous unfinished fragment of a novel. The observer heroine who is in between in this work is Charlotte Heywood but though she is displaced it is a matter of a holiday by the seaside and not a plight. For she comes from the very stable family of Mr Heywood who is indeed first seen working in the fields among his haymakers and who is obviously intended as a simplified or even somewhat mythological figure exemplifying an ideal commitment to the land, to his locale. We are told that the movements of the Heywooods 'had long been limitted to one small circle' (373) and that their way of life is 'stationary and healthy' (374). It is Mr Parker who breaks into that circle when his carriage is overturned near the Heywood's property and it is to Mr Parker's house in Sanditon that Charlotte Heywood is invited for a holiday. The novel opens with that carriage accident and I have commented on that elsewhere.[3] But it is worth noting one or two things about it. Mr Parker is on what turns out to be a foolish and basically misinformed errand—he has been *misled by advertisements* in the papers concerning a doctor seeking a new practice and this has brought him along an inappropriate road in the wrong place. The point is worth making because two things often go together in this work—people make themselves excessively busy in misdirected ways and at the same time they get things wrong. Thus there is a comically inordinate amount of fuss and manoeuvring on the part of Mr Parker's sisters to procure some families to take lodgings in Sanditon. 'I will not tell you how many People I have employed in the business—Wheel within wheel' (387) writes one of them proudly, and in the event it turns out that the two different families they thought they had arranged to come are one and the same family, the confusion coming about through the absurd multiplication of 'busy' communications along a chain of people who are 'extremely intimate' (408) but do not really know each other—a parody of true communal interrelatedness. About all this Charlotte thinks 'Unaccountable officiousness!—Activity run mad!' (410) and Jane Austen later talks of the Parkers' 'spirit of restless activity' (412) a phrase which in manuscript read 'the disease of activity'.[4] Now since Jane Austen certainly did not approve of mere inactivity, indolence and inertia (think of Lady Bertram) we must note that it is a certain *kind* of activity being referred to, and I think we can call it deranged activity, or activity without a stable purposive centre. Mr Heywood has his 'one small circle' and he is clearly a functioning centre. But other kinds of 'circles' are proliferating in the book, particularly in Sanditon which is, remember, in many ways an artificial creation as a resort town.[5] Thus we read that 'the Miss Beauforts were soon satisfied with "the Circle in which they moved in Sanditon" to use a proper phrase, for every body must now "move in a circle"—to the prevalence of which rototory Motion, is perhaps to be attributed the Giddiness & false steps of many' (422). And while I am talking about circles I will remind you that at Sanditon there is a 'Circulating Library' (403) which, notes Jane Austen wryly, if not reproachfully, 'afforded every thing; all the useless things in the World that cd not be done without' (390). A 'demand for every thing' (368) is one of the positive features of Sanditon as described by Mr Parker, and I think there is a connection between a 'want of employment' (412) (Mr Parker has 'no Profession' [371]), an unfocused 'demand' for something or other, and the kind of restless busyness which earns the suppressed but telling description—'the disease of activity'.

Let me return to the beginning. Mr Parker's errand and accident bring together one or two things, among them advertising and medicine. His newspaper-inspired search for a non-existent doctor ironically enough earns him a badly sprained ankle, but I want to use the opportunity of this opening conjunction to suggest that Jane Austen was very aware of the discourses of advertising and medicine and quack medicine, and that whereas Mr Parker is an 'enthusiast' and is mainly interested in 'advertising' and 'puffing' his 'profitable Speculation' (371) in Sanditon, while his sisters are hypochondriac busybodies, Jane Austen could perceive that there was a kind of possible perversion of discourse common to both—for both can become obsessions and as it were take over the speaker until he or she is in the deceptive and fabricating grip of the discourse and out of touch with reality. Let us consider the discourse of hypochondria, and in passing let me acknowledge that other people have noted that there are many references to illness in this fragment and that this, it is usually suggested, is explicable largely in terms of the fact that Jane Austen was herself ill, in fact dying, when she wrote it. That may well be true, but being the artist she was, whatever personal misery or pain she may have been experiencing, in her writing the obsession with ideas of illness is depersonalised and transformed into a social phenomenon which we are invited to consider and find, to use her own words, 'very striking—and very amusing—or very melancholy, just as Satire or Morality might prevail' (396) (note the readiness to oscillate across a spectrum of attitudes). Part of Mr Parker's advertising rhetoric about the virtues of Sanditon is that the sea air and bathing are 'a match for every Disorder, of the Stomach, the Lungs of the Blood; They were anti-spasmodic, anti-pulmonary, anti-sceptic, anti-bilious & anti-rheumatic' (373). Well, no doubt sea air and bathing are good for us but Jane Austen is noting an excess—the language getting out of control. The possible effect of this kind of excess taken in another direction is made very clear in the quite fantastic accounts his sisters give of their imagined ailments. I will quote from one of their letters to Mr Parker:

> your Letter . . . found me suffering under a more severe attack than usual of my old greivance, Spasmodic Bile & hardly able to crawl from my Bed to the Sofa—But how were you treated?— Send me more Particulars in your next. . . . I doubt whether Susan's nerves wd be equal to the effort [of a visit to

Sanditon]. She has been suffering much from the Headache and Six Leaches a day for 10 days together releived her so little that we thought it right to change our measures—and being convinced on examination that much of the Evil lay in her Gum, I persuaded her to attack the disorder there. She has accordingly had 3 Teeth drawn, & is decidedly better, but her Nerves are a good deal deranged. She can only speak in a whisper—fainted away twice this morning on poor Arthur's trying to suppress a cough. (387)

Now the point in all this is not that people do not get ill because of course they do—who better to know it than Jane Austen at the time; and, by the same token, there *is* a need for discourse of symptoms, prescriptions, remedies, and so on. What Jane Austen is depicting, with the incisive unsentimental humour we associate with her, is the way in which that discourse can take over the individual so that what should be in a normal person a reasonable concern for health becomes an obsession with *unhealth* which creates the sicknesses it purports to be concerned with curing. Note the sister's interest in the details of Mr Parker's accident—'send me more Particulars'. And once again let me repeat that Jane Austen attributes both Mr Parker's obsession with advertising some semi-imaginary Sanditon and his sisters' devotion to the terminology of illness to 'want of employment'; as she puts it 'while the eldest Brother found vent for his superfluity of sensation as a Projector, the Sisters were perhaps driven to dissipate theirs in the invention of odd complaints' (412). The problems stemming from 'want of employment' were to occupy many of the great nineteenth-century novelists, in particular as they related to the position of women in society, and here as so often we find Jane Austen anticipating more weighty versions of problems which were to come later in the century. I do not want to give the impression that there is anything ponderous or gloomy about her treatment of this particular brand of *malades imaginaires*. Her touch is as always as light as it is firm. I cannot resist reminding you of the young brother Arthur who, somewhat feebly to be sure, masks a truly fabulous gluttony and idleness under the terms of neurological disorder. Drinking, it turns out, is very good for his nervous condition: 'The more wine I drink (in Moderation) the better I am' (415)—an unforgettable proposition which would not be out of place in *Alice Through the Looking Glass*! At the same time Jane Austen could see that what she calls 'enjoyments in

Invalidism' (418) could have very destructive effects—on self and others. She saw, as other great writers have seen, the dangers and perversities which could be involved in 'quack medicine' and for comparison we can look back to Ben Jonson, or more pertinently forward to Flaubert's Monsieur Homais, the quack chemist in *Madame Bovary* whose interfering intrusions of advice and help— 'unaccountable officiousness—activity run mad' would be a good comment on him as well—are ruinous. He is a man who destroys what he purports to cure. Jane Austen knew about such people.

I have been talking about discourses and may have seemed to have wandered away from the threshold heroine who is 'in between'. I will be coming back to Charlotte Heywood, but I want to mention a third discourse—along with advertising and hypochondria—which is shown to be capable of manufacturing the most ludicrous parodies of pseudo-sense, or more properly capable of generating the most utter nonsense, and I do it with a sense of an appropriate irony considering my present activity and that is— literary criticism! I am referring to Sir Edward Denham's attempts to impress Charlotte. First he begins to 'stagger her with the number of his Quotations, & the bewilderment of some of his sentences.— "Do you remember, said he, Scott's beautiful Lines on the Sea?— Oh! what a description they convey!—They are never out of my Thoughts when I walk here.—The Man who can read them unmoved must have the nerves of an Assassin!—Heaven defend me from meeting such a Man unarmed"' (396-7). Charlotte admits to not remembering any lines by Scott on the sea and as far as I can recall she is right, though there is the odd reference to the 'distant Tweed' and 'Sweet Teviot'. Sir Edward's reply is, well, instructive. 'Do you not indeed?—Nor can I exactly recall the beginning at this moment' (397). He goes on with a lot more of this splendid gibberish until Charlotte begins to wonder not just why he is speaking nonsense but why he is speaking so very *much* nonsense! To Charlotte 'he seemed . . . very full of some Feelings or other, & very much addicted to all the newest-fashioned hard words—had not a very clear Brain she presumed, & talked a good deal by rote' (398). This is all excellent fun but again Jane Austen could see a latent danger in this perversion of a discourse. In relation to Burns Sir Edward says things like 'The Corruscations of Talent, elicited by impassioned feeling in the breast of Man, are perhaps incompatible with some of the prosaic Decencies of Life;—nor can you, loveliest Miss Heywood, . . . nor can any Woman be a fair Judge of what a

Man may be propelled to say, write or do, by the sovereign impulses of illimitable Ardour.' Jane Austen comments 'This was very fine;— but if Charlotte understood it at all, not very moral' (398). What in fact it is is very high order balderdash. But there *is* a moral matter involved here. Asked which novels he approves of, Sir Edward answers that he most admires the ones which 'exhibit the progress of strong Passion from the first Germ of incipient Susceptibility to the utmost Energies of Reason half-dethroned' (403), and then more stuff attempting to justify and romanticise and glorify the imperatives of male lust. But the enthroning and dethroning of reason were genuinely important matters in this period in particular, and in his own fatuous and empty-headed way Sir Edward is in fact participating in the aesthetic discourse of the day, and there were indeed some entirely serious thinkers who wrote against the imperial rule of reason. The point is that a man, say, like William Blake, did it rather better than Sir Edward. What the latter is doing is trying to use the language of literary criticism to dignify, or as we may say 'novel-ise' his intention to seduce Clara Brereton. As a matter of fact it is rather the other way around and here again Jane Austen shows how clearly she understood the problematical relationship between books and life. Sir Edward, we are told, read Richardson at an early age, or rather misread him—and the intention to be a seducer came from the book. His reading, thus, became literally perverted and whatever he read he derived 'incentive to Vice from the History of it's Overthrow, [and] gathered only hard words & involved sentences from the style of our most approved Writers'. The result is 'he felt that he was formed to be a dangerous Man—quite in the line of the Lovelaces'. And Clara in her vulnerable condition suggests the appropriate emulation of the Lovelace fictional rape: 'Her seduction was quite determined. Her Situation in every way called for it' (405). Jane Austen is very amusing about his preformed 'literary' plan of compaign—he thinks perhaps that a good place for the rape would be Timbuctoo 'but the Expence alas! of Measures in that masterly style was ill-suited to his Purse, & Prudence obliged him to prefer the quietest sort of ruin and disgrace for the object of his Affections, to the more renowned' (406). Clara has not the slightest intention of being seduced but this does not put him off: 'He knew his Business' (405) says Jane Austen with the nicest kind of irony, given that she is depicting a world in which everybody is very busy and seems to know their 'business' (both pronunciations) but it is busy-ness gone wrong, 'activity run mad'. Sir Edward is funny because made transparently absurd—but ruined girls are ruined girls, or at least they used to be—and Jane Austen knows that an absurd figure can also be a dangerous one. And, to come back to my point, Sir Edward is in the grip of a certain bad pseudo-literary discourse, as Mr Parker was of a certain bad advertising discourse, and his sisters of a certain bad pseudo-medical discourse. When a person is in the grip of a discourse, particularly if—as in these cases to varying degrees it is— it is a perversion and debasement of a more genuine discourse, then we say that the discourse speaks them and not that they speak the discourse. *Sanditon* is full of people not only dashing around in circles but speaking incessantly. But Jane Austen shows that they are really—*being spoken*. Our heroine who, to come back to my basic point, is in between all these discourses—occasionally somewhat deafened by them but never deceived into them—can hear these perversions and is vigilant over her own inner and outer discourse, trying always to maintain a vocabulary that is at once flexible and firm and the most appropriate one for the occasion. Jane Austen's heroines are often silent; sometimes from necessity, from suffering, from repression, or from sheer lowliness of social or familial position (Anne was a nobody—so her words carried no weight—that is, were not heard). But, for the most part, when they speak—they speak truly and truly speak. So those Jane Austen girls who are in between—in between bad fathers like Sir Walter who 'give them all the negative' and unprincipled young men willing to exploit their vulnerable unmarried condition like Mr Elliot and Edward Denham, as well as more reliable young men like Captain Wentworth and perhaps Mr Parker's brother Sidney—these girls are also in between the various discourses which they have to engage with but which they refuse to be taken over by; they thus become, not only maintainers of good sense, and upholders of appropriate values in a changing world, but very important guardians of the language—as their own author so supremely was.

NOTES

1. We might compare the opening of Anthony Trollope's *The Prime Minister* where the problems of Ferdinand Lopez are all connected with the fact that he 'was an orphan before I understood what it was to have a parent' (1, 27), and a man who is, in the eyes of the English aristocracy, a nobody: 'He had no father or mother, no uncle, aunt, brother or sister, no cousin even whom he could

mention in a cursory way to his dearest friend' (1, 2). Which is why Mr Wharton gives *his* negative to Emily when she wants to marry Lopez after they have fallen in love.

The quotations are taken from Anthony Trollope, *The Prime Minister* (London: Oxford University Press, 1952).

2. *Elements of Semiology*, trans. Annette Lavers and Colin Smith (London: Jonathan Cape, 1967) pp. 21–2.

3. 'Introduction', *Mansfield Park* (Harmondsworth: Penguin), pp. 33–4.

4. See *The Manuscript of Sanditon: Reproduced in Facsimile*, ed. B. C. Southam (Oxford: Clarendon Press, 1975), p. 91.

5. Jane Austen's choice of a resort town for the setting of her novel again indicates her sense that something was happening to the old stabilities of England—not necessarily bad, but certainly changing—as Mr Parker has abandoned his 'snug' old house in an appropriate valley setting for a new one in a fashionable place overlooking the sea. Something may be being gained; something is certainly being lost. The resort town contains a lot of 'Lodgings to let' (383) and while I am not suggesting that there is anything sinister in that, I would remind you of Tess of the D'Urbervilles—a more pitiably displaced and abused girl than any of Jane Austen's heroines—who finds herself taken to Sandbourne, a place of 'detached mansions', the very reverse of a community. It is a 'pleasure city', 'a glittering novelty' (480), a place of meretricious fashion and amusement. ' 'Tis all lodging-houses here' (482) says the postman, and while it is the perfect place for the modern, deracinated Alec, it is no place at all for Tess, the 'cottage-girl' (481). Again there is a strange prescience in late Jane Austen of matters which were to become more sombre and momentous later in the century. Since Sanditon is a resort town it has no natural centre, so you get a kind of unmoored circulation taken to the point of dizziness.

The quotations are taken from Thomas Hardy, *Tess of the D'Urbervilles* (New York: Harper and Row, 1964).

Index

Abrams, M. H., 15, 16, 27
Aikin, John, 165–6, 176
Ainsworth, Harrison, 88
Auerbach, Erich, 86
Auerbach, Nina, xi, 4, 5, 6, 9, 27
Austen, Cassandra, 31, 47, 65
Austen, Jane: critical approaches to,
1–7; *Letters*, 2, 17, 27, 31, 42, 47,
52, 65, 103, 133, 168; limitations,
9–10; relationship to history, 86–7,
90–102; relationship with publishers,
51–2, 65; social attitudes, 2–3, 4–6, 7,
29–30, 66–7, 106–7, 110–12, 120–1,
122, 130, 132; structure of novels, 50
Austen, Rev. George, 52
Austen-Leigh, J. E.: *A Memoir of Jane
Austen*, 28–9, 46, 47

Bage, Robert: *Hermsprong*, 169
Balzac, Honoré de, 88–9, 102
Banfield, Ann, xi, 4, 5, 28, 47, 48
Barrett, Eaton Stannard: *The Heroine*,
172, 179
Barthes, Roland, 187
Bate, W. J., 142
Bayley, John, 95, 103
Beauvoir, Simone de, 146, 149, 158
Becker, George J., 102
Bentley, E. C., 90
Benveniste, Emile, 39
Blake, William, 10, 11
Boswell, James, 102, 141
Brandy, Leo, 102
Brontë, Charlotte, 13, 34, 39, 48; *Jane
Eyre*, 45; *Villette*, 45
Brophy, Brigid, 103
Brown, Lloyd, 107
Brunton, Mary: *Self-Control*, 168;
Discipline, 168
Buck, Anne, 103

Burke, Edmund, 3, 4, 5, 6, 7, 110–11
Burney, Fanny, 30, 68, 70, 86, 123, 169;
Camilla, 51, 70, 164; *Cecilia*, 82;
Evelina, 52, 59, 70, 123–4, 126, 127,
164
Burns, Robert, 191–2
Burroway, Janet, 158
Bush, Douglas, 157
Butler, Marilyn, xi, 4, 5, 6, 7, 39, 47, 48,
49, 65, 84
Byrd, Max, 141
Byron, Lord: *The Corsair*, 11–12, 13, 25;
The Prisoner of Chillon, 11

Carroll, Lewis: *Alice Through the Looking
Glass*, 190
'Catharine', 114–15
Chapman, R. W., 55
Chapone, Hester, 68, 84
Cobbett, William, 42
Coleridge, S. T., 49, 168, 179; 'Kubla
Khan', 11; *The Rime of the Ancient
Mariner*, 11, 15
Collingwood, R. G., 95, 103
Conrad, Joseph, 186
Craik, W. A., 157

Daiches, David, 90
Daly, Mary, 149
Devlin, D. D., 158
Dickens, Charles, 34, 92; *Bleak House*,
89; *Hard Times*, 45, 157
Disraeli, Benjamin, 34; *Shirley*, 46
Donoghue, Denis, 146
Donohue, Joseph W., 158
Donovan, Robert, 144, 158
Duckworth, Alistair, M., 3, 4, 5, 6, 7, 8,
47, 48, 158
Duffy, Joseph, M., Jr, 157, 158

Eagleton, Terry, 1, 3, 6, 7, 8
Edgeworth, Maria, 53, 64, 65, 68, 123, 167, 169, 179; *Belinda*, 69–70; *Helen*, 50–1, 52; *Patronage*, 68
Edgeworth, Richard, 167, 179
Edwards, Michael M., 103
Egerton, Thomas, 52
Ehrenpreis, Irvin, 85
Eliot, George, 46, 91, 93; *Felix Holt*, 45, 46, 48; *Middlemarch*, 91; *The Mill on the Floss*, 30; *Scenes from Clerical Life*, 89; *Silas Marner*, 29, 45, 47
Emma, 38, 42, 48, 84, 87, 184; as novel of social consciousness, 31, 44; attitudes to leisure in, 123, 135–7, 139, 140; attitudes to women in, 107, 108, 110, 115–16, 116–17, 118, 120; generational conflict in, 160, 161, 162, 163, 175, 178; patriarchalism in, 22; publication in volume form, 51, 60, 61, 64–5; relationship to history, 91, 95, 99; Romantic aspects of, 10, 14, 16, 17, 18, 22, 25–6; sexuality in, 67–8, 72, 73, 75, 82–3; social instability in, 180; social ritual in, 3
Engels, Friedrich, 34, 47, 89, 102

Fergus, Jan S., xi, 4, 5, 66
Fielding, Henry, 123; *Amelia*, 82; *Tom Jones*, 68, 87–8, 164
Flaubert, Gustave: *Madame Bovary*, 191
Fleishman, Avrom, 158
Fordyce, James, 105, 106, 107, 109, 121
Foucault, Michel, 66–7, 84
Fowler, Marian, 121
Friedenberg, Edgar, 159, 160
Froude, James Anthony, 88

Galsworthy, John, 92
Gaskell, Elizabeth, 34, 46, 64; *North and South*, 38, 44–5, 48
Gisborne, Thomas, 68, 69, 84, 106, 107, 121
Gladstone, W. E., 91
Glassco, John, 84
Godwin, William, 22, 24, 25; *Caleb Williams*, 14, 15, 16, 19–20, 21, 27
Goldman, Lucien, 1, 7
Goldsmith, Oliver, 93

Grant, Aline, 103
Greene, Donald, 7, 102
Gregory, Dr John, 69, 70, 74, 84, 105, 121

Halévy, Elie, 101, 104
Halifax, Lord, 105
Halperin, John, 158
Hamilton, Elizabeth, 166
Harding, D. W., 4, 158
Hardy, Thomas, 93; *Tess of the D'Urbervilles*, 194
Harrison, Michael, 102
Hauser, Arnold, 86
Hays, Mary: *Memoirs of Emma Courtney*, 168
Heywood, Eliza: *History of Miss Betsey Thoughtless*, 165
Himmelfarb, Gertrude, 104
'History of England', 93, 103
Hobsbawm, E. J., 104
Hogarth, William, 142
Hogg, James: *The Private Memoirs . . . ,* 13, 15, 16, 19
Hough, Graham, 91, 92
Hume, David, 93
Hummel, Madeline, 158

Inchbald, Elizabeth, 55, 68; *A Simple Story*, 54, 70

James, Henry, 50, 65
Janeway, Elizabeth, 149
Johnson, Samuel, 87, 123, 129–32, 134–5, 135–6, 137, 140, 141, 142, 174, 178
Jonson, Ben, 191

Kafka, Franz, 18
Keats, John, 10; *The Eve of St. Agnes*, 11; *Lamia*, 11
Kelly, Gordon R., 103
Kent, Christopher, xi, 2, 86
Kestner, Joseph, 27
Kettle, Arnold, 91
Kilroy, G. J. F., 65
Kingsley, Charles, 88; *Alton Locke*, 45
Knight, Fanny, 70
Knox, Vicesimus, 165

Koestler, Arthur, 18
Krieger, Murray, 8
Kroeber, Karl, 27

Lady Susan, 39
Lamb, Charles, 49
Lascelles, Mary, 85, 102
Lawrence, D. H.: *Lady Chatterley's Lover*, 44, 46, 48
Lennox, Charlotte: *The Female Quixote*, 172
'Lesley Castle', 125
Levin, Harry, 99
Lewes, George Henry, 9, 10, 26, 27, 89, 102
Lodge, David, 90, 158
Love and Friendship, 39
Lukács, George, 48, 86

Macauley, Thomas, 87, 88, 95
Mangnall, Richmal, 93
Mansfield Park, 7, 70, 84, 87, 181, 184, 186; as novel of social consciousness, 30–1, 32, 33–44, 45, 46, 48; attitudes to leisure in, 123, 129, 132–5, 136, 138, 140, 142; attitudes to women in, 107, 108–9, 113, 118, 120, 121; generational conflict in, 160, 161, 162, 163, 173–6, 177, 178; patriarchalism in, 143–58; publication in volume form, 60–1; relationship to history, 93, 96; Romantic aspects of, 12, 16, 18, 25, 26; sexuality in, 72, 73, 74, 75, 76, 77–82, 85; social change in, 29–30; social instability in, 180; social ritual in, 3
Marx, Karl, 89
Maturin, Charles, 24; *Melmoth the Wanderer*, 9, 13, 14, 15, 16, 17–18, 19, 22, 24, 26, 27
McKendrick, Neil, 103
McMaster, Juliet, 121
Meredith, George, 93
Mitford, Miss Mary, 46
Moers, Ellen, 27
Moler, Kenneth, 158
Monaghan, David, xi, 1, 4, 5, 7, 8, 105
More, Hannah, 68, 69, 105, 106, 121, 167

Moynihan, Patrick, 159, 160
Mudrick, Marvin, 5, 8

Nardin, Jane, xii, 5, 122
Northanger Abbey, 35, 59; as novel of social consciousness, 31, 32, 33, 42; attitudes to leisure in, 123, 124, 125–6, 126–7, 128, 142; attitudes to women in, 107, 108, 112, 117–18; generational conflict in, 160, 162, 163, 170–2, 173, 175, 177, 178; patriarchalism in, 21, 22, 24, 145; publication in volume form, 55, 56–8, 65; relationship to history, 93–4, 97–9, 100–1; Romantic aspects of, 10, 12–13, 14, 18, 21, 22, 23–4, 25; sexuality in, 72, 73; social ritual in, 3

'Opinions of *Mansfield Park*', 70
Orwell, George, 18

Paris, Bernard J., 26
Parshley, J..M., 158
Peacock, Thomas Love: *Headlong Hall*, 51; *Melincourt*, 55
Pennington, Lady, 106, 108–9
Perkin, Harold, 103
Persuasion, 27, 42, 59, 84; as a novel of social consciousness, 44; attitudes to leisure in, 123, 137–41, 142; attitudes to women in, 107, 108, 109–10, 113–14, 118–20, 121; generational conflict in, 159, 162, 176, 178; publication in volume form, 52, 55–6, 61–4, 65; relationship to history, 94, 99; Romantic aspects of, 11, 14, 16, 18, 26; sexuality in, 72, 75–7, 80; social instability in, 180–7, 193
'Plan of a Novel', 103
Polidori, John: *The Vampyre: A Tale*, 14
Pope, Alexander, 131, 142
Poston, Carol H., 121, 179
Powell, Anthony, 91
Pride and Prejudice, 41, 65, 84, 87, 184, 186; attitudes to leisure in, 123, 125, 126, 127–8, 133, 136–7, 139, 140, 142; attitudes to women in, 107–8, 109, 112–13, 116, 118, 120; generational conflict in, 160, 161, 162, 163,

Pride and Prejudice (*continued*)
175, 177, 178; patriarchalism in, 25,
27, 144–5, 146, 147; publication in
volume form, 60; relationship to history, 95, 99–100, 102; Romantic aspects of, 12, 18, 25; sexuality in, 71,
72, 74

Radcliffe, Ann, 55, 123; *The Mysteries of
Udolpho*, 13, 19, 20–1, 22, 23, 27,
54–5, 99
Repton, Humphrey, 32
Richardson, Samuel, 30, 68, 69, 123;
Clarissa, 68–9, 70, 124, 135, 151, 164–
5; *Pamela*, 36, 70, 164; *Sir Charles
Grandison*, 82
Robinson, Mary: *Walsingham*, 168–9
Rosemary's Baby, 16
Rousseau, Jean-Jacques: *La Nouvelle
Héloise*, 182
Ruoff, Gene W., 27
Ruskin, John, 33, 48
Ryal, Claude L. de, 143, 158

Sade, Marquis de, 46
Sanders, Scott, 1, 7
Sanditon, 33, 64; attitudes to leisure in,
123, 133, 138, 139, 140–1, 142;
relationship to history, 101; social
change in, 187–93, 194
Scott, Sir Walter, 52–3, 86, 87, 88, 95,
191; *The Antiquary*, 53; *Ivanhoe*, 53;
Kenilworth, 53; *Old Mortality*, 53;
Waverley, 53
Semmel, Bernard, 104
Sense and Sensibility, 84, 132; as novel of
social consciousness, 32–3; attitudes
to leisure in, 123, 124, 128–9, 133,
138, 139, 141; attitudes to women in,
108, 114, 118, 120; generational conflict in, 160, 161, 162, 163, 175, 176;
patriarchalism in, 146; publication
in volume form, 51, 55, 58–60, 61, 62,
63, 64, 65; Romantic aspects of, 10,
17, 18–19, 20, 23, 24–5; sexuality in,
71–2, 73, 99
Shapira, Morris, 65
Shelley, Mary: *Frankenstein*, 12, 14, 15,
16, 19, 21, 24, 27

Shelley, Percy Bysshe, 19; *A Defence of
Poetry*, 16; *Prometheus Unbound*, 11, 15
Sheridan, Mrs Frances: *Memoirs of Miss
Sidney Biddulph*, 165
Sherry, Norman, 158
Simmons, James C., 102
Simon, Linda, 84
Simpson, Richard, 87, 89–90
Smith, Charlotte, 55
Smith, Goldwin, 86–7
Smith, Leroy W., xii, 5, 6, 143
Smollett, Tobias: *Humphry Clinker*, 59;
Roderick Random, 164
Southam, B. C., 26, 27, 62, 85, 103, 158,
194
Spacks, Patricia Meyer, xii, 5, 159
Stein, Gertrude, 66
Steiner, George, 66–7, 84, 95
Stern, Fritz, 102
Stone, Lawrence, 84
Sulloway, Alison C., 26
Swift, Jonathan, 131, 142
Swingle, L. J., 27

Tanner, Tony, xii, 26, 47, 48, 180
Tave, Stuart M., 9, 10, 26, 142, 158
Taylor, Isaac, 167–8
Taylor, J., 179
Thomis, Malcolm I., 104
Thompson, E. P., 104
Trilling, Lionel, 30, 85, 91, 92, 122,
124, 129, 130, 139, 158
Trollope, Anthony: *The Prime Minister*,
193–4

Wakefield, Priscilla, 111
Walling, William A., 27
Walpole, Horace: *The Castle of Otranto*,
48
Ward, William, 99
Warton, Thomas, 49
Watson, George, 102
The Watsons, 29
Wedgwood, Josiah, 98–9
Weinsheimer, Joel, 102, 121
West, Jane, 68, 106, 111, 112, 121, 179
Western, J. R., 103
Whately, Richard, 71, 87, 95
Wiesenfarth, Joseph, 143, 146, 155, 158

Williams, Raymond, 1, 7, 34, 35, 47, 48
Wise, Gene, 103
Wollstonecraft, Mary, 24, 106, 107, 110, 111–12, 120, 166; *Maria*, 9, 22–3, 26; *A Vindication of the Rights of Woman*, 23, 26

Wordsworth, William, 11, 16, 17, 19, 178; 'Nuns Fret . . .', 11; *The Prelude*, 14, 15; 'The Recluse', 15

Yearsley, Ann, 55